ANGELS IN THE MOONLIGHT

A Prequel to The Dublin Trilogy

CAIMH MCDONNELL

McFori Ink

Cover Design by CHAMELEON Studio

Editors: Scott Pack and Julie Ferguson

Proofreader: Penny Bryant

ISBN-13 978-0-9955075-4-8

CHAPTER ONE

Rory Coyne's pulse thundered in his ears. He wasn't great with heights – and when you're standing on the six-inch-wide ledge of a building five storeys up, that's a bit of a problem.

He tried not to look down but he didn't have many other options. Looking to the left or right gave him a view of the Dublin skyline, but from an angle that only emphasised that he was now a part of that skyline. He had tried closing his eyes but his treacherous imagination insisted on showing him the ground rushing up to meet him again and again. He was regretting the four pints he'd sunk before getting up here. Four was either too many or too few. It was certainly not the right amount. He was sober enough to be terrified and drunk enough to want to cry.

A pigeon landed on the balustrade beside him and cooed. He tried to focus all of his attention on it.

The pigeon looked at Rory and then pointedly down at the ground.

"Feck off."

His sweaty hands clung even tighter to the balustrade as the autumn winds tugged at his bomber jacket. The wind was worse than the view. He steadied himself then quickly pulled his left hand away to wipe it on his jumper. The movement was met with a gasp from the crowd below. A sickeningly giddy shock of excitement passed through him before his hand found its hold on the white stone again.

He'd been up here for about twenty-five minutes now. For the first ten, nobody had seen him. When standing on a ledge five storeys up, the options for getting someone's attention are very limited – well, bar the one very obvious and dramatic option. Eventually, some Spanish students had noticed him. A large group of them had gathered, looking up, chattering excitedly for several minutes while the natives tutted and weaved around them. A crowd of foreign students blocking the flow of pedestrian traffic on Grafton Street wasn't exactly an unprecedented occurrence. Then a girl who worked in HMV had poked her head out of an upstairs window to have a cheeky fag and she'd made eye contact. Her scream had really got things moving. There was now a ring of uniformed Gardaí trying to close off the street below, which had immediately drawn a crowd. Rory's situation combined two things Dubliners loved: drama and a free show. A busker had set himself up at the edge of proceedings and was belting out a less-than-sympathetic rendition of R Kelly's "I Believe I Can Fly".

Rory glanced down again. In the middle of the cordoned-off area stood a tall, thin man with a distinctive shock of dark brown hair. He was standing looking up at him, hands in the pockets of his cashmere coat.

"Is that you, Gringo?" shouted Rory.

"That's Detective Sergeant Spain to you, Coyne."

"Ah crap."

It wasn't that he minded Gringo so much. As coppers went, he wasn't the worst. No, it was more what came with him.

"Howerya Rory, how's it hanging?"

He was no longer alone on the roof. The Cheshire-cat grin of Detective Bunny McGarry appeared in Rory's peripheral vision, about twelve feet away, leaning casually over the balustrade as if expecting a neighbourly chat about the football. McGarry was a big lummocks of a man, with a thick Cork accent and a scruffy, second-hand look about him. He was early thirties, six foot two and fat, but in a usable way; he carried the kind of bulk that could slam through a door or be thrown behind a punch as required. His left eye was lazy which gave people the impression he was slightly unhinged. That impression was frequently backed up by his behaviour.

"I knew it." Rory nodded down towards the ground. "Youse two are like stink and shite – never one without the other."

"Poetic as always, Rory," said Bunny. "So, how's life?"

"Stay back, Bunny, I mean it."

"Cool your jets, Rory boy, I've no intention of coming anywhere near ye. I'm just worried about you, that's all."

"Yeah, right you are."

"You've got great sentimental value to me, Rory. Sure, weren't you one of my first collars as a newly-minted guard, just graduated from Templemore."

"You put me through a wall."

"Be fair – that wall collapsed while I was apprehending you. If memory serves, I'd interrupted yourself and Jacko Regan while you were relieving Des Kelly Carpets of some lino. How is Jacko, by the way?"

Rory didn't answer. Regan had been halfway over the wall when Bunny had grabbed a leg. Jacko still blamed that incident for his subsequent lack of offspring. To be fair, the wife had left him when he'd gone back to prison, which hadn't helped.

In one fluid movement, Bunny was sitting on top of the balustrade, his legs dangling over the side. That was the other thing; McGarry moved with more grace and speed than expected. Something in your mind just couldn't accept that a big, hairy-arsed, red-faced ape of a man could move with such dexterity. It was like seeing a baby elephant riding a tricycle.

"I said stay back."

"Calm down, would ye? You want to jump? Jump. I'm not stopping you, but I've been on me feet all day, it's four o'clock and I've still not had me sandwiches."

To emphasise his point, Bunny pulled a tinfoil-covered parcel out of the pocket of his anorak and started unwrapping it. "The car is in the garage again, so I'm trying to save a bit of money by bringing me own lunch in."

"I don't want to talk to you."

"It's nippy up here, isn't it?" continued Bunny, well used to people not wanting to talk to him. "But I suppose there's no buildings to block the wind and that."

"Where's Sergeant Cartwright?"

"Our designated negotiator is at her sister's wedding. Would ye like to leave a message?"

"I want to speak to someone else."

"Alright, alright. Jesus, you're awful jumpy, Rory. No pun intended."

Bunny pulled a walkie-talkie from his other pocket and held it to his mouth. "This is Major Tom to ground control, over."

Rory saw Gringo holding a walkie-talkie up to his lips down below. "Roger, Major Tom. How's it going up there?"

"Well, to be honest Gringo, not great. Mr Coyne seems highly agitated and he'd like to speak to someone else." Bunny pulled the walkie-talkie away from his mouth and addressed Rory. "Would you prefer to speak to Sergeant Spain instead?"

"Anybody but you."

"Hurtful, Rory, hurtful. You might make me suicidal and then I'd totally steal your thunder." Bunny lifted the radio back to his lips. "Sarge, he says he'd much rather talk to you. Are you still a big girl's blouse who's scared of heights?"

"Afraid so."

Bunny put the walkie-talkie down beside him and concentrated on opening his sandwiches. "It's a no, I'm afraid. Don't take it personally, Gringo is generally fierce sociable – for a Dub, I mean."

"You need to start taking me seriously."

"I really don't. In fact, if you take a header off this roof, I get a week's holidays due to 'emotional distress'. I'm thinking of the Maldives, or maybe Greece. Do you know if they do that plate-smashing thing at the end of every meal? I've always fancied a go at that."

"You're a heartless bastard, Bunny. I'm in emotional distress and you're over there making jokes."

"Would you like a sandwich?"

"No."

"Are you sure? They're jam and cheese."

"Yes I'm . . . hang on, what kind of a fuckin' lunatic eats jam and cheese?"

"We're on the doorstep of a new century, Rory, open your mind to new experiences. I had my first cocktail last week. Didn't care for it, mind you, but still."

"I don't give a shite about your manky sandwiches or your gay drinks, alright?"

"Tut tut tut, Rory. There is no cause for lazy homophobia like that. We've been on a course."

Bunny put the walkie-talkie to his mouth and spoke while chewing. "Sergeant Spain, I feel obliged to inform you that Mr Coyne has used homophobic language while conversing with me in the course of executing my duties."

"That is very disappointing to hear, Detective McGarry. Please pass on my discomfiture at the close-minded attitude his choice of language conveys."

"Absolutely." Bunny pulled the walkie-talkie away from his mouth. "Gringo says stop being a prick."

"Why don't you go shag your bum-chum then and leave me alone?"

Bunny had a mouthful of sandwich and didn't immediately respond. Rory watched him chew exaggeratedly before swallowing. "I'll have you know, Sergeant Spain is an unhappily married man, at least for a few more weeks, and I, well, I've not met the right girl yet. Your Aisling is a bit of a looker, come to think of it."

"You leave my wife out of this."

"Widow. You mean widow. Well, soon to be anyway. She doesn't strike me as the type to stay lonely for long. Is she what you'd call high maintenance?"

Rory didn't answer. A wave of nausea was building and he could taste bile at the back of his throat.

Bunny's walkie-talkie beeped. "Have you asked him yet?"

"If you want to ask him, why don't you come up here, Gringo?"

"Because, detective, I am down here, coordinating crowd control efforts to ensure Rory's death plunge doesn't take out any punters or – God forbid – a busker."

"Jaysus," said Bunny. "Do you think we'd get in trouble for moving one of those mimes under his flight path? I really hate those creepy bastards."

"While I sympathise, Bunny, our role doesn't extend to criticism of the arts."

"More's the pity."

Rory regained the power of speech. "Would you two stop bleating on like a couple of old ones, it's really annoying."

"Alright," said Bunny, "take it easy, Rory. By the way, is it the end-of-the-millennium psychosis blues that have you all suicidal?"

"What are you on about?"

"Gringo wants me to ask – he has become a tad obsessed with this, to be honest with ye. He saw a thing on one of those digital channels about how the end of 1999 could be the end of days and now it's all he talks about. Millennium bugs, Y2K and all that. Planes are going to fall from the sky, he says. Cults will be having mass suicides, he says." Bunny looked up from his sandwiches as a thought struck him. "You're not trying to get in before the rush, are ye?"

"Shut up."

"Because it's only October now. Are you not a fan of Christmas or something?"

"I'm in emotional turmoil and this is how you handle it?"

Bunny shrugged. "Well, I've not had the training. They cancelled it for the homophobia seminar. The Minister for Justice gets overheard cracking a shitty joke at some banquet and all of a sudden we're all on a course. Personally, I've always got on fantastically with the gays. Statistically, very law-abiding bunch of lads and lasses."

Beep. The walkie-talkie crackled into life. "What'd he say about the thing?"

"Sorry, Gringo, he says it's nothing to do with the millennium. He's in emotional turmoil apparently."

"Ah, shame."

Bunny pulled the walkie-talkie away from his mouth. "Wasn't it only a couple of months ago that you were trying to jump off the roof of McDonald's up the road there, Rory? You'd think the good merchants of Grafton Street would've learned to lock the doors to their roofs by now."

"They can't," said Rory. "They're fire escapes – health and safety – so they're not . . ."

Rory stopped talking. The four pints of courage he'd downed were making their presence felt, both on his bladder and his queasy tummy. A spasm passed through his oesophagus and he retched reflexively.

"You OK, Rory?"

Before he could respond, his mouth opened and recycled stout spewed forth.

"Christ on a camel," said Bunny. "Look out below!"

Rory's physical outburst coincided with a gust of wind blowing north up Grafton Street, which was very unfortunate for one side of the crowd of spectators below.

"Ah for fuck . . ."

"Ye manky . . ."

Rory wiped his mouth and glanced over to see that Bunny was on his feet and edging towards him. "Stay back!"

Bunny held his hands up and slowly backed away to his previous position. "Relax, Rory, relax. You feeling OK?"

"What do you care? You're useless at this."

"Alright," said Bunny, "how's about you come in off there and I'll even help you fill out the complaint form. Enough of this silliness now, don't you think?"

Beep. "Bunny?"

"Sorry, Gringo, Rory was feeling a bit unwell."

"Well, it's fair to say he has somewhat lost the sympathy of his audience."

A voice rose from the crowd of onlookers. "You'd better jump, ye prick!"

"Hey!" shouted Bunny. "Less of that. Can't you see this poor eejit is in emotional turmoil?" He turned to Rory. "Sorry about that, Rory. Some people have no sense of decorum."

"You'd know," responded Rory, drawing in deep breaths. "Why're you here anyway? Since when is Grafton Street you and Gringo's patch?"

"It's not. We were up here pursuing a report from one of the shops of a gentleman attempting to be intimate with a mannequin."

"Jesus. Is that Andy Dooge again?"

"I would imagine so."

"The perv."

"Don't be so judgemental. He suffers from agalmatophilia, it's a proper thing."

"Is that—"

"With a mannequin. Yes. His shrink gave him a note that he carries around that explains it. Poor little pervert."

Just then a gust of wind whipped at Rory's coat and with a yelp he redoubled his grip on the stonework.

"You're looking very pale, Rory."

"Shouldn't you be trying to talk me down or something?"

"Probably. When you tried to jump off the roof of McDonald's, what did Sergeant Cartwright say to you?"

"She was good, Cartwright. At least she gave a shit."

"Ah, she's a nice girl, to be fair to her. I asked her out there a few months ago. Turned me down very gently. My advice would be, remember what she said to you then and sorta replay it in your mind."

"Thanks a bunch."

Beep. Beep.

"Excuse me, Rory. Yes, Gringo?"

"The round-up is complete, amigo."

"Thank Christ. I'm freezing my knackers off up here."

Bunny shoved the walkie-talkie in his pocket and swung himself around so that he was facing Rory, with one leg now on either side of the balustrade.

"So what's the story, Rory? To use an American phrase, 'it's shit or get off the pot time'. Are you taking the quick way down or coming down the stairs with me?"

"Go screw yourself, Bunny."

"I believe last time, despite Sergeant Cartwright's fine work, it was your Aisling showing up to plead with you that got you to see sense wasn't it?"

"Yeah."

"I'm afraid she's not coming this time."

"How do you know?"

"Because her and . . . hang on," said Bunny, pressing the button on the walkie-talkie and holding it up. "Who was with Aisling, Sarge?"

Bunny held the walkie-talkie out towards Rory. "Her two sisters, her ma, her niece Carol and three nephews, I didn't get their names."

Rory suddenly felt a whole lot more queasy.

"To be fair," said Bunny, "it was a good idea. I assume it was Aisling's – you're not smart enough for this. A man is threatening to jump off a building, so of course the staff and the security guards in the shops are going to be gawping out the windows. Human nature, isn't it? Same as people slowing down to look at a car crash. So while you're out here, pretending you're about to Wile E Coyote yourself, your beloved and her extended family are availing themselves of the five-fingered discount in Brown Thomas's. It's a good scam. Trying the same trick twice though? Greedy. Every guard in Dublin had been briefed in case you tried it again."

"Ah for . . . I told her that but she wouldn't listen."

"Well, the woman has expensive tastes," said Bunny. "Let's get down out of the cold then, shall we?"

Rory sighed. "Fair enough."

Bunny hopped down onto the roof and disappeared from view.

Rory stood there, looking down at his feet.

After a few seconds, Bunny's head reappeared. "Problem?"

"I'm . . . I'm feeling a bit . . . funny. I've been standing here for a while . . . and I . . ."

Rory looked down and suddenly the view began to swim. One image of the crowd juxtaposed messily on top of another. He closed his eyes and felt his head dipping forward . . .

Screams. His eyes opened. There was a moment of giddy weightlessness as the ground swirled beneath him and then . . .

A hand grabbed the back of his jacket. He was dragged back slightly but the coat slipped off him, his limp arms offering no resistance, and his body dipped forward again.

Another hand grabbed his belt.

Then Rory's head cleared, his bladder emptied and he grabbed at the arms around him.

"Alright, I got ye," said Bunny.

Rory tried to turn, pulling his way back towards the shore. Panic gripped his every nerve.

"Calm the feck down—"

One of his feet slipped off the ledge, jerking them both downwards. Rory redoubled his efforts, grabbing at everything, anything – wrapping them in a messy embrace.

LIVE! LIVE! LIVE! The words blared like a siren in his head.

"Stop fighting me, ye gobshite!"

Screams from below.

Bunny McGarry's straining face rushed towards Rory.

And then . . .

Impact.

Darkness.

Nothing.

CHAPTER TWO

Detective Sergeant Tim Spain, who some called Sergeant, several called Gringo and nobody called Tim, looked up from his keyboard and across the desk at his partner of three years. Bunny McGarry had his feet up on the table and was picking at his teeth with an unwound paperclip.

"The suspect then became disorientated and dizzy for reasons unknown . . ."

"Although almost certainly related to him being a gobshite," said Bunny.

"Shut up. It should be you filling out this report anyway."

"Bollocks, Gringo. If you're too much of a wussie to go up on the roof, you do the paperwork. Them's the rules."

"That's a charming way to address a superior officer."

"Sorry, your lordship."

"He subsequently lost his balance and, as Detective McGarry endeavoured—"

"Good word."

"Thank you – endeavoured to drag the suspect to safety, in his panicked state—"

"The suspect's."

". . . the suspect's panicked state, he began to fight Detective McGarry, endangering his own and Detective McGarry's life, leaving the Garda officer with no option but to neutralise the suspect by . . . via . . . through . . ."

"Headbutting him right in the puss and knocking the gobshite out cold."

". . . unconventional but effective means. The suspect was then made safe and received medical attention at Connolly Hospital, see attached, blah blah blah . . . Officer McGarry behaved like a proper legend and even found time to eat his disgusting sandwiches which he is very definitely not allowed to do in the car."

"Done?"

"Done."

"Right," said Bunny. "Well, it's been emotional. I'm off home for a well-deserved curry and an early night."

"My arse," said Gringo. "Have you forgotten what day it is?"

"October thirteenth, 1999. If this is more of your crap about the apocalypse and all that—"

"No, although yes, we should avail ourselves of every opportunity afforded to us before all hell breaks loose but . . . no. October thirteenth? Don't tell me that doesn't ring a bell?"

Bunny looked at Gringo for a moment. "Ah Christ, it's not, is it?"

"It is. It's your birthday!"

"Only it isn't."

"That's your opinion."

CHAPTER THREE

"But my feet are all sweaty."

Mulholland took a deep breath and tried to not say something he was going to regret. "I don't care. You're not taking your shoes off in the car. This is my place of work too, you know?"

Delaney glowered at him from the passenger seat. "How're you going to stop me?"

"That's a dangerous question to ask a man with a gun."

Detective Harry Delaney and Detective Bob Mulholland briefly made eye contact and then looked out of their separate windows. This was their third time being stuck together and they were unlikely to be exchanging Christmas cards any time soon. Delaney had the personal hygiene standards of a mentally-challenged baboon. Every time Mulholland looked at him he had a finger somewhere new – in his ear, eye, nostril, mouth. It was like he'd just been issued with a human head for the first time and he was trying to figure out how it worked. Bob had been forced to put up with a lot but the removal of footwear was the line in the sand that he would not allow to be crossed.

It had already been a long day and it wasn't even lunchtime. The heater in the car was broken and so they were both sitting there in their overcoats, freezing, apart from Delaney's inexplicably warm feet. Escort duty was dull at the best of times – just following an armoured car about while it made its deliveries – but it was now both boring and cold. Bob knew he had drawn this detail as punishment for messing up the paperwork on the O'Byrne case. He had no idea what Delaney had done. Maybe nothing. Maybe somebody had just wanted to remove from their vicinity the sight of Harry Delaney taking his fingers on a magical mystery tour of his own body. Regardless, Bob was stuck with him, same as he was stuck in this damn traffic jam. It was only 1 pm and the Quays were already in a state of gridlock. If there was any sense the security vans and their escorts would be allowed to go up the bloody bus lanes but that had been pooh-poohed by the powers that be. Instead here they were, stuck in a tailback watching four cars go through every time the lights changed. They were also not allowed to attempt to avoid traffic jams. As a security measure, each van had been given three different potential routes and only told which one they were taking that morning. They then stayed on that route, end of story.

Escort had become a much bigger deal ever since the spate of security van robberies over the summer. Nobody just robbed a bank any more. They either did one of those tiger kidnaps where they held a bank manager's family hostage, or they hit a van. With all these dye packs and tracers they had he'd have thought it wouldn't be worth the hassle, but apparently there was at least one gang in Dublin who were ahead of the curve on that.

"Would you look at this fuckin' eejit," said Delaney, extracting his little finger from his earhole and wiping it on his suit trousers.

"What?" said Bob.

"Bloody motorbike, zigzagging in and out of traffic like he's the only one who has somewhere he needs to be."

Bob looked into his side-view mirror and noticed a motorcycle courier on the driver's side, a couple of cars back, weaving his way through the stationary traffic. It was only when the bike had drawn almost level with their car that the thought occurred to him: *If the bike is on my side, how did Delaney see it?* Answer – there were two bikes.

Two simultaneous thunking noises came from behind them. Bob turned to see a suction cup attached to the back-seat window behind Delaney. If he had looked into his wing mirror, he would have seen another affixed to the window behind him. But his attention was firmly fixed on the passenger-side biker, who had now pulled up adjacent to the front wheel. He was pointing a gun at them.

"Jesus," said Delaney.

Bob spotted the movement as Delaney reached for his gun. He slammed his left arm across the other man's body to stop him getting them both killed.

"Don't be an idiot, he's got us cold."

Then, the other biker appeared on Bob's side of the car. He reached onto the roof and grabbed something. It was a third suction cup, which he placed in the centre of the windscreen. From it, a cord stretched to the suction cups on both sides of the car.

"What the f—"

The second biker then withdrew something from his messenger bag and held it up for them to see. Bob had never seen one in real life but he had watched enough movies to know a grenade when he saw one. Like a close-up magician, the biker exaggerated his movements – showing them that he was suppressing the safety lever on the side of the grenade. Then, he carefully placed it into what looked like an over-sized eggcup on top of the suction cup on the windscreen. He withdrew his hands slowly. Mulholland nodded as the biker pointed to the lever that was still being suppressed by the holder. Then, with a flourish, he pulled the pin.

"Jesus H Christ!" said Delaney, blessing himself furiously. Mulholland wordlessly stared at the lever on the side of the grenade; it staying suppressed was the only thing keeping them alive.

Then the biker took an A4 piece of paper from his bag and placed it against the windscreen.

Please Read Carefully
Cord goes slack, grenade goes BOOM
Open a window – BOOM
Open a door – BOOM
Sit still. Turn off engine. Phone the bomb squad.
Have a nice day.

Both bikers then drove off. All in all, it had taken twenty-seven seconds to render the escort car utterly useless.

"I'm getting the fuck out of here," said Delaney.

"Touch that door handle and I'll shoot you."

Bob carefully turned the engine off, gently put the handbrake on and then slowly picked up the mic on the radio. "Control, this is car alpha foxtrot four nine, we have a problem."

Meanwhile, twenty feet away . . .

Frankie Stewart looked at the red light and then turned the newspaper over again. He'd already read it all once and the football news three times. He was going to read it again. This traffic was moving slower than pigs in blankets at a bar mitzvah and they were already behind schedule. He would no doubt get a bollocking. It didn't matter that they were on a fixed route and traffic was traffic, he'd bet any money that arse of a manager at the College Green branch would have a moan at him anyway. Frankie didn't care, his beloved Leeds United were top of the league again. The best young team in Europe, that's what the bloke in the paper had said. They were going to dominate for a decade – easy.

A man in a parka with the hood up walked in front of the van. Pedestrians weaving in and out of traffic wound Frankie up. He'd seen some woman getting nailed on O'Connell Street by a cyclist only last week. Wasn't the poor fella's fault – if people will walk out into the middle of the road without paying attention, they've only themselves to blame. Come to that, it was cold out, but for once it wasn't actually raining. What was this joker playing at with his hood up?

The man stopped and calmly placed an A4 piece of paper up against the driver's-side window.

"What the . . ."

Frankie looked at the picture and then read the words under it. Then he looked at the picture again. He couldn't take his eyes off of it.

Three soft taps brought Frankie back to the here and now. The man was holding a gun in his other hand and was tapping it against the window. Frankie looked into the face under the hood – blue eyes were the only things visible beneath the balaclava.

Frankie nodded, slowly reached forward and pressed the intercom button on the dash.

"Tina, listen to me. You need to open the back doors now."

Tina's crotchety old voice came back over the intercom. "Ara feck off, Frankie, I'm tired of your daft pranks. Are Butch and Sundance outside again?"

Frankie looked at the picture on the sheet again. It was of a nine-year-old girl, looking into the camera while holding up the front page of that morning's newspaper. A copy of the same newspaper Frankie coincidentally held in his hands. She was smiling, happy. She was a dead ringer for her mother when she smiled.

"I swear on my life, Tina, this is real. There's a picture. They've . . ." Frankie swallowed. "They've got my daughter."

Twenty feet behind . . .

Bob Mulholland held the radio mic in his hand. He stared at the grenade on the windscreen and then he watched as the two motorbikes made their way towards the van three cars in front. He watched as its back door swung open and the female guard inside handed out a large bag. One of the bikers put his hand inside it, rummaged around and then tossed a wad of bills into the Liffey. Dye pack.

There was then an exchange of words before the other biker

pushed the guard back inside and leaned into the van. He shook his head at the other biker. Clearly, they had been expecting there to be considerably more bags. They rode off. The second biker stopped briefly to pick up some fella in a parka and they were gone – one driving off down Ellis Street, the other cutting across the pavement on the Bloody Bridge, scattering pedestrians before zooming off down the side of the Guinness brewery.

Out of sight, and all in under eighty seconds.

The only way Bob could be certain it had really happened was he could clearly see the grenade still stuck to his windscreen.

Somewhere nearby, a woman screamed.

CHAPTER FOUR

Bunny took a deep breath and pushed open the door to O'Hagan's. A rapturous cheer greeted his arrival. The pub contained enough Gardaí to comfortably police the All Ireland final, although many of them were already two drinks past an official warning had they been working. Gringo was at the corner table, the king of all he surveyed.

"Here he is," he roared. "Happy birthday, amigo."

Bunny looked around at the assembly. "Half the peelers in Dublin are here."

"What can I say? As soon as they found out it was your birthday, there was no stopping them."

"But it's not my birthday."

"You heard the man," shouted Gringo.

The assembly all raised their glasses. "Cheers!"

One of the traditions of this now annual event was that every time Bunny denied it was his birthday, everyone had to drink.

Bunny McGarry was born on July 26th 1967. However, a few years ago Gringo had fancied a night on the beer with the lads, and his then wife, Sandra, never the most easy-going sort, had been far from keen. He'd got around this by making it Bunny's birthday. Gringo was his only mate in the world and he couldn't leave the poor sod alone on his birthday, so the story had gone. Sandra had bought it and so Bunny's bullshit birthday bash had been born. It was now in its fourth year and, unlike Gringo's marriage, it was going from strength to strength. As word had got around, the number of people attending the celebrations each year had grown. It said something for the mentality of the members of the Garda Síochána that they were far more likely to turn out to celebrate a fake birthday than a real one.

"You should have got here earlier," said Gringo. "Butch has already canaried one of the new kids."

"Ah feck it, I love when she does that!"

"Butch" was Detective Pamela Cassidy – self-described lesbian fundamentalist. The nickname was entirely ironic. While nobody would refer to her as such to her face, she could be accurately described as petite – maybe eight stone and change. Red-haired and fresh-faced with an angelic demeanour, she didn't look like a copper – a fact she used to her full advantage. Rumour had it she had been just short of the officially mandated height requirement at the time she had joined the guards. However, she had also been an Irish judo champion, so someone higher up had made sure that allowances were made. The "canarying" was a tradition that would no doubt give the HR department at Garda HQ fits if they ever found out about it. What it consisted of was Cassidy aggressively coming on to any unaware male recruit. They ran a book on how long it took for the young fella to turn tail and run. Most normally bailed when she started talking about her collection of "implements". Fastest was one minute fifteen, slowest was eight minutes twelve.

"How long did the lad last?" asked Bunny.

"Six minutes."

"Very respectable showing. Who was it?"

"I don't know his name," said Gringo. "He's that big lanky fella by the bar."

Bunny looked over. "Is he normally that pale?"

"I doubt it." Gringo pushed out a stool that he'd been saving for Bunny.

As Bunny sat down, a pint of stout appeared in front of him and he joined in the toasting of his own fraudulent celebration. "Happy fecking birthday to me – ye shower of pricks."

They all cheered and then their attention diverted back to their own conversations.

"Anyway, amigo, I was just telling Garda Clarke here about your heroics today."

Bunny could feel himself blush. Moira Clarke had been at the station a couple of years. She was a nice girl. Bunny had seen her play football for the Garda team at the civil service games last year; she had a good burst of speed on her.

"Ara, heroics me arse," said Bunny. "Don't mind his nonsense."

"He's too modest, Moira, that's part of his charm. He'd be his generation's John Wayne if he wasn't so afflicted with that debilitating Cork accent."

"Feck you."

"Didn't understand a word of that. So anyway, this fella's up on the ledge of the building and he's giving it, 'Leave me alone, leave me alone – I'm jumping, I'm jumping, man!' and Bunny, cool as a cucumber, just hops out there and goes, 'Relax, take it easy, we're all friends here.' He has a very charming way about him when he wants to."

Moira grinned. "Oh, I don't doubt it."

"So he's all like, 'Relax, have a smoke, let's talk about this.' He gives the lad a cig and then offers him a light and as he leans across – *wham* – slams the cuffs on him."

Moira placed her hand on her mouth. "Oh my God."

"And he's like, 'You want to jump, then let's jump!'"

"Jesus!" said Moira. "And where were you when this was all going on?"

"Ah," said Bunny. "Detective Sergeant Spain was down on the ground, supervising from a distance."

Gringo looked affronted. "Grafton Street was packed with innocent women and children."

"And men," said Bunny.

"There's no such thing as an innocent man," said Gringo.

"You're not wrong there," agreed Clarke, before finishing off the last third of her pint with a flourish. "Besides, Gringo, you were right to be careful, what with you being only two days from retirement."

Gringo slapped the table in frustration as Clarke roared with laughter.

"Seriously, Gringo, do you think there's a guard in the country who hasn't seen *Lethal Weapon*?"

"If there is, I'm going to find the poor bastard. I'm going to get this story circulating if it kills me."

"Good luck," said Clarke. "You'd have more chance of convincing people that Bunny has been a ghost this whole time." She stood up. "Same again for the birthday boy?"

"Thanks, Moira," said Bunny, "fierce kind of you."

"Hey, what about me?" said Gringo.

"Why, DS Spain, I'm sure if you sit here long enough, some lucky lady will come bearing gifts of alcohol and peanuts."

And with that she was off and away towards the crowded bar.

Gringo leaned across the table. "You should ask her out."

"Moira?" said Bunny. "Don't be daft. I've a good ten years on her."

"And so what? Women go for the mature gentleman, y'know."

Bunny belched. "I've been called a lot of things in my time but that's a new one."

"First time for everything."

"Besides," said Bunny, "she's clearly gaga for Gringo, like every other lady in a five-mile radius."

"Yeah, apart from the one I married."

"Ah here, none of that. If I'm going along with this bullshit birthday, we'll have none of your moping."

Gringo held his hands up in surrender.

"Besides," continued Bunny, "now that you're about to be re-released onto the market, I can point out that I saw DS Jessica Cunningham on my way out of the station earlier. Apparently she is back from her stint in Galway and is working for Rigger O'Rourke now. You could resume your efforts at being the man who melts her frozen heart."

Gringo actually blushed. "Shut up. I still can't believe I told you that."

DS Jessica Cunningham was mid-thirties, blonde, six foot, athletic and with all the natural warmth of a meat grinder. She was an infamous ball-breaker. Legend had it she once reported a fellow guard for being out of uniform. He had been wearing a Santa hat on Christmas Eve. To be fair, she was very good at the job. She had to be, as her ascension through the ranks certainly couldn't be put down to her winning way with people. This wasn't a woman having to be tough to live in the man's world of policing either; Bunny knew several female guards who managed to do the job and retain membership of humanity. In fact, it was Detective Pamela Cassidy who had come up with Cunningham's nickname. As these things went, it was both apposite and a guaranteed death sentence if you were foolish enough to repeat it in her presence. Robotits was not known for her sense of humour.

All of this meant that Bunny was in possession of what would be a seismic slice of gossip if he ever shared it with anyone. Namely, that prior to meeting his soon-to-be ex-wife, Gringo and DS Cunningham had enjoyed an "arrangement".

Bunny leaned in and lowered his voice. "You never did tell me, what was the sex like?"

"Shut up."

"I mean," continued Bunny, "I'd imagine it'd be a bit like one of those insects where she rips your willy off when she's done with you."

"And to think, I was happy you didn't fall off that building."

"Maybe it was entirely the opposite though. Was she a crier? Were you a crier? I could easily see it ending in tears."

"One more word out of you and this chat will end in tears."

"So we're agreed," said Bunny, extending his pint out. "No more discussion of romance this evening."

Gringo clinked glasses. "Done, ye prick."

They both took a drag on their pints.

Truth be told, Gringo wasn't exactly short of female attention. Tall and slim with brown hair, he bore more than a passing resemblance to a *Star Wars*-era Harrison Ford. So much so, that when he'd worn a waistcoat to Rigger O'Rourke's wedding a couple of years ago, people had immediately taken to calling Bunny "Chewbacca". It hadn't stuck, thanks in no small part to the incident involving Bunny and the swan later in the evening, which had caused people to forget all about the Chewie references.

Bunny had met Gringo on their first day of Garda training down at Templemore, when he'd been assigned him as a criminology lab partner. Initially, Bunny had disliked him on principle. He looked like a bit of a poser – hell, he was a poser – but he'd grown on Bunny over time. Gringo's saving grace was that he never took himself too seriously. They made an unlikely pair. Bunny, the rough-as-arseholes muck savage, and Gringo, the suave and calculating Dublin sophisticate. Beneath the stylish exterior, though, there was a rock-solid man. He'd never been anything but a good friend and – for what it was worth – a loyal husband, as far as Bunny knew, and Bunny would know more than anyone. He didn't know much about these things but it seemed to him that Sandra, the soon-to-be-ex Mrs Spain, had always believed her husband was too good to be true. Her own insecurities had caused her to distrust him. She'd got more and more erratic through eight years of marriage, and then she'd left him for a landscape gardener. Last Bunny had heard, they'd a kid on the way. The divorce hadn't even been finalised yet.

"So," said Gringo, "I've a big night planned."

"Good luck. I look forward to hearing all about it. I'm staying for a couple then I'm off to my bed."

"Would you like to bet on that?"

"No, sergeant, I've more sense than to gamble with you."

CHAPTER FIVE

Detective Inspector Fintan O'Rourke stood outside of the Burlington Hotel and pulled his coat around himself. A middle-aged couple – she in a no doubt expensive evening gown and he in the obligatory tux – were hissing venom at each other at that volume that draws more attention than actual shouting would. DI O'Rourke stood to one side, trying to not be noticed noticing.

"Would you stop showing me up, Dirvla?"

"Me? Showing you up? That's rich! How dare you."

"Christ, you're always like this when you've had a drink."

"Oh, blame it on me, of course. It had nothing to do with you fawning over that hussy like some lovesick teenager. You're pathetic!"

"Can we not discuss this here?"

"We can discuss it in court. If she wants you, she can have you – because I've had enough."

"Would you . . ."

Both parties stopped talking as the distinctive bulk of Commissioner Gareth Ferguson strode out the main doors, a pack of Wellington's cigars already in his hand.

The man smiled. "Commissioner."

He nodded back. "Councillor, leaving so soon?"

"Ah, the wife's not feeling well."

She nodded along enthusiastically.

"Sorry to hear that. Safe home, Dirvla."

A taxi pulled up. "Thank you, Commissioner."

The man held the door open for his wife. "I won't be long, dear, you take care of yourself."

"I'll see you at home, darling."

And with that, she was gone – off to a life of quiet desperation, via a bottle of gin.

Her husband smiled at Commissioner Ferguson, who was now standing beside O'Rourke, puffing a cigar into life. He considered joining them, but veered off back through the hotel's front door when the commissioner met his advance with a simple headshake.

Commissioner Gareth Ferguson was a large and imposing figure of a man. Six foot four with an immense girth, he had the kind of presence normally exuded by heavy artillery. His voice could boom, when so moved, to the point that it could be heard two floors down, and his stare had been known to make grown men cry. The concierge who had been standing behind O'Rourke, to avoid being in the blast zone of the domestic squabble, now noticed he was getting a low-wattage version of the Ferguson stare and scurried away out of earshot.

The commissioner took a long drag on his cigar and then blew the smoke up into the air. "O'Rourke."

"Commissioner."

"Did I hear you ran another marathon there recently?"

"Yes, thank you, sir."

"Nothing in that statement was a compliment." Ferguson gave O'Rourke the kind of look that made him feel like the last sausage at the butcher's. "D'ye know," continued Ferguson, "many would consider me a powerful man. A man who strikes fear into the souls of villains and Gardaí alike as required."

O'Rourke shuffled his feet nervously. "Yes, sir."

"Do you think then, it would have an unduly positive effect on the morale of the country's criminal fraternity if they knew that my sainted wife has banned me from smoking my cigars inside any and all buildings that she is in?"

"Well, I—"

"Understand," said Commissioner Ferguson, "I don't mean rooms, I mean buildings. This hotel contains probably, what, a thousand people right now? Many of whom are smoking, almost all of whom are drinking – not to mention droning on at one another and, in the case of at least one prominent minister who shall remain nameless, farting their way through a five-course meal like a herd of nervous heifers at an abattoir; and yet, to enjoy one of my few indulgences, I have to step outside. The sheer injustice of it is galling."

O'Rourke said nothing, reckoning that he wasn't required for this part of the conversation.

Ferguson took another deep drag and blew a couple of smoke rings into the Dublin night sky.

"Well," he said, "was it him?"

"We're still analysing the crime scene, sir, and taking statements from the . . ."

O'Rourke noticed that he was now on the end of the Ferguson stare. "Yes, we believe it was Tommy Carter and his crew. The level of sophistication involved – we seriously doubt that anyone else would have the capability."

"You've been on these bastards for six months, Fintan, and you'd no idea this was coming?"

O'Rourke took a breath to try and measure his tone. "No, sir, I knew 'this' was coming, I just didn't know exactly what 'this' would be. With all due respect, I told you as much two weeks ago. The problem we have is this crew are impossible to crack. Us knowing who they are doesn't bother them in the least. They are tight, fiercely loyal and they know what they're doing. Hell, seeing as two of them are ex-Army Rangers, we trained them to know what they're doing. As if all that wasn't enough, again, as I told you, the Clanavale Estate is a nightmare. Tommy Carter runs it and we can't get near—"

Ferguson raised his hand. "Alright, Fintan, calm down. I appreciate the difficulties. Tell me about the grenade."

"They strapped it to the front window of the escort vehicle, sir, with an elasticated band around the car, taking the car completely out of commission and rendering the two officers powerless to do anything. If they tried to get out, lower a window or even shoot through one . . ."

"We'd have been scraping them up for a week," finished Ferguson. "Devilishly clever. The chief of staff of the defence forces is inside, I must compliment him on the quality of devious bastards his training is cranking out."

"The Quays had to be closed off for three hours while the device was 'made safe'. Well, that's what we're telling the press."

"Meaning?"

"It was a fake, sir. Albeit a very convincing one. The officers couldn't have known. Carter's crew has used live explosives in the past. The bomb squad was using the robot on it when . . ."

Ferguson pulled the cigar from his mouth. "What?"

"It started laughing, sir. It contained a recording device and—"

"For Christ's sake, Fintan!"

"Sir."

"And how come they had a picture of the driver's bloody child? They've clearly got inside help."

"Undoubtedly, sir, although we believe the photo was doctored."

"What?"

"We're still checking, but we believe it was a school photo of the child holding a certificate. They altered it to be today's newspaper. Any parent is going to—"

"Yes, yes," said Ferguson. "You're not the only one with kids, Fintan."

"We think they must have known the work rotas for the drivers. I've got my people looking into it and . . ." O'Rourke hesitated. This was the bit that needed to be handled with kid gloves. "About the route, sir."

"Ah yes, these so-called 'randomised' routes that these vans are on to prevent precisely this. How did they get around that bit? Let me guess – employed a bloody psychic?"

"Ehm, no, sir. You remember the review of procedures that Deputy Commissioner Geraghty oversaw in the summer?"

"Yes, yes. I remember the argument the two of you had about the resources, too. You banging the table for more bodies for your investigation team, him for his protection team."

"Well, after the job in Tallaght, sir – the one with the fake roadworks – the DC said escort vehicles had to scout the route beforehand to make sure there wasn't . . ."

Ferguson turned his eyes to the heavens. "They followed the bloody escort car?"

"In a manner of speaking. Tracker, sir. The bomb squad found it on the escort vehicle as part of their checks. We've already found one on another of our cars and we're checking the rest."

Ferguson petulantly flicked the stub of his cigar into the nearby bushes. "They were tracking our own bloody cars? This is . . . Christ knows what the hell this is, but I'd imagine we're going to be a laughing stock in the press, that's for bloody sure. And Fintan, political animal that you are, I'm sure some journo somewhere has already got a whisper of the clash between yourself and the deputy commissioner. I would urge you to remember that there is more than enough damage here to end two promising careers."

"This isn't a turf war for me, sir. I just want to take these bastards down."

Ferguson raised an eyebrow. "How noble. Well played. I almost believed you. I don't suppose there are any silver linings to be found in this cloud of shit?"

"Actually, sir, there is one. The van. Ordinarily it should've held about six hundred grand on that run, but a counting machine broke down at the depot."

"You're kidding me?"

"We're getting absolute confirmation, but for all their effort, they only got just shy of thirty-eight grand."

A grin spread across Ferguson's face. "Oh me oh my, it seems Mr

Carter and his boys are going to be having nearly as bad a night as we are."

"Maybe worse, sir. If our intelligence is right, they had big plans for the money. We think they're now short and they might just be a little desperate. We might finally have an advantage."

Commissioner Ferguson pulled up the trousers of his dinner suit and belched loudly. "Well, out with it, Fintan, what do you need?"

"Less of a what, sir, and more of a who."

CHAPTER SIX

"I'm fecking starving."

Gringo continued walking forward but pirouetted nimbly to address the straggling half of the expedition. "For Christ's sake, Bunny, you'd three packets of roasted peanuts back at O'Hagan's, how much food do you need?"

"I'd about a dozen pints too. Them nuts are floating in that much stout, none of them have even hit the sides yet. Can we not stop for a burger?"

"No, because you'll never start again. I know what you're like. You'll be asleep in Maccy D's in under five minutes, ye big baby."

They were walking alongside St Stephen's Green, past the couples with their hands out, vainly trying to flag a taxi. As Gringo spoke, one cruised around the corner with its light on. A gangly lad in his early twenties leapt out in front of it, waving his arms with the kind of frenzy that was normally the preserve of the shipwrecked.

"Get it, Niall, get it!" screamed his lady friend, her high heels in one hand and a wilting rose in the other.

The taxi swerved and honked. Niall stood in the road, angrily gesturing as it disappeared around the corner, its light still on. "Your light is on ye . . . ye . . . ye . . ."

"Bollocks!" screeched Niall's lady friend in assistance.

"Yeah," said Niall, heading back to shore, draped in the body language of abject despair.

"C'mon, Niall, that good taxi rank I was telling ye about is only up around the corner there."

"Ah," said Bunny, watching on, "the mythical good taxi rank, oft spoken of, rarely if ever seen."

"You're not wrong, amigo," said Gringo. "I reckon it's a government-sponsored form of contraception. Why else are there so few taxis in this town? It's their way of keeping the birth rate down. In most other parts of the world, getting the girl to agree to go home with you in the first place would be the tricky part. Here, it's the actually getting there bit that's the challenge."

"Fair point. D'ye think that explains why people who live near the city centre have so many kids?"

Gringo rubbed his chin. "That's a . . . that's a good point. I never thought of that. You're not just a pretty face, amigo."

"Speaking of pretty faces, shouldn't you turn yours around?"

Gringo threw his arms expansively wide while continuing to walk backwards. "I am a man of many talents, *muchacho*, walking arse-first is but one of—"

Gringo was interrupted by a loose paving stone and gravity, his hands grasping for the night sky even as his legs went from under him and his arse ended up deposited in a large pile of bin bags.

He looked up to see Bunny bent double above him, howling with laughter.

"Well, help me up."

Bunny flapped his hand in admonishment. He looked in danger of passing out from a lack of oxygen, grasping at a nearby railing for support.

Two girls walked by, their arms wrapped ineffectually around themselves as they huddled against the biting winter chill.

"Would ye look at that, Janet, someone threw out a perfectly good auld fella."

Bunny looked at the two girls and his hysterics redoubled.

"Who're you calling old?" Gringo put his hands down to try and push himself up and grimaced as something squelched under his right palm.

"Ah for . . ."

Bunny wiped the sleeve of his anorak across his tear-stained face. "Now it really is my birthday. The state of ye."

"Yes, ha ha, lap it up, ye big culchie. Now, help me up."

Bunny extended his hand and pulled Gringo upright. "Is that a new cologne you're wearing there, DS Spain? You're smelling fierce ravishing."

"Yeah, it's called Eau de Cork. Now c'mon, it's not that much further to this place." Gringo started striding along the footpath.

"Seriously? Are you not taking your soggy-bin arse as a sign from God to call it a night?"

"No! In fact, I'm on a mission from God! This place serves until the wee small hours, and you can get food there."

"Really?"

"It's that trick to get around the licensing laws. It's a club, serves food. Well, a sort of sweet-and-sour pot-luck surprise."

"Sounds delightful," said Bunny.

"I've seen you eat how many kebabs? And you still can't tell me what kind of meat is in one."

"Kebab."

They were now back at the end of Grafton Street. The proximity to the events of earlier in the day hadn't struck Gringo until they were just around the corner. He looked down the street and up to the ledge where he'd watched Bunny and Rory Coyne tussle a few hours before.

"Here we are," said Bunny, "back at the scene of the crime."

Gringo stopped and put his hand out. "Just, look, I . . . You know, whatever happens I'll back you up but . . . that shit today, they could be power-washing you off the pavement now."

"Ara Gringo, I never knew you cared."

Gringo's tone dropped enough to wipe the grin off Bunny's face. "Listen to me. That was . . . you freak me out, Bunny. You don't . . .

look, you need to take care of yourself, alright? You might not be too bothered whether you live or die, but I am."

"Ah, would ye calm the feck down, Gringo."

Bunny went to walk off but Gringo grabbed his arm and held him. "Just listen, OK? Since that thing a couple of years ago—"

"We're not talking about that."

"I know," said Gringo, "fair enough. But, since then . . . You're my best friend, ye dozy plank, and I'm the only one close enough to know, but you're not that bothered about getting home safe and that scares the shit out of me."

"Leave me alone, I'm fine."

"There's more to life than this job and an under-12 hurling team—"

"Best under-12 hurling team in the county!" interjected Bunny.

"But still, only a hurling team. You need a little balance in your life and possibly – just throwing it out there – it'd do you the power of good to get laid."

Bunny placed one of his big meaty paws on Gringo's shoulder. "I'm afraid, Timothy, I just don't think of you in that way."

"Yeah, yeah, the night is young. C'mon, talk and walk, I'm getting cold."

Bunny patted Gringo's cashmere coat. "Well, if you will dress for style over comfort."

"Says the anorak boy. C'mon."

Gringo nodded his head towards King Street and they started trudging in that direction, past the waifs and strays staggering home from the pubs and clubs in ones and twos.

"Seeing as we're talking about the things we don't talk about," said Bunny, "you seem to be enjoying the odd game of cards more regularly these days."

Gringo laughed. "I go down to Richie's and play the occasional hand, big deal."

"You were in that game at Daly's during the week, too."

"Having me followed now are you, detective?"

"No, should I be?"

Gringo took a poker chip out of his pocket and flicked it off his thumb. "Relax, amigo. Now that I'm wifeless, I need to find something to occupy my time. I'm thinking of going pro. I need to get me one of those cowboy hats you see the guys on the TV wearing."

"Ah, pro, is it? Is that why you turned down Creevy's offer?"

Gringo looked across at Bunny. "How do you know about that?"

"Christ's sake, Gringo, nobody gossips like coppers. Everyone is busting their bollocks to get an assignment like the Criminal Assets Bureau and you're turning it down?"

Gringo shrugged. "I'm not that bothered. Lots of paperwork. If I wanted to be an accountant I'd have just become one."

"That's bullshit. Look, don't be fecking stupid and let me hold you back."

"You're not. I like working with you. We're a good team."

"Yeah, and if you weren't spending your time keeping me out of trouble with the higher-ups, think where you'd be."

"I'd be lumbered with some stuffed-shirt pencil-pusher. You're an annoying prick, McGarry, but you're *my* annoying prick. We're a team, and besides, I asked around, everyone else understands even less of what you say than I do."

"Is that right, ye little cloth-eared Dublin gobshite, ye?"

"I got none of that."

"Oh, you're a fecking laugh riot, aren't you?"

Gringo furrowed his brow in mock consternation. "Something about a goat?"

"I'll boot your bollocks into a different time zone in a minute."

They turned the corner onto Mercer Street, careful to avoid the remnants of some curry chips that may or may not have been eaten before being discarded onto the pavement.

"Oh, speaking of your love life," said Gringo, "here's your old flame."

Shambling towards them down the pavement came the familiar figure of Mary Murtagh, or "Magpie Mary" as she was affectionately known. Well into her sixties, she'd been homeless since before Bunny had begun to patrol the streets. She wore an old plastic tiara pinned to her blonde bird's nest of a hairdo and, on the back of her ragged coat, a tattered pair of angel's wings that she'd picked up somewhere, probably discarded by a hen do. She always wore make-up, too – enthusiastically if messily applied – although it was a mystery as to where it came from. The overall look reminded Bunny of a doting grandma who had allowed her beloved grandchildren more leeway than was prudent. There had been several attempts over the years to move Mary into stable accommodation, but it hadn't taken. She had her shed down by the train tracks and that was all she wanted. She roamed the streets, her ever-present shopping trolley filled with her most treasured possessions. That was where her name came from: if it glittered and could be found discarded in a skip or sticking out of a bin, Magpie Mary would retrieve and treasure it.

Bunny's first contact with Mary had been a memorable incident. An overly zealous supermarket employee had been sent out with a van to retrieve wayward shopping trollies and had believed his remit extended to the repatriation of Mary's chariot. This had resulted in a screaming fit on Wellington Quay that'd almost led to Mary being sectioned and the supermarket employee being hospitalised. Otherwise, she was a sweet old dear.

"Here she is," said Bunny, "my favourite girl!"

Mary looked up and gave them a dazed smile. "Ah, good evening, gentlemen." Her voice was slurred and slow. Normally, she spoke in a mellifluous Dublin warble of inexplicable poshness.

"You alright there, Mary?" asked Gringo. "Been having yourself a nip against the cold night chill?"

Bunny bowed theatrically before her. "Come, my darling Mary, let me whisk you away from all of this and we shall dance the light fandango in the moonlight, whatever the feck a fandango is."

"Now, Bunny, you know how I feel about that potty mouth."

Bunny clasped his hands to his chest. "I do apologise, m'lady. How uncouth of me." Bunny's voice returned to normal. "How are you keeping, Mary?"

She didn't respond. Her trolley clonked into the railings and she looked down at it, an expression of woozy confusion on her overly made-up face.

Bunny and Gringo glanced at each other.

"Are you alright, Mary?" said Gringo.

She swayed slightly and he stepped forward to place a steadying hand on her arm. He raised the other to her face and gently turned it. Blood trickled from a wound on her temple, a crust of dried blood beneath.

"Christ! What happened?"

"Demons!" she responded. "Demons! Young ruffians tried to take Mary's crown! How dare they!"

Bunny's fists clenched. "Where are they?"

Mary looked around her. "I was . . . there were . . . I'm . . ." She looked up into the night sky, lit by streetlights and weak moonlight, as if trying to navigate by unseen stars. "Where am I?"

"OK," said Gringo. "C'mon Mary, let's get you sitting down for a sec." He led her over towards some steps below a fire exit and gently guided her down. "Right, let's have a look at you." He carefully pushed her hair aside and looked at the damage. "Oh dear, this isn't great, Mary. We're going to have to get you a bit of help."

"Oh no," she replied, weakly trying to push his hands away. "There's no need to make a fuss."

"Nonsense," said Gringo. "It's no trouble at all."

Gringo leaned back to Bunny and spoke quietly. "She's going to have to go to A&E, this looks nasty."

"Right. I'll phone for an ambulance – but this time of night, it might take a while."

"Yeah," said Gringo, then stopped as he noticed a taxi coming around the corner. "Unless . . ."

Gringo strode into the road, forcing the taxi to stop. The driver honked hard in irritation. Gringo whipped his wallet out of his inside coat pocket, opened it and held it up. The driver lowered his window and stuck his head out.

"What the fuck do you think you're playing at?"

"Gardaí," said Gringo, and then indicated towards Mary. "I'm afraid this lady needs to be taken to hospital."

The driver indicated the blonde woman in her twenties in his passenger seat, and her three friends in the back, two male, one female. "I've already got a fare."

"This is an emergency. Drop her down to the Mater Hospital, it'll take you ten minutes."

"So call an ambulance, that's what they're there for."

"I'm appealing to your sense of civic duty, sir. The emergency services are overstretched at this time on a Friday night."

"So are the taxis."

The blonde in the front seat lowered her window and stuck her sour expression out into the night air. "Look, we've a bleedin' house party to get to. Do your fucking job and get out of the bleedin' road."

Gringo gave her a steely-eyed look for a moment. "Very well, madam, have it your way. Detective McGarry – do you have reason to believe that these people might be in possession of controlled substances?"

"Indeed I do, Detective Sergeant Spain."

Gringo gave the blonde a pointed look. "Do you feel a search may be in order?"

"I do," agreed Bunny.

The blonde's expression went up a whole lemon in the sour stakes. "Go ahead ye spanner, see if I—" She was interrupted by the doors on either side of the back seat opening simultaneously and the other passengers hurriedly exiting the vehicle. "What the fuck are—"

A young guy with spiky peroxide blond hair smiled nervously at the assembly. "It's fine, we can walk from here."

"But we—"

"C'mon Karen."

"But—"

"Come on, Karen!" He said the words through gritted teeth as he furiously bobbed his head to the side.

Karen sneered at Gringo one last time, opened her door and clomped off angrily after the rest of the party. "D'ye know your problem, Darren? Ye've no bollocks. You're like one of them you-nicks."

Bunny turned to Mary. "C'mon, m'lady, your carriage awaits." Mary took his proffered arm and unsteadily got to her feet.

"This is nonsense," said the driver, "you can't commandeer my taxi. I've got rights."

Gringo leaned in. "Calm down. Look," he produced one of his cards from his pocket and held it out for him, "how would you like a friend in the police?"

"I've already got lots of friends on the force."

"OK," said Gringo, "how would you like a couple of enemies?" He pointed across at Bunny, who was helping Mary towards the taxi. "That's Detective Bunny McGarry, he's got this whole damsel-in-distress thing going on that, believe me, you do not want to get on the wrong side of."

The driver shook his head in resignation. "She'd better not stink out my taxi."

"You'll live." Gringo produced a pen from his pocket, flipped his business card over and started writing on the back of it. "Sister Elaine Doyle. She should be working A&E, or, if not, the head nurse will know her. Give her this note, tell her it's from DS Tim Spain and she'll take care of her for me."

The taxi driver took the card reluctantly and then watched as Gringo carefully wrote his licence plate down on the back of another one.

"I said I'd do it."

"Good man," said Gringo. "I'll be ringing to check in the morning, so you'd better make sure you do."

As Gringo spoke, Bunny opened the back door and guided Mary in. As he did so, he gave a wave to the five cars that were now waiting behind them.

"Wait," said Mary. "My things! All my precious things!"

Gringo looked at the shopping trolley and then back at the taxi driver.

"Open the boot."

Three minutes later, Bunny and Gringo stood on the pavement, watching the taxi disappear around the corner – its boot open and tied down with climbing rope to hold Mary's trolley in.

"Fancy a pint?"

"Gasping for one."

CHAPTER SEVEN

Bunny gawped at the sign that dangled over the doorway, then at Gringo, then back at the sign.

"No fecking way."

"Don't be so close-minded."

Bunny pointed an accusatory finger at the sign that indicated the establishment was Charlie's Private Members' Club – Dublin's Premier Jazz Emporium. "Fecking skiddle-dee-diddly-wah-wah daddy-o jazz? Have you lost what little mind you have left? You know I wouldn't be caught dead in some wanky jazz club."

"Which is exactly why I didn't tell you where we were going. But look – we're here now."

"No way. Jazz, me hole. I'm not watching some navel-gazing numpty in a turtleneck playing all the right notes but in the wrong order. Goodnight, Eileen."

"You're supposed to be a fan of music."

"Indeed I am," said Bunny. "Bit of Springsteen, nothing better. Johnny Cash is the man. I'll even go you some Led Zeppelin and your man who blew his brains out . . ." Bunny clicked his fingers at Gringo.

"Kurt Cobain?"

"Had some tunes. I've also got a soft spot for Rage Against the Machine."

"Unexpected."

"My point is, I'm a fan of music, but jazz isn't music. Jazz is some cockwomble in a beret, wanking himself off with a saxophone."

"Sax-a-phobic, are we?"

"Don't come that with me, Clarence from the E Street Band is a legend, but he's not doing a twenty-minute atonal arse-clenching solo that sounds like someone sodomising a goose."

Gringo folded his arms. "Would you calm down? We're going in for a couple of drinks. It's a late bar and there's a bit of grub. You do pick the weirdest things to get on your high horse about. We'll just stay for one if you don't like it."

Bunny looked at the sign again, as if he was half expecting it to leap off the wall and bite him. "First sign of a beret . . ."

"Good man." Gringo patted Bunny on the shoulder and started down the stairs. "Rage Against the Machine? Really?"

"Oh yeah. 'Feck you, I won't do what you tell me.'"

"Noted."

Gringo pushed open the door and led the way inside. A wave of warm air, stale smoke and murmured conversation swirled around them. Bunny surveyed the room sceptically. Charlie's was a small-sized bar but a decent-sized basement. Groups of people huddled around tables. There was an undue prominence of beards but thankfully no berets in sight. Gringo exchanged smiles with the bouncer on the door and a couple of patrons on the way in. Bunny assumed he'd been there a few times before although it was hard to tell. Gringo was the kind of person people instinctively smiled back at.

A small bar stood in the corner and to its right sat an equally small stage, which seemed to be ninety per cent occupied by a grand piano. Behind it sat a short man with tightly cropped, wiry silver hair and a face of pained concentration as he worked the keys, coaxing a not unpleasant staccato melody from them.

Gringo leaned into Bunny's ear. "That's the owner, Noel. He's a dab hand on the piano, only . . ."

"Only what?"

As Bunny looked at him, he noticed his head twitch violently to the left and words spasm forth: "Yada, big cocks!"

"He's got that whatchamacallit," said Gringo.

Tinkle tinkle . . . "Yada, fannies. Fannies!"

"Tourette's?" asked Bunny.

"That's the one."

"Is that not a bit of a professional drawback?"

"Not if you own the place. Honestly, you get used to it surprisingly quickly."

A couple got up from the cramped booth in the corner and left. Gringo nodded at it and he and Bunny slipped in. Gringo leaned back against the wall and surveyed the room. "See, amigo, it's not that bad."

"Yeah, so far."

"Yada, big cocks!"

One of the smartly suited group of men on the next table guffawed and repeated "Yada, big cocks." His companions shushed him, even as they shared a grin.

"So far," repeated Bunny.

"It's good that you're expanding your horizons, Bunny." Gringo stood and placed his cashmere coat down beside his stool. "I'll get them in. You, relax – take your anorak off or you won't feel the benefit."

Gringo moved through the tables to the bar. Begrudgingly, Bunny slipped his anorak off and placed it under the table. Then he took his phone out and checked it, for the want of something to do. He had no new messages but he read some old ones, for reasons he didn't fully understand. He considered playing Snake but thought that might make him look like a bit of a sad sack.

The lanky one amongst the suits at the next table guffawed along with every involuntary invective that came from behind the piano.

Bunny noticed some disapproving looks from other patrons that went unheeded.

After a couple of minutes of dead time, Gringo returned and placed two large whiskeys down on the table.

"What madness is this?"

Gringo shrugged an apology. "Look, they don't have stout."

Gringo cut Bunny's tirade off while he was still drawing the breath with which to deliver it. "Chill out, amigo. You like whiskey, remember? It brings out your cheerful side."

"It'll have its work cut out for it," grumbled Bunny.

"That's why I got doubles. Let's see if it can't rise to the challenge. Speaking of which, excuse me while I go water the plants."

Gringo turned and headed towards the door in the corner. As he passed a table, he nodded to a man wearing a long brown coat with a regrettable earring and goatee combination. The man was accompanied by a brunette wearing enough jewellery to start her own market stall. Bunny watched the man whisper something to the woman before he headed after Gringo. Probably nothing. A sip of whiskey and a glance confirmed to Bunny that his interest was being noted by the woman. Bunny looked at his phone again and noted the time. 1:26 am. Give it four minutes. He was suspicious by nature and doubly so of anyone who voluntarily agreed to be in the company of jazz.

Bunny examined the surface of the table, pockmarked with scars and cigarette burns, wobbling under the weight of Gringo's whiskey glass. He guessed the mood lighting was hiding all manner of decor sins.

The song finished and there was an unenthused ripple of applause.

"Yada bollocks!"

There were a few moments of silence, save for the murmured conversation. One of the trio at the next table went to get drinks while the lanky one told a good joke badly.

Then another song began, the piano drifting into a soft,

contemplative melody. Then a female voice chimed in – deep, rich, sensuous and sad all at the same time. It started slow, and built.

Bunny didn't turn around. He sat there, his drink sitting forgotten in his hand as the voice filled the room.

> Caught between,
> What I know and what I mean,
> Helpless to resist,
> Not the one who started this.

> Falling deep into your eyes,
> You know that you hypnotise,
> I can't resist this sweet attack,
> So don't you dare love me back.

The voice swam around him, singing a now wordless melody that seemed to go against the piano and yet, at the same time, fitted it perfectly. They danced in and out of each other in a way Bunny had never heard before.

The lanky one from the next table's voice crashed in like an unwelcome guest, humming along, deliberately out of tune.

"Shush, Victor."

"Should do a bit of Frank Sinatra. Something we know."

Bunny's hand was on the back of the lanky one's neck before he'd even had the thought. He pulled him close and leaned into his ear. "You need to be quiet now."

Bunny pushed him away, with just a touch more force than was required.

The velvety words swam around him once more.

> My heart trapped under,
> My world torn asunder,
> What you do, only you know,
> Why it is, I can't go.

I was gone even as I fell,
No escaping from your spell,
I can't resist this sweet attack,
So don't you dare love me back.

Meanwhile, Gringo stood at one of the two urinals and relieved a pressing concern.

"Ahh, sweet release."

The expected figure of Damo Marsden appeared beside him, leaning against the wall.

"Do you have something for me?"

Gringo looked down. "Not just now, Damo, unless you're looking to take our relationship in an unexpected direction?"

"Very funny. Where's my money?"

"Again, my hands are a bit full at the minute, unless you'd like to hold this for me?"

Marsden sneered and moved aside, leaning against the sink.

Gringo shook extensively and then put himself away. He turned to see Marsden standing there with his hand out. Gringo nodded at the sink.

"Hygiene, Damian. You don't know where I've been."

Marsden begrudgingly moved. Gringo washed his hands thoroughly and reached across for the disposable towels, spending an undue amount of time drying them. Marsden looked at the ceiling and blew out a sigh.

Point made, Gringo tossed the paper towels in the bin and pulled a wad of notes out of his pocket. "Two grand."

"Very funny, you owe me eight."

"And here's two of it. You'll get the rest next week."

Marsden took a step towards him. Gringo was tall, but Marsden's six-foot-five meant he could still tower over him. "I think you've got me confused with the credit union."

"And I think you've got me confused with someone who finds you intimidating, Damian. Don't forget who I am."

"Oh," said Marsden, "don't worry – I haven't. How would your bosses like it if they found out one of their golden boys was running up gambling debts?"

"Try and find out and you'll be in a world of hurt, Damo. Now calm down. You'll get the rest next week."

"Someone pulls this shite, they normally catch a beating."

"Do they?" Gringo calmly looked up into the other man's eyes. He could almost see the calculations running backwards and forward behind his pupils. "Don't bluff me, Damo, you've not got the face for it."

"Yeah, Gringo, well if you know so much about that, how come you're in eight large to me?"

"Bad run of cards is all. Temporary thing."

Marsden took a step back. "That so? How come I'm hearing that I'm not the only one holding your paper then?"

Gringo laughed and threw a lightning-quick punch into Marsden's kidneys, stepping to the side as the taller man crumpled to the floor. He grabbed a handful of greasy hair and pulled his head back up. "If I hear that you've been discussing my affairs again, our next chat will be a lot less polite, Damian. I expect a certain degree of discretion from a man in your position. Do you understand me?"

The response came out as a stringy croak. "Who d'ye think you're fucking with?"

Gringo leaned in and smiled sweetly. "I don't care. You'll get the rest of your money next week. Until then, I expect you to keep your mouth shut. Are we clear?"

Marsden held Gringo's gaze for a long moment and then gave the slightest of nods.

Gringo released his hair and wiped his palm on his jeans. He tossed the two grand onto the floor in front of him.

"There's your money. Don't forget to wash your hands. That floor is manky."

The song was coming to an end as Gringo sat back down. "So have ye—"

"Shush!"

Gringo was taken aback. Bunny was sitting there, eyes closed, his face a picture of serene contemplation.

Gringo glanced at the stage over his partner's shoulder. The black woman who'd served him drinks earlier had joined Noel on stage. She had long dark hair that hung down over her right eye, almost covering that side of her face. She was maybe five four, with brown eyes and full lips. She wore a figure-hugging blue dress that looked like something from the Fifties, but she was making it work. It was strange – it was definitely the same woman who'd served him minutes before, but she looked very different now, as if some internal light had suddenly been turned on. She was not paying the slightest bit of attention to anyone in the room as she sang, standing behind one of those large silver-grilled vintage mics, swaying with the music and humming a soft melody.

As the last notes ended on the piano, the room applauded with genuine enthusiasm, although only one member of the audience was on his feet.

The woman smiled sheepishly in acknowledgment of the applause and moved back behind the bar.

"Glorious. Fecking glorious."

"Eh, Bunny?"

"What a voice, like. Tremendous."

"Yeah. Ehm – everyone else has stopped clapping."

Bunny looked down at his hands as if he'd just become aware of their behaviour. "Oh right, yeah." His face flushed. "Very good." He sat back down.

At the piano, Noel began a jaunty number, unaccompanied save for his own random profanity.

"Anyway," said Gringo, "I know I was in the jacks for a while but I'm afraid you'll have to move. You're in the seat belonging to my jazz-hating friend and he'll be back in a minute."

"Ah shut up. That wasn't jazz, that was . . . I don't know what that was, but it wasn't . . ."

Gringo looked at the bar, where the woman was now back serving once again. "She's pretty damn cute too."

"What? Is she?" said Bunny. "Yeah, I suppose. I'd not really noticed." He glanced at the bar, then looked away, then stole another look.

Gringo gave him an appraising look over his glass as he held it before his lips. "If I believed for one second that you hadn't noticed, I'd be recommending you getting demoted from the rank of detective immediately." He threw the guts of a double whiskey back and winced as the sourness burned at the back of his throat. He held his glass up. "Your round."

"Right, yeah," said Bunny. He glanced up at the bar, confirmed there was one and only one member of staff in evidence. "Give it a minute, I'll . . ."

Gringo laughed. "D'ye know something? You are nothing short of adorable, ye big culchie muppet. You sit here and keep looking all mean and moody, I'll get these. I've just remembered I've not got you anything for your birthday yet."

Bunny's voice became an urgent whisper. "Don't be a gobshite. Sit – don't say anything. Feck, it's not even me birthday."

The last words were swept away in Gringo's wake as he nimbly dodged away from Bunny's grasp. He ruffled the big man's hair on the way past and was gone.

Bunny fidgeted with the bar mat in front of him before ripping the corner off it. Bloody Gringo, could never leave well enough alone. For want of anywhere else to look, Bunny scanned the room. The tall guy with the regrettable goatee was back with his female companion. They seemed to be having an animated conversation, but his eyes followed Gringo's progress towards the bar. The other patrons seemed to be enjoying their drinks, oblivious to the atom bomb of humiliation whistling its way downwards towards Bunny.

He was looking for any distraction, and it found him in the form of the stocky one from the table of besuited gigglers beside him.

He loomed over Bunny. "Hey, what do you think you're doing putting your hands on my friend?"

Bunny didn't even look up. "He was being rude. I asked him to keep it down."

"And what's it to you?"

Bunny picked up his glass and swirled the remains of his drink around in it. "I'm like a modern-day Mary fecking Poppins. I fly around the place giving lessons in manners."

Without moving his head, Bunny glanced to the side. The lanky one and the fat one were a rapt audience for this little play.

"You put your hands on somebody where I'm from, that's fighting talk."

Bunny finally looked up. "That's talk is it? What, are you deaf? Is it some form of sign language?"

"I'll sign language you in a minute."

"Jesus," said Bunny. "No offence, but you are terrible at this. Do you want to go back and send Lanky or Tubs over, see if they might do any better?"

Stocky leaned on the table, in a way he'd probably seen in a movie – one where you intimidated somebody by giving them a wide open shot at everywhere from your knackers up.

He lowered his voice an octave. "You're not taking me seriously."

Bunny leaned back on his stool. "No, no I'm not. A smart man would ask himself why that is. Why I appear to be completely and utterly unaffected by your little hard-man routine here. A smart man might take a moment's pause to consider that. So prove you're smarter than you look there, fella. Go back to your seat and spend the rest of the night discussing with Lanky and Tubby how you could have definitely shown me a thing or two but you decided not to. Give peace a chance – that's what a smart man would do."

Bunny's lips curled into a grimace of disapproval as the foul waft of Stocky's breath washed across him. "There's three of us and one of you."

"Good point," said Bunny. "You might want to call some people."

. . .

The blonde in front of Gringo picked up her drinks and departed, leaving him as the only customer.

The barmaid-cum-songstress ran a cloth across the bar, smoothing out the spillages. "Hey, what can I get you?"

"Can I just say, you've a fantastic voice."

She smiled. "Well, it helps if your audience is drunk, but much obliged."

"My, eh, friend over there thought you were incredible." Gringo pointed over his shoulder.

"And let me guess, he's some big record producer, gonna whisk me away from all this?"

"No, 'fraid not. We are but humble detectives in the Garda Síochána."

"That right? Well, if this is a raid, least you're being awful polite about it."

Gringo held up his hands. "Relax, we come in peace. Besides, you're within the terms of the licence for a private club. As long as you're serving food on the establishment. Speaking of which, isn't there supposed to be some complimentary grub available?"

The woman looked at the door behind the bar. "There's food, but nobody has been complimentary about it. It's a bowl of sweet-and-sour something. Cooking ain't Noel's forte."

"Yada, big cocks!"

"I'd offer you some, only it might count as assaulting a police officer."

"Fair enough. Is that an accent I hear?"

"Damn, I wasn't sure if I believed that detective thing but you won me around."

"I'm guessing . . . Deep South?"

"Correct. Kerry."

"Yeah, I meant America."

"You saying there ain't many dark-skinned maidens from down in Kerry?"

"Not that look like you."

"Oh dear, and you were doing so well. So are you going to be ordering drinks any time soon or did you just come up here to take your twinkly-eyed Irish charm for a spin?"

"Ouch. You are tough."

"And judging by that line on your ring finger, you are married. So what can I get you?"

Gringo leaned against the bar. "Two double Jack Daniel's, please and, for the record, currently getting divorced."

She put two glasses on the bar and started pouring the measures from a near-empty bottle. "Let me guess, she didn't understand you?"

"Nah, I didn't understand her. Que sera, sera. And for the record, I wasn't up here on my own behalf . . ."

"Ahh, wing man. Gotcha. So tell me all about your friend then."

She tossed the now-empty bottle of Jack Daniel's into the bin under the bar and began opening a new one.

"Well . . . he's got a cracking sense of humour."

"Ouch, ding – thank you for playing."

"What?"

"You opened with sense of humour?" She sounded exasperated. "Why not just tell me the poor son'bitch got beaten with the ugly stick and has six months to live. Sense of humour? Damn, son, that is some weak-assed shit right there."

"You put me on the spot. I panicked. What do you want from me?"

"Go for something real. When in doubt, why not try the truth?"

"OK. He's my best friend."

"Why?"

"Because, under the bluster, he's the most honourable and decent man I know. He honestly believes in right and wrong and, in his own fucked-up lunatic culchie way, he actually tries to make the world a better place."

She finished pouring the drinks and placed the bottle on the counter. She held Gringo's gaze for a second and then pointed at him. "See, now that – that was real. You should lead with that next time. Anyway, I'm sure your buddy is quite the catch but I'm not fishing right now."

"Are you sure? You're making a big mistake."

"Honey, this ain't even close to my biggest."

Gringo took out his wallet and withdrew a ten-pound note and passed it across for the drinks.

"Have I mentioned it's his birthday?"

"Ah damn, well, let me close the bar and I'll be right over. Oh wait . . ." She looked around her in mock surprise. "Turns out this isn't a lap-dancing bar."

"Jesus, love, no offence, but you are what we Irish call hard work."

"Honey, I'm what everybody calls hard work." She smiled at him as Gringo waved away the change. "Tell your friend I said 'happy birthday'."

"He's shy, but I'll send him up for the next round and you can tell him yourself."

"Shy? Is this the big guy in the corner we're talking about?"

Gringo turned to follow her look. Bunny was sitting down, but the three guys who had been at the table beside them were now standing over him in a menacing manner.

"Looks like he's making some friends."

"Oh shit."

Gringo had taken two steps back towards the table when the tubby one cold-cocked Bunny on the back of the head with an empty beer bottle and all hell broke loose.

CHAPTER EIGHT

"Aghhhhhhh."

The sound of Venetian blinds being opened ripped into the very fabric of Bunny McGarry's soul, as the ensuing wash of sunlight burned his eyes.

"Wara-ta-fecking-Jesus-bastard-garrr."

"Lovely to see you too, slugger. Come on, rise and shine."

Bunny forced one eye open to see Gringo leaning nonchalantly against the windowsill.

"There he is, wakey wakey."

"Feck off. It's Saturday. I'm off."

"You *were* off. We've been called in."

"The feck we have." Bunny pulled a pillow over his head in a desperate attempt to block out the rest of existence.

"I'm only guessing but, by any chance, when you got home last night, did you happen to get stuck into your emergency booze supply?"

Bunny lifted the pillow ever so slightly. "I . . . Maybe. Remember that bottle of the Portuguese stuff I won in the office raffle?"

"That stuff?" said Gringo. "You know it was the joke prize, right?"

"Well, I'm not laughing."

Bunny's mouth felt like someone had thrown up in it. He hoped it was him.

Vague snatches of memory were returning unbidden. He'd drunk alone while watching *For a Few Dollars More* again on video. Classic. If that couldn't distract him, nothing could. It turned out nothing could, so he had attempted to drink his mind into submission instead.

"How bad was it?"

"What? Last night? Well, amigo, it had many positives. For example, your attitude to jazz has been drastically revised. You also met the woman of your dreams – well, I met her on your behalf. You saw her and I was about to introduce you after some frankly blindingly good build up work when—"

"Ara bollocks."

"Yes. If it is any consolation, you did win the fight."

"They jumped me!" pleaded Bunny into his pillow.

"They did, and I think it is fair to say all three of them learned a valuable life lesson in that regard."

"Ah Christ."

"And look at it this way," continued Gringo, "maybe she is the type that goes for the drunken violent sort."

"Don't."

"Admittedly, at the time, she made some very unkind remarks about you – but that may've just been foreplay."

"I hate you."

"Course you do, now get the hell out of bed. We have a meeting in town in about forty-five minutes."

"How do . . ." Bunny pulled his head out from under the pillow and looked at Gringo. "It's not about . . ."

"Last night?" finished Gringo. "No, no it isn't. That's all fine by the way, although you have promised to get Sergeant Dolan up at Pearse Street station All-Ireland tickets."

"Right."

"And you've got a date with a certain dusky songstress."

Bunny looked up again.

"Well, I say 'date'. You left your coat, phone, keys behind."

"Ahh!"

"Don't blame yourself. You'd your hands full as you were leaving. To be exact, one of your big mitts had one of your assailants by the throat and the other one had bucko number two by somewhere even more sensitive."

"And what were you doing at this time?"

"Who do you think was dealing with the third lad? And I was doing so while reassuring Noel that you'd pay for the damages."

"Was he mad?"

"The thing about a Tourette's sufferer is that it is very hard to tell. Now, do I have to throw water over you or are you getting up?"

"Feck off." Bunny put his head back under the pillow.

"One, two, three, four, five, six—"

Bunny re-emerged. "Hang on a sec . . ."

"Here it comes."

"What's this meeting about then?"

"There you have it, ladies and gentlemen, a fine deductive mind will kick in eventually, even one that's been pickled in cooking sherry."

"Gringo?"

"Your old friend Rigger O'Rourke wants to see us. He's been given the go ahead for something big and he's pulling in a lot of bodies. Armed robbery task force."

"You're shitting me?"

Gringo's nose wrinkled in disgust. "I'm definitely not doing that. Get your arse in gear, Cinderella, we've finally been invited to the ball."

Bunny sat upright, then instantly regretted it. "Christ on a bike."

"There you go, the worst part is over."

"Right, I'm going to have a shower and throw up."

"Good plan, maybe reverse the order."

"You – find me trousers."

"Easily done, you're still wearing them."

Bunny looked down. "Not these ones, my other trousers. They're around here somewhere."

Gringo looked at the mess strewn across the floor. "God, this is clothing? I assumed you'd had a one-night stand with a skip."

"You're not helping."

"I'm not trying to."

Bunny stood up unsteadily. Half a bacon sandwich squelched under his foot. "Ah, breakfast."

Gringo watched Bunny pick it up. "You're not eating that."

Bunny looked at it then extended it towards Gringo. "D'ye want a bite or something?"

"No thanks, I'm good."

Bunny grinned at Gringo. "Armed robbery?"

Gringo beamed back. "Armed robbery."

"I'll be with you presently," said Bunny, before hurrying out towards the bathroom.

"By the way," shouted Gringo after him, "if you're looking for it, the other half of that sandwich appears to be stuck to your back."

CHAPTER NINE

Bunny shifted in his seat. He was feeling more or less human but it had been a close-run thing. His body seemed willing to play ball for now, due to the importance of the situation and on the understanding that there would be a reckoning coming further down the line.

They were in a briefing room upstairs in Sheriff Street station. The chairs were occupied by Bunny, Gringo and ten other detectives, all of whom Bunny was on at least nodding terms with. The room was unpleasantly warm due to the heating being whacked up full tilt. Condensation fogged the windows, obscuring the view of a busy Dublin Saturday morning rumbling by outside. Bunny had a bottle of water that he was clinging to for dear life.

Gringo leaned casually across. "How's the head?"

"I'll live."

The door opened and DS Jessica Cunningham and DS Dara O'Shea strode in purposefully and took seats to the side of the screen at the front of the room. O'Shea was a stocky lad from Meath who couldn't look more like a Paddy if he tried. Shock of red hair, freckles and a wide grin that wasn't so much cat that got the cream as cat who was more than willing to share the cream; sure there's loads of cream, lads, get stuck in. O'Shea nodded and smiled at a few faces he recognised, which seemed to be almost everybody in the room. In contrast, Jessica Cunningham sat down and stared at the back wall with an intensity that implied it was her sole objective of the morning and the room's occupants were a hindrance.

The only other female in the room was Detective Pamela 'Butch' Cassidy, but to say there wasn't much sense of sisterhood between them was an understatement. Cunningham knew it was Butch who had given her the 'Robotits' nickname. Bunny watched Butch shifting awkwardly in her seat. Trying to get back on Cunningham's good side had proven to be a lot like trying to un-hit the iceberg.

Bunny leaned casually across to Gringo. "Looks like you'll be working under Sergeant Cunningham again."

"Try not to speak, ye muck savage. Your breath is like a wino's jockstrap."

Bunny sat up straight and ran his hand across his mouth. The air he captured under his nostrils indicated Gringo might have a point. No doubt he was also keen for Bunny to shut up.

DI Fintan "Rigger" O'Rourke strode in and closed the door behind him. He stood in the centre of the room and immediately commanded it. A tall man with a firm but wiry physique that spoke of his obsession with long-distance running, O'Rourke was quite the high-flyer. For several years, he had been the youngest DI on the force and nothing indicated that he planned to stop his ascent there. You wouldn't find anyone with two brain cells to rub together who would bet against him for the top job one day. Himself and Bunny had been firm friends back in the day, although O'Rourke had long since started hanging out in loftier circles, even before the unfortunate incident at his wedding when Bunny had protected himself from the advances of an irate swan.

"Right," said O'Rourke, "thanks for coming in. You have all been seconded to my team, the major robberies unit, for the foreseeable. I'm DI O'Rourke and this is DS O'Shea and DS Cunningham, who are my right hands. Technically, we are supposed to cover all major robberies that happen anywhere in the state. Don't ask me to define what major means. It's like true love and loitering with intent, you just know it when you see it. That's the theory – here's the reality."

O'Rourke nodded to O'Shea, who turned off the lights and fired up the projector attached to a laptop.

A picture of a man in his early twenties appeared on the screen. He had tightly cropped hair that was gelled down and he wore tinted glasses. He was fairly short in stature but he had the look of a man who could handle himself if required.

"Tommy Carter," said O'Rourke, "the king of Clanavale Estate and the leader of his very own crew of modern-day highway robbers. They have been the sole focus of my unit for the last six months. That farce on the Quays yesterday was them, as was the Prasart van job in July and the Bank of Ireland job in Dalkey. That's just the ones we're certain of this year. Going back over the last two, we like them for several other outings. Basically, if it's high-end and unsolved, odds on it was them. They are ruthless, efficient and sharper than anything we've ever dealt with. Put it this way, if most of the crews working in Dublin are still cavemen banging their nuts off a rock trying to make fire, these lads are sitting around laughing while smoking cigars and scoffing barbecue. They're lapping them – and frankly, us – and you're here to see if we can't catch up."

Nobody said anything but Bunny could feel the ripple pass around the room. Everyone was sitting up a little straighter, bright-eyed. This was the kind of case you joined the force for.

"Carter is only twenty-two, which is an unusually young age to be the head of an outfit like this, but believe me, the lad is anything but typical."

O'Rourke nodded and the picture changed to an old press cutting of a middle-aged man standing defiantly at the front of a crowd of neighbours, like a king before his tribe.

"Tommy is the son of Donal Carter, seen here, a name some of you will no doubt remember." Bunny caught the slightest of glances from O'Rourke. "About twelve years ago, he was the man who announced the Clanavale Estate was a drug-free zone. He rallied the residents and became quite the media darling. Some dealers who

objected to his endeavours tried to burn his house down with his
kids still inside it." Again, just the slightest glance. "Luckily, that
didn't come to pass, thanks to Garda intervention. Donal also did the
unthinkable and won. To this day, nobody deals hard drugs on the
Clanavale Estate, at least not for very long and rarely without it
causing them and the health service some major inconvenience.
These days, Daddy is side-lined, dealing with a serious kidney
complaint, so Tommy runs the estate now – and I mean runs it. It
also means he and his crew are dug in there like termites and we
can't get near them. Patrol cars get their tyres slashed. If you go
around to lift any of them, you've to bring a lot of bodies, or else
your car will be a bonfire. Covert surveillance is impossible and
forget getting anyone close to them. Everyone on that estate grew up
there and they don't leave. It is an island and Tommy is their boy
king."

People shifted in their seats. Coppers didn't like to admit it but
Clanavale was one of those estates – if you went in at all, you went in
the daylight and you went with company. It hadn't always been that
way, Bunny knew better than most, it having been one of his first
beats, but times had changed.

"These are his crew," continued O'Rourke. The picture changed
to a man in his forties with a paunch. He appeared to be standing
outside a pub, smoking a cigarette and glaring at the camera in a way
that suggested that if looks couldn't kill, he was willing to finish
the job.

"Franko Doyle, the self-styled *consigliere*. A friend of Carter senior
from back in the day, he did time for stolen goods once and
housebreaking twice. He's married to Carter's cousin. It's not
technically correct, but Tommy – and hence everyone else – calls him
Uncle Franko. He seems to be the connection with the bigger
criminal world, not that they generally have much to do with any of
it. They keep themselves to themselves and anyone who has tried to
change that arrangement from outside has regretted it."

O'Rourke nodded and another face appeared on the screen. This
time a passport photo of a man in his late twenties. He had shoulder-

length blond hair, tied into a ponytail, and one of those faces that was all sharp angles.

"Meet John O'Donnell. At one time unofficially considered the most lethal man in the Irish armed forces – only he's no longer in the armed forces. A Wexford boy, he rose quickly through the ranks to join the Irish Rangers. Jokes about our army aside, those lads are special forces and are highly regarded amongst their international counterparts. It's a tough gig to get. O'Donnell won commendations, was clean as a whistle and was generally GI fecking Joe. He was their golden boy and they were gutted when he upped and left at the end of his tour a couple of years ago, for no apparent reason. He's been to Somalia on peacekeeping where, incidentally, the Irish Rangers wore US uniforms to blend in. He won some medal in a competition with the Yanks. I asked around; his nickname was, I kid you not, 'Iceman'. Seriously. O'Donnell is an expert in surveillance, counter-surveillance, ordnance and weaponry with a specialism as a sniper. He is, in short, quite the badass, and an absolute nightmare for us."

O'Rourke nodded and the picture changed again, this time to a shaven-headed man in military fatigues, posing with a large knife and a bigger grin. He had a heavily muscled physique below a face with a hint of chubby cheeks to it. Bunny would have laid money he had been a fat kid and was now seriously overcompensating.

"Jimmy Moran, another Clanavale Estate alumnus. Was in the Rangers too, but not for that long. Allegations about his behaviour. The army aren't wild about sharing details with us, but from what we've gathered through backchannels, when his unit were in Canada on a training exercise he got rough with a local girl. Charges were never brought but it was enough to get him dishonourably discharged. His buddy O'Donnell left three months later, and we reckon they both teamed up with Carter straight after."

O'Rourke nodded again and O'Shea turned the lights back on and killed the projector. The detective inspector took a few moments to look around the room, making eye contact with each occupant in turn.

"Those lads – the last two in particular – are serious individuals.

We reckon when they first teamed up with Carter, he was nineteen. Nineteen. I don't know what you were like at that age but I know I was still having a hard time getting served in pubs and finding a young lady willing to do more than hold hands."

A smattering of laughs from around the room.

"Tommy Carter was successfully convincing special forces boys to take his orders. The reason they did? He's smart, really smart. Genius IQ when he was in school. They say he could have been anything. Then, when he was fifteen, an older boy touched his sister in a way she didn't like. Carter, still a runty little fucker at the time, smashed this big lad to pieces and then broke both his arms. Let me clarify – he knocked the bloke out and then calmly broke both his arms. He didn't see any time for it because the lad wouldn't testify. It got Carter out of the school system though. Not that he seemed to care. He isn't some rocket – he is cool, calm and very thorough. He reads constantly – the little shite seems to permanently have a book on him. He plans everything to the last detail. When we were about to bring him in for a chat after the last job, he turned up at the station before we could send for him. He then sat there for eight hours and said nothing except for reciting a bit of James Joyce over and over again. He likes to play with us and frankly he's been doing whatever the hell he wants and we've been helpless. It's about time that changed."

O'Rourke looked around the room again and let the silence linger.

"Ladies and gentlemen, you're here to finally take him down."

CHAPTER TEN

Bunny looked at the sign above the door of Charlie's Private Members' Club and nervously ran his hands through his irredeemably uncontrollable mop of dark brown hair. His palms were clammy, mouth dry and a layer of cold sweat was causing his shirt to cling to his back. The remnants of his hangover were only partly to blame for all this. He'd gone home to change into what he thought of as his best shirt, but it had betrayed him by somehow getting smaller in the three months since he'd last worn it. It was perfectly wearable as long as he remained standing. Sitting down allowed his belly button to play peek-a-boo in a way that was not attractive.

After the morning's briefing, he and Gringo had dropped into O'Hagan's for a lunchtime fried breakfast and a quick straightener from the hair of the dog. They'd eaten mostly in silence. After they'd left O'Rourke's briefing, Bunny had revealed that he was going to ask to be excused from the task force and it had not gone down well. "But," Gringo had pleaded, "half the guards in Dublin would be begging to get on the damn thing!" Bunny had no doubt he was right on that score, and one of those guards would be getting lucky, because his mind was made up. He knew exactly why Rigger wanted him there and he didn't want any part of it.

So he'd headed home, grabbed two hours' fitful sleep and then set about making himself presentable. He'd promised the shirt that he'd give up the takeaways for a month if it'd play ball. His black blazer had at least been a bit more forgiving. He even dug out the shoes he wore for weddings, the ones that squashed his little toe and sliced into the back of his heel.

And here he stood, sweating like a turkey in December, drying his sweaty palms on the back of his shirt to avoid messing up his carefully ironed cream slacks.

Bunny walked slowly down the sloping alleyway. He could hear the murmur of recorded music as he approached. He looked down the short flight of stairs to the basement-level bar and saw that a light was on inside. The door was painted red, chipped in places; the window beside it was grimy and had a wire mesh on the outside. Bunny glanced inside and saw the figure of the woman from last night, her hair tied back in a ponytail as she ran a mop across the floor. As he looked at her blurred silhouette, she wrung the mop out in the bucket and dipped it back into the water. Then she raised her head and looked in the direction of the window. Bunny heaved his big head out of view and turned to go, then turned back, then turned to go again, then turned back and hovered his hand in the knocking position above the red chipped paint.

He looked at his hand and whispered to himself, "Oh for God's sake."

His attempted knock missed as the door opened before his knuckles could make contact. The face of the woman from the night before furtively poked out from around it. Bunny noticed that her hair was suddenly down again, hanging in a dark curtain over her right eye. She was wearing what appeared to be dungarees.

"Ehm, hi, hello, howerya, hi."

She raised an eyebrow and gave him a slight smile, and he noticed up close how big her brown eyes were.

"Hi."

"I'm, ehm, I was, I'm the fella who . . ."

"Smashed up the place last night?" she finished, a playful tone to her voice.

"Yes, I'm really sorry about that. I – you see – not that I'm excusing it, but—"

She held her hand up. "Relax. Noel was pissed at the time but he's calmed down. A couple of the regulars told him the other three-quarters of the fight were disrespecting the music. He can't stand that either. That's not to say we encourage how you dealt with it. We've only got so much furniture."

Bunny followed her gaze as she glanced to his right. The remains of a table and a couple of stools lay shattered and discarded in the small enclave underneath the stairs.

"Ah shitting hell."

"Don't worry about it. Noel's off getting replacements. We might accidentally end up with some furniture where two of the legs are the same length now."

Bunny shifted his hands about nervously; they suddenly felt like unwieldy slabs of meat that he didn't know what to do with.

"I can only apologise, I mean – I'm not a violent person."

She raised the one eyebrow that was visible. "Really? Because you took to it pretty damn fast. You should consider going professional. You got potential, kid."

"They were pricks, to be fair."

"I'm glad to hear it. If that's the way you treat people you like, I'd be worried."

"So where in the States are you from?"

"All of it. I'm a gypsy soul."

"Were you, like, a professional singer over there too?"

She opened the door further to show the wet floor behind her. "I ain't a professional singer over here. Gloria Estefan doesn't have to mop the floors."

"Well you're fantastic, like, at the singing I mean. I was very impressed. Phenomenal stuff."

She smiled nervously. "Yeah, well, you should see how clean this floor is, it'll blow your mind."

"Do you want to be a full-time singer?"

"What? And give up all this?" She gave him a quizzical look. "You ask a lot of questions."

Bunny held his hands up. "Sorry, sorry – nobody expects the Spanish Inquisition."

Her face dropped into a stony stare. "My great-granddaddy was killed by the Spanish Inquisition."

"Jesus, sorry, I . . . hang on!"

She laughed, a soft and surprisingly deep chuckle. "You are too easy."

Bunny grinned nervously back. "Oh, can I give you the money for the new furniture?" He started patting his jacket down, looking for his wallet.

"Easy, big spender. You've not got your wallet, remember?"

Bunny blushed. "Right, yeah."

She picked up his anorak from inside the door and handed it back to him.

"You can drop in and sort it out with Noel during the week. Give him some time to cool off too. He's here most nights, bar Mondays when we're closed."

"What about you?"

"I'm here every night."

"And will you be singing?"

"Serving drinks, unclogging the ladies, breaking up fights – I'm the total package."

"Right," said Bunny. "That's good."

She smiled again. "Is it?"

"Well, yeah," said Bunny. "Can't have the ladies getting all backed up. Then they start using the gents, and sure, chaos ensues."

"It's a complete breakdown in the natural order."

"And as an officer of the law, I'm very concerned about such things."

"That right? You got a peach of a black eye coming up there that says different."

"Well, I . . ."

She looked up into his eyes and fell silent for a moment. When she spoke again, the playfulness had gone from her tone. "Actually, your eye looks a little off, you might want to get that seen to. It don't look right at all."

"Ara, don't worry," said Bunny, pointing to his lazy left eye. "That's always been like that."

"Oh." She looked suitably embarrassed. "Sorry. I put my big ol' foot in it there, didn't I?"

"Don't worry about it. I slammed a lad's head through one of your tables – neither of us is brilliant at first impressions."

"I wouldn't say that. That guy will certainly remember meeting you."

"I'm just saying, I'm not some lunatic going about hurling digs into every mouthy gobshite without the sense his mother gave him."

She gave him a bemused look. "I know some of that was definitely in English."

"Sorry, I, ehm, I was just saying I'm not some drunk bloke who gets into fights."

"Course not, you're just a jazz fan with an admirably low tolerance for rudeness."

"Exactly." Bunny nodded and smiled a wide grin.

"So who's your favourite?"

"Favourite?"

"Jazz artist?"

"Ehm . . . you are."

She rolled her eyes, over a skewed smile that made Bunny's tummy go a tad fizzy.

"And who is yours?"

She stopped and pointed behind her, indicating the music playing inside. "Depends on my mood, I s'pose. Right now, Billie Holiday."

"Oh yeah," said Bunny. "He is great."

She shook her head. "Oh dear. And you were doing so well."

CHAPTER ELEVEN

"Stephen Colgan, wallop the fecking thing! Wallop it!"

DI Fintan O'Rourke heard Bunny McGarry a long time before he saw him. He was parking his car up on Philpott Street when Bunny's distinctive Cork bellow carried over the wall. Fintan double-checked all of the doors, because he of all people knew that in this area you couldn't be too careful. The Celtic Tiger economy may have been raging all around it, but Philpott Street remained steadfastly Philpott Street. Flats dominated it, always looking down in the mouth and overdue a paint job. At its centre sat St Jude's Hurling Club. It had only been set up a couple of years before, on a playing field vacated when a private school decided it would rather bus its progeny out to the suburbs than play on sports facilities it found inadequate for their needs. The land had belonged to the council and McGarry had nipped in before any redevelopment deals could be sewn up.

O'Rourke looked up at the wall over which the sound of ash clattering against ash could be heard, mingled with occasional cheers of support and grunts of exertion. Above it all rose the voice of Bunny McGarry. "Dennis O'Malley, stop chasing the fecking ball around. You're a full back, not a Yorkshire Terrier!"

Fintan passed through the gates, such as they were. "Club" was a grand title for St Jude's: it was one pitch and a couple of Portakabins. Graffiti – mostly unimaginative in both style and content – marked the walls at random intervals. The Portakabins were the worse for it. Someone had tried to distract from what was clearly an enormous cock and balls drawn on the side of one of the structures with the strategic placement of a couple of posters advertising a jumble sale that had already happened.

While pre-teen boys in helmets that looked way too big for them inexpertly hacked a ball back and forth on the field, various knots of parents stood around watching on. Bunny McGarry stood at halfway, red-faced and bellowing. There was notably nobody standing within twenty feet of him, save for one tubby ginger kid who was dunking the top of his hurling stick into the bucket that sat at his feet.

"Davey Ryan, you're the goalie! You're the goalie, son! What are you looking at me so confused for? Are you in the goal right now? Well, get back there!"

Bunny turned to the child standing beside him. "You heard me, Deccie, didn't I say to him before the match, just stay in the goal? How hard is that?"

"He has no understanding of the nuances of the game, boss."

"You're not wrong, Deccie, you're not wrong."

"D'ye want me to tie his leg to one of the posts again, boss?"

Bunny gave the child a look. "No, Deccie, remember we talked about this. Ye can't do that."

"Yes, boss. Sorry, boss."

"Good instincts though. PHILLIP NELLIS! What are you doing sitting down? The ball is in play! I don't care how far away it is, you're playing the fastest team sport on the planet! Get up, wake up and buck up!"

The ginger kid looked behind him to see Fintan O'Rourke standing there. He tugged at Bunny's sleeve. "Boss, the pigs are here."

Bunny turned, an expression of surprise crossing his face. He looked down at the boy. "Deccie, what've I told you? It's the Garda Síochána and you will say that with respect as I am one too."

"I won't tell anyone, boss."

Bunny looked exasperated. "I'm not trying to keep it secret – AH FOR FECK'S SAKE, REF!"

Around midfield, multiple members of both teams had just shambled into each other and descended into a flailing crescendo of limbs and accusation. The referee was blowing his whistle repeatedly but seemed to be having little effect on proceedings.

"Deccie, sponge time. Go easy on the magic juice, we're running low."

The fat kid saluted and huffed onto the field, the precious bucket held in front of him in two hands.

O'Rourke moved forward to stand beside Bunny. "Magic juice?"

"It's just water with a bit of lemon in it but they think it works wonders."

"Right," said Fintan, a smile on his lips. "And which lot are yours?"

Bunny looked sideways at him, indignation etched on his face. "Which d'ye think?"

Fintan nodded his head. Of course. The ones in the red of Cork, naturally. Even without that, he might have known. The team in blue had noticeably better gear and all their jerseys matched perfectly, as opposed to the St Jude's kit, which looked rather patched and mended, showing the strain here and there.

"So," said Bunny, "I didn't know you were a fan of under-12s hurling, Fintan?"

"I'm not – no disrespect. I came to talk to you."

Bunny turned his head back towards the field. "Sorry, Inspector, but I'm a bit busy at the moment. Could you not have given me a ring or something?"

"I couldn't locate your number this morning when I went looking for it."

"Yeah, you must've deleted it. I've certainly not heard from you in long enough."

"I've been busy, and you didn't exactly cover yourself in glory the last time we met."

Bunny flapped his hand above his head in exasperation. "For the last fecking time, that swan came at me like a ... like a bloody—"

"Relax," said O'Rourke. "I'm not here to talk about that. I'm on my way into town to finalise the names for the task force and DS Spain informed me yesterday that you do not wish to be on it. Is he correct?"

Bunny didn't even look at him. "That's correct. Thanks, but no thanks ... C'mon, lads, here we go! CONCENTRATE!"

Everyone having regained their feet and their composure, the referee was preparing to throw the sliotar in again.

Deccie waddled back towards them, still in possession of the bucket and magic sponge. He gave a thumbs up. "All good, boss."

It was a matter of eight seconds between the ball going back into play and it sailing over the St Jude's bar for a point.

"Holy Mary on a moped – Phillip Nellis, will you throw yourself in front of the ball! No pain, no gain, son. The rest of ye, stay in your positions – at least that way the ball might hit off ye by accident on its way to the goal."

"Boss," said Deccie, "the ball's gone out on the road."

"Ara crap, can you go get it?"

Deccie sighed. "On my way, boss."

"Good lad."

Bunny picked up a sliotar from the kitbag beside him and hurled it onto the field.

"Be careful with this, it's our last one."

"Bunny," said O'Rourke, "I need an answer."

Bunny glanced briefly at O'Rourke, clearly annoyed. "You already have one."

"I mean an explanation."

"For feck's sake, Fintan, can't this wait?"

"No. I've a meeting with the commissioner in forty minutes."

"I don't want the assignment – simple. And for exactly the reason that you want me. You know Donal Carter and I have a bit of history."

"I do. The Clanavale Estate was one of your first beats in Dublin, wasn't it?"

"I'm guessing you know the answer to that already. Now, d'ye mind? I'm trying to coach a game here. C'MON, LADS, KEEP IT GOING!"

"Oh for God's sake, Bunny, just give me one minute of your time, please. You're clearly losing this thing anyway."

Bunny turned so fast that O'Rourke took a step back. "What the hell are you talking about? We're up by six!"

Despite his lack of interest, O'Rourke couldn't keep the surprise from his voice. "Really?"

The St Jude's goalie, Davey Ryan, hopped the ball up to restart the game and belted it with everything he had, sending it careening towards midfield. It was then that a slight kid, who'd done nothing up until this point that O'Rourke had seen, effortlessly fielded the ball off his hurl while sending two opponents the wrong way. He then soloed it up the field, the ball seemingly glued to his stick as he wove effortlessly between three defenders before pulling back and in one fluid motion sending it thirty yards through the air to sail over the opposition bar.

Spontaneous applause broke out – some of it, O'Rourke noticed, coming from the parents on the opposition sideline.

"Beautiful stuff, Paulie Mulchrone, beautiful. Keep it going, son. Everyone else – be more like Paulie."

"Wow," said O'Rourke.

"Finest pure striker of the ball you'll ever see. Going to play for the county."

There was then a break in play as Deccie had yet to return with his ball and the other one had skated into the tall grass at the end of the field. The opposition goalie and the referee were leading a search party. As the players from both sides took this as a signal to sit down, chat or bug their parents, Bunny turned to Fintan O'Rourke and looked him square in the eye.

"Tommy Carter may well have turned into a Grade-A villainous little viper and I hope you get him and his crew, but his da is a good man and I don't want to be put in that situation, alright?" Bunny moved closer and jabbed a finger as he spoke. "I know why you want me there, Fintan. When that shower of scumbags decided to burn Carter's house to the ground, it was me that went in and got his kids out. I did the same as you or any other Garda would've done, so let's not make it into something bigger than it was."

"But it was you," said Fintan, "and we can use that."

"Not interested."

"I need to unsettle Tommy Carter, so yes, I'm going to use every bit of leverage I can get."

"Last I heard," said Bunny, "Donal Carter was a sick man, kidneys or something. You have to take his son, fine, but Donal is a decent fella. All he wanted to do was get the drugs out of the estate, and he did. If we'd been better at our jobs, he'd not have needed to."

Bunny turned back towards the field. O'Rourke grabbed his arm and spun him around. "Christ, you're an obstinate so-and-so, McGarry. Fine. So be it. I'm going to tell you the one piece of information that nobody knows aside from myself, the commissioner, O'Shea and Cunningham. We don't want to tip our hand to Carter. I'm trusting you to keep this to yourself."

Bunny gave O'Rourke a long look and then nodded.

O'Rourke lowered his voice further. "The reason we're squeezing Tommy Carter now is that we have it on very good authority that he's about to change business. He's made a deal. We don't know where or when, but we know he has a massive shipment of cocaine coming in."

"Bollocks."

"No, it isn't. I can show you the communications from the DEA in America. Apparently one of his ex-Army Ranger buddies knows some ex-special forces boys in the States who've gone into business for themselves. Tommy isn't his dad, and you said yourself, Daddy isn't well. In fact, the doctors give him about two months at the most if they can't get a kidney, and that's not looking promising. Once he's gone, Tommy doesn't care. He's going to flood the Dublin market with cheap coke and kick off a bloody drug war the likes of which you've never seen."

"But . . ." said Bunny, clearly struggling to fit this all together. "After all they've been through?"

"That's exactly it," said O'Rourke. "You may've pulled young Tommy and his sister out of the fire, but Tommy hasn't forgiven and forgotten those that set it. His dad was anti-drugs, but Tommy is anti a couple of very particular drug dealers – the ones who tried to barbecue him."

"But..."

A cry of victory came up from the far end of the field and a girl of maybe eight years old held the lost ball aloft in her hand.

Bunny turned back towards the field. "Alright, lads, look sharp, keep it going."

The opposition restarted the game.

"LARRY DODDS, get your finger out of your nostril and watch the play."

Deccie reappeared beside Bunny, the other ball clutched in his hand. "He's no appreciation for the nuances of the game, boss."

"You're not wrong, Deccie, you're not wrong."

"Bunny," said O'Rourke, "are you going to ignore what I just said?"

The ball made its way to the far side of the field, where the Mulchrone kid intercepted a pass and got raked across the legs for his trouble.

"REFEREE!"

A twelve-year-old's version of a scuffle broke out, with a lot of pushing and shoving, while the referee almost blew himself to a coronary trying to maintain control.

"Right," said Bunny, "time to use the bench."

Deccie nodded, picked up his helmet and began strapping it on.

Bunny whacked the top of his helmet and bent down to look him in the eye. "I'm sending you on for Des, I want you to mark their number 12 out of the game."

Deccie nodded.

"He's bigger than you, taller than you, faster than you – but you've got something he hasn't got."

Deccie's chubby face lit up. "You're not wrong, boss." He pulled what appeared to be a homemade knuckleduster out of the pocket of his tracksuit.

"What the shittin' hell, Deccie?" Bunny snatched it from him. "This is completely illegal."

"It's not, boss, I looked up the rules of hurling on the Internet at school, doesn't say nothing 'bout knuckledusters."

"What in the . . . this," said Bunny, waving it in his face, "is illegal in this country, never mind in the sport. What have I told you about trying to use your initiative?"

"D'ye know what your problem is, boss?" said Deccie, as he picked up his hurley. "You've no appreciation for the nuances of the game."

Bunny and O'Rourke watched in silence as Deccie ran onto the field.

"Interesting kid," said O'Rourke.

"Ah, he's alright, deep down. He's just a bit . . . overenthusiastic, that's all."

"Yeah," said O'Rourke. "How do you feel about him and all these lads growing up in a city that's about to be awash with cheap drugs?"

Bunny gave O'Rourke a sideways glance. "I think you've still got my number, Fintan. I think you went out of your way to ask me this here."

O'Rourke shrugged. "I'll use every bit of leverage I can get."

CHAPTER TWELVE

Bunny walked down the hallway, his feet squeaking on the polished floors. As he passed each doorway, he couldn't help but steal a glance at the ward inside. They seemed to be large rooms, four beds each, separated by curtains. They were occupied mostly by older people, who looked back at him with vacant expressions of medication, boredom or both. Occasionally someone sat in a visitor's chair by a bed, more often than not in silence. Just sitting there, searching for something to say.

Bunny didn't like hospitals. He didn't see how anyone could.

He took a left, following the signs for the Block C rooms. In this corridor there seemed to be a change in the atmosphere. Private rooms – less hustle and bustle. He caught the odd look through an open doorway, still the same vacant expressions from those in the gowns, the same vain searching on the faces of the visitors. Money didn't buy you an answer, just a nicer room in which to avoid the question.

C43.

Bunny stopped and looked through the small window in the door. The man he was expecting to see was sitting propped up in bed, facing a small TV and flicking through the channels.

Bunny knocked.

"C'mon in."

Bunny pushed open the door. "Hello, Donal."

A quizzical look on the man's face gave way to a warm grin. "Jaysus! Bunny McGarry, is that you?"

"It is, I'm afraid."

"Christ, as I live and breathe. C'mon in, c'mon in."

He patted a chair beside his bed with one hand as the other silenced the TV. Bunny made his way across to it. It'd been maybe seven years since he'd last seen Donal Carter and, given his current location, it was unsurprising that the time hadn't been good to him. His complexion now had a jaundiced tinge to it, and his lips looked an unnatural shade of off-white. Bunny didn't know the exact details, other than it was a kidney thing and it was bad. Donal had always been a vibrant man, bursting with barely-contained energy. The body may have weakened but the same dancing vivacity could be seen in his pale green eyes.

They shook, an IV drip feed stuck into the back of Donal's hand. If you could judge the seriousness of someone's state by the amount of beeping technology behind them, Donal's prognosis was less than rosy.

"How're ye keeping? It must be – what? Seven or eight years?"

"Yeah, about that," said Bunny, sitting down in the chair. "If it's not a daft question, how are you?"

"Ah," he said, indicating towards the machines, "the kidney thing was always coming, y'know, it's a genetic thing, but sure, keeping on. Can't complain. The staff are taking great care of me and – sorry, where are my manners. Of course you remember Eimear?"

Bunny turned, surprised to find they were not alone. In the corner behind the door sat a slight-framed woman with long blonde hair almost down to her waist, a thick textbook in her hands. She waved shyly and spoke a greeting in a voice too soft to hear.

"I do, of course. Sorry, Eimear, I didn't see you there. My God, you grew up to be a fine girl."

Donal beamed pride. "She did indeed. Studying computer sciences now in DCU. First one in the family to go to university."

"Ah, isn't that great. Well done to you," said Bunny. He looked back at Donal. "To the both of you."

Eimear spoke again and Bunny strained to hear. There was a "thanks" in there but it was directed towards the floor. She played with her hair nervously as she spoke.

Donal patted Bunny's hand, "Sure, if it hadn't been for you..."

To his alarm, Bunny noticed Donal's eyes well up slightly. "Ah, don't start that, long time ago now."

"Still."

Bunny shifted nervously. "I was going to get you something but I wasn't sure if you were allowed chocolate or..."

"Don't be worrying about that stuff. Tell you the truth, if I never see another grape, it'll be too soon."

Bunny smiled. "Back in the day, we only ever split a bottle of whiskey round your kitchen table, but I figured that was inappropriate."

"Maybe, but it's not the worst idea. Laura Cole from over the road brought in holiday brochures last week, reckoned it'd be nice to dream about a trip abroad. I've only left the country once, and that was to go see Man United play and they lost!"

Bunny shook his head. "Well, if you will insist on following these foreign sports."

"Ha, don't start all that again. You still doing your missionary work, trying to convert us heathen Dubs to the gospel of the GAA?"

"I am," said Bunny. "Even got my own junior hurling club."

"I heard about that. Fair play to you."

There was a pause in the conversation. Both men looked nervously around the room.

"Fair play," Donal repeated. He glanced over at Eimear sitting in the corner. "Eimear, love, would you mind going and getting me one of those bottles of Lucozade from downstairs, please?" He looked across at Bunny. "Would you like anything?"

"I'm grand, thanks, grand."

Eimear stood, and as she did so, Bunny noticed that under her baggy cardigan she looked unhealthily thin. She hugged it closed around her, smiled shyly and, with a mumble, she was gone.

"She's a great girl," said Bunny.

"Yeah," replied Donal, pride in his voice. "I did something right there."

"You did. Not easy raising two kids on your own."

Back in the day, when they'd been good friends, Donal had once opened up to Bunny about losing Eimear's mother. She'd died in childbirth. They'd warned her of the risk but she'd refused to hear of any other options. In a graveyard out in Glasnevin, his wife and the baby she died trying to deliver lay side by side. Most men wouldn't have come back from that. Donal Carter wasn't most men, and not one cliché of the single-parent father applied to him.

"Yeah, great girl," repeated Donal, and then another lengthy pause hung over the room as both men looked at each other. "So, I take it this isn't a social call?"

Bunny lowered his head. "I'm afraid not. I . . . I wanted to talk to you, up front, about . . ."

"Tommy."

"Yeah."

Donal nodded.

"You know what he . . ."

Donal shifted around in the bed nervously. "I'm not going to say—"

"Oh no," said Bunny, "I'm not asking you to. I'm not officially here or anything. But . . ." Bunny looked back into Donal's eyes. "You know who he is?"

"I know he takes good care of his whole community – and me." Donal waved his hand around. "A bus driver's pension doesn't get you a private room, believe you me. Mrs Grainger from over the road is in one down the hall there too – no widow is going to afford that on her own."

"Alright, but Donal . . . You know how he's paying for it?"

"He runs a launderette and he has shares in a few businesses." It was clear Donal didn't believe it, even as he said it, for all the defiance in his voice. The awkward silence descended again.

Bunny looked around and saw a Sunday paper sitting at the bottom of the bed. He picked it up and pointed at the picture on the front page. "See this, someone robbed an armoured car on the Quays."

"I did," said Donal. "A bank lost some money, no harm in that."

"Yeah, regular Robin Hood stuff. Only . . . men with guns running about, eventually people get hurt. Innocent people."

Donal bristled. "Really? I'd not read of any casualties."

"One of the Gardaí in the support vehicle had a minor heart problem. Not helped by a grenade being stuck on his windscreen. I believe he's on a ward somewhere around here."

"Stressful job."

"And these raiders threatened the kid of one of the van's guards. Just a working Joe from Ranelagh, looking out a window at a gun and a picture of his little girl."

Donal said nothing, just looked away.

"And as great as this Robin Hood image is, that's all it is. It's men with guns taking what they want. And that's saying that stealing is all they're doing."

Bunny looked at Donal. He watched for some flicker of recognition, but there was none there. Bunny would bet his life that Tommy's expansion into drugs would come as a horrible surprise to his father. He felt guiltily relieved that the need to keep the information secret meant he didn't have to be the one to tell him. It'd no doubt break his heart.

"I don't know anything about that," said Donal. "My son doesn't discuss his business with me." Alarm spread across his face before he pointed back at the paper. "Not that I'm saying this is his business."

Bunny put the newspaper down. "Donal, we go back. Long way."

"That's true and . . . you know I'm grateful because—"

"Let's forget about—"

"No," interrupted Donal. "You broke down a door and ran through fire when those bastards tried to burn my children in their beds. I'll never forget that. It's thanks to you I have a family. You're a hero."

Bunny sighed. "I'm really not, Donal. It's my job. And if I have to take somebody down and throw them in prison for a long time, that'll just be my job too." He stood up. "I just, I just wanted to say that because . . . we go back a long way."

They exchanged a sad smile.

"I'll leave you be. Best of luck with all the . . ."

Bunny looked at the machines again and couldn't find the words. He gave a nod and headed towards the door.

"Bunny?"

He looked back at the frail figure in the bed.

"He's not the man you think he is."

Bunny opened the door. "I could say the same."

CHAPTER THIRTEEN

"Herbert W Armstrong," said Gringo.

Bunny continued to look out the window of the car. They'd been parked up opposite 17 Crossan Road, in the centre of the Clanavale Estate, since 7:30 am. On either side of the street were near-identical rows of terraced council housing, which seemed to have been consciously designed with the least amount of imagination imaginable. Most were an eggshell white, save for the occasional stamp of individuality. Number 24 was painted pink. Bunny could only imagine the controversy that must have caused. Numbers 3 and 10 had kitchen appliances in their respective gardens; it was impossible to tell who had stolen the idea for this landscaping innovation from whom.

Bunny looked at number 17 again and tried to picture it as it had been on that fateful night. It had been well ablaze when he had kicked the door in, run through the flames and rescued Tommy Carter and his sister, Eimear. All he had done was his job. What was he supposed to feel now? Pride?

The reality was that he felt nothing. He had always been this way. His good deeds felt like they belonged to someone else. Only his mistakes were truly his.

Donal Carter being Donal Carter, he had rebuilt the house exactly as it was.

"Are you listening to me?" said Gringo.

"I shouldn't think so."

"Herbert W Armstrong," he repeated.

Bunny sighed. "Is he the bloke who lives in number 32 with the rose bushes?"

"No. He's an American fella, predicted the world was going to end in 1936."

"Did he?" said Bunny, watching in his wing mirror as the young woman from number 4 down the road pushed a pram out of her front door. The older sibling of the pram's occupant was running around excitedly, wrapped up in one of those padded anoraks with the hood up that made determining the gender of the child impossible.

". . . and then predicted it would end again in 1943, 1972 and 1975. Can you believe that?"

The mother was now walking up the pavement towards them, her mobile phone out and glued to her ear. The kid was running ahead of her, like one of the less subtle inmates from *The Great Escape*.

"God loves a trier," said Bunny.

"Yeah, but after you've got it wrong three times – like, seriously wrong – who goes, 'OK, folks, I know what I said before, but this time I really have nailed it.' Who has that level of self-confidence?"

Bunny didn't respond. He was watching the kid, he was watching the mother not watching the kid and he was watching the coal lorry that had just swung around the corner.

"I mean, it's almost impressive isn't it? When you think about it."

Gringo was interrupted by Bunny's door opening and his partner stepping out.

He bent down and put his hand out to prevent the kid from running any further. "Woah, easy there, tiger."

The face of a little boy displayed grumpy consternation from under the hood.

He heard the whoosh of the lorry passing and a snatch of radio pumping out something energetic.

"What the fuck do you think you're doing?" Bunny looked up to see the mother racing towards him. "Get away from my child, ye paedo!"

"Relax, love, I was just stopping him in case he ran out in front of the lorry there. I'm a guard."

"That's worse than a paedo!" She snatched the child's hand and pushed by Bunny, a waft of overly sweet, cloying perfume hitting him as she passed.

Bunny sighed and got back into the car, closing the door behind him. "Worse than paedos now, apparently."

"The end is nigh, amigo, the end is nigh."

"Honest to Christ, you have to get a licence for a dog but we'll let anyone have a kid."

"Funnily enough," said Gringo, "that's what I wrote in my last Mother's Day card."

Bunny shifted in his seat. "How's your ma getting on?"

Gringo looked out the window. "Ah, good days and bad."

"I suppose that's to be expected, with the getting confused and all."

"Well, yeah, but it's not like she was a fun gal before the Alzheimer's. I can tell when I go in to see her that the staff at the home hate her. She always spoke to everyone like they were staff – imagine how she treats people who actually are staff."

"I guess."

Gringo didn't speak much about his family, such as it was, and Bunny didn't like to ask. Until the age of thirteen, he'd been brought up on the posh side of the street, packed off to boarding school as soon as they'd take him. Mummy didn't like having him cluttering up the place. Diana Spain was quite the piece of work. The one time he'd met her, Bunny had seen how she must've been quite a looker in her day, but that was before the wind changed and her face got locked into that permanent haughty scowl of disapproval. Daddy Spain, for his part, had been a successful financial advisor and accountant. Celebs, sportsmen, horse trainers; he'd managed the books for some of the biggest stars in the Irish firmament in the

1970s. Then, all of a sudden, the allegations of embezzlement had come. Daddy Spain had reassured the world that it was all a big misunderstanding before going into the garage and giving a hunting rifle the long kiss goodbye. Drunk, Gringo had once spilled forth the details to Bunny, who now knew more than he wanted to. Like the fact that, due to the length of the gun, Gringo's father had pulled the trigger with his big toe. Or that his only son had been back from boarding school for the Christmas holidays and ran in when he heard the shot. As Gringo told it, he didn't remember the blood or anything else, except for the incongruous sight of one highly polished shoe and one naked foot.

Gringo's mother had insisted that her husband had been the victim of a tragic accident while cleaning a gun. Then there had been the quiet conversations. They'd moved out of the large Georgian Village house to a damp two-bedroom flat off Parnell Square that her brother had reluctantly coughed up the rent for. She'd not been able to find what she deemed "appropriate work" and so Mrs Spain had stayed home, marinating in gin and bitterness towards all the friends who had "betrayed her in her hour of need", as she saw it. Little Timothy was taken out of his fancy school, despite the Franciscans being willing to forego the fees if he became a day student. She did not need charity. Instead, he'd been sent to an inner city Christian Brothers school, which his uncle had assured him would be "character building". With his posh accent and ability to conjugate Latin verbs, it had not been a happy experience. It was here that "Gringo" had been born, with the adoption of the Spanish phrases and jovial demeanour to win people over. It was rebranding as a means of survival, and it had eventually become second nature. "Gringo" was one of the lads; "Timothy" was the one the lads picked on. That boy became the man who now spoke without any discernible accent and went out of his way to get on well with everybody.

Oblivious to what was going on in her son's life, Diana Spain had wanted her only son to go into the law. He would then be able to sue everyone and get their money back. Signing up for the guards had been his ultimate "fuck you" to her. Not exactly the area of the law that she had envisioned. Still, when she'd developed the early-onset dementia, he'd taken her in. It had cost him his marriage – or at least hastened its end – but he was her only child and that had been that. Now he had her in an expensive home out in Malahide and went to visit her every week. He gritted his teeth beneath that expansive smile as she told the nurses he was a barrister.

"How long have we been at this?" asked Bunny.

"Just over two hours."

"And how long do we think it'll take?"

"Weeks, if not months."

"I'm bored out of my mind already, I wish something would happen."

Just then Carter's front door opened and he appeared.

Gringo looked across at Bunny in mock amazement. "If I was you, I'd use your next wish on a prettier face." He grabbed the radio. "Control, alpha twenty-nine here. Primary has exited home property and is proceeding on foot. Commencing follow."

"Roger."

"Not even a glance our way," said Gringo. "Hurtful. I do so hate being ignored."

Bunny started up the car. "Let's see where Tommy boy is off to this fine morning."

They drove behind him at walking pace. Tommy Carter never looked back, just waved at any onlookers as if out for a relaxing stroll. He looked the part: neatly pressed slacks, a trim tweed jacket, and his seemingly ever-present glasses with the slightest orange tint to the lenses. His hair was tightly coiffed, his sideburns trimmed perfectly into a stylised point. He looked more like the kind of bloke who'd run a trendy watering hole as opposed to a criminal organisation.

And a pub was where he was indeed heading, The Leaping Trout, to be exact, two streets away. The only licensed establishment on the Clanavale Estate. Painted a tasteful, peeling purple, the car park beside it glittered with shards of broken glass and there were bars on the windows. Signs big enough to be seen from space assured anyone who cared that they had all the live football matches you could possibly want. To the left of the main door sat an incongruous patio table under a large umbrella. Tommy took a seat and, seconds later, a middle-aged man with a gut hanging over his belt appeared from inside, a small cup of coffee in one hand and a couple of broadsheet newspapers in the other.

Bunny parked the car opposite and they watched him sip his coffee.

"Would you look at that?" said Gringo. "How continental. The lord of the manor."

"He certainly doesn't seem fazed by our presence, does he?"

"He hasn't looked directly at us all this time. Maybe he hasn't noticed?"

The tubby fella emerged again, a plate of pastries in his hand. He placed them on the table and then bent down as Tommy spoke a few words to him. He glanced in the direction of the car and then back to Tommy.

"Maybe he has."

The man nodded one more time and started walking towards them.

"Jaysus," said Bunny. "Do you think they offer a drive-through service?"

The man stopped beside Gringo's window, which he duly opened.

"Mr Carter requests your company for breakfast."

"Oh, does he?" said Gringo. "How delightful."

The man pointed at Bunny. "Just you, not him."

"Aww."

Bunny patted Gringo on the knee. "Never mind, sure you've got them sandwiches you made for yourself."

Bunny got out and started walking across the road.

Gringo's voice trailed behind him. "If he's got any pain au chocolat, amigo, nab me one."

Tommy Carter looked up from his paper as Bunny stood over

him. Despite having just requested his presence, he feigned mild shock at him being there. "Ah, Officer McGarry, nice to see you. Please take a seat."

"It's detective, actually."

"Is it?"

Bunny took the chair opposite. "Nice to see you again too, Tommy. My, how you've grown. I can remember when you were knee-high to a grasshopper, and now look at you, an armed robber and thieving scumbag."

Tommy placed his newspaper down neatly and clucked his tongue. "I see you're as direct as ever. I can still remember you and my da getting drunk in our kitchen."

"And I remember pulling your bawling arse out of a burning building."

Tommy gave him an uncomfortably long look and then shook his head. "Ah now, Bunny, well done on getting your moment in the sun and all, but we both know you charged in when we were absolutely fine."

Bunny raised his eyebrows. "Really?" He looked at the man and remembered the frightened young boy, cowering under a dressing table with his baby sister wrapped in his arms. Hunted eyes, red from crying, frozen in a blank stare of absolute terror. He'd had to pry his little hand from the wood and drag him out, kicking and screaming.

"Absolutely," said Tommy. "I'd have got my sister out of there fine. I was just calming her down when you came blundering in."

Bunny laughed and noted the irritation on the other man's face. "Fair enough. Believe what you want to believe."

Tommy turned over the paper and ran his hand across it, removing creases only visible to him.

"Your da seems to be having a rough time of it."

Tommy shrugged. "Indeed he is. I heard you paid him a visit. Are you trying to drag him into this?"

It was Bunny's turn to shrug. "Like you said, we're old friends. It's not his fault you turned out like you did."

"Yes," said Tommy. "I'm a self-made man."

"That's one way of putting it."

Tommy leaned back in his chair. "Anyway, I wondered if we might lay out some rules of engagement?"

Bunny raised his eyebrows. "Such as?"

"My sister Eimear has nothing to do with any of this. I'd like her left out of it."

"Are you in a position to be making demands, Tommy?"

Tommy paused for a moment and gave Bunny a long look. "Consider it a friendly request."

"I wasn't aware we were friends."

"I'm more than prepared to put up with the harassment that DI O'Rourke has decided to visit upon me. It doesn't bother me at all. However, I have always taken a very dim view of anyone upsetting our Eimear."

Bunny remembered the picture in their briefing notes of the boy who'd had both arms broken by an enraged fifteen-year-old Tommy Carter.

Bunny leaned back in his chair. "If she isn't involved, she isn't involved."

Tommy nodded and then picked up a bagel and began slicing into it. "If you could pass on my sentiments regarding my sister to your colleagues . . ."

"Deliver your own threats. I'm not your messenger."

He gave another shrug. "You know your presence is not welcome on this estate. The Gardaí are not required here."

"Is that so?"

"*Civis Romanus sum.* Do you know what that means, Officer McGarry?"

As it happened he did, but he wasn't letting on. "It's Detective, and why don't you enlighten me?"

"'I am a citizen of Rome.' It was the phrase that guaranteed that any Roman could walk the earth in total safety, because everyone knew that if any harm should befall them, vengeance would be swift and terrible. It's the same here. The people know that they are protected, and not by the Gardaí. You boys only exist to protect the folks in the big houses down by the sea."

"I protect anyone who stays within the law."

Tommy gave a quick laugh. "And has it occurred to you *why* you're following me around?"

"Oh, we had quite a detailed briefing on your extracurricular activities, Tommy boy."

"Yes, but why me?" said Tommy, leaning forward suddenly. "I mean, there's millions of pounds of drugs pouring into this city every month – millions. With all that going on, why are you so worried about me?"

"We're after the dealers too. It might take a while, but they'll get theirs."

Tommy laughed. "Yeah, like the ones who set my house on fire. Tell me, have you got them?"

"Well apparently, that fire wasn't much. A ten-year-old boy could have dealt with it."

Bunny noted the annoyance briefly flash across Tommy's face. The implacable façade temporarily slipping. "A ten-year-old boy can't get his own justice – but a man can."

"Is that right?" said Bunny. "Pray tell, how's he going to do that?"

Tommy opened up the paper, signalling that their conversation had come to an end. "It was nice to see you."

"Likewise, I'm sure. You know where I'll be if you fancy another chat."

"I do."

Bunny stood and began to walk away.

"Oh, and Mr McGarry."

Bunny stared ahead to Gringo, who was watching them from the car.

"Detective."

Bunny turned around.

"Our history is nice and all but, just so as you know, it only goes so far."

They locked eyes for a long moment.

"Likewise."

Tommy looked down at his paper again. "I'll see you around."

"Oh, you can count on that."

CHAPTER FOURTEEN

Simone wiped down the counter again. It occurred to her that she seemed to spend an awful lot of time doing that and it was almost entirely pointless; all it did was move the spillages around. Her shift had started at 7 pm and it was past eleven now, and she'd spent about half of that time pretending to be cleaning the counter. It was either that or standing there looking blank, she supposed. First rule of every waitress gig she ever had: look busy or you soon will be.

They had exactly sixteen customers in. Five actors from a show up at the Gaiety, who seemed to prefer coming here to any of the watering holes nearer the theatre, mainly so they could bitch about their colleagues in peace. There was a couple canoodling in the corner, on just the right side of public acceptability. Then there were two women having a heart-to-heart over a couple of G and Ts; she reckoned they had hit "leave the bastard" territory about two drinks ago. In the other corner sat Joan and Jerry, the nice retired couple who came in every Thursday – possibly the only actual jazz fans in the place. They'd be off for their bus in moments. Then there was Nathan Ryan, the head chef and owner of the *La Trattoria* Italian restaurant a couple of streets over, and two of his acolytes. He was tall with sandy blond hair and a tan that nobody had ever got in Ireland. He was a friend of Noel's, or at least Noel thought so. He'd been over glad-handing him as they'd come in, getting them a round of drinks on the house, same as always. Simone had also seen the sly remark and the poorly-muffled smirks as Noel had walked away.

She felt protective of her boss. Noel put a lot of faith in people. It was a good quality, in theory, but she – more than anyone – knew it could come at a real cost. Still, when she'd turned up on his doorstep nine months ago, looking for cash-in-hand work, no questions asked, Noel had been cool with it. Sister Bernadette had mentioned him. Simone was still unclear as to how a nun had known the owner of a late-night bar and neither had been forthcoming with the details. Still, Noel had put faith in her, and she had tried to pay him back. Right now, this was all she wanted. A quiet life and to help keep the lights on in this dingy basement. Noel was in the back room right now, looking at the books, trying to figure out how to appease the bank manager. She'd been around here long enough to know that the more stressed her boss was, the more twitchy he became. Tonight was not a good night. He was a one-man argument back there. He'd not made it to the piano at all, so a Miles Davis LP on the old-school record player in the corner was currently providing the "ambience" that the sign outside promised.

There was a big demand for a late-night jazz bar in Dublin, and all of it came from Noel. She knew enough to know that the little stage crammed in the corner was the centre of the sweet man's world. He loved the music more than anything. She took it as the highest compliment that when she sang with him he seemed to relax, and his various tics and twitches faded away as he got lost in the song, just like she did. A black woman from New Orleans, half a world away, and a Tourette's-afflicted white man in his sixties, who pumped every dime he had into a club nobody wanted, both united by the music. Ain't that a beautiful thing?

That was why after some sweet-talking, Noel had been willing to allow the final two occupants of the bar back in – the big policeman and his charming friend. The little guy had done most of the talking, while the big fella looked all bashful and apologetic. He'd been desperately keen to pay for the damages. Simone glanced over in their direction and caught the big fella looking back. She smiled and wiped the counter some more. They had been in several times since that night a few weeks ago.

"Simone, my darling, looking radiant as always." It was Nathan Ryan, his smile full of TV-white teeth. "When are you going to let me whisk you away from all this?"

She gave him a smile she had lying around. "I told you, I can't cook for shit, honey."

"That's the beauty of my proposal – you don't need to." He lowered his voice. "It's all very hush-hush, but we're opening a second restaurant at a location in Ballsbridge and you can be our front-of-house maître d'. It'd be a step up from here."

She didn't like the way he said it. "I like it here."

"I mean, sure it's . . . charming, but think how good it would be. You'd get an allowance for clothes too."

"What's wrong with what I'm wearing?"

Truth be told, the blouse she had on was sporting a stain from where she'd picked up a not-quite-empty glass earlier, but still. Besides, she'd not noticed Nathan's eyes making it down past her breasts yet.

"Nothing at all, but this place isn't showing off your beauty to its full pot—"

He reached up to push the hair back from the right side of her face and her hand shot up on instinct and slapped it away, harder than she would have done if she'd thought about it.

"Hey!" Anger flashed in his eyes for a moment. "I was just—"

"Sorry, I don't like being touched."

He rubbed his hand. "No kidding. I was just playing."

"I know you were. Noel is your friend, after all."

"Yes, he is."

"And you'd not be seriously trying to take his only member of staff. That wouldn't be nice."

Nathan gave her a smile that didn't reach his blue eyes. "Obviously, yes."

"So, what can I get you? Same as last time?"

He nodded and she grabbed a bottle of Sol from the fridge, opening it with one hand while setting up two shot glasses of Stoli vodka with the other. A lime in the beer, and a sprinkle of black pepper in the vodkas, all done in a fluid series of actions. She'd been a good bartender in places a whole lot busier than here.

"That'll be—"

"Noel said these were on the house."

Simone shook her head and smiled. "'Fraid not honey, that was the last round. These ones are gonna cost you. The man's trying to run a business." She said it with a jovial air, but she was more than willing to pull the drinks back if necessary.

Nathan gave her another smile and then slipped a twenty-pound note out from his wallet.

"Keep the change."

"Much obliged." Cheap, then ostentatious. Pity the girl who fell for this routine.

She turned to the register to ring them up and when she turned back, Nathan Ryan was gone and the big fella stood in his place, smiling sheepishly.

She smiled back. "Hey, slugger."

"Howerya, how's it going?"

"Fine, thank you."

"So . . ." He shuffled his feet as he spoke. "Not to be a Moaning Minnie or anything, but my friend and I came here looking for a bit of live music?"

Simone pointed over at the record player. "That's Miles Davis live at Newport, it don't get no better than that."

"I must respectfully disagree."

"That's right, you think Billie Holiday's 'The Man', don't you?"

He blushed slightly. "Lady Day, as she was known. I love her earlier recordings but some of her later works are a little more hit and miss, when her voice started to fade before her death in 1959. Still, poor girl had a hard life."

Simone tossed her towel over her shoulder. "Well now, somebody's been studying!"

He nodded. "I'll be honest, I'm a late convert to the jazz cause, but sure aren't those the people who turn out to be the most hardcore? There's a bloke in the Liberty Market whose mortgage I've been paying over the last month, what with all the Billie Holiday, Nina Simone, Ella Fitzgerald and Dinah Washington I've been buying. All your fault, by the way."

"Woah there, cowboy – how am I to blame?"

"I was perfectly happy with my Johnny Cash and Springsteen until you started singing. Now I turn up looking for my next hit and you've turned off the supply."

She laughed. "I'm afraid you picked a bad night. Noel is back in the office trying to teach a spreadsheet how to lie – he ain't gonna play tonight."

He looked genuinely disappointed. "Right, so. I'd better console myself with some drinks then."

"Finally your round is it? Seeing as your buddy bought the first three, I was starting to think you were on a date or something."

"Ah no, he owes me a feed of drinks you see. I saved his life in the line of duty."

"Oh really? How so?"

"Shark attack."

"Wow. Is that a regular occurrence on the mean streets of Dublin?"

"No," said the big fella, shaking his head. "Quite the contrary, that's why he was so taken by surprise."

She laughed. "I can imagine. Same again?" She pointed to the bottle of Jack Daniel's and he nodded.

"So where did this shark attack take place?"

"Well now . . ." He shifted nervously. "That's a very complicated story, so it is. I couldn't do it justice right here. I was wondering if, maybe, you'd let me buy you dinner and I can tell you all about it?"

Her reaction must've shown on her face, because she could see the hope in his die and she felt a little guilty for it. "Sorry, I – I'm not—"

"Oh right, no. Of course. You're spoken for."

"No, nobody speaks for me. I am not in need of a man."

"Lesbian?" He blurted it out and then looked instantly embarrassed. "I mean, not that – oh God, nothing wrong with it, and I'm not saying that, y'know, you not wanting to go out with me would mean you were, I was just – and the last girl I sorta asked out, nice girl, like – just happened to be, so I thought I was perhaps on a run of—"

She raised her hand to stop him before he used up all the oxygen in the room.

"No, I'm not a member of that particular branch of the sisterhood, I'm just not interested in a relationship. I'm only passing through and . . ."

"Right. Yeah." He nodded. "But you've not got a fella or that back home?"

She shook her head. "I haven't even got a *home* back home no more, but still. I mean thanks, sincerely. You seem sweet and from the brief bits of your conversation I can understand, I'm sure you're excellent company – if translation services are provided – but I'm not in a place where that's something I'm looking for."

"Right."

"I mean from anyone. Not to blow my own trumpet but I turned down the dude before you and he was throwing in a job." Simone read his expression and felt herself blush. "Not like that."

"Course not," he said. "Right so, you're single, just not interested."

"In anyone," she added quickly.

"Ah right, so it's not that you don't want to go out with me . . ."

"It's that I don't want to go out with anyone."

"You'd rather be alone?"

"Exactly."

"No strings."

"Yep."

"No attachments."

"Free and easy."

"Grand. Well, in that case, I respectfully decline."

Simone stopped and looked at him for a moment. He smiled back at her.

"Excuse me?"

"Your refusal."

"Yes?"

"With the utmost respect, I decline it."

"Run that by me again? There may be a cultural misunderstanding here."

The big fella picked up one of the whiskeys and knocked it back. Then he pulled a whiskey face.

"Same again?"

He nodded.

She poured.

"So, as I was saying, I think you are the fecking bee's knees. You're beautiful, you're smart and you've got a voice that frankly pisses on all the angels in heaven."

"Eloquently put."

"So, if you don't mind, I might politely hang around the place and check in every now and then, just in case you change your mind."

"I see."

"In fact, fair warning, I might even take a crack at wooing you."

"And what would that consist of?"

He shrugged. "I've no idea. I've never really done it before. Chocolates?"

She shrugged. "Diabetic."

"Flowers?"

"Hay fever."

He placed both of his hands on the bar and looked down, breathing out theatrically. He looked up. "Let me guess – vegetarian, too?"

She shook her head.

"Thanks be to Christ. Only veg I can cook is spuds."

"I tried to warn you, I'm hard work."

He pushed himself off the bar and straightened up. "But it seems like you might just be worth the effort."

"OK." She felt the wide smile on her own lips, coughed and looked down. "Well, thank you for the warning. You really are too damn cute, but I think you should maybe direct your full-on charm offensive in another, more deserving, direction."

He nodded. "Thanks for the advice. I respectfully decline that too."

"Damn. I've turned you down once and now you've turned me down twice."

He put a tenner on the counter and picked up the glasses. "Well, I'm afraid you're just going to have to learn to cope with rejection."

"I guess so."

"I'll be off so."

"Wait a sec," she said. "I don't even know your name."

He put the glasses down again and quickly ran his right hand down his jeans before extending it. "Pleased to meet you. I'm Bunny."

She looked down at his hand and then back up at his face. "No momma in her right mind gave you that name."

"Ehm, no." He blushed in a way that was a little bit adorable. "Everyone calls me that though."

"Not any more."

"OK," he said, lowering his voice, "'tis Bernard."

She took his hand and shook. "Bernard, my name is Simone. It is lovely to meet you, and once again, may I politely decline your offer of romance."

"Your declination is again, respectfully, declined." He realised he had been shaking her hand for slightly too long and let it go. Then he picked up his drinks. "Lovely to meet you properly and I look forward to my advances being declined many times in the future."

"OK then."

"Bye."

"See ya."

He turned around and started walking back to his table.

"Wait."

He looked back at her over his shoulder.

"Billie, Nina, Dinah, Ella – you never told me which one was your favourite?"

He winked and continued walking away. "Still you."

CHAPTER FIFTEEN

Simone heaved the door closed and on the third attempt she heard the lock click. The sticking door was one of the things on a long list that Noel promised, at least twice a week, that he was going to fix tomorrow. Normally she didn't lock up alone but the boss had met some friends for an early dinner. He was a bad drinker, or a very good one, depending on your alcohol-related goals. Two glasses of wine and he was giddy as a schoolgirl, three and he started to get messy. In economic terms, he was a very cheap date. When he'd come back to the bar, he'd stumbled down the steps and landed in a heap. He'd then sworn profusely at the stairs and ranted about a non-existent slope that was apparently very deceptive. Simone had cleaned up the scrape on his knee and stuck him in a taxi back to his flat. A stream of invective-smattered promises had assured her he was going to rest his eyes for an hour and come right back. She hadn't held her breath for that to happen.

She locked the two Chubb locks, double-checked everything and then put the keys through the letterbox, careful to give it enough oomph to make sure they weren't reachable by any endeavouring soul with a straightened-out wire hanger and larcenous intent. Noel could get in tomorrow with the spares. He'd do the clean-up and be all apologetic for his no show the night before.

She turned to leave. "Damn it!"

As her right foot hit the first step, a thought arrived just too late to catch its bus. She'd left her damn heels on. She wore two-inch heels behind the bar and on stage, but switched to sneakers for the walk to and from home. It was three miles each way and her feet already ached from standing up all night. The blue crushed-velvet pencil dress she was wearing had been a lucky find in a charity shop down by the Quays. One of her best days in a long time. She'd always loved the dresses of the Fifties, back in jazz's golden era. A velvet dress – when she shut her eyes, she could be singing in the Royal Roost, with Lady Day sitting in the back booth, nodding her approval. The heels had required several more weeks of thrift shop safari. Her old singing teacher, Verna Douglas, had rules on many things, not least of which was that you treated the stage with some respect. Even now, she could hear her deep, sonorous voice as it boomed out in that rundown shack of a community centre: "That stage is a church where you go to worship the Lord, and you will show up on time and in your Sunday best."

Simone sighed. Tips had been slow tonight, so even if she lucked into a Dublin taxi – unlikely at the best of times – she wouldn't be able to afford the damn thing. She'd have to soak her feet when she got home. Welcome to the glamour of showbiz.

She looked at the grey sky as she mounted the steps and tightened the belt on her overcoat. Maybe she'd get lucky and the weather would stay kind. A large truck thumped past the top of the alleyway as she began to walk up the cobbled slope. She cast her gaze downwards; even without the heels, it paid to watch where you walked in this town late at night, lest you walk through the end of someone else's over-indulgent evening.

A hand grabbed her arm from behind. A choked scream escaped her lips as a sickening wash of panic filled her chest. She turned with her fist cocked to see Nathan Ryan, his hands up in the air, an alarmed look on his face. "Woah, easy."

"Christ, Nathan, you scared the shit out of me."

"Sorry, sorry, sorry. I was just passing—"

"Passing? In a dead-end alley?"

"Well," he conceded, "I was nearby. We had a big corporate thing at the restaurant for one of the banks and the CEO gave me this . . ." He pulled out an ornate bottle that had been crammed into his overcoat pocket. "Cognac, Rémy Martin, bloody good stuff. Expensive too. Coupla tonne a bottle."

"Whoop-dee-doo. Who the fuck comes up behind a woman at 2 am? Goddammit!" Her pulse was still racing.

"Alright, sorry. Jesus, calm down."

She could hear the drunken slur in his words now, and noticed that the knot was askew on his necktie.

"How's about a drink to settle your nerves?"

"I don't drink, Nathan."

"Really?" He looked down at the door to Charlie's. "But you . . ."

He was typical of his type, never paying that much attention to the world around him unless there was something in it that benefited him.

"Yeah. I'm sure there's the occasional vegetarian working in an abattoir too."

A grin fell across his face and his left hand dipped into his pocket. "Well actually, I've got a little—"

"I don't do that either." She was fully aware of what would be in his pocket. The man had monumental self-confidence to fall back on, but she'd still noticed how it would occasionally have been given an unnecessary boost when he came back from the toilets, and how his cold never quite cleared up.

"What vices *do* you have?" he said with a leering grin.

"I ain't got time for your bullshit, Nathan. Good night."

"OK, look", he said, dancing around with surprising speed to stand between her and the top of the alley. "I'm sorry. I was a bit of a dick. I didn't think. No offence intended. Cards on the table – I like you, you like me, how about I cook you a nice late dinner?"

"It's 2 am."

"And normally getting one of the finest chefs in Ireland to cook you an individual meal would cost an arm and a leg, but, seeing as it's you, I'm willing to reduce my rates." He threw in a bow and grinned up at her.

She was hungry but not in the least tempted. "There's no need to open your restaurant for me."

"Don't need to. My place is just over—"

Simone took a step back. "Yeah? No kidding. No thanks, Nathan. Now if you'll excuse me."

He straightened up and frowned in a look of genuine consternation. "Why not?"

"Because it's late, you're horny and I'm tired – and I'm only prepared to fix one of those things."

"There's no need to be a bitch about it."

"Yeah, I'm the one who's totally out of line. Good night."

"Look just, just . . ." He spread his arms wide and she stepped to his left to get by him.

He laughed a little and moved to block her. "Just wait a s—"

When his arm appeared in front of her, she instinctively slapped it away.

There was an explosion of glass and overpriced brandy as the bottle slipped from his hand and shattered on the cobbles. A smattering of splashes hit her tights, the liquid cold. She looked down at the shattered glass and smelled the brandy's sweet aroma mingle with the crisp night air. Somewhere in the distance, an alarm was ringing. Nathan's mouth dropped open in an "O" of outrage. He raised his eyes from the bottle to look at her. His lips curled into a snarl. "You fucking bitch!"

"It was an accident."

A klaxon blared in her mind.

Run.

Run.

Run.

She tried to push by him. He moved his frame again, but this time it wasn't playful; hip checked. Her mind raced: she could calm him down, try and say she was sorry. *Trapped* – the word crashed into her mind. Dead-end alley. She put her hands up in an attempt to get by him again, throwing herself at him now. He moved his right foot a step back to steady himself as his left hand grabbed a fistful of her long hair and yanked it hard. She could feel strands pull free from her scalp as her head was snapped backwards.

She looked up into his eyes and both did and didn't recognise who she saw. This man didn't look like Nathan Ryan any more, not a version familiar to her – probably not a version familiar even to himself. She did recognise it though. This was a beast she'd met before.

She went straight for those eyes, jabbing a forefinger into the left one as hard as she could. A sound, half snarl, half howl, escaped from his lips and he wrenched her further backwards by the hair. She didn't even see his right hand as it flew up in a backhanded slap that sent her pinwheeling around.

Her hair released, she stumbled. Head spinning. Amoebas of fractured light skated across her vision. The right side of her face was burning. Burning again. A different burn than before, but burning nonetheless. She staggered backwards down the slope. There was nothing to grab to right herself. The heel of her right shoe snapped off as her legs went from under her. She landed face first in wet plastic. The sickeningly sweet stench of wasted food filled her nostrils. The Peking Palace's rubbish. They closed at midnight.

Her right eye was starting to close.

"Sorry, sorry, sorry," she mumbled. "Please, I'm sorry."

The world kaleidoscoped around her. The throbbing pain in her right cheek whirled sickeningly with the stench and déjà vu. The terror. The helplessness. The guilt. The shame. The *oh no, oh no, oh no.*

Never be a victim again. Never be a victim again. That had been her mantra. She'd sworn it. Damn it. How had she let this happen?

Her hands scrabbled for purchase amongst the wet bin bags. She turned her head to look behind her, causing a sharp pain to shoot through her neck. She squinted to try and clear the blur in her vision.

Over her shoulder, she saw Nathan, one hand over his injured eye, standing over her.

"Cock-teasing whore."

He pulled his hand away and then there was a moment, a helpless moment. In his face she saw the angry sneer twist a little.

She sucked in a lungful of stagnant air. She could scream.

Both of his hands were on his belt now.

Then . . .

In a blur of movement, Ryan was gone. Disappeared, as if simply erased from reality as a terrible mistake.

Simone painfully turned her aching head in the other direction to see a confusion of bodies tumble down the slope towards the dumpster at the end of the alley. Ryan was now on top of the other figure, punching furiously at the back of their head. With a roar, the new arrival reared up and crashed an elbow into Ryan's chest, sending him rolling backwards.

The lights from a passing car rolled briefly across the alley, catching a frozen moment. Ryan, a different kind of animal now. A trapped one. Cowering. His hands stretched out before him, trying to push the night away. Advancing on him, a wild fury in his eyes, was the big fella, Bunny McGarry.

Ryan backed away towards the corner. He picked up a metal bin and hurled it at Bunny, who fended it away with a contemptuous swat of his arm. Then Bunny was on him, slamming Ryan into the dumpster at the back of the alley, his right hand grabbing the other man's jacket collar as his left threw a couple of haymakers into his stomach.

Ryan crumpled to the floor.

Bunny raised his left foot.

"Stop!"

He turned his head and for a moment Simone saw the pure fury in Bunny's face. He looked momentarily confused by her presence.

"Don't hurt him."

Bunny looked between the two of them, then reached down and grabbed the still groaning Ryan by the lapels. The chef was a big man by most standards, but McGarry lifted him effortlessly, turning him around and slamming him back against the dumpster.

Ryan whimpered. "Please, I . . ."

"I am arresting you for the assault and attempted—"

"No!"

Bunny looked down at Simone, still amongst the bin bags. "But . . ."

She tried to get back up. "It was just a misunderstanding."

"What?"

"He was . . . we were kidding around and I . . . slipped."

Bunny looked back and forth between the two of them as Simone gingerly pulled herself up, clinging to the wall. Her dress was damp, her hands were sticky and she could feel a trickle of blood coming down from her right nostril.

Bunny shoved Ryan's head down. "You stay right there."

"Look, I—"

He leaned into his ear. "Nobody gives a flying fuck what you have to say, sonny boy. Move and see what happens. Please, give me an excuse, I'm begging ye."

Bunny took a few steps towards Simone and lowered his voice to a whisper. "You're in shock. I'll call an ambulance and—"

"I don't need an ambulance. I'm fine. It was just a misunderstanding."

Bunny softly laid a hand on her arm. "You're OK, he can't hurt you now."

"Just . . . forget about it."

Bunny looked into her face, eyes filled with concern. "He was assaulting you. He was going to—"

She shrugged his hand off. "I'm fine. I don't want to press any charges."

"But—"

Ryan turned slowly around. "See. I'm . . . I'm leaving." He moved to go, his steps jerky with terror. Bunny surged forward, his left hand cocked back.

"Let him go!" She nearly screamed it.

Bunny looked back at her, eyes filled with incomprehension. She looked down, unable to meet his gaze. "Just let him go. Please."

He reluctantly lowered his fist and Ryan moved swiftly past him. He looked at Simone and then back at Bunny. "You'll be hearing from my solicitor."

Bunny feinted towards him and Ryan almost tripped over his own feet, scurrying away towards the top of the alley and off into the night.

There was a moment of near silence, save for the rumble of distant traffic. Simone looked around, down at the ground. Looking for something, but she didn't know what. She hadn't been carrying a handbag. She checked her pocket for her keys. In the dim light from the distant streetlight, she could see various stains on her blue velvet dress. The hem was ripped.

She was aware of Bunny standing there, unmoving. She could feel his eyes on her, full of questions.

"Thanks for your . . . I'm fine."

He spoke very softly. "You need to see a doctor."

"No," she said, raising her voice, "I do not. Stop telling me what I need to do."

"But he—"

"I'm fine. I was handling it, just – leave me alone."

"But—"

"I'm perfectly capable of looking after myself. I'm not some cat stuck up a damn tree. Who asked you to get involved anyway?"

He stepped back as if she'd slapped him. "I didn't need to be asked. He was hurting you. He was—"

"Just forget it. Leave me alone."

She moved to walk up the alley and stumbled on her broken heel. "Damn it." She reached down and removed first one shoe and then the other, before continuing to walk up the alley.

A stab of pain ran through her left foot as a shard of glass wedged itself into her heel. She yelped in agony. He rushed to her side as she staggered to the wall. Leaning on it for support, she raised her foot to see rich red blood rushing forth, spreading out across the sole of her foot and running across her upturned ankle. "Damn it!"

Bunny kneeled down beside her and cleaned the blood away with a handkerchief. Then he pulled the shard of glass – from the broken brandy bottle – out of her foot, pressing hard against the wound to stem the flow and then knotting the handkerchief in place.

He looked up at her. "I could just drop you to the hospital?"

"No hospitals. Thank you for your concern."

She tried to place some pressure on the foot and winced as pain shot up her leg again, biting her lip until it eased. "Could I get a lift home?"

He nodded and stood up, extending his arms. "C'mon, I'll carry you."

She looked at him. "I meant in a car."

"No kidding. It's around the corner, but unless your feet have become any more glass-proof . . ." He pointed down at the ground where shards of glass twinkled in the faint light.

Reluctantly, she allowed the man whose help she didn't need to sweep her up in his arms.

CHAPTER SIXTEEN

Bunny stared out the window at nothing.

They were in the usual mid-morning lull where a zen level of absolute nothingness happened. Gringo sat in the passenger's seat, Bunny in the driver's, neither of them going anywhere. Across the street, Tommy Carter's house did absolutely nothing.

The first couple of hours of the daytime shift had flown by in comparison. The book they were running on who got post today diverted attention for a good fifteen minutes just after the school run. Gringo was that far ahead, Bunny was starting to suspect he was sending people letters himself. The school run was, of course, invigorating in itself; delightful cherubs and their doting parents scampering by, only stopping to hurl abuse at the Gardaí parked outside their tribal warlord's house. It had been decided by those on high to ignore the verbal abuse, but any spitting or physical contact with the vehicles would need to be acted upon. It was fair to say their presence was not being warmly greeted by the locals. The only upside of the day shift was that it was slightly more exciting than the night shift. Starsky and Hutch never had to put up with this shit.

Bunny pointed out of the window. "I think that grass has got longer."

"What?" said Gringo.

"The grass," said Bunny, pointing to the lawn outside 17 Crossan Road, "I think it's gotten longer."

"We've been here for over a month now, of course it's grown. Welcome to how the world works. Up next – why the sky is blue."

"My point, ye sarky bollocks, is that I think it is noticeably longer. We've been here that long, I've actually watched the grass grow."

"Fascinating," said Gringo, not even looking up from his newspaper. "What's up with you this morning? You're like a bear with a sore head."

"Nothing. Don't want to talk about it."

"Which is it? Is it nothing or is it something you don't want to talk about?"

"Ara . . . I'll tell you later."

Gringo looked at his watch. "Fine, take your time. I won't be going anywhere for at least four more hours. In the meantime, what's a nine-letter word for 'not a jam'?"

"What?" said Bunny.

"Nine-letter word for 'not a jam'," repeated Gringo.

"That's stupid, every fecking nine-letter word is not a jam. Jam is a three-letter word. Put any nine-letter word."

"That's not how it works. It's cryptic."

"'Tis idiotic is what it is. 'Crocodile', there you go – that's nine letters and not a jam."

"The second letter is an A."

"Just spell it wrong and move on with your life."

Gringo tossed the newspaper up on the dashboard. "You know what your problem is? You need to learn to relax. Take a lesson from Mr O'Donnell."

Bunny snorted in lieu of a response.

They'd been on John O'Donnell, aka the Iceman, for most of last week. The subject of their surveillance was regularly alternated to prevent boredom, but seeing as this mostly meant watching a house two streets over from Carter's, it didn't do a great deal to alleviate the tedium. It got lively when O'Donnell went for a run, mainly because he was impossible to keep up with. At least he ran the same route every day, up around the canal and back. The man was a machine. While Moran, his ex-Ranger buddy, was all tattoos and steroid-enhanced muscle, O'Donnell was a lean athlete. Indeed, for two men with similar military backgrounds, they couldn't be more different. Moran, with his shaved head and bodybuilder physique, seemed to view his surveillance detail as a captive audience. He regularly lifted weights topless in the front room; it looked like one of those late-night TV adverts for chatlines. To liven things up, he would occasionally sprint out of the front door and down to the corner of his street, only to stop and walk back home, laughing all the way. He had started to time how long it took the surveillance car to catch up with him. Things like that were how he occupied his time when not entertaining his harem of girlfriends. Two weeks ago, Pamela "Butch" Cassidy and Dinny Muldoon had sat outside Moran's house while he opened the blinds of his bedroom and stood grinning at them while clearly having sex. They had debated trying to take him in for public indecency but he was in his own house and he had been smart enough to keep the girl out of view. Butch had suggested in the weekly briefing that they get a picture of his ma blown up so that they could hold it up if he did it again. That'd put him off his game.

O'Donnell, on the other hand, was like a ghost. He lived alone and had minimal contact with anyone, bar the classes he taught at his dojo. He trained, he read books, he ate, he slept. He didn't even own a TV, which Gringo had suggested was strike one on the psycho scale right there. O'Donnell had never so much as acknowledged his surveillance. The closest he'd come was last week, when he had come out mid-morning and placed a yoga mat down on his lawn. He'd then proceeded to sit there cross-legged for two hours solid, hands placed palm-up on his knees, staring across at the car containing Bunny and Gringo. Bunny had checked the exact weather afterwards: six degrees it had been. And O'Donnell had sat there in a vest and sweatpants, calmly staring at them. It'd been funny to start with – they'd pulled faces, trying to put him off, then Gringo had got out and asked him directions to Leopardstown Racecourse. He'd sat there, barely blinking, staring right through them. By the end, it had become unnerving, which was exactly the point. He was showing them that he was a man of greater will than them. After two hours, he'd suddenly stood up, rolled up his mat and headed back inside, not even a smile or a nod in their direction.

Gringo drummed on the dashboard excitedly. "I just remembered, I've not told you yet!"

"What?"

"Butch reckons Tommy Carter and John O'Donnell might be, y'know . . ."

"What?"

"A couple."

"Bollocks," said Bunny. "Butch thinks everyone is gay. If she was right, we'd be running out of people by now."

"But think about it, we've not seen either of them with a woman."

"I've not seen you with a woman recently either."

"True, but—"

"I mean," said Bunny, "they could be, I suppose, but they're keeping it very quiet if they are."

"Well, like they said on that course, a lot of people are still nervous about being 'out' and all that."

"Well, George Michael came out last year so, y'know."

"Yeah, but George is an international pop star, Tommy and John are criminal hard men, it might not go with the image."

"One of the Krays was gay."

"Was he?"

"Yeah. I read that somewhere. The proper mental one too. Alexander the Great – there's another."

"Leonardo da Vinci."

"Aristotle."

"Ah sure, the Greeks invented it."

"In fact," said Gringo, "get this. Aristotle and Plato were lovers."

"Were they? God, imagine that. Their pillow talk must've been something."

"Oh yeah. Great thinkers the gays, well known for it. And our own Oscar Wilde, of course."

"Well obviously Oscar. Goes without saying. Poor fella got all kinds of abuse for it though."

"Locked up."

"As was poor Alan Turing. The man cracks the Enigma code, basically wins World War Two for the allies, and then they do all kinds of terrible things to him."

"Shocking."

"'Tis not right."

Bunny glanced in his wing mirror. "Speaking of 'not right'. . ."

Gringo peered into his own mirror to see what he was referring to. On the pavement behind them, they could see at least twenty young kids walking in a large group, each dressed in the uniform of the nearby St Kevin's School.

"Youth – and a lot of it," said Bunny. "Is school out yet?"

Gringo looked at his watch. "Nah, it's only just after two. Unless it's some kind of half day or something?"

Gringo got out of the passenger seat to stand by the car and watch the approaching kids. They seemed in very high spirits. He looked at them and then over at Carter's house. "Bunny."

Bunny turned to see Tommy Carter emerging. He was about to turn the key in the engine when he noticed that Carter didn't seem intent on going anywhere. He had a deckchair with him, which he opened and set down on his lawn. Gringo looked in through the open door at his partner. "We're about to get slapped."

Bunny reached down and picked up the radio. "Control, this is alpha twenty-nine. We have eyes on the primary. Carter is currently sitting outside his house and . . . there are a load of kids." He felt foolish as he'd said it. *Mammy, the other children are being mean to me.*

There was a crackle at the other end, then a pause, followed by, "Can you confirm, alpha twenty-nine, is this the same group of children that alpha twenty-seven are seeing? They are on subject Jimmy Moran."

Bunny looked over at Tommy Carter, who shot him a jovial salute and a smile.

"Ara shite, what the . . ."

Gringo moved down the pavement towards the large crowd of rapidly approaching children, mostly boys with some girls thrown in.

"Sorry, kids, you can't come this way."

They ran past him and surrounded the car, joining hands to form a giggling chain of pre-pubescent protest.

Bunny glanced over to see that Carter now had a video camera out and was filming.

"Jingle bells, jingle bells, jingle all the way . . ."

"Alright," said Gringo, in his best authoritarian voice, "move now or you're all under arrest."

Nobody moved. Gringo looked around exasperated, like a supply teacher considering a drastic change in career.

Amidst the enthusiastic if undisciplined carolling, Bunny's radio became a confusion of words.

"Alpha twenty-seven, Moran is on the move, we are attempting to pursue, however car is currently surrounded by . . ."

"Alpha twenty-four on Doyle, we have the same."

Gringo was outside and was trying to move kids from in front of the car by unlocking their hands.

"Gringo!"

He made eye contact with Bunny, who nodded urgently in Carter's direction. Gringo saw the camera and understood. Video of a guard throwing kids out of the way or driving a car towards them – hello, six o'clock news. Gringo shook his head and sat on the bonnet.

"This is control. Doyle and Moran are gone, can you pursue, alpha twenty-nine."

"Negative, control. But I can confirm Tommy Carter is still here."

Wherever the others needed to be, apparently he wasn't required. Bunny pressed the button again. "Any news on O'Donnell, control?"

"Alpha twenty-seven had visual. The same car that picked up Moran got him too. They're gone."

"Roger."

Bunny put the radio down and looked over at Tommy Carter, who was smiling from behind his camera. He gave a nod of recognition in return. They'd been conclusively outplayed. As the song came to a close, Carter stood and clapped. The kids came running over. Bunny counted seventeen of them. They each got a fiver. Not bad for carol singing in November.

CHAPTER SEVENTEEN

Bunny turned off the car's engine and sat still in the front seat, trying to gather his thoughts. It had been three days since the incident with Nathan Ryan. Three days since he had driven Simone home in the car he was currently sitting in. The car, a 1980s Porsche 928S LHD, was his one indulgence. He'd managed to acquire it from an insurance company for a song, seeing as it was technically a write-off. Then he'd pulled in a few favours and spent what Gringo had described as "two decent cars' worth" of cash on getting it restored. He was too big for it and all the rest, but still, he loved it. At least, he loved it most of the time. On that night, it had felt like an utterly ridiculous thing. Like turning up to a funeral in fancy dress.

He looked over into the passenger's footwell for the hundredth time – at the brown stain on the floor where the blood from her wounded foot had seeped through the temporary bandage that he'd constructed. For each of the last three days he'd driven here, pulled up outside the building and then not gone in. He didn't know what to say or how to say it. She had been shaken up, of course she had, he got that. They had driven here in absolute silence, bar some terse directions Simone had given him. He'd stolen glances at her as he drove. Her long black hair had once again hung in a curtain, shielding the right side of her face, where Ryan had hit her, obscuring the damage. She always wore her hair down on that side.

After she had told him to pull up, they'd sat there in the car, enveloped in an oppressive silence. He hadn't known what to say then either. Eventually, she had broken the impasse; her voice had held a strained tone, robbed of its natural mellifluous cadence. "I . . . I do not want this to become a legal thing. Don't arrest him. Just let it be."

He'd looked at the side of her face; in the dim illumination from the streetlights, he'd been able to make out a swelling beginning to rise. She looked down at her hands, clasped in her lap.

"But . . ."

"Promise me."

He'd run through and rejected several things to say. Then she had finally looked across at him with those dark brown eyes.

"Alright."

"Thank you."

He had carried her to the car in his arms, to keep the pressure off her cut left foot, but she politely refused his offer to help her inside. Though she had spoken with anger and determination, he'd been able to feel the tremble passing through her body as she clasped her arms around the back of his neck.

"It's OK, I can make it from here."

"'Tis no trouble, I'll—"

"I'm fine." There had been an edge of exasperation in her voice as she said it. Enough to make him stop offering to help. She had opened the door and moved herself around in the seat so as to be able to stand without placing too much pressure on her left foot. She'd started to rise, but then stopped, as if a thought had struck her. She half-turned. "Thank you."

He'd not said anything, just watched as she limped down the path, supporting herself on the metal railings as she worked her way up the half-dozen steps to the front door. She'd briefly fumbled with the lock before opening the large front door and disappearing inside, without a look back. He'd sat there for a few more minutes, trying to make sense of it all. Then he'd driven back to his house in Cabra, where he'd laid in bed alone and stared at the ceiling all night.

Bunny puffed out his cheeks and looked at himself in the rear-view mirror. He looked exactly what he was – a man who'd hardly slept in three days.

"C'mon, ye gobshite, man up."

With a nod to himself, he exited the car and started making his way up the drive.

The house was in Rathmines, one in a long row of the old red-brick Georgian houses so common in the area. A lot of them were converted into flats, people being less likely to have a football team's worth of children these days, or to require a management team of domestic staff to look after such a large-scale breeding operation.

The first problem he'd expected to meet was figuring out which flat she was in. He climbed the stairs and looked for buzzers that weren't there. He took a few steps back and looked around. He had been sure this was the place, but he was now starting to doubt himself. Most of these big old buildings did look the same and, seeing as it sat back from the road and he'd been rather distracted at the time, maybe he'd got the location wrong.

He had just turned to head back down the steps when the door opened behind him. "I was wondering when you'd finally come in."

The voice had a firm if slightly high-pitched edge to it. Bunny turned around to see a nun of barely five feet giving him an assessing squint over wire-rimmed glasses. Greying hair peeked out from under her veil. She had striking blue eyes that couldn't have dimmed much in the sixty-plus years they'd been skewering people.

Bunny looked down at her and then looked behind him again. "Sorry, I ..."

She moved back to open the door wider. "So, are you going to stand with your mouth dangling open like an idiot or are you coming inside?"

"Sorry, I ... Sorry, Sister, I'm looking for my, ehm, friend."

The nun turned her eyes to heaven. "Yes, Simone. In you come –

or would you rather go back to sitting in your car and gawping like a clueless dunderhead?"

"You're a . . ."

"Nun, yes." She blessed herself. "May the good Mother Mary bless us and save us if this is the deductive might the Gardaí are working with." She waved her hand irritably in the air. "This monstrosity of a place is a nightmare to heat, so can you make a decision quickly, please, as this door is wide open and we're not made of money."

"Sorry. Right. Of course. Sorry."

Bunny stepped inside, onto plush carpet in a large hallway, as the nun started pushing the door closed behind him. "Good gravy, thing weighs a tonne. Don't help or anything will you?"

"Sorry, Sister." Bunny moved across, but too late to be of any assistance.

"C'mon then." The nun, in her dark grey habit, started shuffling down the hall at a surprisingly fast clip. The wall was painted a peculiarly unpleasant shade of orange. The air was an oppressive mix of air freshener and overly central-heated air.

"Sorry," said Bunny.

"Do you start every sentence with sorry? It is tremendously annoying."

Bunny looked around him. "No, I just . . . Sorry."

She turned her head to look back at him. "Quite the silver-tongued devil, I see."

"Yes, ehm . . . Where am I?"

"At last, a coherent question. This house is a retirement home for the Sisters of the Saint."

"The Saint who?"

"Just the Saint."

"But don't all saints have names?"

"Clearly not."

Bunny felt like nothing was making sense, as if he was trapped in one of those stress dreams and he would look down in a minute to notice he had no trousers on.

She pushed open a door to her left and waved Bunny through into a sitting room. A TV sat in one corner, showing horse racing with the sound down. Three sofas, covered in plastic sheeting, were angled towards it and a chandelier with only half its bulbs working hung from the ceiling above. On the left sofa sat a large-in-all-senses nun with a bag of wine gums and, on the right, a nun of even shorter stature than the one who had opened the door. She seemed considerably older, too, although it was hard to judge, as she had her head back, snoring surprisingly loudly.

Bunny's guide spoke to the larger nun in that distinctive loud voice reserved for the hard of hearing. "Sister Assumpta, we have a visitor."

Sister Assumpta smiled a warm smile amidst immense rosy cheeks and nodded at him while chewing aggressively on a wine gum.

The first nun pointed at her sleeping colleague. "And that's Sister Margaret, but she's out like a light. I am Sister Bernadette."

"Hello, Sisters, I am Bunny McGarry."

Sister Bernadette gave him an assessing look. "Really? And that's a name these days, is it? Well, well." She indicated the free sofa. "Take a seat. I'll let Simone know you're here."

"Right, I'll . . ." Bunny quickly placed his hand over his eyes and turned around. "Jesus, sorry, ehm . . ."

"What on earth is wrong with you now?"

Without turning, Bunny pointed back over his shoulder in the direction of Sister Assumpta, who was in the middle of removing her clothing.

"Oh for heaven's sake! Assumpta, dear, this isn't the doctor. Put yourself away, will you? That's a good girl."

Bunny stared resolutely at the door as there was the sound of movement behind him.

"You can turn around," said Sister Bernadette. "Crisis averted."

When he turned back, Sister Assumpta was fully dressed once more and had gone back to staring at the horse racing, seemingly unaffected by the misunderstanding.

Sister Bernadette pointed at the sofa again. "Sit. I'll go and get Simone."

"Right."

Bunny sat down and aimed a polite smile at Sister Assumpta, but it appeared she had entirely forgotten his presence.

After a few long minutes, the door opened and Bunny stood as Sister Bernadette re-entered, followed by Simone. She wore a baggy jumper, jeans and a wary expression. Her left foot was bandaged. The hair on the right side of her face hung down but it couldn't entirely hide the bruising that had blossomed up on her cheek or the swelling on her lip. She looked both younger and older at the same time. Diminished, somehow.

Sister Bernadette clapped her hands together once and looked between the two of them. "Right, well I'm sure you two have a lot to be talking about." She raised her voice. "Sister Assumpta, come with me to the kitchen, dear."

Assumpta pointed at the TV in mute protest.

"You'll live without the gee-gees for a few minutes." She grabbed Assumpta's hand and then leaned across to Simone and lowered her voice again. "I'll leave Margaret here. She's out like a light, and besides, she's not understood either side of a conversation since the Berlin Wall came down."

Simone nodded and smiled nervously. "Thanks, Bernadette."

Bunny and Simone watched them leave and then turned to look awkwardly at each other. Simone gestured towards the sofa and Bunny sat down again. She came and sat beside him.

"How are you?" Bunny asked. Up close he could see the rust-red bruise that started below her swollen eye and stretched backwards into the shadow of her hair.

"I'm OK." She waved a hand at her face. "It looks worse than it is. No broken bones or anything."

"Right. Did you go to the hospital?"

"No." She nodded back towards the door. "Bernadette knows someone."

"Still, though, you should see a proper doctor, to be on the safe side."

Simone gave a weak smile. "Apparently, the old gent was Ireland's leading heart specialist. Bernadette knows lots of people."

"Right. Good. I mean, well ... y'know."

"Yeah." She shifted nervously in her seat. "I just wanted to say ... I'm sorry." Her big eyes, looking wet, flickered up to his momentarily.

"What?"

She looked up again, slightly taken aback by the shock in his voice.

"What are you talking about? You've nothing to be sorry for."

"No, no – I do. You were helping me and I was very rude to you. I'm sorry."

"That's a shower of bollocks."

She raised her eyebrows. "Is this how you normally accept an apology?"

"It is when I don't deserve one. Now you listen to me. You were attacked. You have nothing to be sorry for."

"Yeah, but if you hadn't come along ..."

Bunny moved closer. "Simone, listen to me. You don't have to apologise and you don't have to thank me, alright? None of this was your fault. You need to be clear on that."

She nodded.

Bunny fidgeted. "So, ehm, you're a nun then?"

Simone pursed her lips for a moment, then nodded before turning away.

"Right. Good. Great. Well done you. Fantastic. Sorry about all the ..."

Bunny stopped talking as he noticed Simone's shoulders shaking. Was she crying? Oh God, what did you say to comfort a crying nun? He thought about putting his hand on her shoulder and then thought better of it.

He jumped as she suddenly burst out laughing, holding her hand over her mouth as she turned to him with a glint in her eyes.

"Oh, you cow!"

She laughed harder, pushing at his shoulder playfully as she did so. "Oh, honey, I needed that. You do make me laugh."

Bunny could feel his face going bright red. "Yeah, very funny. Making me look like a right gobshite."

Simone rubbed her sleeve across her eyes and took a moment for her breathing to return to normal. "No," she said, "I'm not a nun."

"Yeah, I know that now. So . . ." Bunny looked around him. "What are you doing here?"

Simone's expression changed again. She looked pensive. "I can tell you some of it, but you'll have to trust me. I'll tell you what I can."

Bunny shrugged. "OK."

Simone looked at the fire as she spoke, and her voice dropped to a low, steady timbre, as if she were delivering a prepared statement that she had practised a hundred times.

"Back in the States, I got into some trouble. Let's just say I fell in with some bad people and some very bad things happened."

"Like—"

She shook her head firmly. "I really can't say." She pointed back at the door. "It ain't just me, you understand. The sisters."

Bunny held his hands up. "OK, but how did you end up here?"

"I was in trouble and running. I had nowhere to go, and I ended up in this church. Hurt. Bleeding. Broke. Scared. What is it they say? No atheists in foxholes? Well, I guess I needed Jesus because nobody else could help me. I collapsed on this altar and, when I came to, there's these two nuns, Mary and Joan. I told them all that had happened and . . ."

Bunny went to ask a question and stopped himself, but Simone still sensed him trying.

"I can't say why, but I couldn't go to the police, OK? I know that's something you find hard but, well, not all police are like you."

"Is that why you wouldn't go this time?"

She nodded. "I can't. The sisters, they got me out of New York. Got me here. I'm not . . . I'm not legal in this country." She shot him a nervous glance. "I know I shouldn't be telling you all this, but I reckon it's better than you going looking. It ain't just me, you understand. I got to protect them. The people looking for me, they won't ever stop, but we reckon they don't know I'm here – not unless someone tells them. I guess . . . Look, it's up to you what you do with that information, but make sure they're left out of it."

Bunny looked into the fire. "I'm not going to say anything."

Simone gave him a long look. "Really?"

He shook his head. "Besides, in this country, nuns are more powerful than the law." He lowered his voice. "And considerably more scary."

"I heard that." The voice came from behind the door.

Simone rolled her eyes and raised her voice slightly. "Bernadette, is eavesdropping not a sin?"

"I'm sixty-six and a virgin. I think God will forgive me a couple."

Simone cleared her throat pointedly.

"Fine." As the sound of her footsteps disappeared down the hall, Bernadette raised her voice so they could clearly hear her talking to herself. "It's our house and they've taken over the only room with a television in it. What do they expect me to do? Assumpta – will you put your clothes back on!"

Bunny smiled. "Never a dull moment around here."

Simone nodded in the direction of the still-snoring Margaret. "You should be here when she wakes up. Swears like a sailor, farts like a 21-gun salute."

"She sounds like a right laugh. Anyway, I should probably get going." Bunny nodded towards the TV and stood up. "Don't want to be in the way."

"Sure," said Simone, standing beside him. "Thanks for coming by."

She opened the door and showed him back down the hall.

"Oh," said Bunny, "I dropped into Charlie's. Noel is very worried about you."

"Yeah, I should ring him. Bernadette says he keeps calling. I just, y'know, don't know what to say."

"You'll figure it out. And when you feel up to it, well, you know your adoring public is always eager to hear you sing."

She gave him a bashful smile. "We'll see."

She opened the door onto the cold early evening air. It washed over them; a welcome relief from the oppressive heat of the house.

Bunny stopped and stood as if transfixed by the view.

When he spoke, his voice came out in a hoarse whisper. "Simone, how bad was the thing that happened in New York?"

She stood looking out into the street for so long that he wondered if she was just going to pretend that she hadn't heard the question. Then slowly she turned to face him. She raised her hand to brush back her long hair from where it hung over her face. Past the swollen eye and the dark bruise lay something worse. A river of callused, burned skin snaked down from above her ear, down the side of her face and onto her neck.

Bunny flinched despite himself.

Simone's eyes remained fixed on the floor as she spoke. "Bad."

CHAPTER EIGHTEEN

Franko Doyle walked slowly down the uneven path that sloped towards the tarmacked area below. This path hadn't been laid down so much as worn into the ground as thousands of pairs of feet chose the same route over decades. It was slippery after the earlier rain, and the winter night was bringing in a chill of frost. That, and the bulky rucksack on his back, was making Franko walk with great care. More than anything, he didn't want to stumble and go on his arse – not in front of this audience. He'd never hear the end of it.

They'd been instructed to meet at 8 pm prompt in the Furry Glen, an area within the bigger Phoenix Park. The main park was neatly trimmed and scrupulously maintained. The Furry Glen was the little corner where they let nature run wild.

The men he was meeting did not like to be kept waiting. It was now twenty past, and he could sense them shooting dirty looks of irritation at him from down by the bench where they were standing. Peter Dylan and Paul Roberts. Dylan was the taller and more muscled of the two. Looked like a heavyweight boxer gone to seed. Franko knew him vaguely. He worked security at a few places – or at least he used to until his recent promotion in the ranks of the organisation he'd affiliated himself with. Paul Roberts was considerably shorter. Franko had only met him the once, and they'd not exactly hit it off. Roberts was the power in the situation, whereas Dylan was only involved as a go-between and a bit of glorified muscle. One of the few things the paramilitaries thought Dubs were good for was talking to other Dubs. As always with the IRA, it was the bloke with the northern accent who held most sway, and that was Roberts.

Dylan had approached Franko and issued the ultimatum. The 'RA wanted to meet him and Tommy Carter for a discussion about unpaid dues and unacquired respect for how things were done. Franko had duly passed the message on.

In the summer, this place would be lousy with school trips and tourists snapping pictures. But as the winter frost started to bite, under the atmospheric lighting, it had a crisp, moody beauty to it. Not that Franko could fully appreciate it. He was too busy watching his feet.

He glanced up to see Roberts's eyes boring into him from above his cigarette. The light above the bench was on, despite this area of the park having been closed since dusk. Getting lights turned on – that was the kind of pull the balaclava boys still had in this town. Roberts sent a cloud of cigarette smoke up into the night to join the gathering fog.

Franko finally reached level ground and covered the remaining distance at a deliberately casual pace. He briefly considered whistling.

"Peter, Paul," he said with a smirk.

"You're late." Roberts's aggressive Northern whine would've probably sounded threatening in any circumstances, but now it was clearly meant to. "And where the fuck is your boss?"

Franko shrugged. "He's parking the car."

Dylan spoke next. "You'd want to mind your manners, Franko."

"Oh, do I?" He casually took the rucksack from his back and laid it on the ground.

"Aye, ye fucking should, ye fat prick. Now where the fuck is Carter?" said Roberts.

Franko looked at Roberts for a long second and then turned to Dylan. "Peter, tell your Northern friend here that I don't like to be spoken to in that manner."

"I'll fucking speak to you however the fuck I want, and if ye don't like it, you can take it up with my bosses."

Franko shrugged. "Who are your bosses these days? I thought with that Good Friday agreement thing youse all signed last year, you were out of the game?"

"The Irish Republican Army is, as ever, here to look after its interests and those of the Irish people."

"Yeah," said Franko, "in that order."

Roberts tossed his cigarette towards the pond and stepped forward. "I came here to talk to the man in charge, not his fat monkey."

"Tommy Carter doesn't just come running when summoned. Out of respect, he sent me to hear what you have to say."

"Respect, my arse."

Franko yawned and then looked over at Dylan. "I can remember when you boys were supposed to be fighting the Brits, whatever happened with that?"

Roberts lunged at him, but Dylan thrust out a large arm and pulled him back.

"Alright, enough of this. Franko, stop playing the maggot."

Franko blew into his hands. "I'm here, I'm cold and I've better things to be doing. Can we move this along?"

Roberts pushed Dylan's arm away and straightened his jacket. "Fine," he said. "Tell your boy king that his actions have been noted. He has been asked – twice – to pay his dues, and twice he has refused."

Franko nodded.

Roberts stepped forward and lowered his voice, despite there supposedly being nobody around bar the three of them to hear. "Furthermore, it is our belief that the weapons you are using have been acquired from us without our permission."

Franko smiled. "Would these be the same weapons that you

acquired from the Irish Army barracks down in the Curragh a couple of years ago without their consent?"

"Nobody steals from us."

Franko laughed. "Well that's clearly not the case now, is it?"

"Are you willing to make reparations or not?"

Franko laughed. "Reparations? That's a good word for it. Reparations." He said it slowly, as if savouring the taste.

Dylan squared his body towards him. "Franko, you'd want to start taking this seriously. Don't go thinking our friendship is gonna protect you here."

Franko didn't take his eyes from Roberts as he spoke. "Friendship? Are you fucking kidding me? You're a joke to us, Dylan. You and all your bullshit wannabe brethren. What kind of a sad sack from Dublin goes off to join the IRA to get bossed around by some Northern pricks as they fight a dead man's war over and over again?"

Dylan shot out a meaty paw and pushed Franko's shoulder. "Fuck you, Franko."

Franko stumbled backwards slightly and looked down at his shoulder. "I really wouldn't do that again if I was you."

"So," said Roberts, "do we have your answer?"

"Yes," said Franko. "In fact, allow me to deliver the exact message Tommy gave me for you. You can take your reparations, your taxes and your stolen guns and you can whistle for it. In fact . . ."

Franko whistled – one long, loud blast.

A half a second later, a red dot appeared on Peter Dylan's chest, fractionally beating the one that appeared on Paul Roberts's. To be fair, thought Franko, Dylan had a lot more chest to aim for.

Dylan looked down and swallowed. "Paul?"

Roberts kept smiling at Franko. "Is this little parlour trick supposed to impress me? Aye, very good. Do you think you're the only one with skilled soldiers at his disposal?" Roberts gave Franko a big grin, then stepped back and raised his voice. "Tony, time to come out and play."

Nothing happened.

For several seconds, nothing continued to happen. As the silence stretched out, Roberts's grin slowly crumbled.

Roberts raised his voice slightly louder. "Tony?"

Franko burst out laughing. "The look on your face." He jigged a couple of steps back and looked around him in mock amazement. He raised his voice into a sing-song warble. "Tony? Where are you? Your Uncle Paul needs you to come out and play!"

Dylan went to say something but Roberts silenced him with a glare. This time though, he did look down at the red dot still shining directly onto his chest.

Franko was still grinning. "So, was Tony one of the three boys you'd hidden in the woods around us here? Or was he one of the two lads down the road in the van?"

"Don't you try and fuck with us."

Franko laughed again. "Try? I think you'll find we already have." He stepped forward and the smile dropped from his face. "Here's the rest of Tommy's message. This is our town now. You try and interfere in our business again and next time there'll be a body count. The only reason you aren't the star attraction in one of your silly balaclava-and-bullets funerals right now is that we chose for that to not be the case. Remember that. Consider this your one and only warning."

He kicked the rucksack at his feet. "This is for you. It's the clothes belonging to your band of five wannabes. I'd hurry if I was you, it's getting nippy and I'd imagine they're feeling the cold right about now, tied to those trees in nothing but their panties. Tell your bosses Tommy Carter says 'fuck you'."

Franko turned and began walking back up the slope he'd come down.

"This isn't over," said Roberts.

"For your sake, you'd better hope it is."

CHAPTER NINETEEN

Nathan Ryan woke with a start.

He'd not been sleeping well for the last few nights. Had it been another nightmare? No, probably not – certainly no residual memory of it clung to his consciousness. It was probably noise-related. He lived in Temple Bar, after all, and even with the penthouse's double glazing, the drunken hollering of the great unwashed could not be entirely silenced.

He looked at the clock. 3:17 am.

The nightmares were ludicrous. While awake, he remembered clearly what had happened. He'd been nothing but charming and the bloody woman had been playing mind games with him. Sure, turning up in the first place might've been a bad idea, but Christ, who didn't have a bad idea every now and then? She had completely lost it and thrown his bottle of Rémy Martin at him. Could've bloody killed him. Then she'd jammed her finger in his eye and his hand had flailed out, entirely in self-defence.

He'd been wearing sunglasses for three days now and pretending he'd poked himself in the eye with his shower loofah. She was damn lucky there appeared to be no lasting damage, otherwise she'd be looking at a serious lawsuit. He tried to pull his mind off that mental track, as it led to an unhappy place. He knew how people would try and make him look. They could throw around some very ugly words indeed. The kind of words that could end a career.

He heard a noise in the kitchen.

"For fuck's sake, Mrs Twinkle!" He'd only got the bloody cat because his ex had wanted it. He'd only kept hold of it for the exact same reason. Truth was, he really didn't like cats. This cat in particular seemed to delight in trying to cause as much damage to his apartment as possible. That was all he needed – another moody bitch in his life.

He threw the duvet back and sat up on the edge of the bed. He had a couple more painkillers in the kitchen. Jackie would have to line him up with something stronger tomorrow. He didn't want to go to the doctor; they'd have questions. No fucker could mind their own business any more.

He tugged his boxers out of the uncomfortable crevice they'd snuggled up in and headed towards the kitchen. The large windows offered an unparalleled view of a rain-soaked Dublin, across which the dawn light would soon be creeping. The sooner he could move on and leave this dump of a city behind, the happier he'd be.

He had half a bottle of Stoli vodka left from the weekend that would help chase the painkillers down, and finally get him some solid kip. He opened the fridge. In its light, he could see the purple bruising on the right side of his stomach that the cheap shot from that raging muck savage had left. That animal was lucky that Nathan just wanted to put the whole unsavoury incident behind him. Several highly-placed police officers were good friends of his. Anyone who wanted to eat at his restaurant on a civil servant's wages had to be very friendly. He was owed favours. As he gingerly ran his fingers over the bruising, his other hand reached for the bottle of vodka.

It wasn't there. He looked into the fridge in confusion. Had he . . .

Nathan jumped as a lamp in the open-plan sitting room behind him was turned on. He turned to see the black leather chair swivel around. A man was sitting there holding Mrs Twinkle.

"Ah, Mr Bond."

Nathan yelped in shock, slamming the fridge door closed and pressing himself up against it. The cold steel against his back made him suddenly aware of his near-nakedness. On instinct, he cupped his hands over his nether regions.

"Are you expecting a free kick?"

On the second look, Nathan recognised the man. Yes! He was that copper, the one he'd seen a few times in Charlie's, mostly in the company of the big gorilla.

"What the bloody hell are you doing in my apartment?"

The man – he seemed to recall hearing someone refer to him by the name of 'Gringo' – stroked the cat affectionately.

"See, Mrs Twinkle, I told you he'd shit himself."

Mrs Twinkle purred disloyally.

Nathan pointed. "That cat does not like to be touched!" Even as he said it, he was aware of just how stupid it sounded.

Gringo turned the cat around and held her up. "She seems happy enough to me." He pulled the cat closer and it licked his face. "She's a happy little puss-puss, yes she is."

Gringo lowered the cat back to his lap. "Although I'm glad you brought up the subject of inappropriate touching."

Nathan's mind raced. His mobile was beside the bed; the flat's phone was on the other side of the sitting room.

"You have been an unacceptably naughty boy, haven't you, Nathan?"

"Look," said Nathan, trying to keep the fear from his voice, "I don't know what that big gorilla told you but he got entirely the wrong end of the stick. It was all a misunderstanding."

"Ahh," said Gringo, "I thought it might be. So you didn't assault a woman half your size and you weren't going to do a lot worse, when the – what was it? Ah yes, 'big gorilla' – showed up?"

"Of . . . of course not."

"Man," said Gringo, "I wish you played poker because you are one god-awful liar, Nathan."

"I'm telling you, he's lying. It wasn't like that."

"OK," said Gringo, moving to scratch Mrs Twinkle under the chin. "Let's ask him."

Nathan followed Gringo's gaze as he turned his head to the front door of the apartment. He nearly jumped out of his skin as McGarry stepped forward into the light from the lamp. He gave a lazy-eyed glower of such hatred that Nathan was in serious risk of losing control of his bodily functions.

"Stay away or I'll call the police!"

Gringo chuckled. "With what? You could also try screaming."

"Briefly," added McGarry.

Gringo nodded. "Briefly. And we are in Temple Bar. I'm guessing the locals are very good at ignoring people hollering in the middle of the night. You'd have to be, to live here."

"You can't do this. You're the Gardaí!"

"Actually," said Gringo, picking Nathan's bottle of Stoli up from beside the chair where he'd left it, "right now, we're just concerned citizens. In fact, feel free to mention our names to law enforcement. We have the most cast-iron of alibis. We're currently enjoying a late, after-hours drink with . . ." He started counting people off on his fingers. " . . . Mr Noel Graffoe, the proprietor of Charlie's jazz bar; a charming retired couple called Joan and Jerry, teacher and bank manager respectively; and, wait for it, wait for it. . . Sister Bernadette – a nun, an actual honest-to-God nun!"

Nathan was only half-listening. He was nodding while gradually moving his right hand back towards where he knew his block of knives would be. Every good chef always knows where his knives are.

Gringo leaned forward slightly, "And you've got to ask yourself, Nathan, how much of an utter fuck-up you are that nuns, actual nuns, are happy – nay, excited – to provide an alibi to a man coming to deal with you."

"I'm sorry," said Nathan. "OK? I'm really sorry."

Gringo turned to McGarry again. "He says he's sorry."

"Does he?" responded McGarry, clearly not concerned either way. "Not as sorry as he's going to be."

Gringo nodded and stroked Mrs Twinkle under the chin. "By the way, Nathan, I moved your knives. We don't want somebody getting hurt now, do we?"

Nathan glanced behind him and his body sagged. "So what is this? The two of you have come here to scare me?"

Gringo shook his head. "Oh no, Nathan. You see, my associate here's attitude towards men who put their hands on women is very well known in certain circles. I mean, don't get me wrong, I, like almost everyone else – and again, Nathan, a nun, a fucking nun! – do not have much time for such men, but he," Gringo said, pointing over towards the door, where McGarry stood stock-still, "is on another level. He seeks them out and does everything he can within the law to bring them to justice, and if that isn't possible, well . . ." Gringo looked down at Mrs Twinkle, who was looking up at him with undisguised affection. "Well, we go play gin rummy with a publican, a teacher, a bank manager and a nun." Gringo chuckled to himself again. "Seriously – a nun."

Nathan flinched as McGarry started moving towards him.

"No, no, no, no, no."

"Ah," said Gringo, still sitting calmly in his chair, "so you do know what that word means."

Panicked adrenalin pumped through Ryan's veins. "So two of you have come here to beat me up? Ohh, big men!"

Gringo laughed humourlessly. "Oh no, Nathan. You see, my friend here has come to punish you."

Nathan slid down the shiny metal front of the fridge-freezer, his hands placed protectively above his head.

He looked up to see McGarry towering over him.

"I'm just here to make sure he doesn't kill you."

CHAPTER TWENTY

Bunny walked into the briefing room and placed one of Pearse Street station's famously bad cups of tea in front of Gringo. Gringo nodded thanks as Bunny slid into the chair beside him.

They'd come straight in after an uneventful day shift on the Clanavale Estate – well, uneventful by the standards of the day before. The night shift had confirmed that John O'Donnell and Franko Doyle had returned home about 1 am. Jimmy Moran had stumbled out of a taxi just before 4 am, with a worse-for-the-drink blonde in tow. Detectives Dinny Muldoon and Pamela "Butch" Cassidy had been on his house at the time. Butch was standing up in the centre of the room, relaying the story to the other members of the task force.

"So, he's got this young one wearing – Jesus, how would you even describe the outfit, Dinny?"

Dinny Muldoon, looking like something the cat dragged in, was nonetheless enjoying his partner's telling of the story. His strong Kerry accent filled the room. "Well let me say this, Detective Cassidy, the young lady in question's outfit, well, 'twould be considered scant."

Butch put one finger to the tip of her nose and pointed at

Muldoon. "Scant. Scant is indeed a good word for it, Detective Muldoon. Her outfit was positively scant-elous."

The chuckles of the assembled company were mixed with groans.

"So anyway," continued Butch, "Moran comes over to the car and he's waving in the window going, 'Y'all right there, officers, have you had a good night' – all this bullshit."

"What a prick."

"Too right, and then he bends this girl over on our bonnet and starts dry humping her."

Butch started enthusiastically acting it out, leaning over one of the desks. "And he's all, 'Oh yeah, she's gonna love it, we're going to be riding all night.'"

"The man is indeed a poet," interjects Muldoon.

"Now personally," continued Butch, "I'd have arrested him there and then for fraud. With the amount of steroids that muppet has probably been on, I'd imagine the best chance of his little ding-a-ling giving anyone a good time is if he dresses it up and does a puppet show."

A guffaw of laughter rippled around the fourteen officers.

"Anyway, enough is enough. We get out of the car and Dinny pulls lover boy aside."

Muldoon leaned forward. "I did indeed. I explained to Mr Moran that he was making a nuisance of himself and that Section 5 of the Criminal Justice Public Order Act 1994 makes it an offence for anyone in a public place to engage in offensive conduct between the hours of midnight and 7 am."

"Jesus, Dinny," chipped in Bunny, "I love it when you get all quotey. How did the muscle-bound bollocks take that?"

"Funny you should ask, Detective McGarry. Not well, but also not as badly as I'd hoped. I was hoping he was going to smack me one and we could get him on assaulting a police officer. No such luck. Instead he's all 'This is harassment! Who am I offending?' Now, I wanted to say me, not least because I've a couple of ten-month-old bambinos at home and let's just say it's been a while since both myself and Mrs Muldoon have been in the same room fully conscious and neither of us with baby sick on us."

"Conjugal visits have been in short supply in the Muldoon household," confirmed Butch. "I feel so bad for him, I've considered letting him come over to my house to watch."

"So did you arrest him?" asked DS John Quinn, a man not renowned for his lightning wit.

"No," said Cassidy, "course not. Rigger said about not leaving us open to harassment charges, tempting as it'd be."

"So what's the point?" continued Quinn, unaware of the eye-rolls all around him.

"Ah," said Dinny, "Detective Cassidy, would you like to enlighten DS Quinn as to the point?" He let it hang in the air as he looked at Butch, giving his double-act partner the dénouement.

"So, while Dinny was having his tête-à-tête with Moran, I'm chatting to his lady friend. Telling her, 'Oh yeah, we've been following himself about, he's under surveillance.' This she knows, by the way. Seems to be getting a kick out of it. Loving the bad boy image and all that. So I says, 'Yeah, followed him to the gym, the shops, the STD clinic . . .'"

Laughter.

"'STD clinic?' she says. And I go, 'Oh shit – I shouldn't have said that, ignore me. It's probably nothing, he might just know someone who works there – who he's gone to visit three times in two weeks.'"

There was more laughter, mixed with a smattering of applause.

Butch took a bow. "So, Cinderella suddenly remembers she has to go home immediately, before Prince Charming turns into a pumpkin."

"Crabs more like!"

"And Moran goes batshit!"

"Ah Jesus, folks," Dinny said through his foot-wide grin, "the look on his face was fecking priceless."

"He was probably in there all night," said Butch, "cursing his massive deltoid muscles that mean his hands can't reach down and grab his little winky."

Cassidy started acting this out to the room's amusement, mimicking Moran's muscle-bound gait that made it look like he was carrying an invisible roll of carpet under each arm.

A cough came from behind her.

The room fell silent.

DS Jessica Cunningham stood in the doorway, looking unamused even by her lofty standards.

"I'm glad to see we're all having a good time. Is there something worthy of celebration I'm unaware of?"

Butch, red-faced and silenced, sat down in her seat as the room shifted nervously.

"We get made to look like clowns by Carter and here we all are, laughing it up." Cunningham stared coldly around the room for a second before moving across to her seat at the front. DI O'Rourke and DS O'Shea came in the door behind her, unaware of the dressing-down that had just been issued.

O'Rourke leaned back against the desk at the front while O'Shea started passing out photocopies.

"OK, folks, thanks for coming in. Look – yesterday was a farce and we all know it. Mr Carter is certainly 'inventive', the little shit, but we knew that." He stopped to look around the room at his team. "I know morale is an issue. I'm not blind to that. We've been on this for five weeks now, but honestly, while it might not look like it, it is working. Yesterday, they had to go to great lengths to get out from under us, and when they did, they'd no alibi for the time they were missing. Any time they pulled a job previously, one of the big problems we had was that the Clanavale Estate would alibi them up to the nth degree. They've not got that when we're on them. We're making it harder for them to work."

This, thought Bunny, was true – up to a point. Whatever they'd been up to yesterday – and every bank, armoured car and Garda on patrol had been made aware of an increased threat of armed robbery – it hadn't been a light-of-day thing. Maybe they were up to something, maybe they just wanted to make the Gardaí look foolish. Either way, they had succeeded.

"We've just handed out some new guidelines," said O'Rourke, holding up one of the photocopied sheets of paper. "I'm asking for more resources. We're going to try and keep a car just outside the estate, so if they pull a stunt like this again, we can pick up the tail. In the meantime, every one of your cars has a video camera in the glove compartment now. If they're going to film us, we're going to film them. We don't want edited footage getting out to make us look bad that we can't counter. Carter is smart but pressure will force him into a mistake. It might not feel like it, but we've got them right where we want them."

CHAPTER TWENTY-ONE

"We've got them right where we want them," said Jimmy Moran.

Tommy Carter placed a finger to his lips and nodded pointedly at John O'Donnell, who was methodically making his way around the front room with the scanning device they'd brought back from Florida the last time they'd been over. A present from O'Donnell's contacts in Miami that was proving useful.

Franko, sitting in the armchair, looked at Moran stretched out on the sofa, his feet on the cushions. The man had no respect for anything, and seeing as Tommy kept his house as pristine as both his father and his mother had before him, that was doubly disrespectful. Moran didn't have the sense he was born with.

"For feck's sake, Tommy," continued Moran, "Johno checked the whole place two days ago. Can we get on with it?"

O'Donnell stopped what he was doing and looked down pointedly at him.

Moran may have been a more imposing physical presence, but he still wilted under O'Donnell's gaze. "I'm just saying," he said, shifting his legs around. Huffily, he took his Zippo lighter out of his pocket and started flicking it on and off, dancing his fingers through the flame.

Tommy stood leaning against the piano that nobody had played in twenty years, not since Tommy's ma had passed. He gave Moran a look that was hard to read. Tommy was always hard to read.

O'Donnell finished running the device up and down the last remaining wall before nodding an affirmative at Carter and going to stand by the fireplace. Tommy turned and switched on the jammer box that sat on top of the piano. Belt and braces. "Right, I'm calling this meeting to order. Let's keep this brief and to the point. Franko, how did the meeting go with our friends from the north?"

"Like clockwork, Tommy. I thought that prick Roberts was going to shit himself when he realised we'd taken out his boys."

"Did he say anything we didn't expect?"

Franko shook his head. "Nah. Usual demands of something for nothing. Thinking they're the big bad wolf. I've not heard anything back since, but I'll keep an ear out."

"OK. Good. From a security standpoint?"

Carter looked at O'Donnell, but it was Moran who answered. "Like a dream. Shower of amateurs didn't know what hit them. I swear..."

Moran stopped talking when he noticed the look on Tommy's face.

"John?"

"Yeah," said O'Donnell, "mostly fine."

"Mostly?"

O'Donnell glanced in Moran's direction. "Jimmy got into it with one of their boys, slapped him around a bit."

Moran leaned forward. "He was acting the maggot, Tommy."

Carter looked at O'Donnell again. "How much?"

O'Donnell shrugged. "Nothing big, but the guy will have gone to A&E."

"Big deal," said Moran.

Carter sighed. "Not a big deal, Jimmy, course not – but the fella's going to hospital. He's going to have visible damage, I assume. Questions will get asked. Even the Gardaí are smart enough to notice somebody with a smashed-up face. We don't want to advertise."

"It sends a message."

Carter didn't move as he spoke. Franko had always noticed that about him. He was unnervingly good at staying absolutely still. "The only messages we send are the ones I say we send. Is that absolutely clear?"

Franko watched Moran shift nervously under the younger man's calm gaze, before mumbling, "Yes, Tommy," and then going back to flicking his lighter.

Franko might have known Tommy Carter better than anyone outside of his immediate family, but even he had to be looking closely to see the flash of irritation that slipped across his otherwise unreadable face.

"Good. Now, how did it go with your friend after?"

Moran perked up. "Really well. Shipment is coming in Monday, 20:37 – just like we expected."

Franko ran his hand through his hair and puffed out his cheeks. "We can't move on that, Tommy, not with the heat on us."

Moran shrugged. "We can run circles around those clowns, what's the big deal? You going soft, Franko?"

"Blow it out your arse, Jimmy." Moran liked to lord his and O'Donnell's hard-man military stuff over Franko every chance he got and he was getting royally sick of it. Moran confused smart with scared way too much.

Moran made to respond but Tommy put his hand out to cut him off. "We don't have time for one of your pissing contests. Franko, how did your little trip go?"

Franko pulled two sheets of paper from under his jumper. "He got us a list of names but it cost double. Rozzers, even dirty ones, don't like giving up other rozzers." It had taken Franko half an hour to calm him down and get the names. Nothing worse than a bent copper with a sudden attack of conscience.

Tommy took the pages. "Good work. You took it out of petty cash?"

"Yeah, but . . ." Franko rubbed his hands together. "That pot is running low, after the expenses and the low return from the last job."

Tommy nodded. "Not a problem, we're good to—"

They were interrupted by a soft knock on the living room door. Tommy put a finger to his lips before raising his voice. "Yeah?"

Tommy's sister, Eimear, popped her head in, glancing nervously around the room. "Sorry, Tommy."

"That's alright, Eimear,' said Tommy, in a soft tone he reserved for his sister and nobody else, "it's only the lads."

They all nodded and smiled greetings at her. She flashed a brief smile, not looking in Franko's direction at all.

"Is everything OK?"

Eimear spoke somewhere north of a whisper but not by much. "I'm going to the cinema with Janet, is that alright?"

"Course. You've got money?"

She nodded.

"Grand. Ring me if you need a lift home."

She nodded again and quickly departed. They waited a few seconds and heard the front door open and close.

"She's awful quiet when we're around," said Moran. "I think she's got a crush on Johno!"

Moran's guffaw died in his throat as the cold eyes of both O'Donnell and Tommy bore down into him.

"Sorry, only messing. No disrespect."

Tommy fixed his gaze on Moran for a second longer and then moved to O'Donnell. "And your end?"

O'Donnell nodded. "All good. On schedule. Which means we need next week to happen or come up with something else fast."

"Don't worry," said Carter, tapping the sheets of paper in his hand, "there'll be a weakness and I'll find it. Just everyone stick to the plan and don't do anything stupid."

They all nodded.

"Now," said Carter, "who wants to see the video of the Garda Síochána's finest being beaten by a bunch of carol-singing twelve-year-olds?"

CHAPTER TWENTY-TWO

Simone looked around Charlie's bar for the third time. All the chairs were up on the tables, the toilet lights were off, the ashtrays were emptied. Noel was currently restocking the bar, having insisted he needed absolutely no assistance doing so.

"OK then," she said, loud enough to be heard over the clanking of bottles.

Noel's head reappeared over the bar and he shot her a smile. "Safe home."

"Right. Yeah. Good." She was nodding although she wasn't sure why. "I'll see you tomorrow then."

Noel looked up from the stock ledger where he was taking notes. "Yes, as already mentioned three times, you will." He said it with a smile.

It was her first night back working since the incident with Nathan Ryan. Noel had come around to the house the day after Bunny had. Or rather, Bernadette had finally allowed him to. He had been trying from the get-go, once he'd realised Simone's excuse of being ill was far from the whole truth. She had sat him down and calmly explained what had happened. He had been all apologies, despite none of it being his fault – at least as far as anyone but him was concerned. His jumble of tics and spasms throughout were so severe, it was hard to figure out where his opinion of Nathan Ryan stopped and the random swearing started. It'd taken both Bernadette and Simone to talk him down from going to the police. He had then inferred that he knew some people who could take care of Mr Ryan. Sister Bernadette had taken him out of the room and given him what Simone could only assume had been a very stern talking to. When he returned, he pointedly avoided the subject of vengeance.

She had been expecting him to insist on driving her home or putting her into a taxi, though she would have turned either offer down flat. She was determined to get back to life as normal. She was expecting him to at least insist on walking her to the top of the alley. As it happened, it seemed there was going to be no struggle on that front either. Simone was glad, and a little hurt.

"OK then," she said, before realising she had already said that. She turned to go, her handbag hanging from her shoulder, clutched tightly under her arm. It had been a gift from Bernadette, as had the can of homemade mace that sat inside it. Simone had made the mistake of expressing scepticism about the potency of such a thing. She had then been horrified when Bernadette had brought Freddy the milkman in and demonstrated it on him. It had taken over an hour for the man to regain both sight and composure. He'd sat at the kitchen table weeping burning tears and gasping as Bernadette had assured him he was doing the Lord's work.

Simone looked down. She had her sneakers on. She had her keys in her pocket. She had her bag. She had her mace. She opened the bag, looked at it, and then put the mace into the pocket of her coat instead. She closed her bag. She double-checked the keys and then looked at the door. A deep breath. First time is the hardest. Just get it done and move on with your life.

She opened the door.

Bunny McGarry was sitting on the stairs outside, looking at his watch. As she emerged, a large smile spread across his face. "How's it going?"

Simone stopped and looked at him. "What are you doing here?"

"I was just passing and that."

"Yeah, I call bullshit." She looked back into the bar to see Noel's silvery hair disappearing fractionally too slowly under the bar. "Look, I appreciate it and all, but I don't need an escort."

"Have I ever told you how much I enjoy a fried breakfast?"

Simone raised her eyebrows. "No, hard as it is to believe, that has never come up in conversation."

"Well, I do. The full Irish, mind. Black pudding. White pudding. Eggs. Sausages. Beans. Mushrooms. None of that fried tomato nonsense but – and this is a recent break with tradition – I will go the occasional hash brown; your nation's finest export, present company excepted."

"Thank you kindly, sir, but – does this have a point?"

"It does indeed. Ye see, I had my yearly Garda physical last week and this fella sits me down and tells me – wait for it – I'm fat."

Simone laid the southern accent on thickly. "Well, I do declare, the very impertinence of the man."

"Oh God, yeah, I'd have slapped him silly normally, but I was unwilling to put down my breakfast kebab. Anyhow, not to blind you with science, but it turns out sitting on your arse for twelve hours a day is bad for you. He wants me to cut down on the booze and the brekkie and start jogging."

"You don't strike me as a jogger."

"Exactly. Only time I run is after somebody, and they're going to regret making me do it, let me tell you." Bunny stood up. "So there we go."

Simone looked around. "Did I pass out there for a minute? I don't see any connection between what you just said and why you're here."

"Simple. I need some exercise, so every night I can, I'm walking from here to a street in Rathmines and back again."

"For the good of your health?"

"For the good of my health." He moved to the side and waved her through. "Now, you can walk behind me, in front of me, or to somewhere else entirely – but I am walking to Rathmines to a house full of batshit-crazy nuns."

Simone looked him up and down before smiling. "OK, but, just so you know there fella, I got a can of mace here, so you'd better behave yourself."

Bunny fell into step beside her as she walked up the slope. "Where'd you get that?"

"Sister Bernadette made it for me."

"Christ on a bike, she is one mental old battleaxe isn't she?"

Simone stopped as they turned the corner. She looked back. The alley stood behind them. Just an alley.

"Everything OK?" asked Bunny.

"Yeah, fine," she replied. "And I dare you to call Sister Bernadette that to her face."

"No thanks, I'd rather try the mace."

CHAPTER TWENTY-THREE

Bunny yawned expansively.

"Someone had a late night, I see."

He looked across at Gringo, sitting in the passenger seat next to him. "You're one to talk. Unless I'm very much mistaken, that's the same suit you wore yesterday."

"I was seeing a lady."

Bunny raised his eyebrows. "Is that right?"

"Yep. Two, in fact. Unfortunately, the other fella was seeing three nines."

Bunny shook his head in disapproval. "You'd want to start widening your range of hobbies."

"Look who's talking. Another late-night walk home with your southern belle, was it? You've been doing that for how many weeks now?"

"A few."

"Any luck in going beyond the walking stage yet?"

Bunny shifted in his seat. "'Tis not like that."

"Yeah," said Gringo, "just good friends. Have you looked at yourself recently?"

"What?"

"I'll tell you what. You're clean-shaven, you've lost at least a stone in weight and are you even hung over right now?"

"Course I am."

"Liar. My point is – you and I are good friends and I can't make you change your socks. You, amigo, are in love and you'd want to do something about it. Slow and steady is one thing, but even glaciers would think you're playing it a bit too cool."

Bunny rolled his eyes theatrically. "Here we go with more romantic advice from the master."

"I'm just saying – you like her, she likes you. It's not rocket science."

"She's not exactly had the best impression of men around these parts so far, 'twould seem rude to make advances."

"Oh for God's sake, Bunny, you're not Nathan Ryan and she, more than anyone, knows that."

"That snivelling gobshite would've been collecting his knackers from another postcode, if you'd let me—"

Gringo held his hands up. "Not this again. I let you do plenty to him. By the way, did I tell you I saw him a couple of nights ago?"

"Really? How was little Nathan?"

"Hard to say," said Gringo. "He just screamed and ran out the door."

"Well, I see him again and he'd better be running fast."

"You're like a messed-up version of Santa Claus, y'know that? Ohh!" Gringo drummed on the dashboard excitedly. "Speaking of which, in a manner of speaking – guess what? The Klan have their own version of Santa Claus!"

"Which clan?"

"The Klan, as in the Ku Klux Klan."

"The shower of racist fucknuggets running around with the pillowcases over their heads?"

"The very same," said Gringo with a nod. "I saw it on TV last week."

"Have you finally moved on from the end-of-the-world specials then?"

"This was on after a fascinating documentary on the Millennium Bug actually. Ask me what he's called."

"Who?"

"The Klan's version of Santa. Ask me what he's called."

"Maybe I don't want to know?"

Gringo pulled a face. "Just ask me."

"Why do—"

"Because," said Gringo, "this is how people communicate. You're going to have to work on your conversational skills if you ever want to sweep a certain lady off her feet."

"Didn't I tell you to shut up about that?"

"She's on your mind, I can tell. All that looking out the window and sighing plaintively."

Bunny waved his hands about in front of him. "We're sitting in a car doing surveillance, ye dozy gobshite. Not only have I no choice but to look out the window, it is what I'm actually supposed to be doing."

"All I'm saying is, you need a bit of coaching, to stop you being all, y'know – you. And I can help with that."

"And how is your divorce going, Gringo?"

"Low blow, amigo. You're embarrassed and you're lashing out. Would you like to talk about your feelings?"

Gringo was grinning across at him now. There seemed to be little he enjoyed more than winding Bunny up.

"My feelings? Ask me hole."

Gringo shook his head. "This is exactly what I'm talking about. You need to be polished up because you are currently a rough – very rough – diamond. I, as your colleague and friend, am willing to *My Fair Lady* the crap out of you."

"Very good of you."

"You're welcome. I'm not going to lie, there's a fair bit of work to do in the wardrobe and personal grooming stakes, but we should get cracking on the conversational skills issue as soon as possible."

"I see," said Bunny. "And your suggestion for a break-the-ice chat with a black girl is 'Howerya, love, did you know the Ku Klux Klan has its own version of Santa Claus?'"

"Ah," said Gringo, "yeah, I'd probably not open with that, alright."

"Oh, you think? Well, thanks very much Cyrano de-fecking-Bergerac – I'll give you a shout if your services are required."

There was a long pause as they both looked out their respective windows at the nothing that was continuing to happen outside.

Eventually, Bunny cracked first. "Well?"

"Well, what?" said Gringo.

Bunny glowered at him, but Gringo let the anticipation build until . . . "Klanta Klaus!"

"Feck off!"

"Seriously. They call him Klanta Klaus. He wears the Santa outfit with the hood."

"Christ on a motorbike. I bet he's dreaming of a very white Christmas."

"You're not wrong," laughed Gringo. "I'd imagine when he's making a list, he's only checking it once. He has a very simple system to cut down on admin there."

"What a shower of limp-dicked dog-botherers."

"Yep," said Gringo. "Ireland has its flaws, but at least we never had dickheads like that."

"True," responded Bunny, "Although I can't help but think the absence of almost any non-white people until very recently really helped to cut down on the racism."

"Fair point, amigo. Fair point."

Bunny reached back and shoved his hand into his bag on the back seat, fishing out the can of Diet Coke he'd brought with lunch.

"Aha!" said Gringo. "Diet! Busted! Look at you, looking after yourself."

"Would you ever shut up."

"It'll be stomach crunches and vegetable smoothies next."

"Would you—" Bunny was interrupted as the can of Diet Coke, which he had allowed insufficient time to settle, exploded upon opening and drenched his trousers. "Ara for feck's sake."

Gringo roared with laughter and applauded. "Fantastic! Bit premature there, amigo. Don't be embarrassed, happens to the best of us."

Bunny rubbed ineffectually with his hand at his trousers, already sticky to the touch.

"Shut up and get me a tissue or something, ye great scuttering gobshite."

Gringo started checking the glovebox as Bunny looked around on the back seat. He looked into his wing mirror as a car came around the corner at a rapid clip and halted with a yelp of screeching rubber on the opposite side of the road.

"Why's Dinny back?"

"Dunno," said Gringo, "but he's a new dad. Odds on he'll have tissues."

They had relieved Detectives Pamela "Butch" Cassidy and Dinny Muldoon at 8 am from what they'd described as a terminally dull night shift. Muldoon had hurried off to try and beat the morning rush hour home to help his missus with the twins. He'd been in a good mood the last time they saw him. Now his face was red and his neck muscles were straining, as if trying to keep his head from flying clean off.

"Maybe he . . ."

Bunny couldn't think of anything but that quickly became irrelevant. Dinny wasn't here to see them. He leaped out of his car and charged to Carter's front door, hammering on it loudly with his fist. "Carter!"

Bunny and Gringo exchanged a glance and then got out of the car.

"Dinny?" said Bunny, "What are you up to?"

He didn't turn around. Even from twenty yards away, the tension in his body was visible, fizzing through him like electricity. A couple of years on the beat taught any sensible copper to recognise the signs.

Carter's door was already opening as Bunny and Gringo broke into a run.

Tommy Carter's face appeared in the gap.

"No!" shouted Gringo, hopelessly late.

Dinny's right fist was already making contact with Carter's jaw as they made it onto the driveway.

The door flew open as Carter was sent sprawling backwards down his hallway, Dinny racing after him.

Gringo nipped through the door just before Bunny.

Dinny was standing over the supine figure of Carter, raining blows down with both hands. Carter had covered his face with his arms but otherwise made no effort to fight back.

Gringo grabbed Dinny's arms to stop the assault.

He was only five ten and whippet thin, but it still took both Gringo and Bunny to drag Dinny out of there, kicking and screaming. "I'll kill you, I'll kill you, I'll fucking kill you!"

When they finally got him outside. Bunny and Gringo let him go, only to have to hurl themselves in front of him again as he attempted to get back inside Carter's house.

Gringo got him in a bear hug and dragged him back to the opposite side of the road, where the Granada still sat, doors open.

Bunny looked around to see a few neighbours out on their steps, gawping. He turned and went back into the house. Tommy Carter still lay on the ground, calmly holding a handkerchief to stem the steady flow of blood from his nose. The beginnings of swelling could already be seen at the corner of his faint smile and under his right eye. Bunny glanced up to see Eimear standing at the top of the stairs, looking terrified.

"Officer," said Tommy, the hint of a smile on his lips, "I'd like to report that I have been assaulted and my life has been threatened."

"I see," said Bunny, a sinking feeling in the pit of his stomach. Bunny looked at Eimear. "And you have witnesses to this?"

Tommy smiled. "I don't need witnesses." He pointed over Bunny's shoulder.

Bunny turned to see the CCTV camera above the door, covering the hallway.

"You can't be too careful."

CHAPTER TWENTY-FOUR

Commissioner Gareth Ferguson stood in his dressing gown and slippers on the balcony, his long cigar clamped in his mouth. He glowered at the traffic below, as if it were personally responsible for all of the inconvenience in his life.

DI Fintan O'Rourke slid the balcony door open and stepped out to join him. Ferguson didn't turn around.

"Shut the bloody door, Fintan. Doctor Jacoby gets a whiff of cigar in his office and I'll never hear the end of it."

As O'Rourke carefully pulled the door closed, Ferguson took the cigar out of his mouth and looked at it. "Honest to Christ, it's only a bloody cigar. You'd think I was weeing on the man's carpet. Bloody doctors." He resumed puffing away.

"Yes, sir," said O'Rourke.

The hem of Ferguson's hospital gown flapped in the breeze under his dressing gown.

"I'm . . . Are you sure this is a good time for this, sir?"

Ferguson glanced briefly back at O'Rourke. "Trust me, Fintan, there is no good time for this chat."

"I know, sir, but, I mean . . . Can I say, I'm very sorry to hear of your . . ."

Ferguson turned to look at him, "My what?"

"Your medical condition, sir."

"Medical con—? Have you lost your damn mind, Fintan? What exactly do you think is wrong with me?"

"Well, sir, obviously you want to keep it private, which I entirely understand. I'm just sorry that . . ." Fintan flapped a hand in the direction of the office he had just walked through. Ferguson turned his eyes to heaven.

"Christ! One of our country's finest deductive minds at work. Look on my works, ye Mighty, and despair! I am here, Fintan, to get a benign cyst removed from my back. The reason I am standing on the balcony of the office of the country's premier neurologist is that his other half is my beloved wife's bridge partner and, having one of only two balconies in this Godforsaken sanctuary for sawbones, he agreed to allow me to use it to have a bloody cigar."

"Oh."

"Yes, so don't go popping your CV in for my job just yet. Do you know what a benign cyst is, Fintan?"

O'Rourke didn't answer, correctly guessing that it wouldn't be required.

"It is a lump of fatty, useless flesh that just sits there and does nothing except look unsightly. In that regard it is like the last Minister for Justice, as opposed to the current one, who is a cancerous little pimple that – unless removed – will one day kill us all."

Another gust of cold wind caused the hem of Ferguson's hospital gown to flap up again. He pulled his burgundy dressing gown tighter and spat on the floor.

"And why the hell do I have to wear this undignified thing with my arse hanging out the back? I'm not in theatre for another couple of hours. What, in the name of all that is good and holy, is wrong with me wearing my fine silk jimmy-jams in the meantime?" Ferguson stepped suddenly forward and looked down at O'Rourke. "Did you just smirk, Fintan?"

"No, sir."

"Any civilised man in his right mind knows that the pyjama is an unfairly-maligned suit of clothing. Well may ye sleep in your nudity beneath the eyes of the Lord, like Adam in the garden of Eden – but when your house burns down, remember lots of strapping firemen with big hoses shall be strutting by you and the missus while you stand there holding your worried little winky as your worldly possessions go up in smoke."

O'Rourke made sure his face was a mask of absolute sincerity. "Thank you for the advice, sir, I shall keep it in mind."

"Yes, you bloody should, Fintan – because I don't know if you've noticed, but your damn house is on fire."

Silence reigned for a few moments as Ferguson turned around and went back to staring at the traffic, flicking ash off the tip of his cigar to dance away on the winter breeze.

"How the hell did this happen?"

O'Rourke pulled a notebook he didn't need out of his pocket and referred to it. "At 8:43 am, Detective Dennis "Dinny" Muldoon returned home, having worked a twelve-hour surveillance shift on Tommy Carter. He found his wife, Theresa, in a highly distressed state. She had just entered the bedroom of their twin babies, Jack and Georgia, to discover two teddy bears with their heads cut off and knives shoved through their hearts."

"Christ!" said Ferguson.

"Someone had obviously broken in during the night. Theresa had been in the room at around 4:30 am to check on them and there hadn't been any signs of a disturbance. And, sir – just for context – I personally know that the Muldoons had been trying to have kids for years. She's had at least two miscarriages that I know of."

Ferguson moved the cigar around in his mouth and twirled his finger in the air in a signal to continue. O'Rourke looked down at his notes again.

"Detective Muldoon, understandably emotional, then immediately returned to Tommy Carter's residence and assaulted him before being restrained by Detective McGarry and Detective Sergeant Spain."

Ferguson pulled the cigar out of his mouth. "And what the bloody hell were they doing that they couldn't get to the man before he got to Carter?"

"Sir, they . . . it happened fast."

"Yes," said Ferguson, "I believe there is a video that attests to the ferocity of Muldoon's attack."

"Sir, can I—"

"No, Fintan, you can't. Muldoon is suspended indefinitely without pay."

"But, sir—"

"The blessed Garda Representative Association can – and will – kick up a fuss, and I've no doubt I'll have Sheila Appleton in my office tomorrow morning doing just that, but video killed the radio star, Fintan, and it may well do the same to Muldoon's career." Ferguson paused and looked up at the darkening skies. "Furthermore, your task force is no longer to carry out overt surveillance on Carter and his—"

O'Rourke stepped forward to push into Ferguson's eyeline. "Sir, you can't. This is exactly what he wants."

Ferguson turned, his bulk forcing O'Rourke to lean back. "And it is exactly what he gets."

"But it was them!"

"Of course it was them, Fintan, I'm not a bloody idiot. However, if you had even a shred of evidence linking Carter or one of his men to this gaudy bullshit with knives and teddy bears I'd have heard about it by now, wouldn't I? Or are you holding out on me?"

O'Rourke pursed his lips and shook his head.

"Then shut up and take your medicine. Either we pull everything off him and his chums or his solicitor gets that tape on the six o'clock news. The video kills us stone dead and you know it, so don't go throwing your toys out of the pram. You got played."

"But—"

"Pull the surveillance – now. You'll have to come up with some other way to get Carter and it'd better be a damn sight smarter than you've been so far. This isn't a shit storm so much as a tsunami."

Ferguson tossed his cigar butt over the ledge of the balcony and then ignored the plaintive "Oi!" that carried up from the street below.

"Either find some way to move forward – or abandon this entire investigation. Either way, move fast if you want to rescue the career you're so in love with."

O'Rourke looked at the concrete floor of the balcony and briefly considered hurling one of the potted plants as far as he could over the railing. "Yes, sir."

Ferguson tightened the belt on his dressing gown again. "Now, if you'll excuse me, I have to get a perfectly harmless lump of flesh gouged out of my back for no other reason than my sainted wife is sick of looking at it. To be honest, I think she's sick of the sight of all of me, but this bit she can do something about."

As he moved past, Ferguson stopped and lowered his voice. "If, in six months' time, Carter and Co are up on a host of charges and bang to rights, then suddenly Detective Muldoon's situation becomes a lot more manageable, and the media would be considerably more sympathetic to his plight. As of right now, well . . ."

"Yes, sir."

"In the meantime, put me down for two hundred in Muldoon's collection."

O'Rourke nodded.

"That's assuming I don't die at the hand of some overenthusiastic butcher boy in the meantime."

CHAPTER TWENTY-FIVE

The screech of car tyres made Simone jump, and she clutched reflexively at the mace in her coat pocket. Bunny's car, that awful 1980s Porsche that he loved so much, was pulled up at the kerb, the man himself trying to extricate himself from it. She still couldn't get over it. In many ways, she had never met a man less concerned with the superficial as Bunny McGarry, and yet he had this ludicrous car which seemed to be in the shop more often than not, and when it wasn't he was far too large a man to get out of it comfortably without the aid of a tin opener.

He moved quickly around the car, his face a picture of concern. "Sorry, sorry, sorry."

"What are you apologising for?"

"I was supposed to walk you home and I wasn't there."

"It's cool, don't worry about it. I'd totally forgotten you were going to." She hadn't. She'd waited around for twenty minutes in the biting December chill. He was normally set-your-watch reliable, and – much as she hated to admit it – she looked forward to the nights when he'd be there. They had become the highlight of her week. His no-show had put her in more of a bad mood than she'd let herself acknowledge. Tonight, of all nights. She'd taken it as a sign.

Bunny looked a little hurt. "Oh right, well, that's good then. Didn't want you worrying. Do you mind if I hop on board for the last couple of stops?"

Simone looked up the street. They were all of a hundred yards from the front door of the Dublin residence of the Sisters of the Saint. She nodded and they fell easily into step, walking in silence for a couple of seconds.

Simone looked up at Bunny, noticing the tightness in his face. "So what happened? You look stressed."

"Ah, I screwed up big time, the whole thing is bollocked to buggery. D'you remember Dinny Muldoon?"

"Was he the guy who helped you steal the goat?"

"No."

"The dude you dangled off O'Connell Bridge?"

"No."

"Don't tell me, don't tell me . . ." She stopped walking, biting her knuckle as she racked her brain. She didn't have that many stories she wanted to tell, but Bunny appeared to have an endless supply. Some of them he'd admittedly repeated, but they were so entertaining she had never minded. Simone clicked her fingers. "The guy you trained with. Y'all put him naked on the train to Belfast as part of his bachelor party?"

Bunny nodded sheepishly. "That's him."

Simone punched the air. "Yes! I passed the pop quiz." Then she noticed his expression. "Ehm, sorry. Is he OK?"

"No," said Bunny, as they started walking again. "He's suspended without pay. He beat the shite out of Tommy Carter. Gringo and I reacted too fecking slow. Couldn't stop him."

"But why would he do that?"

Bunny ran a hand through his hair and puffed out his cheeks. "He's got twin babies at home. Him and the missus had been trying forever. Came back to find her in a state. Someone had broken in, cut the throats of a couple of teddies as a threat."

"Jesus."

"Yeah. Fecking sick. Dinny lost it, just lost it. Came straight over and lamped Carter. Exactly what Carter was hoping for. Got the whole thing on tape. Carter's away and clear and Dinny's going to lose his job. All because we messed up."

"Sounds like you couldn't have known."

Bunny shook his head. "Could've, should've, would've. Been going over it again and again. I'm just coming from Dinny's house. His wife is saying maybe he should leave the force. He'd been in great form this morning when Gringo and I went to relieve them, having a bit of a crack about buying himself a shed at the weekend. Now . . ."

Simone gently placed a hand on his arm. "You can't save everybody, but I do love that you try."

They walked the final few steps to her gate in silence.

"Right, so. Well, the good news is I'd imagine Gringo and I will be back working days now, so I'll be in more often to see you sing. That's assuming I don't get transferred to Donegal as a punishment for messing up."

"Right."

"OK so. I'll probably see you tomorrow."

Bunny extended his arms for their nightly hug goodbye, but Simone placed her hand on his chest to stop him. She looked up into his eyes and then, before she could overthink it, grabbed his tie and pulled him down, drawing his lips to hers. She kissed him hard and then pulled away slightly. Bunny stood and looked down at her with a confused expression.

She started to straighten his tie.

"Shit the bed. What brought this on?"

She didn't look up, just continued straighten his already straight tie. "OK, well, for both our sakes, I'm going to pretend you said something considerably more romantic there."

"Right. Sorry. Yeah."

"And in answer to your question, ye big lug, I appreciate you being the perfect gentleman and all."

"Right."

"But outside of doing something involving tassels, I'm not sure how many more obvious signals I could send."

"I'm a clueless gobshite."

"OK, you should probably just let me do all the talking."

Silence.

"So here's the thing. A priest the sisters know over in Galway is retiring and he's having a party. So, they have all gone there for the night. Tonight . . ."

She ran her hands up and down his tie. "And I was wondering if you'd like to come in for coffee – and before you say anything else, understand that I know you don't drink coffee. So, what do you think?"

She pinched his tie nervously between her fingers. He said nothing.

He continued to say nothing.

Then she remembered she had told him to say nothing.

She looked up into his big, nervously grinning face. He nodded slowly and emphatically.

"OK then."

She grasped his hand in hers and turned, walking quickly down the drive. At the door, she stopped and started trying to locate the key in her bag. She could feel him standing close behind her, his body pressing lightly against hers.

She found the key.

Nervous, she missed the lock the first two times. He grabbed her hand and guided it in. She giggled.

She turned and pushed the door open with her ass while simultaneously reaching her arms up towards . . .

"There you are."

Simone screamed.

Bunny screamed.

A lamp at the end of the hallway turned on, casting light on Sister Bernadette, looking smaller than usual in the oversized armchair. "We're all fierce jumpy this evening."

"Sorry, Sister but what are you doing here? I mean, is everything OK?"

"The blasted car broke down, didn't it? I'm waiting for the AA man to have it fixed and dropped back."

Bunny spoke up. "Eh, Sister, they'd not do that at this time of the night."

She fixed him with a stare. "They do when I ask. Speaking of unexpected deliveries, what are you doing here, Detective McGarry?"

"I, uh, invited him in for a second,' said Simone. "Because you see . . . Noel has had to go away for a couple of days."

"Has he?"

"Yes, and . . . he asked me to flat-sit for him."

"He has cats," chipped in Bunny.

"Yes, cats. And, well, with you three being away, I thought it'd be better than being here on my own."

"We have a cat."

"Of course we do," nodded Simone, "but Brody is a very independent cat." Which was true – he showed up about once a week, peed on something and left. "Whereas Noel's cat . . ."

"Tiddles," said Bunny.

"Tiddles," repeated Simone, giving Bunny a look to indicate further help would not be required, "gets very lonely when Noel's gone. Starts howling."

"I see."

"So I was just grabbing a bag, and Bunny had kindly offered to give me a lift over."

"To the cat," said Bunny.

"To Noel's flat," continued Simone, "where I will be, y'know, taking care of the cat."

"Yes," said Sister Bernadette, "that all stacks up. Well done."

She stood and started walking towards the kitchen, mumbling to herself as she went. "Cat-sitting, is that what they're calling it these days? I don't know."

Simone turned to Bunny and pulled a face.

"Oh Christ," he said.

"Yeah, that was bad."

"Awful," agreed Bunny. "I mean, I was fine, but you're a terrible liar."

"Really? Now strikes you as a good time to crack wise?"

Bunny shook his head vigorously. "No, it definitely doesn't."

"Good."

"D'ye think Noel will mind you sleeping on his sofa?"

She punched him with a little more force than she intended, but no less than he deserved.

CHAPTER TWENTY-SIX

Ben Williams looked at his watch as the wheels of flight AI424 from Antwerp touched down: 8:37 pm – bang on time. He held up the walkie-talkie in his right hand. "Wheels down, on schedule. Be ready." He had another radio strapped to his belt that he could use to talk to ground control via an earpiece.

Ben was a security coordinator. His company moved hundreds of millions of pounds of stock a year and most of it he just monitored from the office, but this was special. The Antwerp flight came in once every six months and for the last seven years he hadn't missed one. It was too important. He'd tried to explain that to his wife, Mairead, but she had refused to see his side of things. Her birthday was her birthday and, while his was a movable feast, like when Karen from work had her hen weekend, it apparently did not work the other way around. That argument had happened last week, and in the five days since, life in the Williams' residence had been like living in Cold War Berlin. He reckoned his only way out of this doghouse, which he still didn't believe he deserved to be in, might involve going big and getting Mairead a diamond. The irony of this wasn't lost on him as he watched flight AI424 come to a stop at the end of the runway and begin its turn exactly on schedule. Its hold contained sixteen million pounds' worth of uncut diamonds. Twice a year, the raw materials for every jeweller in Ireland came through Dublin Airport and it was his job to see that it all ran smoothly.

It was a foolproof system. One van took the stones off the plane and into hangar 3, which had been prearranged to be completely clear. It was under armed guard, with nine members of the Garda Emergency Response Unit in attendance. There the diamonds were divided up and ferried by three armoured vans, each with two armed police escort cars, to their distribution centres around the country. That, of course, was the dangerous part of the operation, especially in light of recent events. This was why there were currently twelve vans in hangar 3. Nobody but him would know which were carrying actual diamonds and which just had empty cases in them. He'd like to see them get lucky on those odds. The bosses hadn't been happy about the extra expense, but nobody wanted to be accused of not doing enough should something go wrong.

When it came to meeting the plane, it would just be Ben and Peter Lovejoy, a long-serving driver, with Derek and Yvonne in the back of the van, two similarly long-serving security guards. For insurance reasons, nobody outside the company's employ could touch any of the boxes. The plane would be stopped in Holding Area Bravo, as that was the point in the airport where there was nothing but clear open ground for 700 metres in every direction. If a vehicle broke through the airport's outer fencing anywhere, the Garda ERU team currently stationed in hangar 3 could move to intercept long before they reached the plane. Once the perimeter had been confirmed as clear, Ben informed ground control, who in turn informed the pilot, who then opened the hold doors. In under two minutes, the van with the diamonds would be back in hangar 3 and under heavily armed guard. It happened so quickly, the passengers on board would not even notice. Clean. Seamless. Foolproof.

There was a beep in his earpiece as the female voice of ground control came through. "Flight AI424 in standby, you may approach."

Ben hit the button on the mic on his lapel. "Roger, control." Then he picked up the walkie-talkie for his team and the Gardaí. "We are go."

Peter Lovejoy started up the engine and pulled out. The head of the ERU team gave him a nod as they passed out of the hangar. Heaven help any member of airport staff who decided to go for a quick smoke behind hangar 3. They would end up staring down the barrel of a submachine gun before they'd opened the packet.

The van made its way across the tarmac and pulled up at the rear of the Fokker 100 idling in Holding Area Bravo. Ben got out and looked around. Nothing but grass and empty runway in all directions. The nearest buildings were half a mile away. Unless the Invisible Man had gone into the diamond robbery business, they were untouchable. His walkie-talkie crackled in his hand.

"Perimeter confirmed," said the head of the ERU team in his ear, who would have been informed in turn by the Garda spotters.

"Roger that," Ben said into his walkie-talkie, before hitting his lapel mic to the tower. "Control, we are go."

"Roger that."

Thirty seconds later, bang on schedule, the rear cargo doors on the plane began to open.

The first Ben knew that something was wrong was when he felt the muzzle of a gun pressing behind his ear.

"Move and you are dead." It didn't sound like a threat. It sounded like a statement of fact. As he stayed absolutely still, a latex-gloved hand ripped the earpiece from his ear and grabbed the walkie-talkie from his hand. While his captor remained behind him, another man in black assault gear – identical to that which the ERU guys were wearing – moved past him. He pointed a handgun through the passenger-side door at Peter Lovejoy.

"Stay perfectly still," said the voice behind Ben.

A thick vest was placed on him, knocking his glasses off his face as it was dragged roughly over his head. Without them, he was as blind as a damn bat. Dark, blurred shapes moved around him. The vest was heavy – too heavy. He knew what that meant. He tried to think clearly. The van was blocking his view of the ERU team, which meant they also could not see him. By now, someone would be getting suspicious – but how long until they moved? Ben hoped the two staff in the back of the van would stay where they were, the last thing this situation needed was a "have-a-go" hero. Gunfire would be nothing but bad news for many reasons, not least of which was that they were standing beneath a large plane, which would presumably still have quite a lot of fuel in it. Above all of these thoughts, one kept recurring again and again: these people could simply not be here. They had literally appeared out of thin air.

A piece of card appeared in front of Ben Williams's face and the voice spoke again. "Read."

"I . . . I can't see without my glasses."

There was the sound of movement and then his glasses were thrust roughly onto his head.

"Read," repeated the voice.

The voice was still behind him, presumably holding the gun. The second man was still covering Peter Lovejoy in the van. A third man in a balaclava and tactical assault gear was standing in front of him, holding the card in one hand and Ben's walkie-talkie in the other.

The gun nudged him on the back of the head again. Ben focused on the card.

"My name is Ben Williams." They knew his name – how did they know his name? "The jacket I am wearing contains six pounds of C-4. There is another twelve pounds of C-4 strapped to the armoured car. Both are on a dead man's trigger."

The man holding a gun on Peter Lovejoy held aloft his left hand, which contained a small cylindrical device, his thumb pressed down on the top of it.

"If the ERU leaves hangar 3 then my driver dies. If anyone attempts to approach the plane, first the driver dies, then the C-4 is detonated. This is not a bluff." Ben wasn't sure if he was supposed to say the next bit but the gun nudged him again. "Ehm, exhibit A."

Nothing happened for about five tense seconds, and then there was a percussive pop. In the left of his peripheral vision, Ben noticed a puff of smoke as a section of the airport's outer fence collapsed. A second later a Toyota HiAce van was through the gap and driving fast towards them.

The card was turned over. "Stand down. Call the bomb disposal unit. There are one hundred and fourteen passengers and crew on that plane. Do not test us."

The card disappeared from view and a hand pushed Ben towards the plane. Once directly underneath it, a cable-tie was cinched around his hands, cutting into his skin as he was attached to the rear landing gear. A few seconds later, just as the HiAce pulled up, he was joined by Peter Lovejoy who was cable-tied to the other wheel. He looked at the vest Ben was wearing. "Is that . . . ?"

Ben shushed him before he could say anything else. He didn't want to do anything to antagonise these men. That was the standard advice from the company. If involved in an "incident" – the word robbery was never used – you should comply with all requests, make no effort at resistance, and instead concentrate only on the safety of yourself and others, and on remembering everything you could to later help police. He had given that course to new staff two dozen times; although it didn't cover what to do with six pounds of C-4 strapped around you.

The driver of the HiAce, wearing a plastic moulded mask that distorted his face, opened its rear doors, revealing two motorbikes. He dropped a ramp and wheeled them out.

Meanwhile, two of the others were quickly moving the black cases containing the diamonds from the plane's hold into the van. In the middle of it all, the fourth man stood calmly with his hand in the air, holding down the trigger. It took them under sixty seconds to load the van.

Nineteen boxes; Ben counted them in by force of habit. He tried to notice other things. Anything. Most of all, he tried not to think about the vest.

The two loaders slammed the rear doors shut. One of them joined the driver in the front of the van, which instantly tore off towards the gap in the fence through which it had entered.

The other loader hopped onto one of the bikes, pulled a helmet on over his balaclava and tossed the trigger-man an identical one. He pulled it on while walking to the second bike, still holding his hand up the whole time. Ben found himself thinking that, by now, the man's arm must be getting tired.

The first motorbike roared off towards the fence.

Ben watched the trigger-man climb onto his bike and kick it into life. Then, for what seemed like an eternity, but may have only been a fraction of a second, he looked into the man's visored eyes. He pointed at the trigger, pressed something on the bottom of it, then casually tossed it towards Ben.

Ben never saw the last bike leave as he fainted.

CHAPTER TWENTY-SEVEN

"You have got to be kidding me?"

DI Fintan O'Rourke looked down into the hole again and then back up at Liam Bains, Dublin Airport's head of security, who looked like he was having the very worst day of his life. They were standing on the edge of Holding Area Bravo, a now empty airplane behind them, its 114 passengers and crew currently in an area inside the airport, giving what would no doubt be utterly useless statements to a hastily assembled team of officers. It had taken the bomb squad nineteen minutes to arrive and another forty to determine that, while the bomb jacket on Ben Williams did contain live C-4, most of the wiring was a complex series of red herrings.

Getting additional officers to the scene had been complicated by the surrounding gridlock. The two robbers who had departed on motorbikes had dropped a series of spikes on the roads in and out of the airport, causing a series of crashes and pile-ups. In the middle of one of these had been a Garda Emergency Response Unit. The Garda helicopter, meanwhile, being unable to fly directly into Dublin Airport's airspace, was currently in the process of looking for a white HiAce van in Dublin, a task that was not so much like trying to find a needle in a haystack as trying to find a piece of straw in a haystack.

The hole was about eight feet by three feet by four feet deep. Just enough of a shallow grave for Bains's career. O'Rourke shook his head again. "What the hell is it doing here?"

"Well," said Dublin Airport's soon to be ex-head of security, "we believe there was originally a hole here for drainage, but it wasn't this big. They must have widened it."

"How? When?"

Bains shrugged. "I don't know. Nobody looks at this area much. They might have been sneaking in and doing it over the space of months."

"And nobody saw anything?"

"It would have been at night."

"Right – because presumably, if it had been during the day, one of your eagle-eyed staff would definitely have spotted it."

Bains shrugged again. He had the demeanour of a man looking for machine-gun fire to walk into.

"Do I want to ask how they got into the hole this evening, with your staff and half the Garda ERU supposedly watching on?"

"The only way I can think of is that they must've got in last night and stayed there."

O'Rourke shook his head again. What? Seventeen hours at least, spent sitting quietly in a hole, waiting for the moment to strike? Who the hell had that level of patience? He didn't need an answer, he already knew.

"Sir?" He turned to see Detective Pamela Cassidy rushing towards him, holding out a phone. "Sir, you've got a call."

"No kidding, Cassidy. We just lost sixteen million quid's worth of diamonds. I've had lots of calls." He'd told the commissioner he'd update him in an hour; everyone else he was ignoring.

"Yes, sir, but you're going to want to take this one."

CHAPTER TWENTY-EIGHT

Bunny lay in bed and watched Simone's dainty finger swirling a circle in his chest hair.

"Promise me something," she said.

"What?"

"Never shave your chest."

Bunny looked down at his chest, an area he had previously paid absolutely no attention to – to the point he wouldn't have been able to pick it out in a police line-up. "Do fellas do that?"

"Some do."

"Why?"

"I have no earthly idea. I think it's to show off how big and strong they are."

"I prefer to do that in more fun ways."

Simone turned and placed her chin on his chest, beaming up at him. "Don't I know it!"

It had been six days since Simone had gone to "cat-sit for Noel". Since that first night, she had stayed at Bunny's house in Cabra. They'd slept in on that first morning, although there hadn't been much sleeping. She'd agreed to come back that night, as Noel's cat, if anything, was going to be even more lonely. From then on, it had just seemed natural for her to be there.

Tonight, they'd finally done the thing they had been dreading. Simone had gone back to Sister Bernadette and explained that she was going to stay with Bunny for a while. He had gone with her in a show of solidarity. Her reaction was not at all what they'd expected.

"Well, it's about damn time."

Bunny and Simone had looked at each other in surprise. "I mean," she had continued, "yes, yes – get married, have babies, all of that, and preferably in that order, but I've seen too much in my life to go telling you what to do with yourselves. Having said that – you, come with me."

She had pointed a crooked finger at Bunny, who had followed her into the kitchen. She'd closed the door behind them and turned to face him. Sister Assumpta was standing over the cooker, watching a large pot of potatoes boil. Bunny gave her a nervous glance, for fear she would start taking her clothes off again, but she seemed oddly entranced.

"Now," said Bernadette, "I've looked into you and you appear to be a good man. A man of honour and integrity. I appreciate your appreciation of natural justice."

Bunny nodded. He knew what she meant, but had never heard it called that before.

Bernadette pointed to the other side of the door. "She is a special girl who has been through some god-awful stuff."

"Exactly what—"

Bunny was stopped in his tracks by a sharply raised hand. "Whatever she chooses to tell you is entirely up to her. I am not a giddy-goose blabbermouth. Now, don't interrupt me again."

"Yes, Sister. Sorry, Sister."

"As I was saying, she's a good girl and she was in my care. I'm now trusting you to take that role on. You mess this up and you'll have me to answer to."

Bunny smiled down at her and patted her arm. "Don't worry, I promise I'll—"

He'd been cut off by Sister Bernadette picking up a carving knife from the table, with more speed than he'd have thought possible, and holding it in front of his eyes.

"Don't patronise me, ye big lump of ham. I've reduced men twice your size to jabbering wrecks."

Bunny's eyes had stayed focused entirely on the knife's blade as it hovered, perfectly still, in the centre of his vision. "Yes, Sister."

"I don't mean you remember her birthday and ask her how her day went. Her past is the past, and hopefully it remains that way, but if for any reason it doesn't, you need to take care of it."

"Yes, Sister."

"Good. Also, you owe me a favour."

"I do?"

"You do." The knife disappeared. "I'll tell you when I need you. I am often in need of a man with your skills. I'm glad we had this talk." She turned towards the kitchen door. "Also, don't forget her birthday. That's just basic common sense."

"Absolutely," said Bunny, and then made a mental note to ask Simone when her birthday was on the drive home. She'd been waiting in the hall, with a look of nervous excitement and one small suitcase.

And so it was tonight. They'd celebrated Simone moving in, without actually ever calling it that. They had been deliberately vague, for fear of verbiage somehow breaking the magic spell.

Simone kissed his chest and looked up at him. "Is there anything you'd like me to promise not to change?"

He rolled her over, his hand on her hip, until he was over her, supporting his own weight as he moved down to place kisses on her forehead, nose and lips. "Nothing. Change nothing. I love you just the way you are."

She looked away, the smile falling from her lips. "Don't." She pushed him gently away as she sat up, her back to him.

"What did I say?"

"Nothing, just . . ." She turned her head slightly, the light from the bedside lamp catching a watery glint in her left eye. "Think that, feel that, if you want, but . . . don't say that word, OK?"

He ran his hand down her back. "I didn't mean to upset you."

"It's not your fault, it's just . . . that's a very easy word for people to throw around, and I can't say it back. I mean . . ." She grabbed his hand with urgency. "Maybe one day, but you're going to have to be very patient with me. OK?"

Bunny sat up and placed his arms around her, enveloping her body in his. Then he brushed back her hair and gently kissed the scar that ran down the right side of her face. She put her hand on the back of his head, pulling him forward until his cheek rested next to hers. Her hot tears trickled down his face.

His mobile rang.

"Ara for feck's sake." Bunny looked at the display. "Work. They always did have an impeccable sense of timing."

She patted him on the cheek. "Get it. Check it isn't important."

Sighing, Bunny leaned back and grabbed the vibrating phone off the nightstand.

"Hello." Bunny listened in silence for about ten seconds. "I'll be right there."

CHAPTER TWENTY-NINE

Strobing police lights danced off the frosty ground as Bunny hurried down the pavement, as if barely resisting the urge to break into a sprint. He had been forced to park up on the North Strand, throwing the car onto the pavement in front of a billboard. Ossory Road was not able to cope with the traffic it was currently drawing, even with it being well past midnight now. Terraced houses, all in slightly different shades of red, lined the road on his left. On the far side was a grey stone wall, behind which lay the train tracks coming out of Connolly Station, and the Royal Canal.

The call had just said that DS Spain was involved in an operation and that an officer was down. Control had no information on casualties beyond that. Bunny had tried to ring Gringo a couple of dozen times in the ten minutes it'd taken him to dress, rush out the door and drive to the scene. No answer. Just the same cheery hello on Gringo's message, time and again.

It couldn't be. They weren't even supposed to be on duty. Since the task force had been scaled down, he and Gringo were back working out of Pearse Street, running down a series of burglaries up at the new apartment blocks on the Quays, as well as a few dozen other cases that had been pushed to one side in favour of the task force. None of this made sense.

He reached the police tape. A young, chubby-faced guard with a shock of blond hair put his hands out. Bunny produced his ID with one hand as he grabbed the tape with the other. The guard moved in front. "Sorry, sir, I'm under strict instructions. There's too many people in there. It is a closed scene."

Bunny looked down at the hand the uniform had placed on him. "Take your fecking hand off me now, or it'll be a closed casket."

The uniform squared up. "I have my orders."

"My partner is in there. So you can take your orders and—"

"It's fine," they both turned to see DI Fintan O'Rourke, a folder open in his hands and with a couple of Technical Bureau guys around him. "Let him in."

The uniform begrudgingly stepped aside. Bunny gave him a look and then nipped under the tape. O'Rourke didn't even look up. "He's over there." He indicated an ambulance sitting under the railway bridge. Bunny could see the back doors were open.

He walked past the metal gates to what appeared to be a small industrial estate. Its courtyard was crawling with yet more Technical Bureau staff in their white suits. The burned-out husk of a HiAce van stood in the centre of it.

Bunny walked around to the back of the ambulance to find Gringo perched on the edge, being examined by an EMT. He wore a dazed expression, and a blanket hung around his shoulders, over a light blue T-shirt with bloodstains down the front of it.

"Jesus," said Bunny. Gringo turned his head at his voice. "What in the shittin' hell?"

Gringo looked down, as if noticing the blood for the first time. "It's not mine, amigo." The EMT, a woman with short brown hair and tight lips, shot an annoyed glance in Bunny's direction.

"This," said Gringo, "is my work wife, doc. He worries about me."

"I'm not a doctor and you're not much of a patient." She turned to Bunny. "Tell him he has to go to the hospital to get checked out properly."

"I'm afraid he can't order me to do anything, doc, I outrank him. Can you give us a sec?"

She shook her head in exasperated disapproval. "Be quick." She grabbed her bag and moved around to the front of the ambulance.

Bunny looked at Gringo. "The feck I can't order you. You're going to the hospital or I'll put you there myself."

Gringo waved him away. "Honestly, I'm fine."

Bunny sat down on the rear foldout step beside him. "What in the hell happened?"

Gringo ran his fingers through his hair and blew out his cheeks. "Myself, O'Shea and Cunningham were out for a couple of drinks after work."

Gringo must have registered the look of surprise on Bunny's face. "What? I occasionally hang out with a couple of fellow officers. That's not that shocking, is it?"

"No, I just thought, what with the history between you and the ice maiden . . ."

Gringo waved it away. "Ah, she's OK, and Dara is great craic. You've been a tad busy with, y'know . . ." Gringo looked down and said nothing for quite some time, before holding his T-shirt out. "This is Dara's blood."

Bunny resisted the urge to speak, giving Gringo the time to get it out in his own words.

"We got the call, said there'd been a robbery out at the airport. Something about diamonds off an airplane, assault team, explosives. It had Carter and his boys written all over it. Dara and Jessica said they'd followed Franko Doyle, months ago, and he'd come to this industrial estate for no apparent reason. Like he was casing the place."

Bunny looked over at the metal gates that he'd passed; he could see the front of a print shop and a bike repair place from this angle.

"They'd thought it might be for a robbery, but they checked and there was nothing in there worth their while. Storage units full of cheap tat from pound shops, that sort of stuff. Anyway, after they hit the airport, Jessica figured, y'know, chance in a hundred, maybe this was where they'd be dumping a vehicle or something."

"So you got lucky?"

Gringo pointed down at his T-shirt. "Does it look like we got lucky?"

"Sorry."

"We got here and saw a van pulling through the gates. They were in the middle of torching it when we raced in, trying to take them by surprise. Dara was in front of me. Got shot in the chest. We returned fire. Shot one of them in the leg, I think. They got to their second car and were gone." He spoke in an emotionless monotone. "I held my hands over Dara's wound, tried to . . . y'know. There was an awful lot of blood."

"Ye tried your best."

Gringo gave a short, bitter laugh and looked over the grey stone wall. His voice came soft and distant. "Did I?"

"We'll nail those bastards for this."

"With what?" said Gringo. "We didn't even get a positive ID, they were wearing masks."

"You said one of them got shot, didn't ye?"

Gringo's forehead creased. "Yeah, they did. I think they did. It was, I dunno, it was . . ."

The sound of a cleared throat alerted them to the presence of DI Fintan O'Rourke. The look on his pale face gave Bunny a sinking feeling in the pit of his stomach. "The hospital just . . . Dara died in the ambulance."

Gringo put his head in his hands, clutching tufts of hair between his fingers, his eyes clenched shut.

DI O'Rourke turned to Bunny. "I'd like a moment alone with DS Spain, please, Bunny."

"Sure."

Bunny moved off towards the opposite end of the crime scene. Police tape was stretched across the road at the far side of the bridge, keeping back a couple of industrious freelance photographers and a few local looky-loos. He leaned against the wall and looked over at

Gringo and O'Rourke, deep in conversation – O'Rourke constantly scanning his surroundings, Gringo's eyes firmly on the ground.

Bunny turned and looked over the wall, at the railway lines lying empty, the canal crawling by like a motorist slowing down to take a gander at another poor soul's worst day. Bunny took a deep breath and tried to process all of this information.

His shock at Dara O'Shea's death was mixed with guilty relief at it not being Gringo. On the drive over, he'd imagined again and again being the one to tell Gringo's mother that her only son had been gunned down on the job.

Then there was his anger. He'd hang that little scrote Carter out to dry if it was the last thing he did.

A movement caught Bunny's eye. There was an abandoned shed on the sloping stretch of wasteland that connected the canal's edge to the higher railway tracks that crossed the bridge above his head. The figure was hard to make out – or at least it would have been if he hadn't already known who was living there.

Maybe she would have the answer to the biggest question that was playing on Bunny's mind. Why was Gringo lying to him?

CHAPTER THIRTY

Bunny knocked on the door of the shed. He'd had to walk around to the bridge and then down across the wasteland, there being no way over the canal directly from Ossory Road.

Silence.

"Mary, I know you're in there."

"Go away," came that familiar voice with its haughty tone. "A lady does not like to be disturbed."

"I'm sorry, Mary, but it's important. It's Bunny McGarry."

A sound of movement inside was followed by the door creaking open a couple of inches, Mary's eye peering out through the gap. Once ID had been achieved, she opened the door fully, running her hands over herself, checking she was still all there and that her tiara was in place. "Oh, Bunny, I do apologise. I did not realise it was you. I am not normally at home to a gentleman caller after dark. Would you mind terribly if I do not invite you in?"

Bunny glanced behind her. The shed was rammed with a cornucopia of shiny tat. A child's mobile dangled from the ceiling, and string held all manner of luminous detritus to the walls, the culmination of Magpie Mary's ceaseless years perusing the dumpsters of Dublin. The floor held a thin mattress, the only furnishing in the entire structure.

"Of course not," said Bunny. "It wouldn't be proper. Perhaps we could have a chat out here?"

Mary smiled nervously and nodded. "Indeed, one moment."

She produced two deckchairs that had seen better days from the side of the shed, unfolded them and set them out. Bunny carefully lowered himself into the one indicated, painfully aware that his bulk could be the straw that broke the camel's back.

Mary sat down opposite him. He noticed that, since he and Gringo had met her a couple of months ago on Mercer Street, she had added a glow-stick necklace to her outfit.

"I'm sorry, Mary, I've not seen you since you had to go to the hospital. I've been meaning to drop in to check on you."

Mary waved his concerns away. "That's quite alright, Bunny. It was very good of you and your associate to show such concern."

"Not at all, Mary," he said, producing his card from his pocket. "In fact, if you ever get any trouble like that from any gurriers, you give me a call. 'Tis a shocking state of affairs."

"Well, yes, although I must say the health service took excellent care of me. It is such a wonder. Whether it be you or I, or the least fortunate amongst us, they give the same excellent care to all. Fantastic."

"Absolutely," said Bunny, noting that Mary considered herself to be amongst the more fortunate.

"Speaking of which," said Mary, looking around herself in alarm, "where are my manners. Will you have a cup of tea?"

Bunny held his hands up. "Oh no, honestly, Mary, it's very late. No caffeine or I'll be up all night."

"If you're sure?"

"I am," said Bunny. He nodded to the flurry of activity still happening on Ossory Road, the patrol car lights still needlessly strobing into the night. "I'm sorry that your night's sleep will have been disturbed by all this."

"Well, yes," said Mary, "there has been quite the commotion."

Bunny nodded. "I was just wondering if, perhaps, you might have seen any of what went on earlier?"

Mary shifted nervously, causing her deckchair to squeak her discomfort. "I don't want to get involved in anything. While I have nothing but respect for you, my experiences of law enforcement in general have not been positive."

Bunny nodded his understanding. He and Gringo had had to step in a couple of years ago to stop two uniforms from evicting her from the shed when an overly-keen new manager down at Connolly Station had decided it was a misuse of Iarnród Éireann's land.

"I'm not here as a guard, Mary. I'm here as a friend." He held up his empty hands. "I'm not taking notes, this is just a chat."

"Well," she said, as if weighing things up, before they tipped in his favour. She leaned in closer, a gossip with a story to tell. "I did see rather a lot of it."

"Is that so?"

She nodded. "I was sitting here, as it happens, enjoying a nightcap."

She looked suddenly nervous, her face clouded by the inveterate drinker's fear.

"As you would," said Bunny. "Something to fend off the cold winter's chill."

She nodded her agreement, a smile of relief crossing her lips. "Indeed. Well, I noticed this van pulling into the industrial estate, and that struck me as unusual, late as it was. Then a minute later, all the banging noises started. I didn't know what it was at first. I thought it might be fireworks. Honestly, the children around here with those blasted fireworks they have at Halloween, you'd be afraid for your life. Demons, they are, pure demons! Why one time, it must have been three in the morning—"

Bunny reached his hand across and touched her on the arm. "Sorry, Mary, not to . . . It wasn't fireworks tonight though, was it?"

She nodded her head and then shook it. "No, it was gunfire. There was quite a bit of it, and some shouting. Some of the language was very uncouth. Then, a car, a blue car, comes hurtling out of there and speeds away up the road – driving very recklessly, I must say."

"I see," said Bunny. "And you're sure you saw nobody go in, between when the van went in and the blue car came out?"

"Oh no," said Mary, "nobody. Not until the lady ran out."

"A lady?"

"Yes," said Mary with a nod. "I was surprised when she pulled the balaclava off."

"What?"

Mary pulled a face at Bunny's shocked tone.

"Sorry, Mary. You were saying?"

"Well, yes. The lady, she had something in her hands. She ran down the road to a car there and then ran back up."

Bunny nodded. Jessica Cunningham. Why would she run back to her car while her partner lay bleeding out on the ground? First aid kit? Perhaps. Surely they'd have had their mobiles with them to ring for an ambulance?

"She came back," continued Mary, "and there were a few more bangs and then, a couple of minutes later, all the police and ambulances showed up. My Lord, the racket!"

Bunny, lost in thought, registered what she'd said a few seconds after she said it. "Wait, hang on – she came back in, and then there were more bangs? You're sure?"

Bunny must have let his tension show, as Mary shifted nervously. "Yes. That's right. I don't want any trouble now. I may have misremembered it. I hope I can trust your discretion in this matter?"

As Bunny spoke, he stared once more over the canal, the silent train tracks and the grey stone wall to the industrial estate beyond. Trying to tie the facts together in any other way than the direction they were pointing. "Yes, Mary, don't worry. This is just a chat between us. In fact, if anyone else comes asking, I'd suggest you say you were asleep and didn't see anything."

"If you think that is best?"

He stood and nodded. "I do. Sorry again for disturbing you."

"That's quite alright."

With a nod he turned and started walking back up the slope towards the tracks. Behind him, he could feel the presence of Ossory Road and its badly kept secrets weighing on his back.

CHAPTER THIRTY-ONE

Tommy Carter moved the armchair to face the window of the front room, sat down and waited. He'd expected to be picked up a couple of hours ago. He didn't know what to make of the fact that he hadn't been. DI O'Rourke was probably being careful. Making sure he had all his ducks in a row. They also now knew that Carter had his house covered by CCTV, and they'd probably correctly guessed that the others would have done the same. The Gardaí weren't going to fall for that trick again, although the tape of Detective Dinny Muldoon assaulting him would still come in handy. When the arrest came, he'd no doubt the officers would be the model of restraint, at least in his house. One of their own was dead; that changed the game.

He had barely slept last night and, when he had, his dreams had been fitful and filled with fire. He had woken to find Eimear standing in his doorway, looking terrified. He must have been worse than usual. His sheets were sweat-covered and his knuckles were bleeding from where he must have punched the wall. He assured her that he was fine and she had gone back to bed. Then he'd sat up, not wanting to return to sleep. Afraid to see O'Donnell consumed by the flames again.

The job itself had gone flawlessly. He, O'Donnell and Moran had waited it out in the hole exactly as planned. They'd had just enough room for one of them to stretch at a time. It had been torture but he'd put up with a lot for sixteen million quid in uncut, untraceable diamonds.

But the van dump had gone completely tits up and he was still trying to work out how. Franko had been driving, with O'Donnell in the back, opening the cases and extracting all the diamonds, exactly to plan. They had no intelligence to suggest there were tracers in the cases but they weren't taking any chances. They had set the incendiary in the van and were transferring to the clean vehicle when the ambush had come. O'Donnell had said it was three shooters, all in balaclavas. He'd put down one of his attackers but he'd been shot in the leg while doing so. Initially, Tommy had assumed the IRA had shown considerably more capacity for surprises than he'd credited them with. Then he'd picked it up on the Garda scanner: the industrial park on Ossory Road, a guard was down. Franko had hit the roof. They'd not identified themselves as Gardaí or made any attempt to make an arrest. Trying to rob a robber, was there anything lower? Still, thought Tommy, if they'd played it straight, there'd have been a heavily armed Emergency Response Unit waiting for them instead of three greedy little pigs, and not even O'Donnell could have shot his way out of that.

Franko had driven O'Donnell to the pick-up with Skinner. That had been the long-standing arrangement. A text to a burner phone and then whoever was injured would be delivered to Skinner wherever he specified. They wouldn't even know where the wounded man would be taken. That was for Skinner's protection. He was clean – no known connections to the crew and no criminal record. He had enough army medic training from his time in the British Forces to be able to give some field assistance. O'Donnell could lay low there and get better – assuming he was going to get better.

O'Donnell was a problem, but not Tommy's biggest. The cops had known where they'd be – only four people, including him, had known that. He'd tried to think of other ways around it but he kept coming back to the same thing: one of those four had talked.

The circle of trust had been broken.

There was movement amongst the numerous Garda vehicles that were congregated outside his house. Tommy caught a glimpse of a large posse heading up the drive.

Someone knocked loudly on the door.

"C'mon in, it's open."

CHAPTER THIRTY-TWO

DI Fintan O'Rourke dragged in a deep breath, puffed out his cheeks and then knocked on the door. He heard the sound of a throat being given a phlegmy and bombastic clearance, followed by Commissioner Gareth Ferguson's familiar boom: "Come in."

Ferguson sat behind his large oak desk, rolling a cigar back and forth in his fingers. He was wearing breeches, a tunic and a shirt with puffed sleeves. The ensemble was completed with leather boots, which were currently resting up on his desk. The commissioner had always had a distinctive sense of dress but this was still somewhat of a departure.

"Ah, Fintan. Excellent. You're tall. Be a good man and pick up that driver there."

The commissioner pointed at a golf club propped up against his bookcase. O'Rourke's look of confusion was met with an exasperated nod. "Get on with it."

Once he had grasped the club, the commissioner pointed up at the roof. "Now, as your commanding officer, I am ordering you to take out that bloody smoke alarm."

O'Rourke looked at the alarm, shrugged and then did as instructed. On the third swing it shattered, falling to the ground in three pieces, accompanied by a couple of golf-ball-sized chunks of plaster and a considerable smattering of dust.

"Good shot. Pull up a chair."

Ferguson pulled a decanter of whiskey from his desk drawer, along with two glasses, and poured them both a generous measure. "We were at a fancy dress ball, of all godforsaken things."

"I see, sir."

"Don't go for obsequious, Fintan, you can't pull it off. I, against my own protests, was Henry the bastard Eighth."

"Who was Mrs Ferguson?"

"Cleopatra."

"But . . ."

"Yes, I very much made that point too. My besainted decided she didn't like her original outfit so she changed. Leaving me in my ludicrous tights and whatever the hell else you call this stuff, playing at being a king while not even being allowed to dress myself."

Ferguson threw back half his whiskey and grimaced. He ran a hand around his face. "And the bloody glue for the beard irritates the skin like a bugger. I sent my new assistant home for a change of clothes, and you'll never guess what the snivelling shit did?"

O'Rourke shrugged. "Went home to his own house and came back in his dress uniform. I shit you not. Thought I was sending him home to smarten up. I don't care if the monosyllabic mummy's boy is the Minister for Agriculture's favourite nephew, I fired the little shit there and then."

"Yes, sir."

"He cried. I mean – there is no crying in policing, that goes without saying." Ferguson swished his drink around in his glass and looked into it as if seeking a divination of the future. "So that concludes the small-talk part of the evening. What in the blue blazes happened?"

"Well, sir, as you know, they hit a plane coming in from Antwerp. A twice-yearly flight where uncut diamonds are brought in. They knew everything – timings, procedures, the lot. They strapped a bomb vest on the Madigan's head of security and cuffed him to the undercarriage of the airplane. Bloody nightmare. They were in and out in two minutes."

"May I ask," said Ferguson, producing a crystal ashtray from another drawer in his desk, "where the hell was the heavily armed, highly trained Emergency Response Unit that I have repeatedly gone to the minister to ask for more money for?"

"The ones who were already present at the airport had to deal with the bomb situation, until the actual bomb squad could be mobilised."

"And?"

"And the rest got taken out with spikes spread on the roads in and out of the airport. That was done by the two members of the team who fled on motorbikes. They brought the whole thing to a standstill – it's a minor miracle nobody was killed in the chaos."

"Yes," said Ferguson, bitterly ripping off the top of his cigar with his teeth and spitting the nub into the bin. "What fucking luck. If these bastards – and let us dispense with the pretence that it might not be Carter and friends – got clean away, one of the many things I don't understand about this shitstorm is how three of your officers then ended up in a gunfight with them?"

O'Rourke swallowed. The "your" was not lost on him. He leaned forward in his seat, running his hand around the back of his neck. "They played a hunch, sir. They'd seen one of Carter's boys casing the location a few months ago, back when we were trying to covertly follow them. They happened to be nearby . . ."

"And why the hell didn't they call for backup?"

"No time, sir. They'd seen them go in, they knew they had the matter of a minute to make a call. For the record, I support their decision."

"Yes," said Ferguson, "well, I imagine we'll both have to spend quite a lot of time explaining that to an inquiry at some point. Charging in against former Army Rangers. Christ."

"Yes, sir. O'Shea caught one in the chest. One of the robbers took one in the leg, then they made good their escape."

Ferguson looked up at the ceiling. "So, can we nail these bastards? Can your officers identify them?"

"Well, yes and no. The raiders were wearing masks the whole time, so neither DS Cunningham nor DS Spain could make a positive ID, but, as I said, one of the raiders was shot in the leg. We just picked up Carter, Doyle and Moran from their houses. They returned a couple of hours ago, and no doubt they'll have a rock-solid, multiple-witness alibi for where they've been. That leaves O'Donnell, who's still out there somewhere, hopefully badly wounded and with nowhere to run. That's how we'll get them, sir."

"Yes," said Ferguson, "assuming Carter didn't put two in the back of his own man's head already."

O'Rourke said nothing. The possibility of that having happened had already occurred to him.

A silence descended on the room for a moment. Ferguson threw his legs off the desk and dragged his considerable bulk to his feet. He belched and then raised his glass. "Devane, Wallace, McCall, McGrath, Hodgson, Murphy, Laidlaw, Murphy again, Smith, Gallagher, O'Shea."

O'Rourke looked up at Ferguson in confusion.

The commissioner lowered his glass. "When you get this job, as you probably will one day, Fintan, those are the names that will haunt your every waking moment. They'll be there, to slip in and rain on the best of days. It's what this job does to you. Some of them will have died as part of a road accident while on duty, others dealing with some raving loon off his meds with a carving knife, or side-swiped by some idiot drunk who thought he could make a break for it rather than blow in a bloody bag. It doesn't matter, every one will be your fault, and I guarantee you, the names will be burned into your very soul."

O'Rourke stood and raised his glass. Ferguson repeated the list. "Devane, Wallace, McCall, McGrath, Hodgson, Murphy, Laidlaw, Murphy again, Smith, Gallagher, O'Shea." They both drank.

Ferguson placed his glass down, picked up his cigar and drew a lighter from his pocket.

"Tomorrow, you and I shall both go and see the widow, assuming she will allow it. Kids?"

O'Rourke nodded. "Two, sir – third on the way."

Ferguson went very quiet, staring at the goldfish bowl in the corner, which was minus a goldfish. Then he sparked his lighter and puffed the cigar into life. "Most of the time," he said around the cigar, "there's no one who you can assuage those voices with. No one to blame. Or if there is, it's some pathetic fool, and that offers no satisfaction. That is not the case this time."

Ferguson drew a long drag on his cigar and blew the smoke out slowly. "This time, I have someone to blame and a pound of flesh to extract. I got off the phone with the minister thirty minutes ago. I offered the snivelling little shit a choice – either we get carte blanche or else he has my resignation, and the assurance that I will go out ugly. He rang his daddy, the whining little weasel, and after some spiel in which he pretended he had some say in it, he gave us the green light."

Ferguson moved around his desk. "We go hard, Fintan, harder than Carter can possibly expect. Everyone they know, everyone they've ever met, we drag 'em in. That estate wants to provide alibis for their wayward sons, fine – but it comes at a cost. If any of them has so much as a parking ticket, they get the full service." Ferguson began jabbing his finger at the air, warming to his subject. "We squeeze and we squeeze until people are queuing up to rat these bastards out to save their own skins. The Irish public, ungrateful and gormless as they may often appear, will not stand for a member of An Garda Síochána being gunned down in the line of duty by some pathetic excuse of a man. We cry havoc, and let slip the dogs of war."

As if on cue, the battered smoke alarm on the floor issued a plaintive, beeping warble.

Ferguson stepped forward, and in one decisive stomp, obliterated it.

"In other words," he said, "Tommy Carter is going down."

CHAPTER THIRTY-THREE

Tara Flynn nervously polished a glass that didn't need it. She'd only been working in O'Hagan's for a week, but she liked the job and she wanted to keep it. Before this, she'd spent a miserable week as a waitress before getting fired, and a worse week as a barmaid in Deegan's – avoiding the wandering hands and paint-stripping halitosis of the owner, Phil – before she quit. This job she liked, and she wanted to break her previous record for employment longevity and make it to day number eight. The currently developing situation, however, might prevent that. They should have closed up and gone home an hour ago, but their "guest" was refusing to leave. Normally, he would have been slung out as soon as he'd tried to start a fight, but allowances had been made. Instead, they'd corralled him into the snug in the back bar and tried to get some coffee into him. Tara chewed her lip nervously. She shouldn't be in charge of coping with this, but Graham, the manager, had phoned in sick and she was the only member of bar staff on. That left just her and the two bouncers: Brian and his uncle Anthony. Brian had been all in favour of chucking their unwanted guest out, but his uncle had preached caution and given Tara the number to ring.

There was a bang on the door. Anthony got up, slid the bolts back and opened it. With a nod, the distinctive figure of Bunny McGarry strode in. She may have only worked there a week, but some men made an impression.

"Where is he?"

Tara pointed towards the snug, "Back there."

Bunny nodded.

"Yeah," said Brian, "and you'd want to tell him to mind his bleedin' manners or he's getting a slap."

Bunny was eye to eye with him before Brian could finish raising his pint to his lips. "Excuse me?"

Anthony rushed over, putting a placating hand on McGarry's arm. "Don't mind him, Bunny, he's only a stupid young fella." He glared at Brian. "He doesn't have the sense he was born with. I apologise."

Bunny looked at Anthony again, then nodded. He turned about on his heels and headed off in the direction of the snug. Once he'd departed, Anthony caught Brian with a vicious clout around the ear.

"What da f—?"

Anthony grabbed a handful of his nephew. "What did I tell you? They lost a man last night. Have a bit of common sense, would ye?"

Tara picked up another glass and gave it a cleaning it didn't need. This was turning into a long day.

"Well, look at the sorry state of ye."

Gringo looked up from staring balefully into the bottom of his empty pint glass. A pint of water and a cup of cold coffee sat untouched on the table beside him.

"Bunny!" he roared enthusiastically. "My amigo. Pull up a stool. Drinks for everybody!" He started pounding on the table.

"Think you've had enough there, fella. You look like something a wino threw up and felt all the better for being rid of."

"Well, I feel fantastic. Thanks for asking. Got a couple of free days' holiday – compassionate leave. That's what you get for having a perfectly good T-shirt ruined by Dara O'Shea's blood." He raised his glass. "Cheap at twice the price."

"You're drunk, and you're being an arsehole."

"Well now, look who's talking."

"Yeah, me, your best friend. And if you keep on like this, your only friend."

"Ha, with friends like you, who needs enemas." Gringo's voice was slurred and his eyes were glassy, his gaze wandering around the edges of the room.

"You're a hoot. Last I heard, you were in giving your official statement, then you disappeared. First I could find of you, you're here trying to start a fight with some student from Trinity College."

"Ah, that prick, ye should've seen him Bunny, just the face alone . . . Him and his face."

"Yeah, he sounds like a monster alright."

Gringo picked up his pint glass. "Can we get some bastard service here? Here, love, why don't you wiggle your fine arse over . . ."

Bunny slapped him across the face. Not hard, but enough to stop Gringo in his tracks.

"I'm not having that."

"Oh yes, I forgot, the mighty moral Bunny McGarry. Defender of ladies's virtue everywhere. Fuck you."

"Back at ye."

Gringo looked down at his empty glass a long moment, a slight tremor in his hand. "Go on, ask me."

"What?"

"You know what."

"Not here and not now," said Bunny.

"Why? Have ye somewhere else to be – or someone else to be in? Don't let me keep you."

Bunny sighed. "You need to listen to me now, Gringo. You don't have time for this."

"For what? I've got all the time in the world." He spread his arms out expansively and grinned a drunken grin.

Bunny thumped his fist on the table. "This! You don't have time for this shite. We've been here before. Hell, I could almost set my watch by it. These are the dark days, where you go down to this place and nobody can reach you. All I can do is follow you down and make sure you don't hurt yourself or someone else. And I'm fine with that, it's what friends are for, but I'm telling you, you don't have time for this bullshit now."

Gringo gave a drunken sneer. "Oh please, impart more of your wisdom, oh wise one. Think you're so clever." His voice became a sing-song. "I know something you don't know."

"Fantastic. Come on, we're going."

Gringo rubbed the pint glass over his forehead. "We're not going anywhere until you ask me the question."

"Like I said, not here and not now."

Gringo slammed the pint glass down on the table. "Yes here, and yes now. Let's really clear the air. It's going to be quite the evening. For me and you and your little black whore—"

Bunny reached across and grabbed Gringo by the shirt collar, pulling him roughly across the table and sending its contents crashing to the floor in a wet crescendo of breaking glass and crockery. "I know what you're doing. You don't mean any of this shite. You just want somebody to give you the kicking you think you deserve. Well, any more bollocks like that and I'll grant your wish. Now come on, we're going."

Bunny stood, grabbing Gringo under the arm. He turned and headed for the fire door down by the toilets. Tara peeked out of the serving hatch, a worried expression on her face. Bunny stopped momentarily. "Very sorry about this." He pulled a couple of notes from his pocket and slapped them onto the counter. "For the damages."

"Put it on my tab," said Gringo.

"He's not normally this much of a gobshite."

"I am, I just keep it hidden."

Bunny propelled Gringo down the hall, kicked open the fire door and hurled him out into the drizzling rain. Gringo staggered a few feet and then flopped against the skip, propping himself up on its grubby side. Bunny followed, slamming the fire door behind him.

"Look, Bunny, we're in an alley. This is where you do all your best work."

"You're not in the least bit amusing."

Gringo turned. "Maybe I'm not trying to be. Go on, ask me."

"I don't want to know."

"Ha. Like hell. I bet you already do. I saw that look in your eyes last night. Your big thick gorilla routine doesn't work on me, remember? I know you. You're smarter than you let on, and we both know you never let anything go. So go on, ask me."

"No."

"Go on. You have questions, I know you do. Whose idea was it? Cunningham's, that's whose. Well, at least she was the one who approached me . . ."

"Shut up, Gringo."

"Her and O'Shea. They knew – knew I was in trouble. I've . . . I can't pay my debts. I can't even pay the interest on my debts. I've a soon-to-be ex-wife and a mother who just won't die. And they have connections, you see. Cunningham knows things. Or at least, she knows a man who does."

"Why didn't you—"

Gringo kicked his foot back into the dumpster. "Oh for. . . why didn't I come to you? This! Because of this! This disappointed brother routine. I'm fucking sick of it."

"I'll tell you your problem, ye fecking idiot, you don't want help. You just want to see how badly you can fuck up."

Gringo staggered forward, close enough that Bunny could smell the stale-booze stench on his breath. "Well, I think I've finally found out. Our simple little ambush was going to get us sixteen million quid in uncut diamonds, clean and clear, while simultaneously taking down that shower of pricks – but it got us nothing but O'Shea dead and me and Cunningham looking at long stretches in prison."

"What did you expect? Why didn't you come to me and talk about this?"

"They wanted to, but I said . . . I said you'd never go for it. You're too moral." He almost spat the last word.

"And you're too stupid. I think you wanted to be caught. D'ye know how easy it was for me to find out? Magpie Mary lives over the canal, saw the whole fecking thing. Two minutes."

Gringo grabbed tufts of his hair in his hands, a moment of clarity amidst the drunken rage. "Oh Jesus."

"Relax. She only talked to me and I told her to keep schtum. Most of the rest of them will probably just dismiss her as some mad old loon. She's not exactly grade A witness material. She's not your problem – the forensics are your problem. I presume you've figured that out?"

Gringo said nothing, just looked at the hazy raindrops dancing on the surface of the puddle in the centre of the alley.

"Cunningham tried her best, I'll grant you that. When you were sitting there, getting covered in her partner's blood, she ran out to the car, didn't she? You couldn't ambush Carter's boys with your service weapons, obviously, so you had other guns, right?"

Gringo nodded.

"So, she ran back, dumped the dodgy ones and the balaclavas in her boot and grabbed your legal ones. Then you pop off a few rounds, because you can't be in a gunfight where you didn't shoot back. That'll muddy the water, but they're going to find more bullets than they've got explanations for. Did you honestly think that'd convince anyone for very long?"

"She said . . . We didn't expect . . ."

"O'Shea to get shot? No kidding. Carter's crew struck you as go-quietly types, did they?"

Gringo lowered his voice. "We had them cold. We knew where they were going to be, so we waited, but . . ."

"But what?"

"I had O'Donnell in my sights, clean shot, but I . . . I couldn't take the shot. And he fired, hit O'Shea. It's my fault."

Bunny lowered his voice. "No, no it isn't. O'Shea knew what he was getting himself into, and the lad who pulled the trigger is the one responsible. You're not a cold-blooded killer."

"Not like you, hey Bunny?"

Bunny looked hard at Gringo, his face twitching with barely suppressed rage. "Keep going the way you're going, Gringo, see what happens."

Gringo spat on the ground and leaned back drunkenly "Oh, I'm just getting warmed up. I'm going to get that bastard Carter, you see if I don't."

Bunny threw his hands up in the air. "Christ, Gringo, would you get a grip. Tomorrow morning, every copper in Dublin is after Carter and his boys. I just heard – they gave them nothing under interrogation and the searches produced zero, so they'll be let go. Ferguson personally gave the go ahead to squeeze the life out of them and anyone stupid enough to be in their general vicinity. If their story of how Gardaí tried to ambush them comes out, it'll be enough to get questions asked – and you two aren't going to have enough answers."

"Christ."

"So you need to stop feeling sorry for yourself, and start thinking. I'll try to help you but—"

"I don't need your help."

"Yeah, you're doing a super job on your own. Look at you, stinking drunk and drowning in self-pity. Part of you wanted this – you know that, right? You want to punish yourself because Daddy left you and Mummy didn't love you."

From anyone else, Bunny would have seen the punch coming. As it was, he only managed to turn his face at the last second, so the impact busted his lip as opposed to breaking his jaw. Gringo was spun around with the momentum of his own swing; Bunny kicked the legs from under him and Gringo landed messily in the large puddle.

"You finished? Or does baby want to continue with his stupid fecking tantrum?"

Gringo looked up at him, something in his expression that Bunny had never seen before. "Think you're so smart, don't you Bunny? You're as big a fuck-up as I am."

"I'm not the one with his arse in a puddle."

"No, you're the one fucking the murderer."

The words hung in the air, silent save for the patter of the rain, steadily increasing in ferocity.

Bunny looked down at Gringo, a confused buzzing in his ears. "What?"

"When she didn't want to press charges on Ryan, I got suspicious."

Bunny could feel an icy cold in his stomach. "What did you do?"

"Do?" he said, defiance in his voice now. "I looked out for you, that's what I did. I got that guy we know at the US Embassy, from the thing, to do some checks. Remember a couple of weeks ago when you were standing at the bar chatting to Simone and I took a picture? Well, that was me being a devious prick. I asked him to run it against their facial recognition. It came back with a partial match, but it was her. Simone Watson is actually Simone Delamere – she didn't even change her first name, for Christ's sake. Murdered a man last year in New York."

"And you just . . ." Bunny took a step towards Gringo, towering over him. His hands clenched into fists.

"I covered it up. Told the guy it was a fool's errand, we'd already definitively identified the woman in the picture as someone entirely different. Told him to get his computer checked."

"Right."

"What were you thinking? Or were you thinking at all? Wasn't your brain doing the driving, was it? Be honest – you didn't want to know. My screw-ups, you're all over. Hers, you'd rather not know."

"Shut up."

"I'm your friend for over a decade but you get laid once and that's all out the window, isn't it? With friends like you . . ."

Bunny looked down at Gringo. "You're full of crap."

"Am I?"

"I'm not your father, go find someone else to take your shitty life out on."

"Fuck you, amigo."

"Right back at you."

Bunny turned and walked towards the top of the alley, wiping the blood from his lip as he went. "We're done, Gringo. You hear me? Done."

"Good. The end is nigh, amigo, the end is nigh."

CHAPTER THIRTY-FOUR

"Ahh, crap." Simone pulled the oven door open to be greeted by a wash of acrid smoke. "God damn it." She waved her hand over the chicken, which was having its worst day since it had died.

She heard the front door open and close behind her. "Hey, babe, I know it's late but I thought I'd try my hand at cooking. Turns out I'm still no goddamn good at it." She tried to grab the baking tray and burned her thumb. "Damn it, damn it, damn it!"

Then the smoke alarm went off.

She grabbed a tea towel and used it to shove the oven closed before turning to flap furiously at the smoke alarm above her head.

Bunny walked into the kitchen behind her.

"Goddamn thing! The numbers on your dial, they aren't the same as they are back in the States. And then the thing, it didn't have things written in . . ."

As the warbling finally ceased, she dropped her arms to her sides and sighed melodramatically. "Ah, who am I kidding? I can't cook for shit."

She turned to Bunny, expecting his warm grin. Instead she was met by a sombre expression. "Baby, what happened to your lip?"

"Oh," said Bunny, raising his hand self-consciously.

"Who did that?"

"Gringo."

"What in the . . . ? That's a messed-up friendship you got going there."

"I think that title has fallen by the wayside now."

Simone tossed her tea towel onto the counter. "What in God's name is going on with you two? Is this to do with that poor guy getting shot last night?"

Bunny shook his head. "Look, sit down would you?" he said, pointing to the nearest chair beside the kitchen table.

"OK, but just let me—"

"Now." He seemed taken aback by the force in his own voice, and added, "Please, just . . ."

Simone took off the apron she was wearing and placed it on the table. She sat down, perched nervously on the edge of the chair.

Bunny drew in a deep breath. "You need to tell me what happened."

"What do you—"

"In New York. You need to tell me everything."

She shook her head. "No, I already said to you . . ."

Bunny closed his eyes for a moment and held his hand up. "I know and . . . I know. But after the thing with Ryan, Gringo got suspicious. He ran some checks."

Simone clenched her eyes tightly shut and lifted her face to the ceiling. "Oh God." She stood. "I have to go. I have to . . . They'll come looking for me." She stood up, looking from side to side, not knowing which way to turn. "Oh God, oh God, oh God."

Bunny moved forward and placed his hands on her arms. "Relax. Nobody's coming. He covered it up – nobody knows. But you need to explain to me. I can't protect you if I don't know what I'm protecting you from."

She looked up into his off-kilter eyes, full of sincerity. "You can't protect me from this."

"I can, I just . . . I know you're wanted for murder. Just, tell me. I'll listen, and whatever it is, I love you."

She looked away. "Please don't say that."

He placed his hand gently under her chin and turned her face towards him. "You don't have to say it back, but you can't stop me from saying it, alright?"

She pushed him gently away. "You should wait until you've got all the facts before calling that one."

She sat down on the edge of the seat again. He leaned back on the counter, and there, amidst the stench of burned chicken, she told him everything.

"I was born Simone Michele Delamere, New Orleans, Christmas Day 1969." She flashed a sad little smile. "I was supposed to change my first name, when I started working for Noel, but I . . . I didn't. I said I messed up but, in truth, it felt like my name was the only part of me I had left. Stupid, huh?"

"Not at all."

"I was the oldest of two girls. Momma died giving birth to Denise. Such a cruel thing, and left my daddy as a young widower who got old fast. He never really recovered. People were always telling me they were this dream couple. You'd see them when they went out dancing and think, *I want to be them*. I guess with Momma gone, Daddy had a hard time wanting to be at all. He wasn't a bad man, just broken. Drank too much and made bad decisions when he did. Ended up in jail. Came out different after the first jolt. Man like him was never meant for that, couldn't cope with it. Just sorta shut down, I guess."

Simone nervously smoothed invisible creases from the hem of her blue dress.

"We stayed with relatives off and on, but, as time went on, it was mostly us. Me and Denise, I mean. I was always looking out for her. Being Mommy, Daddy and big sister all rolled into one. It ain't no sob story, though. We did OK. We both loved music, and New Orleans has always been a town where you can sing for your supper. We started in the local gospel choirs and then as we got older we both sung in local bands, making a good living in the summer, picking up gigs in the French Quarter, singing for tourists. In between, we bussed at restaurants, waited tables, all the things that everybody does to scrape a living."

"Then, when I was twenty-four, something unexpected happened: a happy ending. Denise was singing in a band on those Mississippi cruises when she found her Prince Charming. Surrounded by sweet-talking, fast-living musicians, she fell for the geeky kid doing close-up magic. Card tricks round the tables, that kind of thing. Turned out she was the smart one all this time. Derek Wagner, from Minneapolis. He was an MIT graduate who dropped out of the rat race because he loved doing his magic more than anything. Well, until he met my sister." Simone's face spread into a soft grin. "You should see the way he looks at my Denise. Everybody should get looked at like that at least once in their life. His moon and stars. A beautiful thing. They're off somewhere in the Midwest last I heard. Fell out of touch since . . ."

She met Bunny's eyes briefly and then glanced quickly away, pushing herself back in the seat. "So there I was, twenty-four and suddenly, young, free and single. Nobody I needed to look after and no place I needed to be. Left with the scariest of things – the choice to do whatever the hell I wanted with my life. So, I upped sticks and headed to New York. Broadway!" She fanned her hands through the air, a sad smile playing across her lips. "Me and every other waitress in the five boroughs, right?" She picked up the tea towel to have something to do with her hands. "I mean, I was pretty good, to be fair. On the singing, I got some callback auditions, enough to keep the hope alive. But then they'd ask me to dance."

She moved her feet around as she spoke. "Heel, toe, step, step, twirl . . . I wasn't exactly a natural, so I tended bar, waitressed and went to classes. For that, and the acting. Strangest thing – I hear a song one time, I got it down. Could always just . . . y'know." She shrugged. "But you give me lines to learn . . . I mean, I wasn't awful, I just wasn't a natural. Worst way to be in some ways; just enough hope to keep you going, always something around the corner. So for four years, I kept going around corners, again and again. Never getting anywhere. The human body builds up a resistance to everything eventually – even hope. A girl I worked with got her big break and I found myself unable to be happy for her. I hated myself for it. It was a real low point. Thinking back, I dunno, maybe that contributed to . . ."

The tea towel was now knotted in her hands. She unfurled it and smoothed it out in her lap. "His name was James. He was charming, funny, handsome I guess. Seemed to know everybody, and yet, when he spoke to you, managed to make you feel like you were the only person in the world. He had big dreams, a sharp suit and not a dime to his name, but damn, could the man talk. He would set up that club, that agency, that bespoke butler service for Manhattan's high-flyers. He made you think that not just his dreams were possible, but yours too. We moved in together. He'd been sort of managing a bar, then he'd fallen out with the manager. I was still working though, so we were OK, mostly. Then he was investing in a club and we – he – needed seed capital. I was working two jobs, just for a while. He would soon be raking it in though and I'd be able to give up work, concentrate on my auditions. God, even saying it now, I know how damn stupid it all sounds. Believe me, it's harder to see when you're inside that bubble."

Simone stopped talking, looking down at the linoleum floor, lost in thought. Bunny let the moment stretch out and then he cleared his throat quietly. Simone looked up, a little startled, as if waking from a dream.

"So, James had always dabbled, y'know, with the drugs. Nothing big. He was a party boy. He did it because everyone was doing it. Well, except me. I tried a couple of times, but I couldn't relax. I'm the child of an alcoholic, and we go one of two ways: either we repeat the same destructive patterns or we shut all that down. Still, if he wanted to, now and then, no big deal, I didn't mind. Then the occasional Saturday night became every weekend, and soon enough, it was every day. Got bad when the club failed. It failed because he couldn't keep his shit together, and his response was to lose it all the more. At that point, I was working to pay his coke bills and I couldn't keep up. He was still talking the talk, but that was all it was by then. He started dealing, thinking he was a big, bad man. He was his own best customer though, and soon he ended up somewhere he couldn't talk his way out of. He met some truly bad men and found out he really wasn't one. And so he dealt the only thing he had left . . ." Simone paused and drew in a deep, shuddering breath. "Me."

In the periphery of her vision, she could see Bunny's feet moving towards her.

She raised a hand. "Don't . . . Please. Let me just get through this."

She watched his feet hesitate in the middle of the floor before retreating back to their position beside the counter. His voice was barely above a whisper. "OK."

"He came to tell me he was in real trouble. His hand was broken, which is just a taster apparently. These men were going to kill him unless I could help him. Just one time. A friend of these men knew a guy or – hell, I don't know the ins and outs. I don't even know if James really did. Long and short, there was a really rich guy, the Big Fish they called him, and he was going to be in town. He wanted a girl for the night. Discreet, he said. In other words, he didn't want a hooker. Some, I dunno, some kind of power trip thing, fuck knows. He liked having a woman he wasn't paying for, at least not directly. I'm told he's a little different and, long story short, either I do it or James ends up scattered in various pieces along the East River."

She stopped and rubbed the heel of her right hand into her eye. "And right there and then, like some switch is thrown, I looked at James and saw what he really was – a cheap piece of shit in a shiny suit. Maybe he was always that guy, I don't know, or maybe the sweet guy was still in there somewhere, lost. If he was, I couldn't just leave him to it. So I slept on it. I stared at the ceiling for the night and then I sat him down, said I'd do it on one condition. If I did this, he'd be out of my life for good, never see me again. I'd leave the city and he could not come looking for me. When he accepted the deal so readily, I saw just what I was to him. It was all set up for three days' time. I got sent some clothes, a certain bottle of perfume. Whatever. The night arrived, and some small part of me kept waiting for James to come to me, tell me not to go. Ask me to run away with him. Something.

Anything. I'd have gone too, even then, fool that I was. Instead, he picked me up to drive me there. He gave me a pill and told me to take it, said it'd make it all go by easier. In my head, I was thinking maybe it was like that *Indecent Proposal* film, y'know . . . But it wasn't. The man, he had certain . . . tastes."

She tasted bile in her throat as she said the word and wondered if she was actually going to be sick. She sensed Bunny tense but she couldn't look at him. She knew that she would cry and she'd sworn to herself that she would never cry over this again.

It was he who spoke next, his voice rasping. "What did—"

"No." Her voice was firm. "No. That door stays closed."

She placed the tea towel, folded neatly, onto the kitchen table. "The next day, I went home and booked a flight to New Orleans for two days' time. James was nowhere to be seen. Left his keys on the table, just like I asked. Next day, the men came. I'd never seen them before. Two of them. Grabbed me off the street outside my place and hauled me into a van. Took me to a warehouse. Turns out James and his friends had come up with a plan. Unbeknownst to me, they'd installed a camera in the room and had the whole night, all the . . . they had a recording of it. They were trying to blackmail the Big Fish. He'd been sent a copy of the tape that morning with a demand for . . . I don't know how much money it was about. How much they thought my humiliation was worth. Maybe I don't want to know."

A spark of anger flickered in her chest and she clung to it, because it was the best thing she had here. Being angry was so much better than the other options.

"The Big Fish, he wasn't happy about it, and these men were 'dealing with the problem'. They wanted to know where James was. I'd honestly have told them if I knew, but they didn't believe me. They beat me. They showed me the tape. They asked me why I was lying for that piece of shit. I swore that I wasn't. When they still didn't believe me, well . . ."

She raised her right hand and pushed her hair back, exposing the burned line of skin running down the right side of her face. "The main guy did this, with a poker he'd stuck in a fire."

She felt her stomach start to heave as the sense memory of the stench of burning skin came back to her. "Did it, he said, 'just to be sure'. I looked into his eyes as . . . You've never seen a man look so calm. I can still see those damn eyes."

She sensed Bunny trying to move towards her again but she waved him back. She did not want to be touched.

"The main guy, he went away to – I don't know, what do psychos like that do with the rest of their time, play chess in the park? Anyway, his assistant was just as nasty but nowhere near as bright. He tried to have a little fun with me on his own but he left the knife in his belt exposed. So I . . ." She held up her hands in front of her, as if to say that they had acted of their own accord. "Did I kill the son of a bitch? I suppose I did. I sure as hell stabbed him enough times, and if you want the truth, of all my many regrets, that ain't one. I survived. I did what had to be done. I left him gurgling on the floor, unlocked the chain around my ankle and ran, taking that damn tape with me, because I didn't want anybody, ever, seeing that again."

She rubbed her fingers up and down the edge of the table. "Somehow, bleeding, half-naked, I staggered through the streets. As I was running I realised I couldn't go home. Same with work. They'd find me. What friends I had didn't deserve me bringing this to their door. I had nowhere to go. I saw a church and I staggered in. Just to rest."

She took a deep breath and looked up at Bunny for the first time in what felt like the longest of times. There were tears on his cheeks.

"Then," she continued, "I woke up in a white room, thought I was dead. Wondered if I was in heaven. I remember thinking that I wouldn't have that many bandages in heaven. Then a little tiny nun walked in. She said I was in the care of the Sisters of the Saint. I'd never heard of them. I don't think many people have. After a couple of days, they showed me my picture in the paper. The article was saying I'd killed a man. So, when I couldn't think of anything better, I told them the truth."

"Couldn't you go to the police?"

She shook her head. "The sisters, they never fully explained it, but they've got some contacts. They made some careful enquiries and told me that going to the police was a very bad idea. The Big Fish had powerful friends."

"Christ."

"Yeah," said Simone. "So, a couple of weeks went by, and when I was mostly healed up, they slipped me onto a boat leaving Jersey in the middle of the night and I got slipped off again at the other end. Here. In Dublin."

She stood up. "So there you go. Now if you'll excuse me . . ."

He moved towards her again.

"No, don't."

But this time he wouldn't be stopped. He wrapped his arms around her and they stood there for the longest time, until her tears soaked through his shirt.

Eventually, she pushed him softly away and turned to go upstairs.

His voice was hoarse as he spoke. "I can protect you."

She stopped, nodded and tried to smile, before continuing on her way.

Then, as she walked up the stairs she spoke to him in a whisper not intended to be heard. "You can't save everybody, but I do love that you try."

CHAPTER THIRTY-FIVE

Tommy Carter took a long, hard look in the mirror. There were bags under his eyes. It had been a rough time for him, but appearances were important. He'd spent the majority of the last two days in an interrogation room, sticking to his story. They had released him late last night. He'd been surprised they hadn't been kept for the maximum seventy-two hours. Maybe the Gardaí were getting tired of receiving the same answers again and again. He'd rung Moran and Franko when he'd got home, and they'd both said they'd had a nice trip – code for nothing having happened under interrogation.

They'd had little time to talk about what had gone wrong on the job, but that didn't mean he hadn't been thinking about it. He'd also been wondering how to play this new development. If he used it right, he could end up with allies – albeit unwilling ones – amongst the very people who were trying to catch him.

But first he had to get through the next few days. He, and the other two, could expect 24-hour surveillance and a distinct change in approach. No carol singers were going to get them out from under this time. Still, it was just a matter of patience and will. They had waited them out before; they could do so again.

He glanced up the stairs to see Eimear looking sheepishly down at him.

"Y'all right, sis?"

"I need to go to college, Tommy, but there's guards outside."

He smiled his warmest smile. "Don't mind them, they're only interested in me. I'm heading out and then the coast will be clear. OK?"

She nodded and stepped back into her room.

Tommy gave himself one last scan in the mirror, turned and opened the front door.

There was a barrage of flashbulbs from about half a dozen cameras surrounding him. From behind the cameras came a clamour of voices: "Tommy, were you involved in the death of Garda O'Shea?" "Are you a gangster, Tommy?" "What do you think your father would say about your behaviour, Tommy?"

Tommy pushed through the throng. Four Garda cars were parked on the street, two on either side of the road. He was met at the top of his drive by Detective Pamela Cassidy, flanked by two uniformed Gardaí.

"Ah, Tommy, good morning, sir."

Tommy pointed behind him. "These people are trespassing on my property."

"Well," she said, looking all coy, "that's really a civil matter – unless you think they mean you harm?"

Tommy said nothing.

"I mean, you could ring the station, but we're really busy at the minute. There's a big manhunt on for a cop killer, maybe you've heard?"

One of the journalists interjected. "Where's John O'Donnell, Tommy?"

"That's a good question," said Cassidy, smiling sweetly. "Where is your friend John O'Donnell?"

Tommy didn't like how she said the word friend. He raised his voice. "As I've repeatedly told the Garda over the last two days of ceaseless harassment, I have no idea where John O'Donnell is. The last I heard, he was going rock climbing."

"I see. Do you think the bullet wound might make that tricky for him, Tommy?"

Tommy pushed forward down the path. He was going to keep to his normal routine – he didn't care how many police or vultures from the gutter press followed him. Two more guards began walking in front of him, as the rest of his unwanted entourage followed behind.

Across the road, he saw Bunny McGarry and DI Fintan O'Rourke leaning against the bonnet of one of the cars. He gave them a nod, and both nodded back.

"Anyway," continued Detective Cassidy, maintaining her cheerful tone, as though she was his PA informing him of the day's appointments, "I'm afraid a spot inspection has found that the rear wheels on your car are below specification, so that's a fine, and if you attempt to drive it in its current state, you will face a further fine of up to two thousand pounds and six months in jail. Oh, the Revenue have also asked me to inform you that all of your businesses – the cab companies, the launderette, the pub, the printers – are being audited. So books for the last five years will be required."

Tommy kept walking, maintaining a steady pace. This unusual parade was attracting more looks than normal, which was to be expected. When he tried to exchange smiles with some of the neighbours, though, to show everyone that all was well, that this was nothing he couldn't handle, he was greeted by averted eyes or scowls.

"By the way, Tommy, we don't want you to feel picked on, so everyone on the street is getting audited too. It's a new scheme the Revenue has. Also, a couple of your neighbours have been done for not having an up-to-date TV licence or car tax. Mr Jameson has been arrested for benefit fraud. Mrs Jameson has been arrested for assaulting the officer who was arresting Mr Jameson for benefit fraud . . ."

They had reached the corner of the street now.

"Oh, and by the way, if you're heading to the Leaping Trout pub for breakfast, it was closed down this morning for a rather long list of health code violations."

Tommy stopped, started walking, then stopped again. The cameras *clack, clack, clacked* around him.

"Do you not have anywhere else to go for breakfast, Tommy?" "Where's John O'Donnell having breakfast, Tommy?" "What does a cop killer have for breakfast, Tommy?"

Tommy reversed course, pushing his way back through the throng, past smirking journalists and Gardaí.

"Lost your appetite, Tommy?" asked Cassidy.

As he pushed through the crowd he could see Eimear at the far end of the road, hurrying for the bus stop with a couple of Gardaí and a handful of journalists in pursuit.

Tommy glared in the direction of O'Rourke, who shrugged. "You can't break the rules *and* set the rules, Tommy," he called out. "That's not how the game works."

Tommy turned around and extended his arms to the sides. "You're all supposed to be journalists, why not report some real news? Look at this – harassment by the state. Where are my human rights?"

"Didn't Dara O'Shea have rights, Tommy? What about his kids?" called out one of the reporters.

Tommy started pointing at all the Gardaí in turn. "And look at all this? How can the Gardaí justify all this expense, I wonder? Just to carry out a vendetta against an innocent man."

He looked over at DI O'Rourke, but it was McGarry who answered.

"*Civis Romanus sum*, Tommy. You just didn't realise until now who the Romans really are."

CHAPTER THIRTY-SIX

Jason Armstrong pressed the button to find his car in the underground car park. An electronic beep reminded him that his Audi was parked at the far end, behind the line of SUVs. The squash club was always busy at this time of the morning – people grabbing an early game or just using it as the location for a breakfast meeting. The membership to the Regency Club was inexplicably expensive to the outsider, given that the dimensions of a squash court were the same everywhere, but it was the other facilities that set it apart. It was popular amongst the diplomatic corps, none of whom were, of course, paying for their own memberships.

Jason was in a particularly good mood as he had just beaten Phillipe Albert from the French Embassy for the first time in two years. When it wasn't going his way, Albert had started yammering on about not feeling well, speculating that he was coming down with a virus. Typical French.

Dublin was an anomaly in terms of its importance to the US. It had, to be honest, almost no economic significance, and even less of a military one, yet it was still a big deal politically. It was the dotty old grandma of American politics. Every presidential candidate had to win its approval before they could even consider asking the electorate for its hand in marriage. As foreign postings went, Jason thought, the fact that everyone spoke English was a bonus, although not one that made up for the weather.

He tossed his squash gear into the trunk and then hopped into the driver's seat. Before he could put the keys into the ignition, the passenger door opened and a man slid into the seat beside him. He was wearing a fedora hat and sunglasses that a dreary Dublin day in December most definitely did not require. His skin was dark. If Jason had been forced to guess, he'd have said Cuban descent.

"What the—?"

"Mr Armstrong, there is no need to be alarmed."

The use of his name caused Jason to pause. "Who are you?"

"You are Mr Jason Armstrong, graduate of Yale Law School. Currently you are serving as assistant security attaché at the US embassy here in Dublin. You have a wife, Samantha, and two beautiful children, Jacob and Jemima."

"I know who I am, what I want to know is who you are and what the hell you are doing in my car?"

"Excellent questions. I would ask you to keep your voice down while I explain. We do not want to draw attention to ourselves."

"Oh don't we? How about you get the hell out of—"

Jason's words were cut off by an elbow being jammed down hard into his testicles, forcing him to double over as exquisite pain surged through his body. His head bounced off the steering wheel, causing the horn to issue a plaintive parp.

A hand guided him back to a seated position. "Up you get, that's it. Breathe. Breathe. Good boy."

Through tear-drenched vision, Jason looked at the man again, who was calmly smiling at him as if nothing had happened.

"Now, you keep quietly breathing there while I answer your questions. Firstly, who I am is unimportant, but if you would like a name then let us go with Mr Lopez. As for what I am? I am a man who fixes problems. A plumber, of sorts." He stopped and smiled to himself, as if the thought amused him. "I am here because I require your assistance."

"Fuck you." Jason hadn't meant to say that; the words had been involuntarily expelled from between his gritted teeth.

"I am going to pretend I didn't hear that. All I am asking for is a little courtesy towards a fellow American patriot. In particular, with regard to the matter of a certain Simone Delamere, who turned up when you did a search on a face and name last week."

"That was nothing. It was a case of mistaken identity."

"I see. Who asked you to do the search?"

"I'm not telling you that, you—"

This time, Mr Lopez grabbed Jason's fingers and held them in such a way that rods of pain shot up his left arm.

"Aghhh."

"You are making this unnecessarily difficult, Mr Armstrong. Now I have to do the vulgar thing." He pulled a brown envelope from his jacket pocket and tossed it onto the dashboard. "That is a series of pictures that were taken of you when you were down in Key Largo two years ago on a 'golfing trip'. But you're not golfing in those pictures, are you? No, you are having sex with someone who is not your wife. In fact, the someone in question is not even a woman, although he is wearing some of your wife's clothing, as are you. I'll admit, that's a new one to me, but I am not a man who judges, Mr Armstrong, I am just a man who fixes problems. You, for example, have the problem of these pictures existing. I will fix that for you, and all I ask in exchange is that you tell me everything about the person who expressed an interest in that woman. As long as you tell me everything you know, and ha – believe me, I can tell if you don't – then your problem will go away. In fact, I will open this door, leave your car and disappear from your life entirely, providing that the next words out of your mouth are the ones I want to hear. Do you understand?"

Jason Armstrong nodded.

"Excellent. I am so happy to hear that we can help each other get rid of these trifling problems. I do so hate problems. You may begin speaking – now."

CHAPTER THIRTY-SEVEN

Jimmy Moran looked out the window of his taxi as the city whooshed by in the rain. He'd asked the driver to deliberately go the long way around, just so they could go up the north side of the Quays. When they'd passed the point where they'd hit the security van a couple of months before, he'd popped his head out and waved at the three Garda cars following him. They'd stuck to him like glue for the last few days and he wanted to wind them up. They had managed to get the gym he went to closed down for some sort of "building code violation" bullshit. They could do what they liked – it'd take more than that to break him and Tommy Carter. Franko Doyle, on the other hand – well, Jimmy had been telling Carter for a long time that Franko was the weak link. If it had been Jimmy in the van that night instead of bloody Franko, O'Donnell would never have taken a hit. No doubt about it. The last Tommy had heard, he was recovering all right and, more importantly, the cops and all their searches hadn't got close to finding him. They had nothing.

That was not to say the last week hadn't been without its stresses. His ma's boyfriend, Rick, had been nailed for cheating on his benefits and she'd been done for stealing Sky TV with that dodgy dish Jimmy had got her for Christmas. The pigs were making a nuisance of themselves. It had also been over a week since Jimmy had last got his end away. He had a rule: never have sex in the three days before a job. He wanted to be sharp, on edge. And in the five days since, due to his permanent entourage, it'd not really been possible. He'd tried to convince Carol to come over but the cops outside had put her right off. She was on parole and didn't want any hassle. He'd phoned around, but nothing. That was why the text from Wendy had been so appreciated. She was only a six to look at but she was a wild one in the bedroom. A proper nine with the lights out. She'd even come up with a way he could get away from his chaperones. Jimmy was buzzing. He threw a rapid punch combo at the back of the passenger's seat in front of him.

"Hey!" said the taxi driver. "What are ye at?"

"Nothing, old fella. Relax."

The driver had already had a full-on freak-out when he'd arrived to pick Jimmy up and been greeted by his police escort. He'd tried to refuse to take Jimmy anywhere, but Jimmy had been having none of that and got in before the dude could drive off. Jimmy knew his rights. Couldn't chuck him without a reason.

Jimmy looked at the meter. Just ticking over seventeen quid. He opened his wallet and slid out a twenty note. They hit a red on the pedestrian lights coming off the Ha'penny Bridge – perfect. As the vehicle came to a halt, the door automatically unlocked. He watched the lights closely, still on red. A few boisterous lads on a night out and a couple, hand in hand, crossed the road, heading over the bridge towards Temple Bar. The green man changed to amber. He put his hand on the door handle. Red man. Jimmy shoved the door open while simultaneously tossing the cash into the front seat. "Thanks, ye miserable old prick."

He was gone. Running. Down Liffey Street, past the statue of the old ones sitting on a bench having a chat. Behind him, he could hear car doors opening and raised voices. As he turned the corner into the North Lotts, he glanced back to see three uniforms charging after him, but they were only just turning onto Liffey Street. He ran the twenty yards to the black metal gates of the Bachelors Walk

Apartments. He looked up and down. There it was, the key, just where Wendy had said it'd be, dangling from a piece of thread at the top of the gate. He ripped it down and quickly stepped across to the pedestrian entrance.

In. Open. Shut.

He stood on the other side, just out of reach as the three uniforms slammed against it.

Jimmy Moran laughed heartily. "Look at the state of ye!"

"Open this gate."

"Or what? Sorry, boys, I'm off for a night's riding and you are not invited."

He thrust his hips a couple of times and then bowed. As he turned and walked into the internal courtyard, he could hear one of the cops yammering into his radio. "Subject is in the Bachelors Walk apartments. . ."

He moved quickly. It wouldn't be long before they buzzed a number on the intercom and somebody didn't think the "This is the Gardaí, open up" line was bullshit.

He rushed across to the door she had told him about and found it propped open with a rock. He kicked it away and closed the door behind him. She was on the fourth floor but he didn't bother with the lift. He was buzzing. He'd fucked the police and he was about to fuck her.

At the top of the stairs he turned right. Like she'd said, the door was open. That'd been her last text. *Remember, 416 – the door will be open. I'll be in the bedroom waiting!*

He slammed through the door, rubbing his hands together, and was down the hall in two strides. He pushed open the bedroom door.

There she was, on the bed, tied up. Gagged. Blindfolded. Wendy you kinky b...

That she was still fully clothed barely had time to register before he heard the click behind him. He knew the sound instantly.

"Don't move," said a Northern voice.

At the far side of the room, the wardrobe door opened and a man in a balaclava stepped out, a gun in his hand too.

On the bed, reacting to the noise around her, Wendy gave a plaintive mumble through her gag. The man in the balaclava looked down at her, without his gun veering an inch from Jimmy.

"Relax there, love, it'll be over soon." The man stepped forward and addressed Jimmy directly. "Take three steps back into the sitting room. Try anything and you're a dead man."

Jimmy did as instructed. He could hear the man behind him moving back too, staying far enough away to prevent Jimmy trying anything. Two guns to zero; his odds weren't great.

As he stepped into the front room, the second man spoke again. "Against the wall."

"Who the—"

"Against the wall. Now."

Jimmy moved back. The wardrobe man nodded at his compatriot, who took his balaclava off.

"Remember me, do you Jimmy?"

It took him a moment, but he did. The last time he had seen him, Jimmy had been tying him to a tree in the Phoenix Park, giving him a few slaps because he didn't like his attitude.

The wardrobe man took his balaclava off now too. Him, Jimmy recognised straight away. Paul Roberts, the IRA boy. The last time Jimmy had seen him had been through the sights of a sniper rifle.

"It was my nephew's birthday last week, so I decided to get him you."

Jimmy looked around as casually as he could. Scanning for anything he could use. "You know Tommy Carter will have you both for this, don't ye?"

Roberts laughed. "Oh, Jimmy, who the fuck do you think set this little date up? We don't know what skanks you're banging."

"Look at his face," said the nephew, "he's only just getting it. Beautiful."

"Why don't you go and f—"

In a couple of hours, neighbours would describe the thump of the body hitting the floor and how they dismissed it as somebody just moving furniture.

CHAPTER THIRTY-EIGHT

DI Fintan O'Rourke walked down the driveway, gravel crunching beneath his feet. He nodded at the Garda protection detail sitting outside in their car and then rang the doorbell. He had been summoned. In fact, "summoned" was putting it mildly. He had received a voicemail full of screamed invectives that added up to a very detailed description of the unusual and entirely unpleasant acts that Ireland's highest-ranking Garda officer was going to perform upon him, his ancestors and at least one family pet.

O'Rourke braced himself as the door opened. He was prepared for everything up to – and including – actual physical assault. What he was not prepared for was a petite blonde lady with a kindly smile and a glass of ice.

"Hello. You must be DI O'Rourke. Have I got that right?"

"Yes, hello. I take it you are Mrs Ferguson?"

She nodded. "Well, somebody has to be. He's down at the end of the back garden. I sent him down there to that god-awful hot tub he insisted on putting in last year. I do it when the swearing and gesticulating get too much. I'm not having him breaking another vase."

"I see."

"This way, he can smoke his awful cigars and I can pretend not to know. I will warn you, Gubby is in quite the mood."

Gubby? The commissioner was known by many names, none of them complimentary, but that was a new one to O'Rourke.

Mrs Ferguson pushed the glass of ice towards him. "Here, take this. He'll need it for the bottle of whiskey I also don't know about. You can go around the side of the house. The gate is open."

"Right."

"Oh, and announce yourself as you do. He's been drinking and he does have that frightful gun thing of his with him."

She smiled and closed the door. O'Rourke remained looking at it for a moment, then down at the glass of ice in his hand. It hadn't been a great day and it seemed unlikely it would be getting better any time soon.

He walked around the house, which was large and well appointed, situated in Seapoint. With the security light on, he could see that it had finely manicured lawns, with several playful gnomes sprinkled around the place. He was guessing that was more Mrs Ferguson's touch than the commissioner's, although who knew what "Gubby" got up to at the weekend.

O'Rourke walked down the side passage, which opened up onto a large rear lawn, surrounded by deciduous trees that sloped down to a gazebo containing a hot tub.

"Ahem . . . hello Commissioner. It's DI O'Rourke, sir."

"Who? I know an O'Rourke but I'm pretty sure I demoted him back to uniform about an hour ago."

"Yes, sir. May I come down?"

"Yes, yes, get on with it."

As O'Rourke started to walk down, another security light flared into life above his head, illuminating the entirety of the back garden. More gnomes stood stock-still, as if interrupted in the midst of nefarious doings.

As he approached the hot tub, O'Rourke could confirm that in its bubbling waters sat the Garda commissioner, a cigar in one hand, a glass of whiskey in the other and a look on his face that wouldn't so much kill as wipe out an entire village. He also noted what appeared to be an air rifle leaning against the hot tub. He felt rather thankful that his boss was a keen drinker and smoker who only had two hands.

"Ah, Fintan, how good of you to join me. Thank you oh so very much for taking time out of your busy schedule."

O'Rourke decided that saying nothing was the best course of action, to allow, as much as possible, Hurricane Ferguson to blow itself out.

"I'm sure you've been very busy," Ferguson continued. "I know I have. I've had the Minister for Justice on three times, the Taoiseach himself, not to mention every bloody journalist in Ireland. They've all somehow got hold of my private mobile number."

"Yes, sir."

"I'd probably still be getting calls, only . . ."

Ferguson transferred his glass of whiskey to the hand that already held his cigar, and then reached into the water and pulled out a mobile phone. "Surprisingly robust little blighter. Harder to drown than you'd think."

Ferguson threw the phone off into the darkness. The security light behind O'Rourke shut off, leaving the underwater lighting of the hot tub as the only illumination.

"I see you've brought your own drink."

O'Rourke looked down at the forgotten glass of ice in his hand. "Sorry, sir," he said, holding it out. "Your wife sent this ice down, for your whiskey."

Ferguson shook his head. "Bloody woman, knows everything. It's not natural." He leaned forward, grabbed two of the ice cubes and dropped them into his glass. Then he picked up the bottle of Jameson from the edge of the hot tub and poured a large measure into both his glass and the one in Fintan's hand.

"Cheers," said O'Rourke, on instinct.

"What the—? Bloody cheek." Ferguson snatched the glass out of his hands. "Christ, you misread that situation. No drinkies for you."

O'Rourke could feel himself blush as Ferguson downed the first of the whiskeys. He drew a long puff on his cigar and O'Rourke waited as he blew a smoke ring into the cold night sky.

"So," Ferguson said eventually, "how exactly does an individual under blanket surveillance – unprecedented surveillance, surveillance that in all probability breaches the Geneva Convention on human rights – how, in the name of thundering Christ, does that individual get shot dead?"

"Well—"

"And not by some eagle-eyed sniper, mind you. No, at close range by someone standing as near as I, the soon-to-be-ex-commissioner of the Garda Síochána, am to you, the soon-to-be most overly-qualified traffic warden in history. How on earth is that allowed to happen?"

"Obviously, there were serious errors on our side."

"Ye think?"

"We have recovered his phone. It appears that the attackers had taken the woman hostage earlier in the day and then lured Moran there with a series of text messages from her phone that promised him intercourse, in rather graphic terms."

"Really? Was an orgy mentioned, because that's what happened isn't it? He got fucked, we got fucked and, I assure you, your beloved career is looking well and truly on the monumentally fucked side of life."

Ferguson took a sip of his second drink. "An hour ago, the Minister for Justice ordered me to pull you off the case and then, once the headlines have moved on, accept your resignation."

"Yes, sir."

"I told the minister to shove it up his well-upholstered arse. It seems my career and yours are now inextricably linked."

"Thank you, sir."

"Don't. The wife wants me to take early retirement and go on a trip around the godforsaken Mediterranean on a bloody boat. This may be my masochistic way of giving her what she wants." He stopped to take another sip. "I get seasick."

O'Rourke had no idea what to say to that.

"Do we have any idea who did this?"

"Not as such, sir, no, but it is very early days. There was some chatter about Carter having fallen out with the IRA. Then there is his long-standing unpopularity with the drug-dealing gangs over his family's control of the Clanavale Estate."

"Do we think anyone knows the thing we haven't said? About Carter's imminent move from being gamekeeper to poacher in that regard?"

"If they do know, they're not saying much."

"By the way, in order to save your sorry arse, I did have to promise the Taoiseach that we were weeks away from the biggest drugs bust in Irish history, not to mention making the bastard Yanks very happy. So that'd better happen. That is the only thing we've got going for us. If your intel on Carter's next move is wrong—"

"It isn't, sir."

"You'd better be right. The chance of having his belly tickled by the Yanks for striking a blow in their ludicrous drugs war is the only thing stopping the T from firing us both. Personally, I think kowtowing to the damn Yankees is degrading, but nobody wants my opinion – only my job."

O'Rourke turned around as the security light behind him came on again.

Ferguson's voice dropped to a whisper. "Speak of the devil! Out of the way, Fintan."

O'Rourke sat down on a plastic lawn chair as Ferguson knocked back his whiskey and then reached for his air rifle. He scanned the area and saw a grey squirrel looking around nervously as it haltingly scurried across the lawn.

"Little grey Yankee bastards. Coming over here, wiping out the ginger natives, then scoffing the nuts out of my bird feeder." O'Rourke heard the soft slosh of water behind him as the commissioner drew himself carefully up onto his feet in the hot tub.

"You know there's a thing you can get—" O'Rourke had made the mistake of turning around and he turned quickly back again.

His boss was drawing a bead on the grey squirrel as it surreptitiously glanced around at the base of the bird-feeding table.

However, that wasn't what had caused O'Rourke's consternation. It appeared his boss enjoyed hot-tubbing naked. He had just made unfortunate eye-to-eye contact with the most senior penis in Irish law enforcement.

O'Rourke focused all of his attention on the bird table. The squirrel had made his way to the top of it.

"The trick is . . ." said Ferguson in a whisper around his still-clenched cigar, "to get the little bastard when he least expects . . . it."

On "it", several things happened: Mrs Ferguson opened the patio doors, which spooked the squirrel into running, which forced Commissioner Ferguson to hastily try to reacquire his target, which led to an overcompensation and the commissioner, who, in his defence, was really very drunk by this point, shooting one of the columns of his own gazebo, resulting in a ricochet, a surprisingly girlish squeal and a very undignified fall from the hot tub.

There then followed a small amount of blood and a large amount of swearing.

CHAPTER THIRTY-NINE

Simone wrung the mop out and then slapped it down onto the floor with considerably more force than necessary. It had been a long day, following a sleepless night that she'd spent staying absolutely still, sensing Bunny beside her in the bed, awake too and wanting to talk. She'd kept her eyes closed and her breathing low. As far as she was concerned, she had done more talking the night before than she had ever wanted to.

Her every instinct told her to run. It was what she had always known she would have to do. Dublin was only ever supposed to be the first stop. As she'd sat in that shipping container for two weeks, reading the same three books until the torch's batteries failed, she'd thought of little else. She'd learn French. A non-English speaking country was always going to be safer. The French loved their jazz too; it was where Lady Day had had some of her best times. She could find a little bar in the middle of nowhere and . . .

Do what she was doing now. She looked around Charlie's Private Members' Club. Damn, she really did love it here. Even the name. Noel had explained that he'd picked it because nobody would go to a jazz bar called Noel's. It was small, smelly, had three areas of persistent mould and a Ladies toilet that didn't work properly for more than a week at a time. She had never been supposed to sing, she was just employed to tend the bar. Then, as Noel had played one afternoon, she had been humming along softly to *Cry Me A River*. At least, she thought she'd been humming. Noel had finished the song and looked at her with those eyes, full of that look of childlike excitement that she'd come to know so well. "You didn't tell me you could sing?"

And she had; she had broken that rule. She had let herself believe that it was OK now. It had been almost a year. They probably thought she was dead.

It wasn't the only one of her rules she had broken. The last thing she had wanted was a relationship. Bunny – that had been the biggest mistake. He had . . . what? Crept up on her? Hardly. He'd clearly announced his intentions. She'd been so damn confident, thought he'd just been a charming distraction. Then he had gotten under her skin.

If she could go back in time and talk to her younger self – and Lord, how many times had she imagined she could do just that – there was so much she would say. If she had the chance to say one thing though, it would be "Don't mistake fireworks for fire." That was what James had been. Bright colourful lights and explosions that generated no heat. Love at first sight wasn't love at all; it was just biology. Fire was a different thing. It warmed you against the cold and illuminated your way on the darkest of nights. That was Bunny, the brightest part of her day. Her warmth. She liked being with him. She liked who she was when she was with him. That was why she couldn't leave. She wanted to. Needed to. Every fibre of her being was screaming for her to do just that, but she couldn't. Damn it all to hell. She lov—

Her train of thought was interrupted by a bang on the door.

It was 2 pm; the only person wanting to get into Charlie's this early would be its owner.

"You promised you were definitely going to see the accountant this after—"

Simone opened the door and froze.

The eyes from her nightmares looked back at her.

He shouldered through the door, sending her sprawling back onto the floor.

"Hola, Simone. Nice to see you again. Please do not scream, you know how I do so hate problems."

CHAPTER FORTY

Despite the church being empty, save for one old dear up near the altar working her fingers around a set of rosary beads, DS Jessica Cunningham sat on one of the angled pews on the side. This allowed her an unfettered view of the back and side doors. She had been here for over two hours – long enough that she had already had to politely bat off a couple of enquiries from the nice old priest to check if everything was okay, one approach to see if she'd like a nice cup of tea and another of an offer of confession.

The confession had briefly tempted her but she had politely declined. While watching the doors, though, she had offered up half-remembered prayers for the soul of Dara O'Shea. They had never been friends, at least not in the conventional sense, but they'd worked together for several years. Long enough that they'd insisted she take a few days off after the trauma of his death. She had been able to kick up the pretence of a struggle, despite the time off being exactly what she needed. Not to grieve, although she was sad for Dara and his family, but because they had needed time to think and rework the plan. Everything had gone to hell but it was salvageable. She'd have help.

Franko Doyle came through the back doors, nearly knocking over a stand full of pamphlets in his efforts to remain unseen. He clocked her, blessed himself the wrong way and then moved up the central aisle towards her. She had picked the location carefully. Franko stood out like a sore thumb, precisely because nobody would expect him to be in a church at 11 am on a Tuesday morning. That meant there was no chance of anyone seeing them together – which was precisely the point.

Franko dipped his knee towards the altar in a half-arsed genuflection and then slipped into the seat beside her.

"Christ almighty," said Franko. "This is fucking ridiculous, do you know that?"

"Keep your voice down and mind your language. Remember where you are."

"Remember where I am?!"

The old woman at the front of the church looked around with a frown. Franko looked down sheepishly and repeated himself in a softer voice. "Remember where I am? Do you have any idea what I had to go through to get here?"

She glanced at him briefly. "How did you get here?"

"How did I . . . I went to the GP and then nipped out of the window in the toilets, cut myself an' all," he said, lifting his right arm to show a blood-red stain seeping through the dark blue of his Dublin GAA tracksuit top. "I'm going to need one of them Tetris shots now. I wouldn't have made it out at all, only a couple of smackheads kicked off in the reception."

"That was lucky."

"Not really. I'd had a word. Your half-dozen piggies in uniform that were following me ain't exactly the brightest."

Cunningham turned and gave him a sharp look. "Mind your manners."

"Mind me . . . Are you kidding? After your screw-up?" Franko shook his head in disbelief. "You were supposed to hold us up and nick the diamonds, not start a bleeding shoot-out at the O.K. Corral. It's a miracle I'm still alive."

Cunningham thought it unlikely that anyone's god would waste a miracle on someone like Franko Doyle, but she kept that to herself. "Things didn't go to plan."

"If that isn't the mother of all understatements. You've messed this up totally." Franko shook his head. "Totally."

"Calm down, Franko. Our agreement is exactly as it was."

"How do you figure that?"

"You just need to tell us when and where the deal is going down—"

"No way!" The old woman glanced around again but this time Franko didn't lower his tone. "You're off your rocker."

"Tell us when, we'll intercept Carter and the diamonds and we all get taken care of."

"Bollocks."

Franko was prevented from any further speech by the elbow that dug into his ribs, knocking the breath from his lungs.

Cunningham gave a polite wave to the old lady even as she spoke through gritted teeth. "Calm down and stop acting like a damn baby. Remember why you're doing this."

Franko held his hand to his left side, in a way that Cunningham considered rather OTT. When he spoke, it was at the requested lower volume. "I don't want drugs on the street. Me and Tommy's da—"

"Oh please," said Cunningham. "Lie to yourself all you like but don't waste my time. You'll do whatever I say, because when Eimear Carter was nearly fifteen, her Auntie Jenny took her on a shopping trip to London."

"Don't—"

She ploughed on. "Only it wasn't that, was it, Franko? She was getting an abortion. She was a scared kid. Didn't want to tell her dad, it'd break his heart. Didn't want to tell her brother, as he would break the entire world, seeking the bloodiest of vengeance against the man who'd defiled his beloved baby sister."

She pulled a brown envelope from her pocket. "I've still got the paperwork if you'd like to see it? Where a scared fourteen-year-old girl misunderstood a question and named you as the father."

"That wa—"

"A mistake, yes, you said."

"How do you even have that? Them things are private."

"A friend in MI5 owed me a favour."

Franko scratched at his scalp irritably, sending a light snowstorm of dandruff down onto his tracksuit top. "That's a violation of my civil rights."

"Oh please."

"It wasn't like you think."

"I don't care, but best of luck explaining it to Tommy Carter. A man who, as a teenager, broke the arms of a guy who tried to touch his sister. *Tried*. You must believe he's mellowed an awful lot since then to consider not doing everything I tell you to. And you must believe that he's suddenly developed a sense of humour about who tipped us off – seeing as last night, by my reckoning, he had the person he thought it was killed. Are we all caught up now?"

Franko drummed his fingers on the pew. "You think you're untouchable, don't you, Cunningham? What if I went to the press, told them what really went down. They'd love –"

Franko stopped speaking. He held his breath and stayed perfectly still. The sharp blade of a knife poking into his scrotum will do that to any man.

"Listen carefully, Franko. Don't you ever try and threaten me, or I will do my gender a great service. The scariest person you know is Tommy Carter, but I'm a close second. Think about that before you speak again. Now, there's a mobile phone in a bag under your seat. It has one number in it. When you know the time and place for the deal with the Mexicans, you text it to that number, then you destroy the phone. Do that, and you and your beloved manhood might make it to Christmas. Am I absolutely clear?"

Franko nodded slowly.

"Then go in peace to love and serve the Lord."

CHAPTER FORTY-ONE

Bunny McGarry stood on the sideline while sixteen twelve-year-old boys looked up at him with a mix of awe, fear and incomprehension.

"Hurling is a simple game, lads. It's about two things: focus and determination. And skill, obviously. Three things."

"And fitness, boss." Deccie, the sub-cum-assistant manager, piped in.

"OK, four things: focus, determination, skill and fitness."

"And discipline, boss."

"And discipline, of course. Focus, determination, skill, fitness and discipline. Those five things."

"And teamwork, boss."

"For Jesus' sake, Deccie, where are you getting this stuff from?"

"You, boss. You said that last week. Teamwork – you did a whole big speech on it."

"That's right, I did. OK, it's about those six things: focus, skill, fitness, discipline, teamwork and . . . What was the other one?"

A voice from the back: "Intelligence."

"Phil Nellis, you stay out of this. I never said intelligence."

"Actually, boss, ye did," said Deccie, "you did a whole thing about it on the bus home a couple of weeks ago."

A clamour of voices rose up from the huddle in agreement.

"Alright, fine," said Bunny. "Them seven things."

"And being respectful to women."

"What?" said Bunny, his exasperation growing, "I never said that!"

"No, he's right, boss, ye did."

"I mean, I know I did, but that was more of a life lesson than a thing particular to hurling."

"You also said always wash your bollocks."

"Now hang on," said Bunny. "Hold your horses. I mentioned the importance of personal hygiene, but don't go around telling people I said anything about the state of anybody's bollocks. That's the kind of thing that can be entirely misconstrued. What I was saying was—"

Bunny was interrupted by the referee in the centre of the pitch blowing the whistle to get the teams out for the second half. "Ah, for God's sake. My point was . . . emh, Deccie, what was my point?"

"Give the ball to Paulie."

"Well yes, do that. Go get 'em lads."

The ragtag bunch of players scampered out onto the field.

"Deccie, I worry our team talks aren't hitting the spot."

"It's the lads, boss, they lack an appreciation of . . ."

Bunny joined in: "The fundamentals of the game. Right as always, Deccie. How are we nine games unbeaten?"

"Cause Paul Mulchrone is fucking deadly at hurling, boss."

"You're not wrong, Deccie, but go easy on the swearing."

"You've sworn ninety-seven times in this game so far, boss."

"I most certainly have not."

"I've been counting, boss."

"Why are you doing that?"

"We're running a book on it. Fifty pence a man, closest guess gets the lot."

"Why the hell are ye telling me this? Wait, no, don't say it. I'm a detective. What was your guess?"

"A hundred, boss."

"You're a devious little fecker, Deccie, d'ye know that?"

"Ninety-eight. Go easy, boss, we've the whole second half to go yet."

Deccie turned to look behind them and then tugged at the sleeve of Bunny's tracksuit. "Boss, the five-oh's here again."

"The what?"

"The po-po. The fuzz."

Bunny looked down and placed a hand on Deccie's shoulder. "Do we have to have the chat about the dangers of drugs again? You promised me you'd have no more to do with that reprobate cousin of yours."

Deccie shook the hand off. "What am I supposed to call them, boss? You said not to say pigs."

Bunny turned to see DI Fintan O'Rourke standing behind him. "Oh, for feck's sake."

"Ninety-nine."

"Right, that's it, Deccie. Give me a lap."

Deccie clutched his hands to his chest, his face all wounded innocence. "What did I do?"

"You're a smart lad. You'll figure it out while you're running."

Deccie mumbled something unintelligible.

"I heard that," said Bunny. "And think of it this way: you won't be able to hear me swear from the other side of the pitch."

"Are you mad? People can hear you swear from space, boss."

Deccie started running down the sideline at an unexpectedly fast pace, putting him just out of the reach of Bunny's lunge. Behind them, the ref threw the ball in, and it quickly made its way to the skinny little kid that O'Rourke recognised from the last time as Paulie Mulchrone. Three of his opponents ran into each other in a vain attempt to tackle him. He soloed and then unleashed a shot of such ferocity that the opposition goalie dived out of the way of it.

"GOAL!" screamed Bunny. "See lads – that's what I'm talking about. Focus, fitness, determination, teamwork, skill, intelligence and discipline."

"And he's got very clean bollocks."

"I heard that, Deccie! Two laps!"

O'Rourke cleared his throat loudly.

Bunny looked behind him in irritation. "It's Sunday, the day of rest."

"You don't look what I'd call 'relaxed'."

"That's because it's my day off and my boss just turned up."

"Well," said O'Rourke, stepping forward, "I've been informed that you've taken yourself off my task force, which means I'm no longer your boss."

"I decided it wasn't for me."

"What the hell are you on about?"

"All this strong-arm stuff. Not my bag."

"Really? If you prefer a more subtle form of policing then those fitness reports of yours I've read have been very misleading."

"Look," said Bunny, "I've never as much as taken a sick day in my whole time on the job. I'll be in tomorrow, working my normal caseload. There are lots of other crimes happening that don't involve Tommy Carter."

"This'd be the same Tommy Carter whose crew killed one of my officers last week and tried to kill your partner?"

Bunny shifted on his feet. "Ex-partner. DS Spain and I have decided we'd rather work apart."

"Oh for Christ's sake, Bunny, I've enough to be doing without being a marriage counsellor now, too."

"Nobody's asking you to do that, Fintan. Now if you'll excuse me."

"No," said O'Rourke, "no, I won't." He moved forward and grabbed Bunny's arm, pulling him closer. He lowered his voice. "Is there something you'd like to tell me?"

"Yes. Get your fecking hand off me now. I wouldn't like to knock out a senior officer in front of the kids, but I will if I have to."

O'Rourke withdrew his hand but gave Bunny a long, searching look. "What are you hiding? If you know something that I don't, now's the time to tell me."

Bunny met his stare with one of his own, his good eye seemingly focused on O'Rourke while the lazy left one watched the match.

"There's nothing, sir."

"You're sure?"

"Yes, sir."

O'Rourke shook his head. "You're messing up your career on this one, Bunny. It won't be forgotten."

"Thank you, sir."

O'Rourke sighed. "Fine. Have it your way." He started walking back towards the gate.

He had got all of three feet before Bunny's voice was raised behind him. "Phil Nellis, pull your fecking finger out!"

"One hundred!" came the shout.

"Right, Deccie, three laps. Let's see you count them!"

"Do ye know what your problem is, boss?"

"That I lack an appreciation of the fundamentals of the game?"

"No, you're a bollocks."

"FIVE LAPS!"

CHAPTER FORTY-TWO

Bunny kept his left hand firmly on the doorbell, even as his right pounded on the door.

"C'mon, open up. I just want to—"

He took a step back as the door opened a fraction, and through the chained gap, Sister Bernadette's intense little face, with those piercing blue eyes, peered out. "Oh, it's you."

"Yes, Sister, sorry to disturb you, I just wanted to—"

"Hang on, hang on."

The door closed and Bunny could hear the chain being slipped off inside. The door reopened, slightly wider this time, allowing Sister Bernadette enough room to properly get her glare on. "It's past midnight, what on earth is the meaning of this?"

"I'm sorry, Sister, it's Simone. She isn't in work and she didn't come home. Noel says he's not seen her all day, although he . . ."

"What?"

"He says he thinks she mopped the floors this morning as they'd been done when he got in. Look, is she in there?"

"No."

"Would you tell me if she was?"

"Not if she didn't want me to."

"I'm an officer of the law, y'know."

"And I'm an officer of God. If you'd like to meet him a lot sooner than expected, try and get in this door."

"I just need to know she's OK."

"I'm a nun. I'm not in the business of giving men what they think they need."

"Look, I'm not playing around here, Sister."

Bernadette stood back and swung the door open. "Neither am I."

Behind her, Sister Assumpta's large bulk dominated the hallway. She was pointing a shotgun straight at Bunny's head.

Bunny looked at Bernadette, then Assumpta, then back to Bernadette. "What kind of fecking nuns are you?"

"Ever seen *The Sound of Music*?"

"Yes."

"Not that kind." Sister Bernadette beckoned Bunny closer, and he leaned in, as if he expecting to be told a secret. Instead he got walloped on the earhole.

"Ouch!"

"That's for the bad language."

"Jesus!"

She stamped on his toe. "And that's for the blaspheming."

"Mother of . . ." She couldn't weigh much more than a bag of spuds but she had somehow managed to concentrate her entire mass on the area of his big toe. Bunny bit his lip and swallowed enough expletives to give him indigestion.

He gathered himself and took a deep breath. "I'm sorry, Sister. I'm just worried about her. Something has happened. Or maybe she thinks she's not safe any more, because . . ."

Bernadette widened her eyes. "You know, don't you?"

Bunny nodded.

Bernadette blessed herself.

"I don't care though. I believe her and I'll do everything I can to protect her, just . . ."

Bernadette looked him up and down. "I believe you would. You're one of the good ones."

Bunny looked at Assumpta, who was still regarding him down the barrel of the shotgun. "Is there any chance you could tell her that?"

Bernadette looked back at her wingman, as if just remembering she was there. She pushed the barrel of the gun up. "Relax, Sister, it's not him." Then she turned back to him. "Now look – she isn't here, and no, you cannot check, because we have guests. You'll just have to take my word for it. If she comes back here, we will of course take care of her, but we've not seen her in a few days."

Assumpta nodded, giving the first indication that she was in any way following the situation.

"Maybe she will be back home when you get there," said Bernadette, with what probably passed for her version of a soft smile. "There's no point getting yourself in a tizzy about this."

"OK," said Bunny, running his fingers through his hair. "Well, if you see her, just tell her I'm worried about her."

"I will. Good night."

"Good night, Sister."

The door started to close.

"Wait."

Bernadette poked her head out. "Now what?"

"A minute ago, you said 'it's not him' – who were ye expecting?"

Bernadette looked around and then lowered her voice. "We have a guest upstairs from Donegal. She rang her mother a couple of days ago and told her where she was, which we discourage as a rule, but anyway. Apparently her mother is the kind of woman who views the sanctity of marriage as more important than her daughter being used as a punch bag by some muscle-bound buffoon. Calls himself a weightlifter of all things. He's been banging on our door all day with flowers and threats, neither of which we're taking. Seems the overly-aggressive type. I'd bet he's on those god-awful steroid things. They make you go gaga apparently."

"And they shrink your penis." It was the first words Bunny had ever heard Sister Assumpta speak. He couldn't be sure, but he thought the accent was Italian.

For a moment, he and Sister Bernadette looked at Assumpta's broad, friendly face in dumbfounded silence.

"Well," said Bernadette, "someone has been watching the channels further up the dial again."

Bunny turned his attention back to her. "Did you call the Gardaí about this . . ." Bunny paused, not wanting another clatter around the ear. "This fella?"

"Yes," Bernadette said with a grimace, "and as soon as he actually tries to carry out one of these threats, they'll be right over. It's a wonderful system. He's been sitting out there for two days in his van, staring in. Poor girl is terrified. But don't worry, we've dealt with worse than him. You've got no idea."

Bunny took one of his cards out of his pocket. "Well, if you ever need help."

Bernadette took it. "Oh, don't you fear, Detective McGarry, I have plans for you." She took his card between her nimble fingers and disappeared it into some unseen pocket in her habit. "Good night."

"Good night, Sister."

She closed the door.

Bunny looked at his phone again. No missed calls.

Maybe she was right. Maybe Simone would be at home when he got there.

He turned around and headed back to his car.

As he glanced up the street, he noticed a blue van with a large, shaven-headed man sitting in the front seat.

He had to get home. Bunny got in the car and drove off.

He got all of two hundred metres before he pulled a U-turn. Five minutes either way probably wouldn't make that big a difference.

He reached into the back seat and grabbed the hurley that was lying there. "C'mon, Cathleen, we've to make this quick."

A brief conversation ensued, which achieved its goal of the muscle-bound fella swinging first. What followed was a vivid and impactful demonstration of why muscle was no match for God-given natural malevolence.

CHAPTER FORTY-THREE

Bunny sat in his armchair and looked at his phone. He'd spent a restless night checking it every fifteen minutes, while trying to call Simone at least once every half hour. It was now well into the next day and what little hope he had held onto was fading fast.

Maybe she'd decided to run, to get going before her past caught up with her again. If he could just talk to her . . . He kept coming back to the clothes upstairs. She could have taken them if she'd wanted to go – he'd been out at the St Jude's match for several hours, what with the game itself, taking the boys for fish and chips and then dropping people home, having the odd word and dealing with a few issues.

Her clothes being left behind meant one of two things: either something unexpected had happened and she had been forced to bolt immediately, or she had left them so that Bunny wouldn't become suspicious. Neither option appealed. He hated the idea that she might somehow now see him as someone else she had to run from. He kept going over everything he had said again and again, finding fault. If she'd asked, he'd have gone with her. There wasn't much holding him here, after all, especially not now. If only he had found the right words. He had never been smooth though, that was Gringo's forte.

Speaking of which, while he had been waiting for Simone to either call or pick up, he had received several calls and texts from Gringo. He'd apparently been informed that Bunny had left the task force and he wasn't happy about it. He was undoubtedly bathed in remorse for his performance in O'Hagan's a couple of nights ago, but Bunny wasn't interested. His ex-partner's text messages seemed to indicate he was going through the five stages of grief, but Bunny himself had just hit anger and so, on the fifteenth call, he finally answered.

"Would you ever feck off? We've said all we have to say to each other."

"Alright, look, I'm sorry about the—"

"I don't care. I'm waiting for an important call. Hopefully it's not too late to fix the damage your big fecking nose caused."

"What the—"

Bunny hung up and looked down at the phone. Then he nodded. Good, that was that dealt with. Gringo and he were through – he could clean up his own damn messes from now on. Bunny didn't want any involvement in the slurry pit DS Spain had dived head first into. Whatever he and Cunningham thought they were pulling, it had gotten Dara O'Shea killed and they were in all kinds of trouble. He was going to forget everything he had either figured out or heard from Gringo, but that was as far as it went. He had more important things to worry about.

Gringo tried to ring back. Bunny hung up on him. When the phone rang immediately after, he was on his way to hanging up again when he noticed the number. Simone.

In his rush to answer it, Bunny fumbled it and had to dive onto the carpet to retrieve the phone. "Hello, Simone, is that you? Are y'alright?"

There was a pause and then a male voice spoke. "No, it is not Simone."

"Who in the shitting hell are you?"

"I am . . ." There was a pause, and when the voice returned, it sounded amused. "Who I am is unimportant, Detective McGarry.

What is important is that I have something you want, and you have something I want."

The accent was foreign – Spanish, maybe?

"Let me speak to Simone."

"You are in no position to be making demands. Try to remain calm, Detective. There is a way here that everybody can get what they want."

"I want to speak to Simone now or I'm going to—"

The line went dead. Bunny looked at the phone in horror. As he tried to pull up Simone's number to ring back, it rang again.

"Hello."

"Do not test me, Detective, or the next time I hang this phone up, you will never hear from me or Simone again. Do you understand me?"

"Alright, yes, look, I . . ." Bunny started to chew nervously on his thumbnail. "Look, I just need to know she's alright. I mean, how do I know that she's not . . . that you've not just got her phone?"

An exaggerated sigh. "Very well."

There followed a few seconds of movement, then Bunny's heart leapt into his mouth as a piercing female scream reverberated down the line. Simone. Bunny clenched the mobile tightly in his hand, clammy with sweat.

The voice returned. "Please do not make me do that again. I do so abhor violence."

"When I get my hands on you, you twisted little goat-humper, I'm going to—"

He spoke in a sing-song. "Hanging up, Detective . . ."

"No, alright. Don't."

"May I expect full and docile cooperation from here on out?"

"Yes."

"Good. Now, as I said, Simone tells me you have something I want. Do you know what it is?"

Bunny's mind raced, running through everything she had told him two nights ago. If this man just wanted revenge, then he already had Simone. Which could only mean one thing. "The tape."

There was silence at the other end. It may have only been a matter of seconds, but it stretched out in front of Bunny, filled with the sound of his own blood rushing in his ears, the pressure on his chest as he held his breath.

Finally. "Yes, Detective. The tape. You have it?"

"I do."

"Then it is your lucky day. I will trade it for Simone. She is of limited use to me and, frankly, I am already growing bored of her."

Bunny's mind was a cacophony of stomach-twisting images that he tried to ignore. He needed to focus.

"You may be tempted to seek assistance from your associates in law enforcement in this matter. I urge you strongly not to. My colleague is watching your home as we speak. I will save us some time. I assume you will insist on an in-person swap of Simone for the tape?"

"Yes."

"Sadly, as expected." The voice sounded cheery. "There is so little trust left in the world, don't you find?"

Bunny said nothing.

"Once we have finished our conversation," the voice continued, "you will take the tape and meet my colleague outside, where he will take you to—"

"I need time to get it first."

The caller sounded as if he were disciplining a rambunctious child. "No. Simone told me the tape was there. If it is not, then we are done."

"No," said Bunny, trying to think on his feet, "It's here, it's just . . . I need to knock part of a wall out to get it." He was remembering how a particularly industrious drug dealer in Glasnevin, accused of attempted murder, had hidden a gun in just such a way. If it hadn't been for the metal detectors – and his wife's preference for the bloke he had tried to kill – they would never have found it.

There was a pause on the other end. He could sense the calculation taking place. "Very well, you have ten minutes."

"Twenty. I've not got anything bigger than a hammer and I doubt you'll let me go and get a lend of a sledgehammer."

"Fifteen. Work fast. As soon as this conversation is done, you will toss your phone onto your front lawn."

"I can't."

"Goodbye."

"No, wait, I mean I've not got a front lawn. I'll smash it on the paving stones if you like."

Another sigh. "Very well. And, before you check, your home phone line has already been disconnected. The first hint of suspicious activity and we are gone, do you understand me?"

"Yes."

"Anything out of the ordinary."

"Alright, I get it, just . . . don't hurt her." Bunny could hear how defeated and desperate he sounded. He wished he was putting it on.

"Drop the phone. Your fifteen minutes has already started. Do not test me."

The line disconnected.

Bunny walked to the front door, opened it and smashed his phone on the paving stones outside.

Connor Gilsenan, a slightly odd young fella of six or seven, was standing a few doors down outside his granny's house, whacking her wheelie bins with a stick.

"What did ye do that for, mister?"

"Reception was shite."

"Ah yeah, fair enough."

Bunny went back into the house and slammed the door behind him. He had been careful not to look directly, but he had caught a glimpse of the man sitting in the silver Audi about fifty feet up on the other side of the road.

He had fifteen minutes. He also did not have the tape the man was looking for.

CHAPTER FORTY-FOUR

DI Fintan O'Rourke stood in a pew three from the back and fiddled nervously with his tie. He didn't like funerals as a rule and he had been to too many. Yesterday, he had been at Dara O'Shea's. The family had requested not to have the full-on state affair that was on offer, so the only coppers there had been him and Cunningham, not in their dress uniforms. Jessica Cunningham had been quiet, even by her high standards of frosty silences.

For today's funeral, he had also foregone the dress uniform, but that was more a matter of personal safety than personal taste. This was Jimmy Moran's funeral. To say it presented a logistical difficulty was an understatement. The entirety of the Clanavale Estate seemed to be packed into St Joseph's Church. The first two rows were crowded with family, Jimmy Moran's grieving mother at the fulcrum, leaning on what looked like a daughter for support. Behind the Morans were Franko Doyle and his family, and beside him were the Carters. Eimear looked as uncomfortable as always, no doubt made worse by the presence of their father, Donal Carter. Jimmy's casket was a closed affair – very understandable, given the direct gunshot wound to the head – but Dara O'Shea's hadn't been. O'Shea had looked better dead, O'Rourke thought, than Donal Carter looked alive. His skin was a sickly yellow colour that only existed in nature as a warning to others. But he had insisted on being there, apparently, and Donal Carter had never been a man easy to dissuade from anything.

The body language before the service had been fascinating, the older Clanavale residents coming up to pay their respects to Donal, the younger showing their deference to Tommy, their boy king.

The church was oppressively hot and overcrowded. Regardless, the elderly priest was clearly determined to milk his rare full house for all it was worth. Tomorrow his morning mass would be lucky to hit double figures, and that was allowing for the inclusion of dogs.

As the congregation stood, O'Rourke noticed that Carter senior couldn't make it to his feet this time.

Beside O'Rourke, Detective Pamela "Butch" Cassidy fidgeted nervously. He couldn't blame her. Beneath the heavy pall of grief at a young man's death, the church was simmering with a low-level yet palpable resentment of their presence. In truth, O'Rourke didn't want to be there any more than they wanted him, but he had no choice. Tommy Carter and Franko Doyle were still the primary persons of interest in the death of a guard and the theft of sixteen million in uncut diamonds. Someone had to keep eyes on them at all times. O'Rourke was there because he wouldn't send one of his people into a hostile environment that he wouldn't go into himself. He had chosen Cassidy to accompany him partly because he had judged the local grunts as being marginally less likely to hit a woman, and partly because she was a former All Ireland judo silver medallist, which meant they were a lot less likely to enjoy the experience if they tried.

Outside, there was a heavy Garda presence but they had been instructed to stay out of the way as much as possible. It was a tricky balancing act though, as this was now a lot more than simple surveillance. Someone had taken Moran out, and they still didn't know who. If this was the opening shot of a gangland war, then funerals were traditionally a popular location for the follow-up. Then there was the fact that Moran had been the best friend of John

O'Donnell, currently Ireland's most wanted man, who was considered armed and embarrassingly dangerous.

O'Rourke wasn't a religious man, but he mouthed along to the prayer and then glanced behind him before he sat down. This wasn't the first funeral he had attended where his presence was not welcome. Without a word, he moved the half-finished, sticky-to-the-touch bottle of children's fruit juice that had mysteriously appeared where his backside was about to be. He actually heard a groan of disappointment as he did so.

That small victory was forgotten as Tommy Carter stood and made his way towards the altar. Cassidy and O'Rourke shared a glance.

With no notes, Tommy Carter took up position behind the lectern. He removed his orange-tinted glasses and slowly looked around the room, making eye contact with as many people as possible. Then he looked down at the mahogany coffin in repose before him.

"Jimmy Moran was no angel – I'm not going to stand here and tell you otherwise. He was a man with his strengths and weaknesses, just like the rest of us. None of us are perfect, are we?"

Heads shook and nodded, depending on whether you were answering the question or agreeing with the statement.

"Jimmy was full of love – for his mum, Gina, for his sisters, Carol and Sarah, and for his brother, Derek. He also loved his community. He would have done anything for a neighbour in need. You could knock on his door and he'd be out there, helping you start your car, fix a window – you name it. Since we were young fellas, me and him have always cleaned out Mrs Byrne's gutters every year" – an old lady in the fourth row nodded, teary-eyed, into a tissue – "although that was for purely selfish reasons. We were both demons for those fabulous fairy cakes we all know she makes." A smattering of half-laughs. "That's what this estate has always been about, looking after each other. Jimmy's da, Patrick – God rest him – he stood with my da back in the day, in order to keep this estate safe. Nobody else looked out for us, so we looked out for each other. We still do. When the dealers were kneecapping poor Terry Flint back in 1990, where were the Gardaí? When Gerry Fallon and the other drug-dealing scum tried to burn me and my sister alive in our own home, where was the police?"

O'Rourke felt it pass through the congregation. Felt eyes burning into them from all sides.

"And when Jimmy Moran, a man who loved his community, and lest we forget, served his country in the army with distinction . . ."

Yeah, thought O'Rourke, *right up until the dishonourable discharge.*

"When he was brutally executed, where were the Gardaí? The Gardaí who, despite him not being under arrest or charged with anything, were following him everywhere. You've all seen them, following us about."

Nods.

"They've been harassing this whole estate. When your car gets done or your purse gets snatched, where are they? I'll tell ye, nowhere to be seen. But now? They've invaded, haven't they? That's because to them, we're not people – no, we're just criminal scum. We're only here to be fitted up and looked down on, isn't that right?"

With each question, the murmurs of agreement grew louder and louder. O'Rourke's eyes remained fixed on Carter.

"So where were all these Gardaí, who you've all seen following us around, when poor Jimmy Moran got shot? I'll tell you – they were right there. They say they can't figure out who shot Jimmy. Course they can! It was them."

Curses and glares were now coming at them from every direction. O'Rourke felt Cassidy shifting nervously beside him. He spoke, barely moving his lips. "Hold your ground."

"Remember this," continued Carter, "when people ask you what happened, remember this. The Gardaí were the ones who invaded our homes. The Gardaí were the ones who harassed us in the street, and the Gardaí" – he paused for effect – "were the ones who fired the first shot in this war when they executed Jimmy Moran."

CHAPTER FORTY-FIVE

Bunny was having a difficult moment in the bathroom when the doorbell rang. He looked at his watch – it hadn't even been ten minutes. He angrily heaved up his trousers and was still fastening the belt as he opened the door.

"It's not been—" He stopped. Gringo stood before him, looking like a kid who had just been called to the principal's office. "I've nothing further to say to you."

Gringo held his arms out in a supplicatory gesture. "Look, I'm sorry."

Bunny's eyes unconsciously flicked to the silver Audi still parked up the street, and to the watching eyes . . .

Mr Frock picked up his mobile and dialled the number. He held the phone to his ear as he continued to watch the action taking place down the street.

After two rings – "What?"

"Your friend has just had a visitor."

"Who is it?"

"I don't know. A geezer."

"A what?"

"A man."

Frock had only met the man who called himself Mr Lopez a couple of days ago. It had been an unusual request through the usual channels. An American needed a hired hand over in Ireland for a few days – a week at the most. It paid better than triple the normal rate. Suspiciously well, in fact. All that was required was that he provide a gun and be available 24/7, discretion expected and assured. Frock hadn't been wild about them kidnapping the woman, but he could live with it. Nobody paid that well for an honest day's work. Now he was watching the big Paddy bloke he'd been instructed to pick up standing on his doorstep, waving his finger in another bloke's face.

"What are they doing?" asked Lopez.

Frock watched as the big fella pushed the other guy.

"Arguing I think and . . . woah."

"What?"

"The big fella just sucker punched the other guy. They're properly going at it now."

"This appears to be a nation of savages."

They were rolling around on the ground now.

"Your guy is winning."

"Oh good," said Lopez, dripping sarcasm, "I am pleased."

They grappled some more before the big fella, McGarry, regained his feet first. Frock had been in more than enough fights, both in and out of the service, to know what that meant. The one who's down normally stays down. A couple of good kicks and it'd be good night, Irene. Instead, the big ape picked up a nearby bin and hurled it down at the other man.

A little kid who'd rushed over to watch proceedings raised his arms and hollered, like the manager in one of those ridiculous American wrestling things. McGarry said something to him that sent him scurrying, then turned around and re-entered the house, slamming the door behind him.

Frock made a decision there and then. Normally he didn't like letting anyone else drive, but this time he would make an exception.

That way he could keep McGarry's hands busy on the wheel so the big dumb ape couldn't try anything.

McGarry's visitor slowly staggered to his feet, blood streaming from his nose. His shirt was half ripped off him and he looked dazed.

Frock lowered the window slightly to hear what he was shouting.

"I'll be seeing you again, Bunny, you hear me? I'll be seeing you again."

He limped off in the opposite direction, like a whipped dog.

Frock put the phone to his ear again. "He has dealt with the situation, the other guy is gone."

"Very well. Pick him up in four minutes and keep a close eye on him."

Yeah, thought Frock, *no kidding*.

CHAPTER FORTY-SIX

"Pull in here."

"Grand," said Bunny. "The meter says thirty-two quid, but sure, just call it thirty. Seeing as the banter has been such good craic."

"Shut up."

It had been about an hour since the silver Audi had pulled up outside his house and its occupant had honked the horn. Bunny had appeared, holding an Arnott's bag containing a videotape. He was wearing his anorak, as the encroaching evening was laden with dark clouds that promised an unhappy night.

He stood looking at the man standing beside the car. Well built, but not excessively muscled, forties, smart enough to be wary, experienced enough not to be jittery. There was the waft of ex-military about him. He was maybe six foot two and carried himself like a man who had been in a fair few fights and had come out mostly on the right side. Bunny knew how to recognise those people because he was one of those people.

Bunny had jangled his leg and awkwardly pulled at his underpants. "Apologies. That gobshite earlier caught me a dig right in the Martha and the Vandellas."

"If you've any weapons on you, you'll be checked at the other end." English accent.

"Only my devastating wit."

"Get in, you're driving."

The English bloke had sat in the back seat as Bunny got into the front.

"Check your rear-view."

Bunny adjusted the mirror enough to see the gun that the man held under a newspaper.

"We clear?"

"Clearer than a nudist's sexual preference."

"What?"

"Cause, ye see, you'd be able to see who they—"

"Shut up and drive."

Bunny put the bag with the tape in it under his seat and adjusted himself, trying to get comfortable. "Where to, guv?"

Over the next hour, his passenger had only given Bunny directions, guiding them up into the Wicklow Mountains via the M50. All attempts at casual conversation had been met with a firm "shut up". There seemed to be no way to either wind him up or win him over. Either would have done. Bunny placed great stock in an enemy being too annoyed to think straight. This guy was not going to play ball. If anything, he seemed slightly bored with the whole thing.

"Get out of the car."

The sporadic rain was in the middle of one of its more sustained outbursts. They were in a lay-by at the bottom of a valley, densely forested hills on either side.

His guide, the gun now tucked into the pocket of his dark grey overcoat, nodded towards a worn and muddied path that lay between the fir trees. As they trudged forward, Bunny could just make out the sound of the occasional car whooshing by in the background. If anyone noticed the Audi at all, it would be as a brief flash of soon-forgotten silver on their way to somewhere else. This area was no doubt popular with hill walkers and tree huggers in the summer months, but in the fading light of a shitty December day, it only existed as somewhere on the line between two points.

About twenty yards in they came to a clearing. Bunny could see stone steps leading up the south face of the hill. A brook, giddy with winter rains, rushed by under the wooden bridge that lay at the foot of the steps.

"Stop."

Bunny did as instructed.

His guide stepped in front of him and dialled a number on his mobile. "We're here." He nodded and carefully extended the phone out to Bunny, his gun in the other hand, pointed at Bunny's centre mass.

Bunny took the phone and clamped it against his ear with his shoulder, leaving his left hand free to pull at the posterior of his trousers, his right hand still clutching the carrier bag.

"Detective McGarry, thank you for coming. Is everything alright?"

"Grand, yeah. Sorry about that, I'm having a bit of testicular discomfort due to earlier ructions."

Bunny shoved his left hand back into the pocket of his anorak.

"I trust you have brought the tape with you?"

Bunny held up the carrier bag. "Yep, I did. There she is – and this is as close to it as you're getting until I see Simone."

The voice laughed. "I think you have greatly overestimated your negotiating position, Detective."

"I'm not so sure. Let me tell you about Bibi Baskin."

"Who?"

"She was a goldfish. You see Gringo, my very much ex-partner, said it wasn't healthy for me to be living alone – said it was making me grumpy. So, he went off one day and bought me a goldfish."

"Bibi Baskin?"

"That's right. Named after the thinking man's thinking woman off the telly. Do you know Irish TV? Probably not. Anyway, she's a fine looking red-headed woman, and the fish was sort of red so—"

"Is there a point to this?"

"Yes," said Bunny, rolling his eyes at his guide, as if his boss was a little hard of thinking. "So Gringo got me this fish, but I'd to go buy Bibi an aquarium and all this stuff. Jesus, it adds up. Few hundred quid all told, but I went for the whole nine yards, as you Yanks say. Anyway, first week in, I come home and Bibi – and I still don't know how this happened – has jumped out of her tank, died there on the floor."

"Oh dear. Is the point of this story your lack of success in protecting the women in your life?"

"No, no, not at all. The point is, I'd bought all this gear, including this thing for cleaning the algae off the tank. The guy in the shop really did a sales pitch on me, said it would make my life so much easier. 'It makes tank cleaning a joy' – I distinctly remember him saying that."

The voice sounded slightly irritated now. "What is your point?"

"Well," said Bunny, pulling his left hand out of his pocket to produce a black object, which he held a foot above the bag, "the point is, that algae doodah is how I happened to have a decent-sized magnet in the house. And videotapes and magnets don't get on."

"So, let me get this straight, detective: you are threatening to destroy a tape that I came here to destroy?"

"Ah, well then, if all you want is the tape destroyed, then I'm as screwed as screwed can be. Thing is, I'm guessing a man like yourself would rather own this tape than just destroy it. I'm guessing it has a value in still existing and in you being the one that has it. Am I right?"

"And you think your little magnet is enough to destroy it before Mr Frock puts a bullet through your head."

"D'ye know, I've no idea, and I'm betting you don't either. So, will I tell Frocky boy here to shoot me in the head and we can both find out?"

Mr Frock pursed his lips and looked at Bunny.

The voice sighed. "Very well, Detective, let us play your game. You can keep your magnet and the tape, but I shall not be allowing you to go any further with the weapons I'm sure you will have on your person."

"Ye can frisk me if you like."

"And allow you the chance to 'try something'? That will not be necessary. Please hand the phone back to Mr Frock."

Bunny switched the magnet to his right hand and then quickly tossed the phone at Frock.

He calmly took a step backwards and let the phone fall onto the muddy ground, his gun never wavering from covering Bunny. Then he leaned forward and picked it up, mumbling something under his breath that sounded a lot like "asshole".

Mr Frock listened for a few seconds then hung up the phone.

"Strip."

"Excuse me?" said Bunny.

"Strip."

"Y'know, I get that there was some obvious sexual tension between us on the drive over, but I'm kind of seeing someone."

"Strip."

"Seriously? It's pissing rain and nearly freezing."

"Like I care. You want to play silly buggers, fine. Strip."

"Alright, but, before I do, I want you to remember it is cold and you're not seeing me at my best."

Bunny put the bag containing the tape on a nearby rock and held the magnet over it while he stripped. It was a slow process, by the end of which he was slick with rain and shivering.

"Can I keep my shoes on?"

"No. Nothing."

"I'm really starting to go off you."

Mr Frock tilted his head in the direction of the stone steps. "Up there."

"You first."

"Move."

"I'm serious. You stay in front of me. I'm not having you being tempted to shoot me in the back of the head when I can't see it coming. I want you where I can see you or . . ." Bunny looked pointedly down at the magnet and the plastic bag containing the video tape.

Frock grimaced and slowly walked backwards over the wooden bridge, Bunny following about six feet behind. He made no effort to maintain his modesty, preferring to hold his hands up in such a way that the magnet would fall into the bag containing the tape if he dropped it or Frock dropped him.

Frock started to climb slowly up the steps, still facing Bunny.

"So, Frock, is that a German name?"

Frock said nothing.

"In the British Army with a German name, dear oh dear. Were the other children mean?"

By the time they reached the top of the stairs, Bunny was unable to stop shaking as the cold went through him. The granite was hard and slippery beneath his feet as the rain teemed down, the sound of it washing all others away. Bunny glanced around into the trees, a random thought popping into his head as to what the wildlife must be making of all this.

At the top of the stairs was a forest clearing that sloped down towards where Bunny now stood. Four picnic tables were dotted around, and Simone was sitting behind the one furthest away from Bunny. Her right hand was handcuffed to it. Her hair clung wet around her face, which looked puffy and swollen. Her eyes welled when she saw him and she turned away. She was wearing the overalls Bunny recognised as the ones she wore to do the cleaning in Charlie's.

Leaning against one of the other tables was a dark-skinned Latino man holding a golf umbrella over his head. He was wearing a black sheepskin coat over a cream suit that matched neither the weather nor the environment, and a pair of dark glasses that were the definition of optimism for Ireland in December. He completed the outfit with a handgun held nonchalantly in his right hand.

Mr Frock moved towards the top of the clearing, to provide wide cover while also sheltering beneath the treeline from the worst of the rain .

"Ah, Detective, we meet at last. You may call me Mr Lopez."

Bunny ignored him and moved awkwardly towards Simone. "Are you alright?"

"Ah-ah. Far enough, Detective."

Simone looked up and nodded at Bunny. When she spoke, her voice came out in a croak that barely carried amidst the thundering rain. "I'm sorry. So sorry, so sorry."

Bunny spoke softly. "Look at me, Simone."

She raised her head slowly and her eyes met his.

"Whatever happens, you've got nothing to be sorry about."

"This is all very touching," said Lopez, "but this rain is playing havoc with my shoes, so can we move this along?"

Bunny turned to address the man for the first time. "I want you to know – if this goes really well, I'm looking forward to watching you die slowly."

The man smirked. "And if it goes really badly?"

"Then you get to die quick."

This at least wiped the smile from his face. "I'm bored of your histrionics. Put the tape on the table and back away."

"No."

"Do it or I will shoot you in the leg."

"I always wanted to ask you . . ." They both turned at Simone's interruption. She looked at Bunny. "That night in the alley outside Charlie's when Ryan, y'know . . ."

Bunny nodded.

"Why were you there?"

"I was . . . I dunno. I was hoping to accidentally bump into you or . . . something. Daft, I guess."

She shook her head. "No. It would've been nice." She gave him that lopsided smile that made him forget everything for the briefest moment. "I wish things had worked out differently."

"But they didn't," said Lopez, taking a step towards Bunny. "Let us be realistic, Detective, there is a very good chance that the tape you are holding isn't the correct one. I would be a fool to think otherwise. I let this play out as I wanted you to deliver yourself to me, and you have, naked and helpless. The more likely options are that you either don't have the tape or you have it hidden elsewhere. If it is the latter, I will take my time and get that information out of you. I am very good at getting answers – it is a skill I have. Incidentally, your lady friend broke a lot more quickly this time than she did last time. I don't know what that says about her feelings for her ex-beau compared to you."

Bunny refused to rise to the bait. "And if I don't have the tape?"

"Then I will enjoy greatly confirming that answer. I like my work."

"Ah sure, enjoy your job and you never work a day in your life. Isn't it lucky you're a scum-sucking psycho cockwomble?"

"Sticks and stones, really? I mean, coming here, what was it? Some ludicrous romantic gesture or did you have any kind of a plan?"

"To be honest with you, I was sorta hoping I'd be able to pull something out of me arse."

"And how is that working out?"

"It's really too early to tell. Although, you're wrong, there's a third option for what's about to happen."

"Really?"

"Oh yes, amigo."

And then Simone screamed.

21.8 miles away, seventy-six minutes previously . . .

Gringo rang the doorbell, took a deep breath and looked around. A young kid was standing a few doors down from Bunny's house gawping at him, having taken a break from walloping stuff with a stick.

Something crunched under Gringo's feet. He looked down to see what appeared to be the remains of a mobile phone, and then the door opened.

Even by his standards, Bunny looked pissed. "I've nothing further to say to you."

Gringo held his arms out in a supplicatory gesture. "Look, I'm sorry."

Bunny stepped out onto the doorstep; Gringo moved backwards.

"Now isn't the time to be sorry. D'you have any idea the trouble you've caused?"

"Amigo, I'm sorry."

Bunny pushed Gringo, causing him to stumble. "Not as sorry as you're going to be."

"Look, I'll do anything to make it up to you."

"OK."

Then Bunny swung a punch straight into Gringo's jaw.

Gringo spun and the world roulette-wheeled around him. As he hit the ground, he was dimly aware of the kid whooping excitedly. Then Bunny was on top of him, his big arm wrapped around his throat.

Bunny pulled him closer and whispered in his ear. "Act like we're fighting."

Gringo choked a response that came out as nothing more than a strangled cough.

Bunny loosened his grip slightly while simultaneously kneeing Gringo in the back. "What?"

"I said, we *are* fighting."

"So hit me."

Gringo slammed his fist into the side of Bunny's head.

"Ouch, me fucking ear, ye fucker – good. They've got Simone. Silver Audi. Follow it."

"But—"

Bunny grabbed a handful of Gringo's shirt, heaving on it to send three buttons pinging away.

"What the—?"

"No time. Do it."

Bunny pushed himself back onto his feet. Gringo remained on the ground, bleeding, dazed and confused. He watched as Bunny picked up a nearby bin and hurled it down at him. He raised his knee to deflect it away without too much damage.

In the background, Gringo heard the little kid whooping with delight.

"You – get the feck out of here or I'll skin ye alive."

Gringo could hear the kid's feet slapping lightly on the pavement as he hotfooted it to a safe distance.

Bunny turned around and re-entered the house, slamming the door behind him.

Gringo slowly staggered to his feet, blood streaming from his nose. His shirt was half ripped off him and he felt like he might throw up.

He stumbled out of the gate, trying to look only slightly more dazed than he felt, but aware enough to clock the silver Audi briefly, and the man sitting in the front seat.

Gringo turned back towards the door.

"I'll be seeing you again, Bunny, you hear me? I'll be seeing you again."

He limped off around the corner to where his car was parked.

Then he drove off.

He went around the block and parked up on the main road, where he could keep an unseen eye on the silver Audi.

At Simone's scream, everyone in the clearing turned towards her.

This allowed Gringo almost, but not quite, enough time to cover the ground between the treeline and Frock. When all eyes had been on Bunny, Simone had clocked Gringo making his way around the clearing.

Unfortunately, while her attempt at a distraction did partially work, it still gave Frock just enough time to identify where the real threat was coming from. He ducked down to the side, meaning that the blow from the large log Gringo swung two-handed at him only landed on his wrist, sending the gun skittering off into the trees. Frock went down but he had the presence of mind to lash out with his legs, taking Gringo with him.

Lopez moved towards Bunny, his gun aimed directly at his head, stopping his attempted charge before it could start. "Don't."

Lopez looked around, confirming that the cavalry was limited to one unarmed man.

"Was this your big plan?"

"Well, to be honest, I thought he'd have a gun."

"How disappointing for you."

Lopez glanced from Bunny, to the fight unfolding between Gringo and Frock, and back again, the gun still resolutely trained on him, allowing Bunny no opportunity to try anything. "I think we shall let this play out. If your friend wins, I'll shoot him. If my man wins – well, it's just one more body to bury."

"No offence," said Bunny, "but you're not exactly a people person, are ye?"

As they rolled down the hill, Gringo lost all sense of geography. His whole world now consisted of him and the man he was grappling with. He attempted to fire a knee into where he hoped his opponent's groin was, but a twisting leg deflected the blow. Frock's left hand was down around his ankle. Gringo saw the flash of steel. His instinctive movement stopped the knife from embedding deep in the meat of his leg, instead only slicing the edge of his thigh. The focus shifting again, he desperately clamped his hands around Frock's left wrist as they rolled down the hill. His opponent was bigger, stronger and armed. Gringo was running out of ideas.

They rolled and rolled again – Gringo's head slamming into the leg of a wooden picnic table as Frock's knee simultaneously drilled into Gringo's groin. Instinctively, Gringo released his grip on his opponent's arms. He saw Frock over him, fire in his eyes as he drew the knife back above his head.

Frock roared in frustration as a female hand grabbed a fistful of his hair and yanked him backwards.

Gringo kicked his legs, freeing himself from under the bigger man.

Frock turned, his knife slashing through the rain and catching Simone's arm, momentarily painting a slash of red blood across the downpour, accompanied by her plaintive scream.

Gringo hurled his full weight against Frock's back, sending his opponent slamming chest first into the picnic table, sandwiching Frock's blade-wielding hand between the table and his body.

Gringo felt the sickeningly sweet squelch as the knife passed through the resistance of the other man's chest to the heart below.

With a gurgling gasp, Frock's last breath passed from his body.

Gringo fell backwards onto the soft wet grass and lay there gasping. The other man's body rolled off the table, the knife still protruding from his chest.

He looked up to see Simone awkwardly trying to use her handcuffed hand to stem the flood of blood from her upper left arm.

"You OK?"

"I'll live."

"That is very unlikely." Lopez's voice carried through the rain. Gringo turned to see the gun pointed directly at him. "I mean, on the upside, you have saved me from paying Mr Frock the second half of his fee, but still. Too many people, too much complication. Time to revert to plan A, which is to prove to my employer that Miss Delamere will never be a problem."

Lopez's chain of thought was interrupted by the sight of Bunny in his peripheral vision. "Are you quite alright, Detective?"

Gringo looked across. It did appear as if Bunny was, well, showing undue interest in his own back passage.

"'Tis the cold," said Bunny, "It's playing havoc with my haemorrhoids."

Lopez grimaced. "We can't decide when we go, but we can decide with how much dignity. Goodbye, Detective."

"Sláinte!" shouted Bunny, falling backwards.

The last thing Mr Lopez saw was Bunny McGarry, his legs spread wide as he fell backwards, his right hand appearing between his legs, followed by a bright flash from his groin area.

Then a 130-grain bullet travelling at 685 feet per second, producing 111 foot-pounds of ballistic energy, entered Mr Lopez's brain via his right eye, and put a severe crimp in his plans for the evening.

CHAPTER FORTY-SEVEN

"Up your arse?!"

Bunny, still shivering under the sheepskin overcoat he'd borrowed from a dead man, looked at Gringo. "Would you please stop saying that?"

The rain having finally stopped, the three of them were sitting at one of the picnic tables in the near-darkness. Simone was trying to warm Bunny up as best she could, holding him tightly, running her hands up and down his body. He was cold – numb, in fact – but the feeling of her close to him was warming him in other ways. Gringo had found the keys to the cuffs in Lopez's coat, which Bunny was now wearing. Gringo had gone back to his car and returned with a bounty that included a first aid kit, two powerful torches, half a pack of Jammie Dodgers and a bottle of whiskey that he had in the boot. He had also brought his used and smelly football kit which Bunny was currently squashed into, his own clothes having been turned into a sodden mess by the rain. Simone had used the first aid kit to bandage the wounds on her own arm and Gringo's thigh as best she could, though both would need stitches. Then they had sat in silence and passed the biscuits and whiskey around.

"But where did you even get a derringer pistol from?"

Simone rolled her eyes. "Up his ass. Get over it."

Gringo stopped, a Jammie Dodger halfway to his mouth. "Had it . . ."

"What?"

"Had it been up there a while?"

"What are you yammering on about?" said Bunny. "Do you think I've been walking around for ages with that" – he pointed at the four-inch long, one-shot derringer pistol that was now lying on the table in front of them – "stuck up me port tunnel? No! I put it up there when these guys gave me fifteen minutes to turn up outside my house with a tape I didn't have. I figured it was the only advantage I had – surprise."

"I was surprised," said Gringo.

"Exactly."

"Because you pulled it out of your arse."

"Gringo – how many times have you frisked someone for weapons?"

"Hundreds."

"And have you ever checked their arse?"

"No."

"*Quod erat demonstrandum*," said Bunny, with a wave of his hand.

"Although now I've seen you pull that trick . . . I'm still not checking arses. I'd rather just get shot. I mean – up your arse!"

"Oh Lord," said Simone. "I'm starting to miss being tortured."

Bunny gave her a squeeze and a quick peck on the forehead. While Gringo had been gone, she had reluctantly given him a few details about what the last day had been like. She had only cried when explaining why she had given them his name, speaking through sobs. "It was either you or the sisters or Noel, and I figured you might be able to defend yourself."

He had told her she'd made the right decision. The thought had popped into his head that the sisters were a lot more capable of defending themselves than anyone might imagine, but he left it unsaid.

"By the way, on the subject of what happened outside your

house," continued Gringo, "where did you learn to pull a punch? You nearly broke my jaw."

Bunny smirked. "I had to make it look realistic." He took a slug of whiskey and passed the bottle to Gringo.

"Where did you get it from?"

"What?"

"The derrière pistol. And you should totally copyright that name, by the way."

"Yeah, I'll get my lawyers right on it. It was a present from my uncle Bunny. I think he brought it back from the Spanish Civil War or something."

"Wait, Uncle Bunny is real?"

"Of course he's real, sure, haven't I been telling you about him for years?"

"I thought he was someone you made up to liven up boring stake-outs in the car."

"Do you think I make up family members to entertain you, ye clueless gobshite?"

Gringo drummed his hands on the tabletop excitedly. "There really are a long line of Bunny McGarrys? Like through history?"

"Yes," said Bunny, exasperated. "Haven't I been telling you about them for years?"

"Well, now I have a whole lot more questions."

"Hang on to them," said Bunny, standing up. "We need to start sorting this mess out."

The light was rapidly fading and there was work to be done. Gringo and Bunny had only exchanged a couple of words before Gringo had gone back to the car, but he had been running it through in his head, and he could tell Gringo had been too. If Simone's past was to have any chance of staying hidden, they couldn't go through official channels. If the people chasing her were as powerful as she feared, and what had happened over the last couple of days certainly seemed to bear that out, then there was only one option.

"There's something else I don't understand," said Gringo.

Bunny leaned on the table. "I'm not going through it again."

"Not that," said Gringo, nodding at the derringer, "although, yes, also that. No. I mean the tape." He pointed at the Arnott's bag sitting in the middle of the table. "What the hell is this tape?"

"Never mind," said Bunny. "All you need to know is that this isn't the one they were looking for. This is the 1992 All-Ireland final between Kilkenny and Cork."

"Did Cork win that?"

Bunny gave Gringo a sour look. "Course not, I wouldn't risk a tape of one of the ones we won, ye lunatic."

"Right, that is the first thing you've said that does make sense."

"Come on," Bunny said to Gringo, before placing a kiss on Simone's forehead. "You stay here, love."

"Are you sure? I can help."

"You're alright," said Gringo. "This is ditch digging, it's what his people were made for."

"Yeah," said Bunny, "and this gobshite is overdue an honest day's work."

They had never directly said it, but when Gringo had returned from the cars, the decision had been made. He'd taken the keys to Frock's silver Audi and returned with two shovels, requisitioned from the dead man's car boot along with two newly-purchased torches. A full gravedigging kit.

They looked around and then Gringo pointed in the direction away from the steps.

"Makes sense," said Bunny with a nod. "I guess we keep walking until we find a spot. Dig the hole first, and . . ."

Gringo nodded, turning on both of the torches and handing one to Bunny. They then each picked up a shovel. "There's that many bodies buried in these mountains, we'll be doing well to find a fresh spot."

Bunny looked over at Simone. "We won't be long."

They walked into the woods, scanning the ground before them with their torches as they went.

"Do you think she'll be OK?" asked Gringo.

"Yeah," said Bunny. "She's tougher than she looks. And I'm going to take care of her, if she'll let me."

"She's lucky to have you."

"We'll see. Hey, I've a question for you. How come you didn't have a gun?"

"Jesus, amigo, I'm on compassionate leave after what happened with Dara. They gave me the number for a counsellor; they're hardly going to let me take a gun home."

"Ah right," said Bunny. "Yeah. Course. Sorry. How's all that going?"

"Counselling?"

"No. Y'know, the Carter stuff..."

"You don't want to know."

"I don't, but look, I owe you for this. You're ... whatever help you need, you just ask."

"No," said Gringo, shaking his head firmly. "The kind of debts we owe each other never get wiped away, we both know that. But this – this you don't do."

"For God's sake, you're in the middle of helping me bury a couple of bodies."

"Yes, amigo – of two bad men who had come here to do a very bad thing. Two men who I accidentally led to your door. We're both members of the blessed Garda Síochána and, regardless of the views of a court, what we just did and what we're about to do are the right things. I'm fine with that. Hell, it's good to be back on the side of the angels for a little while. The nightmare I got myself involved in by joining up to somebody's get-rich-quick scheme is nothing to do with you and I'm not having you dragged down with me."

"But—"

"But nothing. You've not just got yourself to take care of now, and she, God help her, deserves you. And you deserve her, for that matter. I'll fix what I have to, but you stay out of it. That's the final word, alright?"

"Alright."

They came to a small opening amidst the trees, sheltered on one side by a looming rock face. Someone had graffitied a large clown's face on it.

"Clowns give me the creeps," said Bunny.

"Can I remind you that we're here to bury some bodies."

"Fair point."

Gringo tested the ground. "Seems soft enough."

Then the clouds parted and a soft silver moonlight fell down upon them, illuminating the clown's fading grin.

They both started digging in silence for a couple of minutes, until . . .

"Seriously though, up your arse?"

CHAPTER FORTY-EIGHT

Butch didn't like it – any of it.

They had been watching the newly re-opened Leaping Trout pub in the centre of the Clanavale Estate for the best part of eight hours now. It seemed the whole estate was in there, except for those who were standing around drinking outside the front doors. The pub sat on what was effectively the central square, with roads leading off it at each corner. Butch, as site commander, had positioned a squad car on every side. She had also requested more support but there had been none available. A couple of Northern Irish politicians were down on a visit to herald the new spirit of co-operation, and the Gardaí had to make sure none of the numpties got anywhere near them and set Anglo-Irish relations back a generation.

Her orders had been very clear: be respectful, but be visible. Their role here was twofold: firstly, to make sure there were no further attacks from whoever was on the other side of this possible gang war; and secondly, not to let Tommy Carter or Franko Doyle out of their sights. The reality was, Butch hadn't actually laid eyes on either of them for a good six hours, since she had seen them enter the pub. It had occurred to her more than once that if the place had some kind of tunnel running beneath it, they were going to be made to look like idiots again.

Last she'd heard, DI O'Rourke had spent most of the day on the phone to the press, vehemently denying Tommy Carter's accusation of Garda collusion in the death of Jimmy Moran. Somehow, Carter had put them on the back foot yet again. Her and DI O'Rourke's walk out of the funeral would live long in her memory. The looks of pure hatred, the overpowering threat of imminent danger, regardless of it being in a church. The only experience that came close to it was the time she had escorted a child killer into court.

Since then, the mourners had been drinking fairly solidly from what Cassidy could see. There had been comings and goings, and an increasing amount of looks in their direction from the group of men congregating outside the doors of the pub.

She looked across the top of the car at Paul Norman, a uniformed guard so young he still had acne. She tried to give him a warm smile. "Relax. I've not seen a fella look that terrified since my one attempt at heterosexual dating."

He tried to smile back but looked in danger of ruining his undies. Cassidy internally scolded herself. She must remember that her sense of humour was an acquired taste. God, she missed Dinny Muldoon. The sooner they could nail Carter, the better.

She looked across at the drinkers sitting outside the front door of the Leaping Trout. The predictably dull attempts at "banter" had been directed her way, but she had long ago become impervious to such things. Once you had slammed a couple down, the rest of the herd learned the lesson. Right now though, she would have welcomed it. Instead, she was getting excited looks and surreptitious conversations held in huddles.

Sometimes, as a copper, it felt like your fate was entirely out of your hands. You knew what was coming in your very bones, but you were powerless to stop it. So far tonight, the only thing they'd had in their favour had been the policeman's best friend: the weather. Persistent rain, often quite heavy, had kept the mourners mostly inside and the Gardaí out of their line of sight. Now, the damn clouds had cleared to a cold crisp night.

Her mobile rang. DI O'Rourke.

"Cassidy, how's it looking?"

"Not great, sir. The rain has stopped and the locals are looking restless."

"Any sign of our two boys?"

"Negative, sir. They were last seen entering the Leaping Trout at 3:45 pm, nothing since."

"Are we sure they're in there?"

Cassidy hated the question. "We've not seen them leave, sir, so I assume so."

"Right. They'll be closing up soon anyway."

"I don't know about that."

"But the licence—"

"Respectfully, sir, do we want to go in and enforce closing time in this situation? It'll be depicted as us not showing . . . Shit!"

"What is it?"

A cheer rose from the drinkers. A group of what looked like teenage boys appeared out of one of the laneways off Sunnyvale Road. She was guessing at their ages based purely on their builds, because she couldn't see any faces.

"Males in masks, sir."

Another group appeared, clambering over a wall into Didsbury Road. Freddy Krueger mixing with a couple of *Star Wars* Stormtroopers, Homer Simpsons and at least three devils. In another context, they would have looked funny. In this one, they were anything but.

"What are . . ."

Cassidy ignored O'Rourke, reached into the car and grabbed the radio handset. "All cars, be alert, be alert. Masked youths, men, coming up Sunnyvale Road, maybe twenty, and another dozen or so on Didsbury—"

A rock hit the pavement to her left, coming from the crowd behind her on Sunnyvale Road. "Jesus, boss!" exclaimed Norman.

"We're OK," said Cassidy, not believing it for a second.

She put the phone back to her ear. "Sir, masked men throwing stones. Currently blocking two routes out of the estate. Didsbury and Sunnyvale are closed off and— SHIT!"

She barely registered the movement in the crowd at the mouth of Didsbury Road before there was the brief flash of a flame igniting. She watched the Molotov cocktail spiral through the air, scoring a direct hit on the patrol car parked on the left side of the pub. She saw Riordan and Brennan scamper away from it. Unhurt, at least for the moment.

The two groups of masked men roared, as did the drinkers outside the Leaping Trout. Cassidy could see more of the pub's patrons rushing out, now that the festivities had started.

The crowd at the top of the Sunnyvale Road started chanting. "Jimmy! Jimmy! Jimmy!"

The others soon took it up.

"Bugger this."

Cassidy swung into the driver's seat, tossing her phone onto the dashboard. Norman hopped into the passenger seat beside her. "All cars, pull back now. I will pick up Riordan and Brennan."

She could faintly hear DI O'Rourke demanding an update over the phone, which she ignored.

A glance in the rear-view mirror showed her the crowd at the top of Sunnyvale Road, Darth Vader standing before them with a lit Molotov cocktail in his hand. He hurled it at them. Luckily, Darth wasn't anywhere near as good a shot as the first guy had been. Instead of hitting their car, it veered into the drive of a house two doors down, setting somebody's ice cream van ablaze.

Cassidy walloped the button to turn on the blues and twos, while simultaneously slamming her foot down on the accelerator. As they pulled away, she caught the briefest glimpse of Darth Vader getting smacked upside the head by Homer Simpson. Somebody clearly liked ice cream.

The crowd coming from Didsbury Road were heading towards

the burning Garda car. At least they were – until they noticed the other Garda car heading straight for them.

"Butch?"

Most of the twenty or so figures turned in their direction. The smarter ones got out of the way, the cockier ones stayed in the road, chanting with arms aloft.

"Butch?!"

Cassidy had long ago decided that the best way to bluff was not to bother. Cocksure bravery was no match for physics. At a point, even the dumbest of them realised she wasn't stopping. Bodies scattered as she threw the car into a sharp right turn. One fat kid in a gorilla mask got a thump off the back end as the car fishtailed around the corner, but he would live.

"CHRIST!" Norman, on the other hand, looked liked he'd aged a decade in the previous fifteen seconds. He had his eyes closed and appeared to be having a one-sided conversation with Jesus.

As she screeched the car to a halt, she saw a third group of trick-or-treaters at the top of Crossan Road surging towards them. Rocks started raining down on the car, mostly from the front. The Didsbury Road crowd were temporarily distracted picking each other up. Brennan and Riordan dived into the back seat, Tony Brennan getting a half brick to the shoulder for the privilege of being second.

Before the door had even closed Cassidy floored it. The crowd behind had regrouped and were running towards them. The bigger concern lay in front. One kid in a mask she didn't recognise was holding yet another Molotov cocktail as his mate tried to light it. She headed straight for them, banking on their fear trumping their bravery.

Adrenaline pumping, Cassidy was dimly aware of Norman in the passenger seat, working his way through Hail Marys like they were going out of fashion.

"Hang on!"

The kids got the cloth to light when Cassidy was about thirty feet away. She could see the whites of their eyes as they looked up to see their intended victim barrelling towards them. The chucker dropped his payload, setting his soon-to-be ex-buddy's leg alight in the process. They dived in opposite directions, as did their cohorts. If this was bowling, it would have been a strike – not that they actually made contact.

As the car hurtled through the sprouting flames, Butch's professionalism slipped momentarily and she punched the roof. "Yippee ki-yay, mother-humpers!!!"

As their car hurtled up Crossan Road, they passed a couple of motorbikes coming the other way. She had got her people out successfully, but Butch would stake her life on the fact that they had just lost their grip on the whereabouts of Franko Doyle and Tommy Carter.

CHAPTER FORTY-NINE

Franko Doyle was getting royally sick of bloody motorbikes. Every one of Tommy's plans seem to involve them in one way or another.

The two bikes had come haring down Crossan Road in the opposite direction to the fleeing coppers and then stopped outside the pub. Franko took the helmet he was offered and hopped on the back of one of the bikes as Tommy did the same on the other.

He then hung on for dear life as the bikes took off. They sped past the bottom of Crossan Road, and up ahead he saw the bike with Tommy on the back drive through the four-foot wall of flames caused by the dropped Molotov. Franko was grateful that his rider felt less of a need to showboat, instead easing off the speed slightly and going around. Franko caught a brief glimpse of Deirdre Duffy's young fella, all of fourteen, crying his eyes out as others looked down at his scorched legs. There'd be hell to pay over that.

They raced down one of the laneways off Crossan Road, then took a left and a right, before skipping down another laneway and coming out on a green in the Parnell Heights Estate opposite.

Tommy's bike stopped and he dismounted, pulling off his helmet. He seemed to be breathing funny. The rider of his bike took off his helmet, revealing himself to be Mick Kitchener. Tommy knew his dad.

"Wahoo!" yelled Mick. "That was a fucking rush, man."

Tommy then slammed his helmet into Mick's face. The kid collapsed off the bike, his hands held to his shattered nose and bloodied mouth, a look of terrified incomprehension in his eyes.

"What the fuck?" said the other rider, who, Franko suddenly realised, was a bird. Through all the leather, he'd not noticed. He didn't recognise her at all. "What the hell did you do that for?" she said.

"Are you questioning me?"

Franko managed to get himself between Tommy and the girl as he surged towards her.

"She's not, she's not. Relax, Tommy."

Tommy's eyes were wild in a way Franko hadn't seen before. If he didn't know better, he would have thought he was on something. A demented smile seemed to be frozen upon his face. His breaths were short and fast, like a greyhound after a race.

"You OK, Tommy?"

Tommy took a moment and then pushed Franko away. "I'm fine. I just don't like unnecessary risk." He turned and walked a few paces. "Franko – a word."

Franko dutifully followed him, glancing back to see the girl helping Kitchener up as he spat out a couple of teeth.

Tommy turned to look at Franko, the wildfire now gone from his eyes.

"You're clear on the plan?"

Franko nodded.

"And you remember the location?"

Franko nodded again.

"OK then."

"Is O'Donnell going to meet us there?"

Tommy stopped and looked down at the ground for a moment. "John's dead."

"What?"

Tommy shrugged. "Skinner contacted me yesterday, said he wasn't getting any better and the wound had become infected. He dealt with it."

"Jesus."

"Problem?"

Franko looked at Tommy's face, back to its normal emotionless veneer. "No, I just . . . Are you OK?"

"Why wouldn't I be?"

"You were, y'know . . ."

Franko stopped talking.

After a moment, Tommy nodded, walked over to Kitchener's bike and got on. Kitchener tried to speak, but showing admirable survival instincts, the girl pulled him away before he could say anything.

Tommy kicked the bike into life. "She'll take you where you need to go."

Franko nodded and Tommy rode off towards the main road.

"What the hell is his bleedin' problem?" said the girl.

Franko watched him ride away. "You don't want to know."

CHAPTER FIFTY

Gringo stood under the shower and let the almost scalding water drill into his face.

They had eventually got back to Bunny's place at one in the morning, having developed a new appreciation for the level of commitment the criminal fraternity had shown to bury so many bodies in the Wicklow Mountains over the years. Even in the soft ground, digging a hole eight foot deep had taken a lot of time. He also now understood what the phrase "dead weight" meant. If he ever had to do it again, he would make sure that the dead bodies walked themselves to the hole before being relieved of their mortal coils. They had been careful to cover the ground with leaves, and the winter weather should do the rest. By the time the summer ramblers returned, they would have no idea what they were walking on.

Gringo was clear on the why and what of the things they had done, but the who had held one last nasty surprise. The big fella, Frock, had been carrying no ID on him. Lopez, however, had. A card in his wallet identified him as an FBI agent called Daniel Zayas. Gringo had tried to make the case that it might be fake, but neither of them had been convinced. That was only going to be bad news.

Gringo had slipped the wallet into his coat pocket. He was going to dump it somewhere later on, that was what he had told himself.

Both he and Bunny knew that to make the bodies harder to identify, they could remove teeth and destroy the fingerprints. They never directly discussed it, both knowing that, somehow, that would feel like crossing a line too far. Later that night, they had added to their growing list of criminal misdeeds. Bunny drove Frock's Audi to just off Gardiner Street and left the keys in the ignition. By now, nature would have taken its course. It would either be in pieces or an entirely different colour with an entirely different number plate.

Overall, Gringo was surprised by how he felt about the whole thing – or, rather, how he didn't feel. Numb, that was the word. Two men who would have killed them – and in fact had intended to, judging by their gravedigging kit – were dead, and he and Bunny had disposed of their bodies. Gringo had killed one of them. A few weeks ago, that would have seemed an unconscionable act, but that was a whole other life now.

The one positive in so comprehensively messing his life up was that it had provided a wonderful clarity. You don't notice the pinpricks when there's a large sword dangling over your head.

He had been drowning in debt. The cards had started out as a hobby, a bit of excitement to liven up his week, some escapism to temporarily free himself from the crumbling ruins of his marriage. Then, the worst thing that could happen, happened. He had won. Suddenly, he could afford to cover the cost of his mother's extortionately-priced care home and his bills from the divorce and still have a bit left over. Life was good. It was that simplest of traps: when you won it was skill and when you lost, well, it was just a temporary run of bad luck. His addiction had been an invisible, odourless gas, and he had been too stupid to realise that his downfall had been softly whispering into the world around him.

Still, right now, he didn't give two shits for a couple of psychos who could and would've killed him, Bunny and Simone given half the chance. Maybe that would change, but he doubted it. No, the ghost that haunted his dreams was that of Dara O'Shea. Gringo still didn't know how, but Jessica Cunningham had broken Franko Doyle and he was willing to give them everything. Once they'd decided they needed some help, they had then carefully approached Gringo. They had known all about his debt. How bad it was. Everything. They told him they could make it go away in the short term, and he could make a whole lot more in the long term.

Gringo's back ached, his side was a rather spectacular collage of purples, browns and blacks, and the knife wound on his thigh hurt like a bastard. Before getting in the shower, he had removed the bandages to have a closer look. While it was three inches long, the wound was thankfully not that deep. When they'd got back, Simone had insisted on cleaning it thoroughly. Gringo had popped a couple of painkillers and the next thing he knew it was after 3 am. He'd woken up on Bunny's sofa, a duvet over him and every inch of his body in pain.

It felt like he hadn't slept properly in an age. For weeks now, his nights had been filled with variations on a theme. Dreams where he was being dragged – behind horses, a car, a juggernaut – and once, memorably, an elephant. All the time, being dragged helplessly forward. You didn't need a doctorate in psychology to understand what was going on.

The water started to turn cold and Gringo realised he had used up the remaining contents of the tank. Bunny and Simone had already been in. They were downstairs cooking a fried breakfast. It was half three in the morning but Bunny had always been a firm believer in the all-day breakfast principle. Before hopping in the shower, Gringo had watched them for a little while. A silent negotiation had been taking place between them, Simone trying to show Bunny that she was fine while Bunny tried to hide his aching need to protect her under a sheen of nonchalance. Given where they had started from, he wasn't sure if they had ever reached a state of normal before the roof had fallen in. Still, there was something there. It hurt a little to be around. Not that he wasn't happy as all hell for Bunny – he truly was. Gringo's own marriage had been an exercise in mistaking lust for love, and being around the real thing was painful. Like seeing sunlight after spending so long underground.

Bunny had woken him with a cup of tea and an apology. He'd said he'd debated letting him sleep, but had reckoned rightly that Gringo would want to hear the news they had just received from Butch. Under the cover of a near-riot, Carter and Doyle had disappeared off the grid. Gringo had checked his phone, on which he'd seen the text message he had been dreading.

Feeling slightly more human after his shower, Gringo re-bandaged his leg, dressed and went downstairs. He could hear Simone in their bedroom, softly humming a melancholy tune.

"There he is – Sleeping Beauty," said Bunny, working away industriously over the cooker, the aroma of frying meat filling the downstairs.

"Fresh as a newborn lamb."

"Praise Jesus!"

Gringo leaned against the counter and lowered his voice. "So look, what do we do if someone comes looking for those guys?"

"Don't worry about it," said Bunny, inexpertly flipping a fried egg.

"Bunny?"

He turned to look at Gringo for the first time. "I said don't worry about it."

"Yeah, but—"

"Listen to me – leave it alone, alright? If anyone comes looking for them, I will handle it. You weren't there, it has nothing to do with you."

Simone entered the kitchen, wafting a hand in front of her face. "Damn, is there any food in this house that didn't die screaming?"

"I certainly hope not," replied Bunny, giving her a wide grin.

"Yeah, because a bit of healthy living would kill you."

"I'll have you know, my granddad had the full Irish fried breakfast every day of his life. Never did him any harm."

"Really?" asked Simone. "Would that be the same granddad who died before you were born?"

Bunny shrugged. "Maybe."

"Yeah, nice try, buddy. You could also do with some more regular exercise."

"I'm game if you are."

"Bunny! Mind your manners." Simone flashed Gringo an embarrassed smile. "So, how're you feeling?"

"I'll live," replied Gringo.

"Not if you eat too many of his breakfasts you won't."

"Well, I'm in luck there. I've got to go."

"What?" said Bunny. "Don't be daft. It's the middle of the night!"

"I know, but I've got an early meeting about something."

"Please," said Simone, "stay. A good breakfast is the very least I owe you. If it helps, I've got some Bran Flakes stashed away?"

"Christ," said Bunny. "*Et tu, Brute*?".

"Oh shut up. You're going to start eating like a grown-up. End. Of. Story."

"She's right, amigo, you need to keep yourself regular. There's no telling what other weapons you might have stockpiled up there."

"Ha ha, very funny."

"I'll talk to you tomorrow."

A look passed between Bunny and Simone.

He turned from the cooker to address Gringo directly. "Look, if this is the Carter thing . . . we can get you out of it. Let me help. Just, tell me."

Gringo raised his hand.

"It's not. And anyway, like I said, not your problem."

"But—"

"But nothing."

Gringo gave Simone a hug and threw a playful punch at Bunny's belly. "Enjoy your breakfast in the middle of the night. I'll talk to you tomorrow."

Gringo sat in his car and dialled the number.

"Finally."

"Something came up."

"Well I'm sorry to have to drag you away. What did he say?"

Gringo glanced back towards Bunny's front door. "Like I told you, he's not interested."

"For Christ's sake. He knows too much."

"It's fine."

"No, it isn't."

"He's not going to say anything, alright?"

"I am not putting my future in the hands of that—"

"You don't have to. Look, I have things on him, he has things on me. Call it mutually-assured destruction."

There was silence on the other end, long enough that Gringo was tempted to see if the call was still connected.

"Get over here now and we will discuss this further. The clock is ticking."

CHAPTER FIFTY-ONE

Tommy Carter leaned back against his jeep, hugged his windbreaker to himself and watched the eastern sky lighten to meet the new day. He had been here since 5:30 am, spending most of the time lost in silent contemplation. There was something reassuring about the sea – so immense and powerful, entirely disinterested in your existence. It had been here before him and it would be here long after him. For a mad moment, he considered walking down the jetty, taking his shoes and socks off and going for a paddle. He quickly dismissed the idea; it was a starkly cold December morning, and besides, he was here on business.

It had been a long road, with more than its fair share of bumps along the way, but it was all about to be worth it. By the time the sun was high in the sky, their enterprise would have taken a massive step forward. He turned to look back at the sea once more. In thirty minutes, a luxury yacht containing seventy-two bales of the purest Colombian cocaine would be offshore. Their contacts had insisted on coming in at dawn, which made unexpected sense. Any activities that happened at night were suspicious almost by definition; the first light of dawn was when the good people went about their industry. In this case, their speedboat would be bringing ashore enough coke to dominate the Irish market indefinitely and make some very serious friends over the Irish Sea. Tommy already had two names, one in Liverpool and one in Glasgow, who would eagerly take large chunks of the shipment off his hands. Gerry Fallon had spent the last decade establishing himself as the undisputed kingpin of the Irish market, but that was about to change – and fast. He would live to regret trying to burn down Tommy Carter's house, but he would not live to regret it long.

After he had concluded the morning's business, Tommy would disappear for a couple of days. Unless they wanted to charge him with anything, the Gardaí wouldn't even get to hear his alibi as to where he had been. Needless to say, it had been put in place months ago and refreshed given the current circumstance. It would just be a matter of waiting the Gardaí out. They had nothing, and what is more, with dirty cops having tried to ambush O'Donnell and Franko, they might soon realise that looking too hard at the evidence might lead somewhere they didn't want to go. Carter smiled to himself. If his opponents hadn't got greedy, he would probably have been behind bars by now. A valuable lesson. From now on, he would be one step removed from the action – once this deal had been made and his future secured.

Brònchluich Beach had been his most careful selection. Never one of Donegal's most scenic beaches, it might get some customers on a Saturday in August but on an early morning in December it should remain deserted. Two miles from the nearest house, it was of no interest to joggers, fishermen or anyone else. And if that were to change, Tommy had some hi-vis jackets in the boot and a plausible story about a water pollution warning.

He looked to his right, where the beach sloped upwards to become a gorse-topped cliff, waves crashing against the rocks beneath it. In the summer, according to his research, local youths often dared each other to take the fifty-foot leap from the cliff's edge into the waves below. That had stopped a couple of years ago after a tragedy had left a Spanish exchange student in a wheelchair. Now there were signs warning of a dangerous drop, and some fencing to prevent anyone from taking the required run-up. There had once been a lighthouse at the top but it had been knocked down in the Eighties as unsafe, and now a meteorological measuring station perched up there, looking like an overly ambitious child's science project. The fact that it hadn't been vandalised proved the location's remoteness from the curiosities of local youth, now that reckless self-endangerment was no longer possible.

The Moran situation had been a disappointment. He and O'Donnell had quietly discussed his behaviour several times over the last year. He was too flashy, and the last thing their organisation needed was a big mouth. All the time they had served together in the army had made O'Donnell deeply reluctant to deal with Jimmy Moran. Even after he had taken a bullet in the thigh in the ambush, O'Donnell had tried to make the case that the leak might not be Moran. Still, Moran's death had given Tommy just what he needed – a way out from under the surveillance. It had required him making at least a temporary ally of the IRA, but it had been worth it. He had taken a grim satisfaction in turning the loss of Moran into a win. The leak was plugged and they had made the Gardaí look like fools yet again. As for O'Donnell, well . . .

Tommy heard an engine behind him and turned to see a blue van appearing from behind the line of sand dunes. It was really more of a one-lane track than a road, skirting the bottom of the slope that lead up to the cliff before meandering down to the beach, but it served their purpose. Tommy looked at his watch. Exactly on time. The van pulled up behind his jeep on the jetty, and Franko Doyle opened the door and got out.

"Any problems?"

"No, Tommy, all good. Picked up the van just where you said it would be. Any contact with the boat?"

"Ship."

"What?"

"It's a ship, Franko. A vessel of its size is a ship. The launch that'll be pulling up is a boat though."

"Whatever. Any word?"

Tommy shook his head. "No, but then there's not supposed to be. Radio silence. Don't worry, everything is in hand. You just be ready to do the unloading."

"So," said Franko, leaning back on the front of his van, his hands nonchalantly in his pockets, "you've got the diamonds then?"

"You've an awful lot of questions this morning, Franko."

"Course I do. I'm in this too, you know. There's only you and me left, Tommy, you need to stop with all this secrecy bollocks."

Carter gave Franko a long, hard look and then pulled his jacket around himself tighter. "Yes, Franko, I've not turned up to the drug deal without the necessary. I don't have a death wish."

Franko stretched his arms out as if to yawn and then snatched the handgun from his overcoat pocket. "Glad to hear it, now give me the stones."

Tommy stayed still, looking Franko directly in the eye. "Uncle Franko, I do hope this is some kind of a joke."

Franko smiled at him. "Do I look like I'm laughing?"

"And after all I've done for you."

"Oh please. Treating me like your lackey, always thinking you're so bleedin' smart. You're an obnoxious little prick and you always were."

The back doors of the van opened and Detective Tim "Gringo" Spain got out on the left side, his gun pointed at Tommy's head, quickly followed by the similarly armed Detective Sergeant Jessica Cunningham, who took up station on the other side of the van.

"I see you've brought your new friends, Franko."

"Yeah," said Franko. "Not so clever now, are you, Tommy?"

"No, I guess I'm not. I honestly didn't think a man I'd known since birth, who my father called his brother, could so easily betray me."

Franko spat on the ground. "Oh please. You betrayed your da a long time before I did. Or have you told him you're going into the drug-dealing business?"

Tommy shrugged. "You should know, Franko, O'Donnell always thought it was you – the leak, I mean." As he spoke, Tommy looked in turn at the three guns trained on him and the eyes behind them. "I actually defended you. You did a very good job of setting Moran up, I'll give you that. More subtlety there than I would expect from you."

"It's a bit late to try and butter me up."

"Oh no," said Tommy, with a slight laugh, "I was just explaining. You see, I promised John that, if I was wrong, he could deal with you personally."

"What a shame then that he died before he had the chance. I'd have loved to deal with that arsehole and all."

"Died? Where did you hear that he had died?"

"You told me."

"Did I?" Tommy smiled again. "Well, that must've been the truth. We don't lie to each other, do we, Uncle Franko? But could you imagine? Imagine that, right now, you're bang in the sights of a world-class sniper whose best friend you had killed. That wouldn't be fun, would it?"

"Bullshit."

Tommy could see Franko resisting the urge to look around. A bead of sweat was trickling down his forehead. He blinked twice. Tommy was aware of the cops behind Franko nervously scanning the horizon. The dunes, the cliffs, the sea.

The moment continued to stretch out around them. Nothing happened.

"Any last words, Uncle Franko?"

Franko licked his lips nervously and then curled them into a sneer. "You're full of shit, Tommy. Thinking you're some kind of la-di-da genius. You're just trying to mess with me head—"

It was an unfortunate choice of words, as a fraction of a second later, Franko Doyle's head exploded.

A bullet from an Accuracy International Arctic Warfare bolt-action sniper rifle can comfortably take out a target at a range of eight hundred and seventy yards in the hands of an expert. At a range of less than two hundred yards, and in the hands of John O'Donnell, Franko Doyle's fate had been sealed since the moment he pointed his gun at Tommy Carter. O'Donnell slammed the bolt action back, and loaded his next bullet.

Gringo dived for cover behind the van and heard Jessica Cunningham do the same. As he looked around, he saw Tommy Carter disappearing behind his jeep. But he was not their biggest concern right now. They needed to find cover from the sniper. The problem was that unless you knew where the danger was coming from, cover wasn't cover. Apart from the two vehicles, they were forty metres from any other protection. It might as well have been a mile.

"Where the hell is he?" said Cunningham, from the far side of the van, panic in her voice.

"I dunno."

Gringo scanned the dunes at the end of the beach. In films, you would see a reflection off a telescopic sight or at least the flash of a muzzle, but he doubted John O'Donnell was dumb enough to make a simple mistake, and a muzzle flash would almost certainly mean it was too late.

Gringo looked down at Franko – or rather, at what remained of him. He had fallen to the left, in the direction of Gringo's side of the van, so . . .

He heard the sharp thud of a bullet hitting the other side of the van followed a half a second later by the report of the shot. Then came the thump of Jessica Cunningham's body hitting the ground.

"Jessica?"

Gringo spotted movement in the corner of his right eye, and let loose a couple of shots to send Tommy Carter diving back behind his jeep. A bullet whistled off to Gringo's left in response. Gringo's heart was pounding so hard, it felt like it might erupt from his chest. O'Donnell must be to their right up on the cliffs. Which meant he had an elevated angle on the beach.

"Throw down your gun and you'll live, Detective."

"Fair enough, Tommy, sounds reasonable."

Carter's head briefly appeared around the front bumper of the jeep and then disappeared just as quickly as a bullet thunked into the front wheel.

"I think you've got a flat, Tommy."

"Very funny, Detective Spain. O'Donnell wants you to know – he's hoping to shoot you somewhere that'll cause you to die a slow and painful death."

"Honestly," said Gringo, "you shoot a guy in the leg – once – and he really takes it personally."

Several hundred yards away, a sheep was calmly regarding a figure crouched down beside it, holding a pair of binoculars. This was an unusual sight in the sheep's world but, as it appeared to be neither a threat nor edible, the sheep opened its mouth and resumed chewing on some grass.

There was a loud cracking noise in the distance. It was beyond the sheep's field of reference, but it was the sound of a shot from an Accuracy International Arctic Warfare bolt-action sniper rifle.

"Ah, shittin' Nora on a lilo."

The figure rushed back to his vehicle, which allowed the sheep to carry on with its business in peace.

It was too quiet.

Gringo flattened himself against the ground as silently as he could. He couldn't see anything beneath the van. There was no movement by the jeep either. He tried not to look at the body of Jessica Cunningham, motionless beside the rear driver's-side tyre of the van. Her body was crumpled, as if she were nothing more than a dolly callously dropped by a bored child.

The wind blew in from the sea, the cold breeze whipping the scents of salt air and seaweed around him. Gringo ran his gaze back and forth, the grip of his Glock 22 pistol moist with sweat. He tried to keep his breathing steady. Tried to think. The only thought that occurred to him was that, right now, John O'Donnell could be calmly making his way through the dunes, looking for an angle. If he was lucky, Gringo wouldn't even have time to realise before the bullet hit.

The silence was becoming oppressive.

A flash of movement, then the front windscreen of the van

shattered as a sniper round ripped through it. Glass tinkled down around Gringo. He saw the feet of Tommy Carter quickly stepping over Jessica Cunningham's body. Gringo squeezed off three quick shots beneath the underside of the van and Tommy Carter screamed. His body hit the concrete and he rolled, instinctively firing off a couple of shots in response.

Another sheep stood halfway up the slope that led to the top of the cliff. She had been standing at the top, perusing the gorse bushes when a loud noise had issued from the piece of nearby ground that wasn't ground and it had frightened her and the other two sheep off. Her brethren had scattered down below but she had become distracted by a tempting tuft of grass.

Another loud noise came from atop the cliff, but she wasn't so bothered any more. It was further away and it was starting to lose its shock value.

Then there came the roar of a ferocious-sounding beast. The sheep turned to see something large, black and angry careening off the one-lane road and heading straight for her. The sheep didn't know it, but it was a 1983 Porsche 928S, with black paint and a red leather interior. Sheep may not be nature's greatest survivors, but an instinct nevertheless grabbed her and she started running as fast as she could back up the slope.

Above her, the ground that wasn't the ground suddenly stood up.

John O'Donnell had been trained not to get distracted, to live in the moment that existed only when staring down the sights of a rifle. An old instructor used to put himself an inch from his ear and scream all manner of abuse at him while he calmly picked out and dispatched assigned targets on a range.

Still, in the back of his mind, his inner sentry screamed the alarm. O'Donnell withdrew his right eye from the sight and opened the left one. He looked down the slope to see the improbable spectacle of a black Porsche bumping messily up the hill towards him. A panicked sheep rushed along in front of it, inadvertently leading a charge it wanted no part of.

O'Donnell dropped to a knee – clumsily, due to the wound in his right thigh – and put a bullet left of centre through the windscreen, shattering it before passing through the tacky red leather of the driver's headrest.

There was nobody in the driver's seat.

Quickly and smoothly, O'Donnell slammed the bolt back and loaded another round. After a moment's thought, he attempted to put it through the engine block of the car. The car bounced up on the uneven ground and the bullet instead passed through the number plate.

The sheep rushed by O'Donnell as he dived to his right, the car narrowly missing him as it destroyed £327 of Irish Meteorological Service monitoring equipment.

The sheep, having found herself somehow trapped between the devil and the deep blue sea, stopped at the edge of the cliff and looked in horror at the rocks below. The 1983 Porsche 928S, with black paint and a red leather interior, had no such moment of existential crisis as, with a defiant roar, it threw itself off the cliff towards the unsuspecting sea below.

The sheep bounced up onto the bonnet and for a moment found herself standing on top of the beast. Then she was flying, which is an unusual state of affairs for a sheep.

John O'Donnell watched the car as it sailed off into the sea, a surprised sheep bouncing over its bonnet. He started getting to his feet to look over the edge.

Ninety seconds before, Bunny McGarry had found himself with no weapon. At least in the technical sense.

He was, through his job, allowed and often required to carry a gun. Unfortunately, that gun was in the locked cabinet in their squad's office, as he was technically on leave.

He did own a derringer, but he had possessed only one bullet for that and it had already been used. In all honesty – though he hadn't admitted it – he had been pleasantly shocked it had worked at all. If he was to be of any use in this situation, he would have to metaphorically pull something out of his arse, as opposed to literally.

He had nothing, save a car that for once wasn't in the shop and a hurling stick. To be fair, he had frequently used the hurley as a weapon – it worked well in close combat situations. It was, however, singularly unhelpful in a battle with a sniper. Actually, that was not entirely fair. Broken in half, it had held down the accelerator pedal on his 1983 Porsche 928S, allowing him to crouch down in the passenger seat and lean across to work the clutch pedal with his right hand and the gearstick with his left. He had used the belt off his trousers to tie the steering wheel into a fixed position as, ducked down as he was, steering was not much of an option. He had to hope his initial aim was good. He had managed to get the car up into third, roaring unhappily as it hurtled off the cliff, as if attempting an impractical bid to be the first car to jump the Atlantic Ocean.

Bunny didn't actually see the car leaving the ground, having rolled out of the passenger door moments before. Rocks bit at him and gorse bushes ripped at his skin, but he had no time for that. He was on his feet as quickly as possible and running.

John O'Donnell saw him coming and began turning, his sniper rifle still in his hands.

Somewhere in Bunny's mind, the calculation must have occurred without him being consciously aware of it. His opponent had a sniper rifle and undoubtedly a sidearm. He was highly skilled in both armed and unarmed combat. Though he had a wounded leg, the advantage still very definitely lay with the ex-Army Ranger.

That was why, as O'Donnell had almost completed his turn and was bringing his rifle up onto his shoulder, Bunny lowered his, extended his arms out and executed a perfect hip-height rugby tackle on his opponent. He did not bring his opponent safely to the ground, however, as the momentum carried them both off the cliff.

There were rocks below, landing on which could undoubtedly kill a man.

As much as Bunny had a plan, he was very much hoping to be the second man to land, as opposed to the first.

Tommy Carter sat propped against the back wheel of the van, breathing heavily. Just dragging himself to this position had been agony. He had been shot through the instep of his left foot and in the shin of his right leg. Standing was utterly impossible. The effort to drag himself three feet had caused him to scream in agony.

"Detective?"

There was no response, although he had heard movement. He guessed that DS Spain was still alive but, if anything, was in an even worse state than him. One of the shots Tommy fired off must have connected with something meaningful.

Tommy Carter being Tommy Carter, he had been running and re-running situations and permutations in his head.

Distracted by his own screaming, he hadn't seen what had happened on the cliff, only the whoosh of a car hitting water had attracted his attention. He had then, through watering eyes of agony, seen two figures collide and disappear over the edge of the cliff. Since that moment, there had been precious little movement.

The sun had risen high enough that it was dazzling his eyes as he looked over at the cliffs, running things through for the third time. What if the authorities turned up? Life in prison. Defeat. And if the representatives of the Cruz Cartel come ashore? Assuming they hadn't seen a car go hurtling off a cliff and thought better of it? Well, if you met a seriously wounded man who had sixteen million pounds worth of diamonds and no means of escape, you'd wish him well, put a bullet in him, and depart with your merchandise and your payment. It was what he would do; he couldn't criticise them for it.

His only chance was John O'Donnell, so it was with great interest that he watched as a figure emerged from the waves and started walking towards the shore.

Tommy Carter smiled.

"Good morning, Bunny."

"That's Detective McGarry to you."

McGarry looked like a drowned rat. Tommy raised his gun.

"Is John O'Donnell dead?"

"Judging by the crack when he hit those rocks, I'd imagine so, or else he's going to be one hell of a limbo dancer."

"You are showing insufficient respect for the man with the gun, Detective."

"Ah well," said Bunny. "If I need to have an epitaph, that'll do. Where's Gringo?"

Tommy waved his hand in the vague direction of behind the van. "Don't you want to beg for your life?"

Bunny shrugged, causing his belt-less trousers, soaking wet, to fall down.

He looked down at them, a look of resignation on his face.

"Are you going for slapstick, Detective?"

Bunny shook his head. "To be honest with you, the last twenty-four hours have been like riding a bull who's dipped his knackers in Deep Heat, so if it is all the same to you, if you're going to shoot me, just fecking shoot me. I'm too tired for this crap."

Just then, a sheep who had frankly had more than enough of this shit, emerged from the water and ran up the beach on unsteady legs.

For a moment, Tommy Carter and Bunny McGarry both watched it as it ran off towards the dunes.

"Well," said Tommy, "there's a thing you don't see every day."

Bunny hauled up his sodden trousers and started trudging up the beach, his shoes squelching on every step. "Put the gun down. We'll phone you an ambulance. You'll be fine."

Tommy Carter shook his head. "No thanks." He moved the gun to train it on Bunny. "Stop walking. Listen. I want you to promise me something."

"What?"

"Tell them . . . tell Dad . . . tell them to give him my kidney."

"Wait—"

Bunny barely had time to put his hand out as in one swift motion, Tommy Carter turned the gun around, stuck it in his own mouth and pulled the trigger.

Gringo watched the waves as they pushed and pulled against the land. He looked up at the sky, and suddenly it was blocked by Bunny McGarry looming over him.

"Jesus, Gringo."

Bunny fell tǫ his knees beside him.

Gringo found his voice, barely above a whisper. "You came?"

"Ah, I'd nothing else on for the day. And I went through your messages while you were in the shower."

"Nosy bastard."

Gringo was aware of his hands, clutched to his stomach, being moved to one side. They were sticky. Bunny pulled his sodden Johnny Cash T-shirt off and pressed it to Gringo's wound.

"Aghhh!"

"Sorry."

"What're you getting naked for? Trying to take advantage of a dying man?"

"Shut up, DS Spain. Need I remind you of your sensitivity training. Besides, who says you're dying?"

Gringo smiled. His life had been slipping through his fingers for what seemed like a long time now. Whatever the bullet hit when it passed through his stomach had caused a foul stench. He had been glad when the wind had changed and brought the salty tang of the ocean to push it away.

"It's OK, amigo."

"Hang on, I'll – I'll ring – shite, I've not got my phone. I'll get . . . There'll be a phone here somewhere, you just hang on."

Bunny got up to leave but Gringo grabbed his hand. When he spoke, his voice was croaky and distant, as if hearing a recording of himself from another time being beamed across the water. "I'm sorry about . . ."

"Don't be—"

"Listen, ye big idiot."

Bunny kneeled down beside him, his big, warm face tear-streaked. Gringo tried to smile again. He could taste blood in his mouth.

"You were a good friend and I'm sorry for . . . y'know."

"Forget about it."

"Take care of Mum if you can."

"Sure you'll be doing that yourself, let me just—"

"And take care of yourself. You deserve a good life. Your sins are no worse than anyone's and your good deeds should count."

"Save your strength."

Bunny looked down, blinking to try and push away the tears. His lips kept moving as if starting and rejecting something to say.

Gringo's voice was a whisper to himself. "The end is nigh, amigo."

Bunny looked around, desperation singing through his veins. "Just let me call the . . . Let me . . . I can . . . They can send an air ambulance or . . ."

When he looked down again, he was alone on the beach.

CHAPTER FIFTY-TWO

Bunny kept his left hand firmly on the doorbell, even as his right pounded on the door.

"C'mon, open up. I just want to—"

He took a step back as the door opened a fraction. Through the chained gap, Sister Bernadette's intense blue eyes peered out. "Oh, it's you." Her voice was softer than normal. "Hang on."

The door closed and Bunny could hear the chain being slipped off inside. It reopened, and Sister Bernadette glanced around him and then pulled her head back inside. He wondered if she was telling Sister Assumpta that she and the shotgun could stand down. Her face returned to the gap.

"Is she here?" asked Bunny.

"No."

"Would you tell me if she was?"

Bernadette didn't respond; instead she gave him a sad smile.

Bunny hadn't seen Simone for two days now, not since he had left to follow Gringo. The plan had been to follow from a distance, to make sure Gringo didn't get himself into any more trouble than he was already in. He'd felt he owed it to him, for all the good it had done.

The doctors had insisted on holding Bunny in hospital overnight for observation. They claimed he was showing the symptoms of concussion. Considering how hard he had hit the rocks – though nowhere near as hard as O'Donnell, who had borne the full brunt of the impact – a concussion, a sprained wrist and a few choice additions to his already impressive collection of bruises had been one hell of result. He also had a bit of swimmer's ear.

At least part of the reasoning behind Bunny being kept in became clear that night, when he was woken from his sleep by DI Fintan O'Rourke. Being officially concussed, Bunny had been unable to give any form of a statement. In hindsight, this had allowed DI O'Rourke some precious breathing space. Bunny had listened quietly as he had laid it out. It was couched in diplomatic language, of course, but the reality was that Rigger and his bosses had figured out what was going on. Bunny was still unsure if they had been suspicious beforehand, but the carnage on Brònchluich Beach must have made it alarmingly obvious. Three of their officers – that they knew of – had gone into business for themselves, trying to rip off Carter as opposed to bringing him down. The scandal would rock the force for a decade at least, further damaging public trust. Officers O'Shea, Cunningham and Spain would also be demonised in the press, with their families losing their benefits and living with their shame.

But there was another way. A gang of vicious cop killers and thieves had been brought to justice. The actions of a few brave officers had resulted in the largest drug seizure the state had ever seen. The *Wings of an Angel* luxury yacht had been boarded fifteen miles off the coast by the Irish Navy with backup from the Brits, and seventy-two bales of pure cocaine had been seized. All Bunny had to do was to support the version of events O'Rourke would lay out and any mumbles of doubt amongst his colleagues would be drowned out by the marching band warming up for the proverbial parade. O'Shea's family, Cunningham's husband and Gringo's mother would receive their full death benefits and be warmed by memories of a fallen hero.

Bunny had agreed to it. He had been so far beyond tired and he would rather have Gringo remembered as a hero than a pariah.

The next day he had given his official statement to DI O'Rourke and Butch Cassidy. Now and then Butch had looked slightly suspicious, but she didn't probe. Thanks to the mountain of evidence against Tommy Carter, Dinny Muldoon was due back on full duty in the morning, so she had some skin in the game too.

Bunny had lied through his teeth, engaged in a massive cover-up, and then they had popped him in the back of a patrol car and dropped him home.

Simone hadn't been there.

Which had led him here, to the doorstep of the Sisters of the Saint, once again.

Bernadette looked up at him. "I'm afraid she has gone."

Bunny sagged against the doorframe. Knowing it had been coming didn't make it any easier.

"Don't go looking for her, it isn't what she wants. I think you should respect that."

"But..."

Bernadette took something from the small table beside the door and handed it to him. A letter. "Would you like to come in?"

Bunny shook his head.

Bernadette gave him a long, lingering look. "Take care of yourself, Detective. You're one of the good ones."

As she closed the door, he turned and sat on the cold stone steps.

Then he opened the letter.

My dearest Bunny,

This is the hardest letter I have ever had to write. I'm so sorry about Tim. I know you will have done everything in your power to try and save him, just as you did for me. Please don't beat yourself up about it. You can't save everybody, but I do so love that you try.

I have tried and tried to think of a way around it, but the reality is that my past is always going to keep coming after me. I'm sorry I dragged you into it, and I can't in all good conscience continue to do that. With every fiber of my being, I'd love to stay with you here for the rest of my days, but it wouldn't be fair. You're a good man and you deserve better than this.

Please don't try and find me. I hope you get what you truly deserve in this life. Thank you for giving me the happiest time in mine, at a time when I thought I could never be truly happy again.

I love you,

Your Simone

EPILOGUE

Three weeks later

"Phil Nellis, what in the name of Christ on a llama are you doing? Put your helmet back on, fella, would ye? For Jesus's sake! I can't imagine severe brain damage would impact you much, but the sight of a sliotar ripping your gormless noggin off might upset the other children!"

"D'ye know what his problem is, boss? He has no appreciation of the fundamentals of the game."

"You're not wrong, Deccie, you're not wrong."

"Also, he's thick as pig shit."

"Deccie! You can't say that."

"But you said it last week, boss."

"Well – you're not allowed to repeat the things I say."

"How's that fair?"

"Who the feck told you life was fair, Deccie?"

"You did, boss."

"Well . . . exactly. Proves my point."

"What does?"

"Are you giving me cheek, Deccie?"

"No, boss."

312

"Michael Dolan, do not kick the ball! We have given you a large stick for a very good reason!"

"D'ye know what his problem is, boss?"

"Yes, Deccie, I've a very good idea."

"Boss, the—"

"What?"

"The you-know-what are back, boss."

Bunny looked over his shoulder to see DI Fintan O'Rourke standing behind him.

"Ah," said Bunny, "it's the pigs."

"But, boss—"

"You're not allowed repeat things I say, remember, Deccie?"

"This is bullshit!"

"Welcome to life. Now – head over the far sideline and shout at Larry Dodds every time he shoves a finger up a nostril."

"Every time? Jesus, I'll lose me voice." Deccie stomped off disconsolately down the sideline.

"Bunny."

"Detective Inspector, I should warn you that if you repeatedly turn up at under-12s hurling matches without a child, I am supposed to report you to the authorities."

"Duly noted. I hear the insurance company wrote off your car?"

"They did. And I bought it back off them for scrap. Terry Frisby is currently drying it out for me. He reckons he can get it back up and running, given time."

"That's wonderful news. And speaking of things taking time . . ."

"Is that what they call one of them segues, inspector?"

"I guess it is. Are you coming back? The offer still stands."

Bunny turned briefly to look at DI O'Rourke before returning his attention to the game. "What's the matter, Fintan? Would you rather have me in the tent pissing out? Is that it?"

"You're a good detective. We need you."

"Yeah," said Bunny, "I'm surprised that wasn't mentioned more on my fitness reports."

"Your skills have been re-evaluated. In fact, the commissioner would like you to know that, if you come back, your name will be on the next list of detective sergeants."

"I don't care about that."

"Sure you do. It'll give you a whole new rank of people to shout at."

"Vinny Curry, tackle the fellas in a different colour jersey to the one you're wearing. We have been over this!" Bunny kicked one of the kit bags lying in front of him, then he glanced behind him as if he had forgotten O'Rourke was there.

"Well, I delivered the message."

"You have."

"I'll see you soon."

"I wouldn't bet on that."

O'Rourke gave a little laugh. "Actually, I would."

Bunny turned to look at him.

"You're a natural copper, Bunny, there's nothing else you know how to do. It's in your blood. I'll see you back in work Monday morning."

"We'll see."

"We will."

A WORD FROM CAIMH

Hey there reader,

Thanks so much for checking out *Angels in the Moonlight*, I hope you enjoyed it. If you're a new initiate into the cult of Bunny then you're in luck, the first two books of *The Dublin Trilogy* are awaiting your hungry eyes. If you've already devoured them, then you can either read the sequel to *Angels in the Moonlight, Dead Mans Sins* or head to back to the future and read the final part of the Trilogy, *Last Orders*.

If you'd like to find out more about the arse-kicking Sisters of The Saint, you can find a novella called *Sisters Gonna Work it Out* in my short fiction collection *How To Send A Message*. The paperback is $10.99/£7.99 but you can get the e-book for free by signing up to my monthly newsletter at www.WhiteHairedIrishman.com. You'll get a monthly e-mail from me with info on my forthcoming books, freebies and frankly, far too many funny animal pictures.

Thanks for reading,

Caimh

ALSO BY CAIMH MCDONNELL

Visit www.WhiteHairedIrishman.com to find out more.

THE STRANGER TIMES: C.K. MCDONNELL

There are dark forces at work in our world so thank God *The Stranger Times* is on hand to report them. A weekly newspaper dedicated to the weird and the wonderful (but mostly the weird), it is the go-to publication for the unexplained and inexplicable . . .

At least that's their pitch. The reality is rather less auspicious. Their editor is a drunken, foul-tempered and foul-mouthed husk of a man who thinks little of the publication he edits. His staff are a ragtag group of misfits. And as for the assistant editor . . . well, that job is a revolving door – and it has just revolved to reveal Hannah Willis, who's got problems of her own.

When tragedy strikes in her first week on the job *The Stranger Times* is forced to do some serious investigating. What they discover leads to a shocking realisation: some of the stories they'd previously dismissed as nonsense are in fact terrifyingly real. Soon they come face-to-face with darker forces than they could ever have imagined.

The Stranger Times is the first book from C.K. McDonnell, the pen name of Caimh McDonnell. It combines his distinctive dark wit with his love of the weird and wonderful to deliver a joyous celebration of how truth really can be stranger than fiction.

Printed in Great Britain
by Amazon

35575345R00182